THE HOURS COUNT

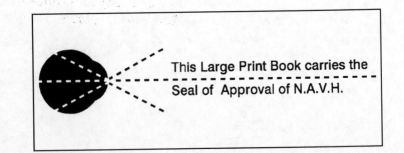

This Large Print Book carries the
Seal of Approval of N.A.V.H.

THE HOURS COUNT

JILLIAN CANTOR

WHEELER PUBLISHING
A part of Gale, Cengage Learning

GALE
CENGAGE Learning·

Farmington Hills, Mich • San Francisco • New York • Waterville, Maine
Meriden, Conn • Mason, Ohio • Chicago

GALE
CENGAGE Learning

Wheeler Publishing Large Print Hardcover.
The text of this Large Print edition is unabridged.
Other aspects of the book may vary from the original edition.
Set in 16 pt. Plantin.

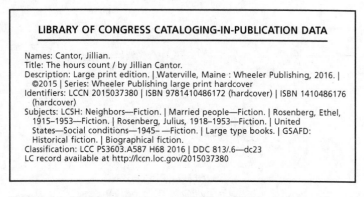

LIBRARY OF CONGRESS CATALOGING-IN-PUBLICATION DATA

Names: Cantor, Jillian.
Title: The hours count / by Jillian Cantor.
Description: Large print edition. | Waterville, Maine : Wheeler Publishing, 2016. |
    ©2015 | Series: Wheeler Publishing large print hardcover
Identifiers: LCCN 2015037380 | ISBN 9781410486172 (hardcover) | ISBN 1410486176
    (hardcover)
Subjects: LCSH: Neighbors—Fiction. | Married people—Fiction. | Rosenberg, Ethel,
    1915–1953—Fiction. | Rosenberg, Julius, 1918–1953—Fiction. | United
    States—Social conditions—1945– —Fiction. | Large type books. | GSAFD:
    Historical fiction. | Biographical fiction.
Classification: LCC PS3603.A587 H68 2016 | DDC 813/.6—dc23
LC record available at http://lccn.loc.gov/2015037380

Published in 2016 by arrangement with Riverhead Books, an imprint of Penguin Publishing Group, a division of Penguin Random House LLC

Printed in Mexico
1 2 3 4 5 6 7 20 19 18 17 16

For G, B, and O, with love

The hours count.
The minutes count.
Do not let this crime
against humanity take place.
— Pablo Picasso,
on the Rosenbergs,
L'Humanité, May 1951

Always remember that we were
innocent and could not wrong our
conscience.
— Julius and Ethel Rosenberg,
in their last letter to their sons,
June 19, 1953

June 19, 1953

On the night Ethel is supposed to die, the air is too heavy to breathe. The humidity clings to my skin, my face wet with sweat, or maybe tears. It is hard to tell the difference. To understand one thing from another anymore. It's as if the world were ending the way I always imagined it would. And yet I'm still here. Still driving. Still breathing, somehow, despite the heavy air, despite what I have done. The sky is on the edge of dusk. No mushroom cloud. No bodies turned to dust.

I'm driving Ed's Fleetmaster up Route 9, the road to Ossining, along the sweltering Hudson. There are a lot of cars, all headed the way I am, slowing me down. I push anxiously on the gas, wanting the miles to speed along, wanting to get there before it's too late. I hope the car will make it, that I haven't damaged anything that will cause it to stall now at the worst possible time.

I wish I could've left earlier, but I had to wait until I was able to take Ed's car. I suppose you even might say I've stolen the car, but Ed and I are still married legally. And can a wife really steal a car from her own legal husband?

So much has already been stolen from me, from all of us. From Ethel. And that's why I'm driving now.

My stomach turns at the thought of what might happen to me when I tell the truth at last. And I glance in the rearview mirror at the backseat. For so long, I have taken David with me everywhere, and it takes me a moment to remember he's not here. It's just me in the car and David's gone.

But Jake will be there, at Sing Sing, I remind myself. He has to be. And if I can just see him one last time, one more moment, then it will make everything else I am about to do, everything I have lost and am losing by doing this, all worth it.

I think now about the curve of Jake's neck, the way it smelled of pipe smoke and pine trees, just the way the cabin on Esopus Creek smelled. I inhale, wanting him to be here, to be real and in front of me again. But instead my lungs fill with that thick air, the dank smell of the Hudson, a humid summer afternoon turned almost evening.

A few fireflies begin to gather just outside my window, their bodies glowing, a little early. It's not quite dark. Not yet the Sabbath. I'm almost there, so close, and I will the darkness to hold off. Just a little longer.

Up ahead, there are dozens of red tail-lights and I realize that traffic has come to a standstill. I stop and put my head out the window. Farther up the road, it looks like there are barricades set up. Police with flashlights, though I'm hoping FBI, too. I switch on the radio and listen anxiously, wanting so badly for there to be good news. A last-minute stay. A decision to halt things until after the Sabbath has passed. More time.

I switch the stations, anxious for something. Anything. But all I get is music: Ella Fitzgerald singing "Guilty." It feels like a cruel joke, and I switch again. At last I find news, but it's not good. President Eisenhower has denied a stay of execution, saying Ethel and Julie have condemned tens of millions of people to death all around the world. *No.* Ethel and Julie are still set to die at eight p.m. An hour from now.

I switch the radio off, pull the car to the side of the road, and kill the engine. I take a cigarette from my purse and light it with shaking hands. I inhale the smoke and for a moment consider not getting out of the car but just waiting here in the line of traffic. But I know I can't.

I push open my door and step out into the steamy air. I stomp out the cigarette with my worn heel. I stare at the back window and picture David there on the other side, staring back at me, his round brown eyes like the pennies he so loved to stack. "Come on now," I would tell him if he were here. "We have to hurry if we're going to find Dr. Jake."

His mouth would twitch slightly at the mention of Jake's name, and I'd wonder if maybe it might even be a little smile.

Jake's here, I tell myself instead. *All I have to do is find Jake.*

And I shut the car door and begin running up the road.

1947
1

The first time I ever saw Ethel Rosenberg, she was round and bright as a beach ball. She stood on the sidewalk in front of our building at 10 Monroe Street in Knickerbocker Village, clutching a bouquet of yellow roses in one hand, her little boy in the other, and despite all her brightness and girth I might not have even noticed her at all if it hadn't been for David, who decided at the very moment we walked by her to reach up and swipe the roses from her hand.

I saw them in a blur, yellow and green flashes tumbling all over the sidewalk, and then Ethel let out a short, startled cry.

"David!" I yelled at him, realizing what he'd done. "What's wrong with you?" David was almost two, but he wasn't prone to tantrums, fits of rage, or grabbing things from strangers on the street. But then I realized what it was — the yellow. David was recently infatuated with the color, drawing circles for hours with his yellow crayons. *Suns,* I would tell him, begging him to repeat the word after me, but he kept drawing his yellow circles without even the slightest sound.

I bent down to gather up the flowers, and I noticed David was crying silently. He hated it when I yelled at him, and I immediately felt bad for being so cross. It was exactly what Dr. Greenberg had told me not to do, and here I was, doing it anyway. "I'm so sorry," I murmured, handing Ethel back her flowers. "He didn't mean to . . ."

"Yes he did," her little boy shot back at me. I judged him to be older than David, though I couldn't be sure how much, and he spoke to me like that, so clearly and completely. And *rudely* . . .

I nodded at him. David had meant to. But what else was there to say?

We had lived on Monroe Street only a week by then — David, Ed, and I — and I had thought, however stupidly at the time, that it might change us. The outdoor playground, the scores of other children, the loving families that nested all about Knickerbocker Village like indigenous birds, that somehow we would become shiny like all the rest of them just by virtue of living here. But aside from the steam heat, the laundry room, and the elevators, nothing was different in Knickerbocker Village than it had been in our efficiency above my mother's apartment on Delancey Street.

"It's all right," Ethel said. "They're only flowers. And you've gathered them all back up. No harm done, see, John?" She handed the bouquet to her boy and she turned back to me. She patted David on the head and his sobs worsened, shaking his shoulders, but he still did not make a sound. "You're new around here?" she asked, turning back toward me, her voice clear and sweet now.

I hugged David close to my hip, willing him to stop so that we might have a moment to befriend someone in the building. So far the other mothers at the playground had eyed me and David with trepidation. And why shouldn't they? When David would only sit by himself, silently stacking rocks in even piles, while all the other children laughed and shouted and ran around the courtyard together.

"I'm Millie Stein." I reached out for her hand to shake it. "And this is my son, David." Her grip was firm but delicate, yet her fingers looked decidedly swollen, like the kosher sausages Mr. Bergman sold in the butcher shop.

"Millie," she said. "Nice to meet you. I'm

Ethel Rosenberg. And this is John."

"You live here, in Knickerbocker Village?" I asked her. "I haven't seen you at the playground yet."

She looked down. "We don't get to the playground too often these days," she said softly. I assumed it was because of her large, heaving belly, her being so firmly in the family way — about eight months along, I judged — remembering how uncomfortable I'd been at that stage and trying to imagine feeling that way with another child to tote along.

But at the mention of the word *playground,* John suddenly clung to Ethel's bright dress, twisting it between his fingers. "I want to go to the playground," he whined. Ethel shook her head, and he began to cry. Not the way David cried, silently, but loud, disturbing cries, reminding me of the feral cats that used to run around outside our apartment on Delancey, howling at all hours of the night in hunger or pain.

Ethel offered me a fleeting smile, and then she quickly pulled John and her round body back toward our building. "I've got to get him inside, but maybe I'll see you around," she called over her shoulder.

I could hear John crying even after she walked inside, the sound coming through

16

the brick walls like a siren.

David, however, had stopped. His eyes followed after them with what I imagined to be curiosity.

David and I were on our way to visit Mr. Bergman that morning we first met Ethel and John, and after parting ways, David and I continued walking slowly down Monroe Street toward Market Street and Kauffman's Meats, the kosher butcher shop once run by my father and, since his death five years ago, run by Mr. Bergman, his business partner.

I watched our footsteps making shadows on the sidewalk, overrun quickly by people humming by all around us. Now that the war was so firmly over, the city moved again. People smiled, the crowds on the sidewalks bright flashes of warmth and laughter. People everywhere were happy. Or at least it seemed that way to me. Every woman I saw seemed to have the bright pink stain of love and happiness across her cheeks, a look I tried to replicate myself with Helena Rubinstein blush, but somehow when I saw my own face staring back at me in the mirror, it never seemed quite the same.

Mr. Bergman set aside a brisket for me

every Friday, free of charge. His best cut, he said, and we both pretended that that was why David and I came to see him each week. The truth was, the inside of the shop, the smells of meat, Mr. Bergman's thinning gray hair and thick gray beard, still seemed to be a familiar little piece of my father.

"Mildred! And boychik!" His voice rang out across the counter as we walked in through the glass front door, and the bell clanged cheerfully behind us. The sound startled David and he jumped a little. *He is not deaf,* I reassured myself yet again despite Ed's insistence that he must be.

Mr. Bergman waved and I waved back. David clung to the side of my dress until Mr. Bergman leaned across the counter. "I have a present for you, boychik." He opened his hand to reveal a yellow gumdrop and David took it and chewed it greedily.

"You spoil him," I said, but I smiled, enjoying how this moment felt normal for David. I remembered the gumdrops Mr. Bergman would sneak to my sister, Susan, and me when we came into the shop as girls.

"And for you," he told me, "a bigger cut this week. Because I hear you are having company tonight to enjoy the Shabbos."

I nodded and thanked him. It was the first Friday night in our new apartment, and everyone from my family was coming to us tonight: my mother, Bubbe Kasha, Susan, Sam, and the twins. Whenever there was a family get-together, we normally all flocked to my sister Susan's house, so this would be a first — everyone coming to me.

"How is the new place?" Mr. Bergman asked as he handed my brown-paper-wrapped brisket across the counter and David chewed happily on the candy.

"Wonderful," I said, though I had not yet decided for myself whether it was truly wonderful or not, but it certainly did have a lot of nice, modern features. "There's an elevator that takes us all the way up to the eleventh floor."

"Your mother told me."

I smiled, unsurprised. I was sure all of Delancey Street had heard about the elevator multiple times, even the feral alley cats. Which was a change for my mother, whose usual favorite topic of conversation was my older sister Susan, her adorable baby girl twins, and her recent move to the suburbs in Elizabeth, New Jersey.

"And how is Ed?" Mr. Bergman asked, his voice taking on a slightly higher pitch, a peculiar end note. I often thought Mr. Bergman saw Ed the way Ed's mother, Lena, saw me. With disdain and mistrust. Though

I couldn't imagine that Mr. Bergman knew much about me and Ed, beneath the surface, it was almost as if some shadow of my father still existed within him. He worried about me.

"Ed is well," I said. Our weekly dance.

Mr. Bergman frowned. "And he isn't having a problem at work with this loyalty oath everyone is talking about now?"

"Why should he?" I asked, though I swallowed hard, not willing to admit to Mr. Bergman that I had already worried as much but had been afraid to broach the subject with Ed myself. Ed clung to his Russian past like a winter coat, something that enveloped him absolutely even though it had been four years since he'd come to America.

"I just thought . . . Well, never mind." Mr. Bergman waved his hand in the air. Behind us another customer demanded service by clearing her throat loudly and talking in Yiddish to what looked like her mother. Mr. Bergman held up his hand to indicate he'd be with her in a moment.

"Millie," he said, leaning over across the meat case so he could lower his voice to a whisper. "I'm worried about you. Things are not the same as they used to be for a Russian Jew in New York. It's not like it was when our relatives came over forty years ago." Mr. Bergman shook his head. "They say Stalin is the next Hitler, you know? And what will happen if he gets the bomb?"

"You worry too much," I told him, and I grabbed my brisket and David and headed back toward Knickerbocker Village.

2

Mr. Bergman was not the only one who worried about the bomb. The truth was, I thought of it often — we all did — the idea that this utterly destructive *thing* could come suddenly, and seemingly out of nowhere, all the way across the ocean from Russia, instantly turning New York City into dust. We could be the next Hiroshima, Nagasaki. And no amount of blush could hide this fear.

As David and I walked through the front entrance of 10 Monroe Street, I imagined the bomb coming just then, the imprint of our bodies etched forever wordlessly in the ground where the two thirteen-story brick buildings of Knickerbocker Village once stood, our remnants just shadows, nothing more. In midtown, Ed's body would become a shadow beneath his office building. And somewhere across the ocean, Stalin would be laughing at us.

But it didn't happen, and David and I rode the elevator back up to the eleventh floor as peacefully as we'd come down an hour earlier, stopping at each floor along the way, as David wanted each button to light up yellow. I allowed him to do it if only to keep him from crying again.

On the long ride up, I thought about my sister, Susan. She and her husband, Sam, had retreated to the suburbs of Elizabeth last year shortly before the twins were born. Susan told me there was safety in the suburbs, that no one would think to bomb there because life was more spread out, slower, less people as targets. And *Time* magazine had recently reported the same thing. Not that I was surprised, as Susan was always right — or, at least, she acted as if she were. I wondered if Ed and I would've been safer and happier there, too, rather than here in Knickerbocker Village, but Ed had insisted on staying in the city so he'd be closer to work and to his mother. And since Susan had left, I knew I needed to stay, too. Someone had to be close by for my mother and Bubbe Kasha. Besides, Ed was giving me steam heat, an elevator, a playground, and, at some point, even a nursery school for David. And our one-bedroom apartment here on the eleventh floor was quite an upgrade from our tiny *one-room* apartment on Delancey.

And as Ed said, with an accusing lilt to his thick Russian accent, why did we need any more than this with only one child?

Time had also reported that the American family was thriving as never before, that the average man and woman now hoped for three children. Susan was well on her way, but *three*? I couldn't imagine. I could barely even imagine two, of taking care of David and a baby, and so I had taken special and quite secret steps to make sure this would not happen.

Ed was none the wiser. Ed, who had repeatedly told me that all the fears about the bomb here were silly.

It's never going to happen in New York, he always said, waving the concerns away with the trail of smoke from his cigar, and I didn't understand how he could be so certain about a city he had known only for a short time. *Women have many babies,* he told me. *That's what they do.* He whispered it in my ear at night like a love song, in his thick Russian accent, just before he took his pants off and rolled on top of me.

When the elevator at long last stopped on the eleventh floor and the door opened, David and I nearly ran right into Ethel again, as she was waiting to ride the elevator down. But this time, she was alone.

"So we meet again," Ethel said, and she laughed, as David and I stepped out. I wondered what had happened to John and how Ethel managed to be going out without him. Since David had begun showing some peculiarities in his behavior, my mother had lost interest in watching him, so now he was always with me. Sometimes I dreamed about the solace of being alone, even if only for an hour. And I was torn for a moment between feeling jealous of Ethel and excited that she lived on the same floor as us. Perhaps we really could be friends, and I imagined David playing with John, me sharing afternoon coffee with Ethel. It had been a while since I'd had a friend this close by, not since before David was born. On Delancey all my old friends had married before me and moved or we'd drifted apart, and in the room above my mother's apartment our only companions had been her and Bubbe Kasha.

But Ethel propped open the elevator door with her thick fingers and seemed a bit impatient for us to get out, shuffling her feet as if she were in a hurry. David reached for the elevator buttons again, and I grabbed

for his hands. "No. No more buttons, darling," I told him, and he shrank until his
eyes caught onto Ethel's dress, the same
bright yellow-and-red one as earlier, but
now I noticed her brown curls were also
topped with a dramatic red hat. Ethel was
quite short, a few inches shorter than my
very average height, but she held herself in
such a way that I hadn't noticed it earlier
on the street.

"I have to run," she said, pushing past us
into the elevator. "I have studio time and
I'm late."

"*Studio time?* You're on the radio?"

"Oh, no." She laughed. "I'm making a
recording for my John so he'll have my voice
to listen to when I'm in the hospital for the
new baby."

"Oh," I said. "How lovely."

She smiled and touched her free hand to
her hat shyly, in a way that made me think
someone else had told her this was not such
a lovely idea. I wondered about her husband
and if he was like Ed when it came to
money. I guessed not. Studio time sounded
expensive.

"I should have you and John over sometime," I said as I watched her press the button to go down to the ground floor.

But before she had time to answer, the

26

elevator doors shut and Ethel was riding down to her studio.

Our apartment was dark, the air inside quiet and cool. Ed was still at work, and I prayed David would actually lie down and take a nap so I could have a little time to myself.

I switched on the lights, unwrapped the brisket, and put it in the oven, and after I settled David into his crib, which I understood he was getting way too big for but was trying to follow Dr. Greenberg's advice to coddle him just a little while longer, I lit myself a cigarette and sat at our scratched wooden table. The Sabbath was only a few hours away, and Susan and Sam and the twins would arrive before sundown. They never took the twins on the train into the city, but tonight they had decided to make an exception in order to see our new place.

I inhaled the smoke from my cigarette and then exhaled. My sister and her babies and all their glowing perfection. Motherhood seemed to suit Susan, made her even prettier than she always had been, which I might have once thought impossible, but, no. Caring for the girls gave her rosier cheeks and a new sheen to her vibrant black hair and even made her laughter sound brighter. And never mind that she'd carried *two* babies at once, the extra weight had dropped off her waistline just like that and now her figure looked more perfect than ever. The twins were only nine months, but they already babbled and smiled and had started to make sounds that vaguely resembled *dada. Sam is just in love,* Susan had gushed the last time I'd seen her a few weeks earlier when we'd taken the train out to Elizabeth for Sunday brunch. And why wouldn't he be? His children — and his wife — were perfect, and thinking about it made me well up with both jealousy and sadness.

Motherhood had done no favors for my figure. I was always a slightly heavier, slightly shorter, slightly duller version of my older sister. My mother used to tell me my features were ordinary — and not unkindly, just a statement of fact. I'd always had nice clear skin and pretty pale brown eyes, but I was neither tall nor short, beautiful nor ugly, the kind of woman who can blend into a crowd and be utterly forgettable. My most distinguishing feature was my shoulder-length medium brown curls, often impossibly unruly. I loved David, but my waist was a few inches thicker than it once was, my curls were forever a mess, and the last time Susan saw me she took one look at the bags under my eyes and told me I wasn't sleeping enough. Yes, David was exhausting. He would be two soon and had yet to utter even a single sound. Ed claimed his ears must not work, or possibly his brain, and Dr. Greenberg said it was me, that I was too cold with him, too cross with him. *Indulge him a little more, why don't you,* he had said, the entire weight of his bald head sinking into his frown.

And yet I'd tried everything: coaxing him, playing with him, listening harder, hugging him more, punishing him, yelling at him. I read *Parents* magazine with a rapt hunger for answers that were never there. I learned about illnesses and tantrums, but nothing at all about what to do with a child like mine who just would not speak.

I heard a knock at the door, interrupting my thoughts. I checked the time, but it was only three thirty, too early for anyone to arrive for dinner and too early for Ed to be home from work. For a moment, I wondered if it was Ethel back from the studio and wanting to take me up on my offer for coffee. "Coming," I called, but not too loud so as not to wake David, and I squashed out my cigarette, stood, and smoothed down my dress with my hands, then smoothed my curls.

I opened the door and saw my mother

standing there in the hallway, looking as if she'd just swallowed a lemon, a frown so big enveloping her plump cheeks that it seemed to weigh them down, to make her entire face sag. "You're so early," I said, opening the door wider, "I don't have anything ready yet."

She pushed past me into the apartment. "Dinner is canceled," she said. "Susan just sent me a telegram. Thank goodness she figured it out."

The telephone operators had been on strike for two weeks, rendering our new shiny black telephone entirely useless. We had been promised a party line as part of our forty-six dollars a month rent, which also included electricity. It was an excellent deal, according to Ed. Not so excellent when the phone was unworkable because of the operators' strike.

"Canceled?" I asked, trying not to let the disappointment I felt seep into my voice.

"There's a smallpox outbreak in the city," my mother said. "Susan heard on the radio and she can't bring the twins into the city under these conditions."

Susan had yet to bring the twins into the city under any conditions, and I fought the urge to roll my eyes. "Smallpox outbreak?" I'd heard nothing of it yet, but I hadn't listened to the radio all morning. David did not like the sound and he would cry when I'd turn it on — more evidence that he could at least hear. I'd asked Ed for a television, hoping that David would be drawn more to it, the visual stimulus, but he'd yet to oblige what he called my *expensive whims.*

"There's going to be inoculation clinics in the streets starting Monday," my mother said. "We'll go. You'll come for me in the morning."

"Is that really necessary?" I murmured, thinking ahead to the way David would react to an inoculation in the street. It had been bad enough when Dr. Greenberg had inoculated him for whooping cough in the office, after I'd read the terrifying article about it in *Parents.* David had clung to the examining table and kicked and cried such hard, silent tears that I thought his entire small body might burst.

"You should want to die of smallpox instead?" my mother asked, putting her hands on her wide hips. She wore her pale gray dress like a sack, and her hands revealed the lumpiness of her large stomach underneath.

Would I want to die of smallpox? It seemed closer, more immediate than Stalin's bomb, but I also imagined the process would be slower and more painful. Should the bomb come and take us, I might never even know what happened. And it would take me and David, instantly and simultaneously. What would happen to David if I should die of something else on my own?

"Of course not," I said to my mother. "I'll come by for you Monday morning." I paused. "You'll still come for dinner tonight, though? And Bubbe Kasha, too?"

"Oh goodness no. I feel like I'm risking my life just having come here. All these people living here in one place. All the germs that could be in that . . . *elevator.*"

"Well, then you should have sent a telegram," I said, unable to keep the annoyance I was feeling with her from my voice. I had been looking forward to the dinner with my family, my sister — perfect babies and all — and now it would just be Ed and me and David. Alone. I had a brisket enough to feed at least ten. And there was no option to skip Shabbat, not for Ed anyway.

"You should want for me to spend money on a telegram when I can use my own two feet?" She waved her hand in the air, blew me a kiss, and then as quickly as she'd come she was gone.

From the back room I heard the sounds of the crib bars rattling. David was awake.

3

I was raised Jewish — and only the second generation in America at that. My grandparents came over from Russia in 1901, but for them, and later for me, our religion always felt more cultural than spiritual. Growing up, Shabbat dinner was something we'd attend at Bubbe Kasha's and Zayde Jerome's apartment, but not every week. Only when my father felt like it. Some weeks he was too tired and wanted to stay in our apartment and rest, which to him meant eating my mother's terrible split pea soup, smoking a cigarette, and then listening to Jack Haley on *The Wonder Show*. As he always said, he could believe in God *and* listen to the radio on his night of rest.

To be married to a kosher butcher who doesn't even want to attend Shabbat dinner, my mother would say and cluck her tongue, and then she would light our candles. She always lit the candles and we'd always say a quick prayer. But then she would smile and pull up a chair next to the radio and eat pea soup there with our father, and Susan and I would hear the two of them laughing from the bedroom in the back of the apartment.

But Ed grew up back in Russia, much more religious than I did here. He insisted on a formal Shabbat dinner every Friday night. We used to go to the one at his mother Lena's apartment, which was regularly attended by Ed's younger brother, Leo, Leo's wife, Betty, and their two daughters, but more recently I had told Ed that I would make the dinner for us. Back on Delancey Street my mother and Bubbe Kasha would walk up the steps to join us each week.

I had offered, not because I wanted to make the dinner or even cared so much about the ritual of Shabbat, but because I didn't enjoy attending the dinner at Lena's, the way her piercing green eyes bored holes into me. It was as if they knew my secret and she hated me for it, though there was no way she could know — Ed had no idea about the diaphragm I'd gotten from Dr. Greenberg. And I'd told no one, not even my mother or Susan.

But then I understood that wasn't what it was at all. The last time we'd been there, two months earlier, Lena had taken me aside just before dinner. "I raised boys, you know," she'd said, her voice curling, so I didn't want to point out that, technically, she'd raised only Leo. Ed had grown up in Russia with an aunt and had moved to America as an adult to join Lena, only four years ago. "And neither one of them had the . . . problem that David has." She frowned, and her green eyes felt hot against my face, as if they really and truly could burn me.

"David is fine," I shot back at her. "Dr. Greenberg says he's just taking his time to develop, that's all." That was, of course, only part of what Dr. Greenberg had said, but that was the part that had to be right.

She wagged her finger in my face. "You don't love him enough," she said, but it wasn't clear whether she was referring to David or to Ed. I didn't answer, and when we got back to Delancey Street that night, I told Ed that I would cook us Shabbat dinner from then on. I blamed it on my mother and Bubbe Kasha, who was getting old and had a hard time with her memory, and so far they had joined us each week.

But now, tonight, I had a brisket in the oven, enough to feed ten, and no one coming to dinner.

■ ■ ■ ■

Ed walked in the door just after five, just after I'd gotten David settled with a pile of brightly colored blocks on the floor by our window overlooking Monroe Street. I'd pulled all the yellows out and had given them to him, and he sat there and stacked them over and over again, seemingly contented, lulled by their brightness. The brisket was done and I had it on the table, along with our Shabbat candles. I smoked a cigarette nervously, waiting for Ed to arrive, watching out the window at all the men in suits rushing by on their way home from work. From this high up, they were tiny, and they all looked the same, cloaked in dark suits, dark hats, and I could not make out which one was Ed until I heard the door opening, and then I knew I'd missed him entirely.

He entered the apartment wordlessly and walked toward the narrow kitchen. I heard him rustling in the cabinets, pulling out a glass and pouring his vodka. And then he entered the living room, glass in hand.

He didn't lean in to kiss me, as my father had always done with my mother when he returned home from work each evening, or even stoop down to pat David on the head, as I remember my father doing with me. Instead, he simply sat on the couch, downed his vodka, and then he said, "Where is everyone?"

"They're not coming." I squashed my cigarette out in the ashtray on the coffee table just next to where Ed rested his feet.

"What do you mean not coming?" he asked.

"There's some kind of smallpox outbreak, I guess," I said. "So Susan didn't want to bring the twins into the city, and my mother and Bubbe Kasha thought it better to stay home." I tried to read his face, to judge his reaction. But his expression was blank, his gaze fixed straight ahead on the beige wall, and I couldn't tell if he was angry or just tired. I thought about what Mr. Bergman asked, about whether Ed was having trouble with work now that everyone was making such a big deal out of Truman's loyalty oath. Ed's Russian accent, even four years after he'd come to America, was so thick, so obvious, that it worried me that it would brand him now that everyone had started worrying about Stalin and Russia and American loyalty in a way they hadn't before. "I have the brisket ready," I added. "And the candles."

He finished off his vodka and put the empty, sweating glass down on the coffee table. "You should have telephoned me at work," he said. "Then I would have had time to let Mother know she would have three more at the table tonight."

"I couldn't," I said quickly. "The phone operators' strike, remember? No calls are going through." Though the truth was, I wouldn't have called him at work anyway. And now it would be too late to go to Lena's, there was no way to telephone her, and besides, the brisket was already done. Ed would not let a cooked brisket go to waste. "Come on," I said to him, sitting down on the couch next to him and gently reaching my hand around to the back of his neck. "Let's eat." Ed had a thick neck, and I could feel it was knotted with tenseness. I rubbed it softly with my fingers, hoping it would calm him.

David picked that moment to accidentally knock his stack of yellows over so that they scattered all about the floor. I watched as his mouth turned from content to aghast in a matter of seconds, and his face turned bright red, his eyes welling with tears.

Ed pulled out of my grasp and he stood, clearly agitated now. David kicked the floor, making loud, booming thuds over and over again. "Do something with him, would you?" Ed demanded. And he walked back into the kitchen.

I went to David and held on to him, trying to soothe him by picking the yellows back up, stacking them again, but this time David knocked them back over intentionally. I wasn't supposed to yell. I was supposed to give him extra love, Dr. Greenberg had said, so I hugged his small body to me tightly. I rocked him back and forth and back and forth until his breathing evened and his crying stopped. "I wish you could just tell me what you were thinking," I whispered into his soft curls. "Wouldn't that be a whole lot easier for both of us?" But the only sound I heard came from the kitchen: Ed pouring another vodka.

I led David to the table, where I handed him his cup of milk, and then I walked into the narrow kitchen and put my hand on Ed's shoulder. "Come on," I said to him. "Let's sit down and light our candles and eat. David has calmed down, and the meat is growing cold. We can still celebrate the Shabbat together as a family in our nice new apartment."

Ed finished off his second vodka, and I could feel the tension ease from his shoulders. He put the glass in the sink and nodded.

Later, Ed and I lay on opposite sides of our hard mattress, not quite touching. The room was still, but I could hear the even sounds of David asleep, breathing in his crib, and the sounds of the neighbors next door, who I hadn't met yet, their bed springs squeaking up and down and up and down. It was clear what they were doing in there, and I hoped it wouldn't give Ed any ideas.

Ed wanted another child, another boy, so very badly. We had been married only a month when I got pregnant with David, and we had barely known each other but everything had seemed like a grand adventure to me then. Playing house with a man and a child in the one-room apartment above my mother's — it was such a relief to be doing what I always thought and dreamed I would — leaving my days as a working girl at the factory behind for a quiet domesticity.

My marriage to Ed was something my mother and Lena cooked up one evening a few years ago at a Hadassah meeting. Lena had for years tried to bring Ed to New York, but it was not as easy to emigrate from Russia in the '40s, during the war, as it had been when Bubbe Kasha and Zayde Jerome

41

came in 1901 with my mother. Lena had finally gotten him here at the end of '43 and then she had to marry him off, of course. Ed had been living in New York only a month when I first saw him, and he was ten years older than me. Back then I'd still been working at the Cupid Garment Factory with Susan. The work there was easy, and though I took no particular joy in sewing, I liked the camaraderie with the other girls there, all just like me, young, unmarried, unfettered. But my friends at the factory started getting engaged one by one, including Susan. I feared I might become a spinster, stuck sewing forever. Ed appeared to be the answer to everything.

It didn't hurt that he was very nice to look at. He was tall, with a thick head of brown hair. He had very nice broad shoulders and a squarish nose that sat firmly in the center of his face. The first time I ever saw him, inside Lena's threadbare apartment, he was sitting at Lena's worn table, looking at me shyly, his hands shaking a little as we were introduced. He was nervous in front of me at first, a quality I found endearing.

I wasn't lucky — or even beautiful — like Susan, who had known and loved Sam practically forever. He'd grown up down the street from us on Delancey and he'd gone to high school with us. We'd always known he and Susan would get married, and they did, just after he came home from the war. But I'd had no one, and with all the men gone, and my thirties rapidly approaching, it had seemed I might never find anyone, that I might live on Delancey with my mother and Bubbe Kasha forever. And then I saw Ed there at Lena's kitchen table so eager to please me, for me to like him, and a few weeks later, when he asked, I agreed to marry him.

I never thought about the years and years that would stretch ahead in our marriage, making the life that lay ahead of me sometimes feel like an impossibly long and arduous void. I didn't know about the way Ed would drink too much vodka when things bothered him or the way Ed would need another child that I might not be ready to have. Ed was so happy when David was first born. Ed's younger American-born brother, Leo, had so far given Lena only two granddaughters, and here Ed, always trying to prove himself to Lena after so many years away from her in Russia, had produced the first grandson, a boy to carry on the family name. But since it had become clear that David might not exactly be a normal, perfect boy, Ed had become obsessed with having another. It felt to me he wished to throw David away as you would wayward garbage. Ed had grown so cold and distant with David in a way I could not understand nor accept, that it often occurred to me now how little I had ever really even known Ed — or loved him — at all.

Suddenly his hand reached across the bed for my thigh, and I noticed the bed springs were now silent in the apartment next door. Ed's fingers pushed up my leg gently, but in a way that now made me feel sick to my stomach. If we didn't have another child, Ed would not be able give up on David.

"Not tonight . . . I'm bleeding," I said to him.

"Again?" He moved his hand. "Maybe you should see the doctor, Mildred." He sighed. "Maybe there is something wrong with you?"

"There's nothing wrong with me," I said, wondering how long I could keep this up without Ed growing suspicious. It had been six months of us "trying" so far with nothing happening. "Dr. Greenberg says it just takes time, that's all. David isn't even two yet."

But Ed didn't say anything else and his silence hung there, an emptiness between us, as I wondered what he was thinking, if he knew I was lying. He rolled over and I could feel the weight of his back, leaning into the mattress. A few minutes later, he was snoring.

4

On Monday morning, my mother, Bubbe Kasha, David, and I waited in the pouring rain in a very long line on Monroe Street to get our smallpox vaccines. I was flanked by David and Bubbe Kasha, while my mother stood just in front of us, complaining about her hip hurting, as it always did in the rain. Bubbe Kasha was confused, as she tended to be these days, and kept asking why we were in line.

David, blissfully now, said nothing and clutched tightly to my hand as I tried to shield both him and Bubbe Kasha from the rain with my umbrella, all the while getting soaked myself. There were so many people and we were packed tightly in line, water rushing over us. My brown dress was soaked and my bones ached, and I thought maybe smallpox would be better than this, especially since my mother kept talking, as she always did. "I hear the man who started this epidemic carried it in from Mexico and then spread it all through the city like a sewer rat. Imagine, the gall of some people." She was talking too loudly, something she had begun doing lately, which I took to mean her hearing wasn't as good as it used to be, and several strangers in line stared at her suspiciously. She seemed not to notice and shook her head, right into my umbrella, sending rainwater tumbling over both David and Bubbe Kasha until I repositioned.

I thought about the poor man, maybe drawn to the sunshine and beauty of Mexico, who'd come back to New York only to die of a terrible disease and then be blamed for it.

"Good thing Susan and the babies aren't in the city," I heard my mother saying, "in the middle of all this filth. You and Ed will probably find your way out to the country eventually, too, and then I suppose we will be forced to come live with one of you. Won't we, Mamaleh?" Bubbe Kasha did not respond and neither did I.

"What are we in line for?" Bubbe Kasha asked me for what felt like the hundredth time, and I calmly explained to her again about the smallpox and the necessary inoculation. But I knew I could tell her anything now and she would simply nod her head.

She had been my sanctuary, growing up. It was her apartment I'd run to when I was upset with my mother or Susan — or both. She was the one who showed me how to knead the challah in a way that made me always feel better. She was the one who dropped butter cookies in the pocket of my dress even before the candles were lit for Shabbat dinner. "You're too skinny," she used to whisper even though it wasn't true. "I need to fatten you up."

I hugged the umbrella under my shoulder so I could reach down and squeeze her hand now, and for a moment her thin, frail fingers clutched mine, squeezing back, the way they used to when I was a girl and my mother would prattle on and on about Susan's many accomplishments. Susan got high marks in school, while mine were decidedly average, and she sang a solo every year at the end of school performance because she had such a lovely voice, while I was in the chorus. I was just plain old dependable Millie, the one who helped my father out in the butcher shop and who helped Bubbe Kasha around her apartment, while Susan was too busy with all her many activities. But with a slight squeeze of my fingers, a knowing smile cast my way, Bubbe Kasha told me that I was appreciated, that she thought I was special, too.

"Finally," my mother exclaimed, and I looked up and saw that at long last we were at the front of the line. My mother pulled Bubbe Kasha away from me and pushed up her sleeve. Then did the same thing herself. Their pale, wrinkly arms hung there in the rain, waiting to get inoculated, and it was at that moment that I thought to move the umbrella to look down at David. His eyes were wide and his mouth had dropped open a little. He was not dumb, I reminded myself again. He understood exactly what was happening, what was about to happen to him. I saw it in his eyes, the fleeting recognition, the memory of the whooping cough vaccine that morning not too long ago in Dr. Greenberg's office. *He understood* even if he didn't say it.

"It's all right, darling," I leaned down and whispered in his ear. "It's just a little poke. But it will keep us from getting sick."

"Ouch!" my mother yelled too loudly as the needle hit her arm. "That hurts."

David's eyes widened farther, and he struggled out of my grasp and began running through puddles right into Monroe Street. It took me a second to understand what was happening, that David had gotten away from me and was in the street, and then I ran after him, a yellow taxicab swerving and honking at me.

There were so many people in line that it wrapped around the block, past the entrance to our building, and it was raining so hard that I struggled to see, to make sense of where I was looking. David. *My David.* I couldn't see him, and certainly I wouldn't be able to hear him.

"David!" I screamed. "Don't run. Don't move. You don't have to get a shot!"

In response, I heard only the rain hitting the sidewalk, the squeal of car brakes in the street, my mother's voice yelling, "Millie, get back here. Should you want to die of smallpox?" She was oblivious to what had happened, and I didn't turn back to tell her.

My heart pounded so loud and hard, louder and harder than the rain, and I turned frantically in circles looking for him — in the street, across the street, then back by the entrance to our building. "David!" I screamed his name again and people in line looked at me, but no one left their place to ask who I was looking for, why I was screaming. "My son!" I shouted at them. "Have any of you seen my son? A little boy?"

David was so small and he couldn't talk. How would he ever find me again? What had I done, taking him to get inoculated in the street and not watching him carefully enough?

"Millie." I heard a familiar woman's voice saying my name and I looked up. It was Ethel. John clung to her hip, and she was holding on to David, his small legs wrapped around her rotund belly.

"David!" I grabbed him from her and held him tightly to my chest. His tiny arms clasped my neck in such a way that I knew what he wanted to say even if he couldn't: *He loved me, and he was sorry.*

"I saw him wandering in the street" — I realized Ethel was talking — "and I grabbed him."

She walked in through the front entrance of our building as she talked, pulling herself and John out of the rain, and I followed her, David still clutching tightly to my neck, me clutching back. "Don't you ever do that again," I said to him, not sure if he understood or not, but the way he curled his head into the crook of my neck I hoped he did.

The elevator doors opened and Ethel and John stepped in. I ran to catch up with them. "Thank you," I said to Ethel. She nodded, holding John tightly to her hip but staring straight ahead as if she didn't want to talk to me now. What she must think of me!

The elevator doors shut, and we began moving slowly up to the eleventh floor. "Really," I said to her, "we were waiting in line for the smallpox inoculations and he got startled and . . ." My voice broke and I couldn't hold back the tears. To think what had happened, what might have happened.

"Of course," Ethel said. "I did what anyone would have done."

I thought of all the strangers waiting in line, staring anxiously at me as I screamed for David. "No, really," I said. "I owe you . . ."

The elevator doors opened again and Ethel and John stepped off onto the eleventh floor. They walked to apartment G.E. 11 at the end of the hallway, down a few doors from ours. Ethel pulled her key from her pocket and fumbled to get it in the lock. I was soaked to the bone and my teeth were chattering. David's tiny body heaved with shivers, but I got off the elevator and ran after her.

I reached up and touched Ethel's shoulder, and she turned to look at me again. "I can imagine what you must think of me," I said, and she shook her head as if to say she didn't think anything of me. John tugged at the bottom of her red dress, impatient, and she put her key back in the lock. "Would you at least come over for a cup of coffee after we all change into dry clothes? Let me thank you," I said. "The boys could even play . . . maybe."

She hesitated momentarily. "I don't think so."

"Another time, then?" Though I understood there would not be another time, that whatever I thought about Ethel and me becoming friends would not happen now after she had seen firsthand what kind of mother I was. After this, Ethel and I would be nothing more than strangers who would pass each other by in the hall, getting on and off the elevator.

"You never let me have friends," I heard John say as we walked down the hallway toward our apartment. His voice sounded so crisp and perfect and clear that it surprised me. Granted, he was obviously older than David, but it was as if I'd forgotten the way normal little boys sounded. That they had voices, demands.

"Millie," Ethel called down the hallway after me. I turned back to look at her, and from farther away, I noticed her stomach was so big that there barely seemed to be anything else to her tiny frame. "Why don't you come here for a cup of coffee after you dry off. John has so many toys. David might enjoy playing with some of them."

Ethel's apartment was quite similar to mine, right down to the linoleum squares in the tiny, narrow kitchen. The exceptions were the large upright piano in the living room, the views of the courtyard and the East River, and the multitude of toys scattered all about the floor. She was right about John having so many, and with that, the piano, and her studio time, it seemed Ethel and her husband had a lot more money than Ed and I had.

Now that we were in dry clothes, David seemed tired, and he still clung to my neck and sucked his thumb. We sat at Ethel's table while she brewed some coffee in the kitchen, and John tossed a ball against the hard floor, trying to get David to join in.

"Why doesn't he say anything?" John implored me, frowning.

"He just . . ." I didn't have an answer that I could give a child. Or anyone. "He just doesn't talk yet," I said, brushing the damp brown curls from David's forehead. "He's younger than you."

"He doesn't need to talk to play with you," Ethel said to John, putting two steaming cups of coffee on the table. I was still chilled, my curls were still damp, and the steam felt wonderful against my face. "Why don't you show him some of your things?" Ethel said.

I pulled David from my lap and put him on the floor, but he reached right back up for my neck. "Do you mind if I sit down here with him?" I asked Ethel.

"Not at all." And she joined us on the floor, too. John handed David the ball he'd been bouncing, and David pulled his thumb from his mouth to use his hands to examine the ball carefully. It was red with yellow squares, and I watched David's eyes widen with interest.

John pulled the ball back and began bouncing it again. And David reached his arms back, trying to recapture it. "Make sure you're sharing," Ethel said to John. He squirmed and pulled out of Ethel's grasp.

"It's all right," I said, sensing John was on the edge of a tantrum. "There are plenty of toys to go around here." I searched the floor for something else yellow, saw a bright yellow bird stuffed animal, and picked it up and handed it to David.

John bounced his ball without complaining, though the repetitive noise of it against the floor was dreadful, and David seemed content to turn the yellow bird over and over again.

Ethel glanced at me and struggled to get off the floor. I stood up, gave her a hand, and then we both sat back down at the table. She put her hand across her large belly and looked at me carefully as if she were judging the plain features of my face and the wild way I could feel my curls reforming as my hair was drying, maybe even judging me.

"So how long have you lived here?" I asked in an attempt to keep the conversation away from my terrible faults as a mother.

"Five years this month."

"And you like it here?" I wanted her to tell me that she did, that Knickerbocker Village held all the secrets for any family to be happy.

She shrugged. "It's fine," she said in a way that made me think it was not fine at all. "We're settled here, I guess. For now. It's close enough to my husband's work."

"Where does your husband work?" I asked.

"Oh, Julie's an engineer. He started his own machinist shop last year with my brothers." She shrugged again but didn't volunteer anymore. "I think Julie knows your husband, actually. Ed Stein, right?" I nodded and opened my mouth in surprise, but then she added, "Politics," in a way that made me think she paid about as much attention as I did to the meetings Ed sometimes attended.

"You and your husband must be very excited about the new baby," I said, now wanting to get the subject off Ed though I was thinking of him, of the way his fingers reached across the bed for my thigh the other night, the way he wondered if something must be wrong with me.

John chose that moment to throw the ball hard across the floor. It hit my toe and it stung, even through the leather top of my shoe. "Ouch!" I reached down and grabbed my foot.

"John!" Ethel admonished. "Tell Mrs. Stein you're sorry. That it was an accident."

"It wasn't an accident," John said calmly. "I wanted to hit Millie." He walked over and picked the ball up and began bouncing it again.

"I'm sorry," Ethel said to me across the table. I was surprised that she didn't yell at him more, but I kept my mouth shut. "I think he's nervous about the new baby. He's very attached to me." Her voice dipped in a way that made me wonder if she was nervous, too, and I remembered how she said she was making him a recording of her voice for when she went off to the hospital. Maybe it was not glamorous at all but practical, a method of self-preservation.

"I'm sure it will be fine," I said, though as my toe throbbed a little from John's intentional ball toss I wasn't so sure.

"I suppose so," she murmured, fingering the edge of her coffee cup. "But it's much harder then I ever thought . . . Being a mother."

Our eyes met in a way that said we understood each other at that moment, that there was nothing else I needed to say. Ethel knew. She didn't judge me harshly for what had happened earlier. *She knew.* What it was like to love a little person so much, and also for that little person to cause you so much angst.

She looked away first and took a careful sip of her coffee.

"There's something wrong with him," I blurted out, my voice low. "My David — he won't talk."

"He's young," Ethel said.

The way she said it, so assured, it almost made me believe it. "The doctor says I don't love him enough. But I do."

"Of course you do." Ethel's voice softened, and she let go of her coffee cup and leaned across the table and patted my hand.

The ball bounced furiously on, pounding in my head. "John, darling, please," Ethel said, but the bouncing didn't stop. He kept on going. David stared at the ball as if it mesmerized him, up and down and up and down. The yellow flashed by him again and again.

Ethel turned back toward me and rubbed her temples. "You're different than the other women around here," she said. "All the others would've left by now." She glanced at John, at the dreadful bouncing of the ball.

"It's just a little bouncing," I said, forcing a smile, forcing myself to drown the noise out. Because now I understood why Ethel said the other day that they hadn't been to the playground much. There was something about John. Maybe not as obvious as David's silence, but it was there nevertheless.

Ethel smiled at me. "I'm glad to have met you," she said. "It's nice to know another mother on the floor."

"You saved David's life," I said.

"Not at all. He was walking back toward the building when I caught ahold of him. Maybe he's not saying anything yet, but it's all up there." She pointed to her head.

I knew that David was not dumb. I did. I knew that as well as I knew the ins and outs of his facial expressions now, his silent tears.

But it hadn't occurred to me that it might actually be the truth, more than a mother's wishful thinking. Or that David had not been trying to run away this morning, to disappear, but that he had simply been trying to run back home. And it suddenly felt so good to hear Ethel say this about my David. "Still," I said, at a loss for words but feeling I needed to add something. "He's not even two . . ."

"I took a wonderful parenting class last fall," Ethel said. "If you want, I can get you the information on it."

"Sure," I said, though I knew even as I said it that I could not ask Ed for money for a parenting class. But I didn't want Ethel to think that I wouldn't make every possible effort. She was right, being a mother was hard. Harder than I'd ever imagined.

Suddenly the bouncing of the ball stopped, and John ran over to the table and crawled up onto Ethel's very swollen lap. He buried his head deep into his mother's chest, not saying anything, and Ethel kissed the top of his head. "Are you needing a nap, darling?" Ethel said quietly into his hair, such tenderness and love in her voice.

"We should get going." I finished off my coffee. "But thank you for having us."

Ethel smiled. "We'll have to do this again."

"And if you ever need anything, anything at all," I said, "I'm just down the hall."

5

The telephone operators' strike appeared to be over because as I turned the key and entered my apartment I heard the telephone jingling. *My mother.* Of course. I'd just left her there on the street in the rain with no explanation and she was probably frantic by now.

"Yes, we're fine," I lied to her, ignoring her rush of questions, after I picked up the telephone. "David got over his fear and we got right back in line again. I just . . . couldn't find you . . . Of course we got inoculated." The evidence of my lie would be obvious on our unmarked arms, but I hoped when she saw us next, she would have forgotten, she would've moved on to something else.

I put David down for a nap and then I stared out the window and smoked a cigarette. The rain continued and Monroe Street blurred down below, awash with water and people waiting in line to be inoculated. What would happen to us now, David and I both susceptible to some strange disease carried in from Mexico?

Or maybe, I thought again, watching the water drip quickly down the windowpane, the bomb would come and take us instead, just as we were now. Just like this.

Ed was in a foul mood when he came home that night.

I thought it was because of the rain, still coming down furiously, still beating on the windowpane and Monroe Street below, when he stormed in, slamming the apartment door behind him in a way that made me jump.

It was late, later than usual. David was already asleep in his crib, and I hoped the door slamming wouldn't wake him, which would only agitate Ed further. Ed smelled of vodka, so I assumed he hadn't come straight home from the office.

I thought I should find him a dry shirt or that my hands should find the back of his neck to massage it, but he tensed when I looked at him and he looked back in a way that frightened me a little, so I did nothing. "Can I get you anything?" I asked him.

"Get me something?" His voice curled

and his accent thickened the way it did when he was upset. He frowned at me and I felt I knew what he was implying: I was good for getting him one thing only, and I hadn't yet gotten him that.

He sat down on the couch, loosened his tie, and sighed, and I tentatively sat down next to him. "I'm sorry," he said after a little while. "I did not mean to be so . . ." He didn't finish his sentence, and I wasn't sure if it was because he couldn't find the right word or he just didn't want to.

"David found his way back to the building today," I told him proudly, leaving out the other parts about me losing him in the rain and him running into the street on his own. "He's really very smart," I added.

Ed nodded but didn't comment. I wasn't sure what I was expecting, but I felt vaguely disappointed at his nonreaction. "I am having trouble at work," Ed said instead.

"Trouble?" I heard the unnatural way my voice rose.

"They should want to get rid of me."

"Get rid of you?" It had been there in the back of my mind and yet I hadn't imagined what would happen if Ed would lose his job. I couldn't go back to the factory now. What would I do with David? And how would we be able to pay the forty-six dollars a month for this apartment if Ed didn't have a job?

"I thought for so very long that America was the land of opportunity. That you could be anything you wanted here." He sighed again. "But the truth is, you can't. You can only be what *they* want you to be."

"Is it the loyalty oath? Why don't you just sign it?" I asked.

"It's more complicated than that, Millie."

I waited for him to say more but he didn't, so I added, "It's just a piece of paper. It doesn't mean anything."

Ed shrugged. "There is an issue of trust."

"Trust?"

"I don't want you to worry. Everything will work out, okay? People still need a good worker. Even a Russian one." His voice curled on the word *Russian,* and, as he said it, I thought that I wasn't so sure.

"Mr. Bergman would always have a place for you in his shop," I said.

"You should want for me to work with raw meat all day?" I didn't understand why this would be so bad. My father did it every day for years and he had always been a happy man. "You don't worry. I have friends of my own, you know."

By *friends* I knew Ed meant the men he attended political meetings with, or had before it had become so unfavorable to be

65

labeled a communist. I went to a democracy meeting once a few years ago with my friend Addie, who worked at the factory with me, but the truth was, I didn't much like the other women there. They were trying to organize a rally for youth labor rights — a worthy cause, I agreed. But the women spent most of the meeting arguing with one another over who should have what role in the whole thing, and I'd left the meeting with a headache. When I got home, Susan and my mother had both reminded me that being involved in such things would only make me less likely to find a man. Which seemed funny now, seeing as how Ed was involved, and I wondered if he would like me more if I were involved, too. But since I'd had David, I had neither the time nor the energy to think about saving the rest of the world. Politics felt large and faraway. And I didn't know Ed's *friends,* as he called them now. They were not the kind of friends we'd ever had over for dinner. But I remembered what Ethel said earlier about how her husband knew Ed, and now I wondered if Julius was one of them. "Do you know Julius Rosenberg?" I asked. "I met his wife Ethel the other day."

"Yes," Ed said. "I have known the Rosenbergs for a few years."

"Why didn't you ever introduce me to Ethel?" I asked, feeling offended, as if Ed did not think me good enough to share with his friends. "She's very nice."

Ed shrugged. "I didn't think you should have any interest in politics."

"Well, I don't, really," I said. "But it seems Ethel doesn't either. And they live down the hall from us here. They have a little boy, too."

Ed shrugged again.

"Why don't you just sign the silly oath?" I repeated to him. "Wouldn't that be so much easier than finding another job?"

Ed reached up and touched my cheek. His head moved in close to my face, close enough so I could feel his breath on my neck, and it was hot and smelled of vodka. "There is more to this than an oath, Mildred." He kissed my cheek softly, and his finger strummed across the top of my collarbone, down my chest, across my stomach, until it stopped there. "But don't worry yourself. I will figure everything out. You should only concern yourself with staying strong and healthy and growing us another child," he said.

6

A few weeks went by and the smallpox epidemic passed, David and I still remarkably alive, no worse for the wear, David still remarkably silent.

On a sunny day two weeks after I'd seen Ethel, David and I walked to Mr. Bergman's to pick up an extra brisket, and then when we got back off the elevator on the eleventh floor we walked down to the end of the hallway and I knocked on the door to G.E. 11.

After a few moments, Ethel opened the door. She looked exhausted. Her body seemed entirely the breadth of the baby, and her face peaked and wrinkled in an almost unnatural way. "I brought you this." I held out the brown-paper-wrapped brisket, my excuse for stopping by.

"Oh, Millie," she said. "How thoughtful of you." She took the package from me, hesitated, and then asked if we'd like to come in, which was what I'd hoped for. The brisket was not so much thoughtful as it was selfish. These past weeks had stretched out, one lonely, quiet day after another, interrupted only by short, silent walks to the playground, where the other mothers had stared at me and David without inviting us into their conversations.

Ethel's apartment was dimly lit, the shades still drawn though it was midmorning, and toys were scattered all about the floor. I scanned the room for John and soon found him in the corner by the window, where he appeared to be . . . setting an envelope on fire.

"Ethel!" I pointed toward John and pulled David back behind me instinctively. Ethel sighed in a way that told me that this was not entirely surprising to her and then walked heavily — the weight of a the baby pulling her so far down now — to scold John about the matches. She appeared ready to give birth any moment, and it seemed John was not at all ready for what was to come.

"This was so kind of you to bring me a brisket," Ethel said, waddling back toward me, matches and half-burned envelope in hand. She put them down on the console table and took the brisket and placed it in her refrigerator. "Would you like a cup of coffee?" she asked.

"If it's not too much trouble," I said.

"Not at all." I wasn't sure I believed her, but she was already pouring the water, so I let her go ahead.

David sat on the floor with John, watching with his mouth open while John tossed his blocks around carelessly and then laughed. Ethel ignored him, and I hoped David wouldn't get any bad ideas. But it was so nice to be in someone else's company that, for the moment, I didn't even care.

"You know Julie might have a job for Ed," Ethel said nonchalantly as she handed me the coffee, as if this were a conversation we were in the middle of, not one we were just beginning after not seeing each other for weeks. I had yet to meet Julie, but a picture of him and Ethel, looking happy in their bathing suits, sat on top of the piano. They fit each other, I thought, simply from the way he had a sweetly protective arm around her shoulders, which looked altogether different than how Ed had ever had an arm around me. "He's had trouble, too," Ethel said, and shrugged. "He knows what it's like. That's why he started his own business."

"Julie is from Russia, too?" I asked.

Ethel laughed and I smiled at her, until I realized maybe she was laughing at me. Ed had said he'd known the Rosenbergs for years — and, in fact, there was a whole world that Ed and Ethel and Julie belonged to that I did not. I was the one left out. It occurred to me that maybe politics wasn't as large and distant as I'd once thought but that it was about connections and friendships, things I sorely lacked these days. "I'm sorry to sound like such a ninny," I said. "I just haven't been that involved in politics." I hoped Ethel wasn't going to think I was just some silly, stupid woman she couldn't be friends with now.

"I used to. Before John." Ethel waved her hand in the air. "But who has time for that now, right?" She reached across the table, patted my hand, and smiled kindly, so I knew she wasn't laughing at me — not in a mean way, anyway. "Julie's having a get-together here next week. You should all come," she said, and I promised her that we would.

But the next week Ethel gave birth to another baby boy, and they would not have a get-together at her apartment again for months.

June 19, 1953

I run up the side of Route 9, past cars at a standstill, people honking on their horns, impatient. Where do they think they're going? Why are they here? It can't possibly be for the same reason I am. Mostly, they are here as onlookers or protestors, I think, or a strange combination of both. I hate them all for slowing me down, for blocking my way.

I should've come sooner, but I never believed it would come to this. I never believed that Ethel would actually die for something that she didn't do. I can't wrap my head around it even now, in this moment. *Ethel will die by electricity.* Not a bomb, nor disease, but by current being forced through her body so hard that it will stop her heart.

The thought nearly stops mine, and I have to stop running. The night air is so thick. I am breathing hard and sweating, but I stop to catch my breath and then I keep running. I hit a barricade. Policemen are lined up behind it, shining flashlights at the cars. Thankfully, mine is too far back for their lights.

"Miss!" one of them yells at me, shining his light in my eyes, and I hold up my hands in an attempt to shield them. For a moment, I think he knows what I have done today, that it is spilled across my face. But, of course, he can't possibly. That is not why he's shining his light on me. "You can't go past this point," he says.

"I need to!" I shout at him. "I have to talk to the FBI."

"Now, miss . . ." The police officer steps forward and places a large hand on my shoulder. I pull away.

"I have information for them," I say. One of the other officers laughs and I understand he is laughing at me: I sound insane.

"Look," I say, "Ethel is innocent. I have to —"

"Miss," the officer interrupts, pulling harder on my arm. "You need to stay back behind the barricade. No one is allowed past this line for any reason."

My face is wet, I realize, and it's not sweat. I am crying. Crying so hard that I can't see what is in front of me. The police officers, the barricades, the lights blur into fountains of black and orange and yellow. I hear laughter. They are laughing at me and they are laughing at Ethel. Somewhere, a church bell chimes. Seven fifteen.

And then there is a hand on my shoulder. Not the big, rough hand of an officer but a familiar, gentle hand.

I hear his voice. "What are you doing here?"

Jake.

And everything else suddenly turns still and silent. Jake is here, just like I knew he would be. I close my eyes and see if I can smell the familiar scent of him, the pines, the cabin in the woods. But all I smell is smoke from the flares burning off to the side of the road. "Millie," he says. "You shouldn't have come."

1948

7

The air hung heavy in Ethel's apartment, filled with cigarette smoke and excited voices. About a dozen people were crowded in, far too many for the small space. Julius, Ed, and the other men talked loudly — yelling, really — but there were so many voices that I caught only a few pieces of conversation. They disliked President Truman and they felt Wallace would do a better job. I didn't mind Truman myself, despite his silly loyalty oath. Ed and I had listened to his State of the Union address on the radio last winter and I had found it inspiring, all the goals President Truman had for the country. But I could hear Ed's voice cutting clearly across all the others now: "Freedom and equality . . ." His voice curled on the words, and Julius clapped him on the back, while another man laughed and nodded in agreement.

Ed worked for Julius at Pitt Machine

Products now, Julius's reorganized business, so Julius was not only Ed's friend and our neighbor but also his boss. But I hadn't seen Ethel much lately since the new baby came. David and I had stopped over here a few times for the children to play and for Ethel and me to share a cup of coffee. Ethel always seemed so exhausted, overwhelmed. Her back and her low blood pressure had been giving her trouble and on some days kept her in bed all day. I'd thought maybe I should try to find another friend for us in Knickerbocker Village. Yet none of the other mothers at the playground were friendly to me or David, who was turning out to be tall for a three-year-old and who still wasn't talking. David and I had taken a few desperate day trips on the train to see Susan and the twins, but that had made me feel even worse, to watch her beautiful, whole girls, their voices ringing clear with the word *Auntie* now. They had just turned two. And I felt besieged by all of Susan's inquiries about *why* David wasn't speaking yet. *What* was wrong with him?

Then yesterday, out of nowhere, Ethel had shown up at my door, inviting us all to come to the get-together tonight. "It's been so long since I've been to a political meeting," I said, unwilling to admit that I'd only ever gone to that one with Addie. "I'm not sure I'll know what to say to everyone." Ed had gone to meetings often when we were first married, and I would ask him about them when he came home. But he never wanted to discuss them with me and he would only say that they were *fine.* Over the years, his meetings had become fewer and farther between, and as I had David to worry about, I'd stopped bothering to even ask him about them. But suddenly I felt ashamed that I hadn't asked more questions or had more knowledge. I was afraid that I would appear hopelessly out of it at the Rosenbergs' get-together.

Ethel laughed. "Nonsense," she said. "It's more of a party anyway. The men can talk politics, if they want, and you and I can catch up." She had a lightness in her voice that I hadn't heard from her yet and I wondered if, underneath, that was truly her. Ethel the woman, not Ethel the frazzled mother.

So now Ethel and I were crammed into her tiny kitchen, pouring glasses of kosher wine into wide goblets. I poured with one hand and held on to a very tired David with the other hand. Frank Sinatra came suddenly from the phonograph, drowning out the voices of the men. The phonograph was controlled by a restless John, up far past his bedtime, but I preferred Sinatra's smooth singing voice to that of my husband's.

"You can put him in my bedroom, if you want," Ethel said, interrupting my thoughts and pointing to David. Her Richie was a quiet, gentle boy, in nearly every way the opposite of John, and he was already asleep in his crib.

I hesitated, wondering if David would get upset if I put him down in Ethel's unfamiliar bedroom. But he yawned and shoved his thumb in his mouth, and I thanked Ethel and followed her to their dark back bedroom to get him settled on the bed.

"There," Ethel said, putting a hand on my arm. "Now you can join the land of adults again. Come on, have some wine. I want to introduce you to my brother, David, and his wife."

"I'll be out in a moment," I said. "I just want to make sure he'll be okay in here."

Ethel nodded and walked back out toward the front room. The apartment was tiny enough that I could hear all the loud voices of the men still talking about Truman and Wallace and the sounds coming from John's phonograph. One of the men asked him to turn it down, but then it seemed he turned it up in response.

Frank Sinatra seemed to be shouting, his voice at odds with the voices of the gravelly sounding men in Ethel's living room. David's eyes were closed, but he stirred a little on the bed, restless, and I stared at him hard, willing him to settle himself so that I might have some time alone in the company of adults. After a few moments, he was motionless, and he looked peaceful and perfect, lying there in the darkness, just like any other three-year-old boy, like a boy you would expect to open his eyes and call for you, and sometimes I thought maybe David would. That the words would just come to him one day magically, seemingly out of nowhere.

I heard footsteps behind me. "I'm coming, Ethel," I said softly so as not to wake David.

"Oh, I'm sorry," an unfamiliar man's voice answered and I jumped and turned around. I could make out only his shadow in the darkness of the bedroom, but I could see he was tall, with a thin frame. "I was looking for the bathroom," he said.

"I'll show you," I told him.

I touched David's soft cheek one last time, listening for the sound of his even breathing, and then I walked into the light. Outside the bedroom, I adjusted my eyes to see if I recognized the man. But I supposed he had blended in with all the others I didn't know when I'd walked in, and I looked at him now for the first time. He had pale skin, with dark brown, curly hair, and dark brown eyes to match. "I don't think we've met," I said.

He smiled at me and his eyes softened. "I'm Jacob Gold."

"Nice to meet you, Mr. Gold," I said.

"Actually, it's *Dr.* Gold," he said, and I immediately thought he seemed much too young to be a doctor, and nothing at all like the stodgy Dr. Greenberg, who I had not been back to since he'd suggested that maybe David would be better off somewhere else, not with me. "But you can just call me Jake," he added.

"I'm Millie Stein," I told him.

"Ed's wife?" he asked, and I nodded, realizing that that was how I'd be defined here among Ed's friends. "Nice to meet you, Mrs. Stein." He held out his hand to shake.

"Please," I told him, "call me Millie." I took his hand and it was solid, his grip firm, wrapped around mine. He smiled and let go of my hand.

"Oh, there you are." Ethel grabbed my arm, and I turned around to find her pulling me back toward the front room. "I've finally gotten John to lie down, too. He was exhausted. He fell asleep on the couch in the middle of everything." She laughed. "But you and I are free for a while. Let's have fun, shall we?"

I noticed the absence of the shouting phonograph, and the room felt calmer now — the men spoke in lower tones as if they were afraid to wake a sleeping John. Some nights I could hear the phonograph in my apartment. John was playing it so loud, so late, and more than once Ed threatened to go complain, though we both knew he wouldn't. Julius had been Ed's friend first, but now he was also his boss, and though Ed said he was not making as much money as he was before, he didn't complain, not about the job anyway. Only about what he called my *frivolous spending* when I asked him for money for clothes and shoes for a quickly growing David. "Where does he go?" Ed asked, disgusted. "What should he need new things for?"

I noticed Ethel was humming now as she held on to my arm. She appeared lighter without her children — happy, even. She grabbed a bright red hat from the hook on the wall and fashioned it atop her curls. "It's like I can pretend I'm young again." She laughed.

81

"You *are* young," I told her.

She laughed again and waved her hand in the air. "Did I ever tell you how I wanted to be on Broadway?" she asked. "I really thought I'd do it, too."

I tried to imagine it, the small, motherly Ethel as a big stage star. Maybe that explained the piano, which I'd never heard anyone play for real.

"In high school my class voted me most likely to be America's leading actress by 1950," she said.

"You still have a few years," I told her.

She swatted me lightly on the arm and smiled. "Oh, Millie, the dreams of a young girl . . . I'm a mother now. But, anyway, I can't say I'm sorry."

I saw Julius catch her eye from across the room, and he smiled at her. I first met Julius last summer just after Richie was born when I'd come over to see the baby and bring Ethel a casserole. Julius was not as tall as Ed, though he towered over Ethel, and he was quite slender, with an oval face, dark hair and a mustache, and round wire-rimmed glasses. He was holding the baby when I'd come by that day last summer, rocking Richie in a gentle way that had put him to sleep. "Ethel is resting. But I know she'll appreciate your kindness," he'd said

82

in a hushed voice, trying so ardently not to wake her or the baby. I'd been immediately taken with — and, I'll admit, a bit jealous of — his sweetness and obvious love for his family.

Since then, I'd seen Julius from time to time, getting on or off the elevator on his way to and from work, but always dressed in a suit, walking briskly, and looking quite serious. Now his face appeared softer again, and he seemed kinder and gentler, the way he'd looked that first time I met him.

Ethel smiled back at him and dropped my arm to walk toward him through the crowd of men. Ethel leaned in and gave him a big kiss squarely on the lips. I could suddenly see them as a young couple deeply in love, holding on to dreams of bigness and life together. And it seemed that this tiny apartment in Knickerbocker Village, even with the elevator and the steam heat, was not enough for them now, not what they had hoped for once. I could imagine the two of them and their boys running across a green lawn in New Jersey just like Susan's.

I walked toward them and Ethel pulled away from Julius for a moment and introduced me to the other people standing nearby. A man named Mortie Sobell, who waved with a friendly smile, and Ethel's younger brother, David Greenglass, a round man smoking a cigarette who simply nodded at me, and his wife, Ruth, a pretty woman with a serious expression who was the only woman tucked in among the men, talking politics with them. Ruth looked me over once quickly and then took a drag on her cigarette and jumped back into the conversation. They were talking about Elizabeth Bentley, and I remembered reading about her in the paper, a quite pretty woman who'd claimed to be a spy for Russia who'd now turned back to our side and wanted to help keep the United States safe. She'd testified before the House Committee on Un-American Activities over the summer.

"Oh, she'll say anything," Ruth said, blowing a ring of smoke in front of her. "Doesn't matter if it's true or not."

"Can you blame her?" David said. "She's trying to save herself."

I wanted to jump into the conversation, but I wasn't sure what to say. I felt I didn't know enough about Elizabeth Bentley to make a comment, so instead I said, "Are you all members of the Communist Party with my husband?"

Ruth exchanged a look with David and took another drag on her cigarette. "We're

Democrats now," she said. "Davey only wanted to come tonight because he likes his sister's baking so much." She motioned to a tray of cookies resting on the coffee table. "And because we needed a night out with adults." She laughed.

"You have a child?" I asked, relieved that I could ask about something relatable.

"Yes," Ruth said. "A two-year-old boy. We left him with my sister." She leaned into her husband and put her head on his shoulder. "Just you and I tonight, dearest. Just like when we were young and in New Mexico."

"God-awful desert," David chimed in, though he pulled Ruth closer and kissed the top of her head.

I was about to ask why they were in New Mexico when I heard Ed's voice, and it startled me. "There is my Mildred." He'd snuck up on me. Ed's words were too loud and slurred. He was already drunk, and the room seemed to get quieter, everyone staring at him now. He grabbed my arm roughly, holding on too tight, the way the vodka made him do sometimes.

"What are you doing?" I asked, trying to yank away and feeling embarrassed that Ruth and David and Mortie were all seeing this after I'd only just met them. But Ed pulled me closer to him, not letting go. I could feel the eyes of the others — all watching me. "I should want to give my wife a kiss," he said, his breath hot against my neck. "Is that so wrong?" He pulled my face close to his and pressed his lips against mine. He smelled of vodka, kosher wine, and cigar smoke.

"Stop it," I whispered, trying to pull back but unable to get out of his grip. "Not here."

"I know what you've been doing." He said the words so quietly that it took a moment for them to register. And then he let go of me so quickly that I stumbled a little, and grabbed on to the edge of the console table to catch my balance.

I looked up and saw Ethel staring at me now, her eyebrows raised in surprise. "I'm going to go downstairs, outside, for a bit," I said, trying not to cry. "Will you keep an eye on David?"

"Now?" she said. "Millie, it's late."

I glanced at Ed, who was already talking to Mortie Sobell as if I weren't even here, as if he hadn't just grabbed me. *How could he possibly know?* "I just need some air," I said.

"But . . ." She hesitated, and I guessed there was more she wanted to say but she stopped herself and then said instead, "Take as long as you need."

Out on the sidewalk below, the air was much too cold for early September, and I'd not stopped by my apartment for my coat. I shivered, and pulled at the sleeves of my gray dress, but I could not go back inside, up the elevator, to Ethel's. And Ed.

I had the urge to walk, to go up the street and get on the subway and ride it somewhere. Anywhere. But I didn't even have my purse with me. And besides, where would I go now at this hour? And even if I should ever want to leave here, I couldn't go alone. I would never leave David behind.

I could still feel the impression of Ed's fingertips on my wrist. I looked down and saw slight purple marks. I could also feel his lips against mine and I reached up and touched my mouth as if to brush the memory away. *I know what you've been doing,* he'd said. I shivered again and wondered if it was possible, if he'd finally figured out about the diaphragm.

I hoped he was talking about something else, some imagined ill I'd committed against him. The more time that passed without me finding myself with a child, the more distant and angrier Ed became.

But I knew if he had discovered my secret now, there was not much I could do about it, and it terrified me to think what might become of David should we ever have another, more perfect child. It terrified me to think that maybe Dr. Greenberg was right, that it was me. My fault. And it was bad enough that I was ruining one child.

I felt a hand on my shoulder and I flinched. "I didn't mean to startle you . . . Again . . ." I turned and there was the doctor I'd met upstairs.

"Dr. Gold," I said.

"*Jake,*" he reminded me gently. "I was about to head home and I noticed you standing out here. Is everything all right, Mrs. Stein?"

"*Millie,*" I corrected him, too, and he smiled at me. "Yes, of course. Everything is fine." I shook his hand away from my shoulder and forced a smile. "I just wanted some fresh air. That's all. It was quite loud in there. And very smoky. Is the party over?" I wondered if everyone had left Ethel's. If Ed had noticed I was gone. If David was still sleeping.

"Not yet," he said, and I wondered why he was leaving early but didn't ask. "Can I walk you back up before I go?"

I shook my head. "I'll be fine. I live here,

too, so I think I can find my way." My words came out sounding short and angry, and I felt a little bad for being rude to this man who was practically a stranger and trying to be kind. "Thank you," I added. "But really, I'll be okay."

He pulled a card from his coat pocket. "Here," he said, "take this. If you ever want to talk . . ."

My hands were shaking with cold, but I held up the card to the streetlamp to read it as Jake walked away.

Dr. Jacob Gold, it read. *Doctor of Psychotherapy.*

8

The next morning, I didn't wake up until after Ed had left for work, a rare day when David slept past the first moments of sun slanting in through the tiny bedroom window, and Ed had moved carefully enough around the apartment so I hadn't even heard him leave.

I awoke disoriented at first, David so still that I thought he wasn't here at all until I saw him sleeping heavily on the mattress across the room. I remembered Ed's ominous whisper in Ethel's living room last night and I looked down to my wrist, where the purpling imprint of his fingers seemed singed into my skin.

When I had finally ridden the elevator back up to Ethel's apartment last night, Ed had already left. I'd assured Ethel that everything was okay and I'd carried a sleeping David back home to find Ed passed out and snoring in our bed. It felt like a gift not to have to talk to him then, or this morning either, a momentary reprieve where I could gather my thoughts and figure out what to do next if he had, in fact, discovered my secret.

I stood now and tiptoed to my small wooden dresser, a relic from Bubbe Kasha's old apartment. I opened the top drawer and searched below my underthings. I felt it there — in the small, nondescript box where I always kept it — undisturbed. And last night felt like nothing more than a dream, Ed's words nothing more than the ramblings of a drunk man. *He knows nothing,* I told myself, and then I said it out loud as if hearing the words would make them real. I walked into the kitchen and made myself some coffee and then

I went to the window and watched the street below. The sunshine fell upon the men walking to work and the women pushing carriages, making everything appear ultrabright, and the world beneath me seemed a thing of excessive beauty, the unreal world of storybooks. I wondered if Ethel might want to take her boys outside to play with David today before the weather turned and got too much colder.

The sound of knocking at my door startled me, and I nearly spilled my coffee. It was early, before nine, but maybe Ethel had had the same idea.

"Coming," I said, but not too loud so as not to awaken David, and I peeked my head in the back bedroom to see if he was still sleeping. It was so unusual for him to be this undisturbed that for a moment I wondered if he was ill. But then I heard the knock on the door again and I ran to answer it before the noise woke him.

An unfamiliar woman stood in my doorway, her hand raised to knock once more. She was short and quite round, wearing a too-tight brown suit, her graying hair pulled back into a taut bun. She looked at me and she frowned, and I realized that I was still in my robe. I pulled it tighter across my chest. "Can I help you?" I asked.

She tried to peer past me into the apartment, which was quite untidy. David's blocks still scattered across the floor. And had it not been for the fact that I was in my robe, I would've stepped out into the hallway and shut the door behind me so she wouldn't see our mess. Up on the eleventh floor we didn't get wayward visitors, unexpected guests, or salesmen. So I felt certain this woman had knocked on the wrong door by mistake until she glanced at me, frowned again, and said, "Mrs. Stein?"

"Yes," I managed, startled that she had, in fact, come to the right place. I noticed she was holding a thick notebook and a pen. "Can I help you?" I asked again, my tone sharper than before.

"I'm Zelda Weiss from the Jewish Children's Home." She paused. "Your husband called us."

"Yes?" I managed to say again.

"He felt your son might benefit from being placed in our care."

I know what you've been doing, Ed had said, his fingers marking my arm with their forcefulness, and now he was exacting his revenge? Zelda Weiss was standing at my doorway at such an early hour because she wanted to take David. Ed wanted David sent away.

I stepped back and slammed the door, latching the chain. I pressed my back against the door, and I could hear my ragged breaths rattling in my chest. I wouldn't let her in. I wouldn't let her near David.

"Mrs. Stein." She rapped on the door again. "I would just like to talk with you about your husband's . . . concerns about . . . We can help you, you know."

I pressed my back harder against the door, and I watched my coffee cup tremble in my unsteady hands. From the back room I heard the sounds of David awakening now. Surely he would not have slept through my slamming of the door. I could hear him kicking the wall, the steady, uneasy thumps reverberating in my brain. It was his way. His way of saying that he was awake and he needed me. I understood it. I understood him. And no matter what Ed or anyone else thought, he would not be better off with someone else.

"Mrs. Stein!" Zelda Weiss called again through the door, her voice sounding tighter, stretched by impatience. "I am going to slide my card under the door . . . I'll be back later in the week. Perhaps it will be a better time for you. And we can talk then."

I watched the card come across the floor and then I picked it up. It would never be a better time and I would never talk to her. I ripped the card up and threw the ugly pieces in the trash, and then I walked into the bedroom and grabbed ahold of David.

"Good morning, love," I said into his unruly curls, my curls. *My* son. "Mommy is here." I held on tight, even when he struggled to break free of my grasp.

Though it wasn't Friday and I didn't need any meat, I got David dressed and walked with him toward Market Street and Mr.

Bergman's shop. If anyone would understand, or would have the desire to help, it would be him. I had considered calling my mother or Susan, but I worried they might agree with Ed, that they might tell me now, with David already three, I was holding on to nothing. I pictured the cool look in my sister's hazel eyes as she might tell me that sometimes you had to be willing to let go. But I wasn't. I wouldn't. I never would.

I held on to David's hand extra-tight as we walked. And I talked and talked, enough for the both of us. I smiled and hugged him along the way as I thought about how Dr. Greenberg said I was too cold. That *I* was the reason David refused to be normal.

I remembered Ed had been to see Dr. Greenberg for his yearly physical last week, and now I wondered what Dr. Greenberg had said to him. Had he told Ed what he had told me, that he believed David might do better in *another environment,* or had he simply told Ed about the diaphragm? Probably both. And I felt even more certain Ed had called Zelda Weiss to get even.

As we walked, I couldn't shake the feeling that David and I were being followed, that someone — Zelda Weiss? — was watching us, judging me. I glanced uneasily behind my shoulder, and for a moment I thought I recognized a man on the street, that doctor from last night, Jake. But then I turned around again and he was gone, and I told myself no one was watching us. That now I was becoming paranoid.

"Boychik, what a wonderful surprise!" Mr. Bergman called out when we walked in his shop and up to the counter. But even his kind, booming voice couldn't cheer me up.

"Mildred," Mr. Bergman said as he passed David a yellow gumdrop. David swallowed it hungrily, and I realized I hadn't fed him breakfast yet, a thought that only made me feel worse. "I don't have a brisket set aside for you today. Do you need something? I can go in the back and see what I can find."

I shook my head, but I didn't realize I was crying until Mr. Bergman pulled his handkerchief from his pocket and handed it across the counter. I used it to wipe my eyes, and Mr. Bergman put his hand on mine. The shop was quiet this morning, a Tuesday, unlike the pre-Shabbat bustle of a midday Friday that I was used to when I usually came in here. I worried that business wasn't as good as it once was when my father was alive.

"Bubbelah, what's wrong?" he said gently. "Is it Ed?"

I nodded, and I wondered how Mr. Bergman could be so wise. But he had never seemed to like Ed. Before our wedding he'd told me his concerns, that Ed and I had such different pasts, that Ed was so much older than me, that none of us knew Ed nearly as well as we knew Sam, but I had brushed them all away with a flick of my wrist and had chalked up his worries to a fatherly sort of overprotectiveness.

He scowled now. "Damn Reds he's got himself mixed up with."

I thought of the party last night at Ethel's. Ed's friends. Ethel's friends, too. *Reds,* as Mr. Bergman said with disdain as if a simple color could be worthy of so much hatred. I thought of the way Julius had held on so sweetly to Ethel last night and the kind way that that doctor, Jake, had asked me if I'd needed anything as I'd stood out on the night street in the cold. "What do you mean?" I asked him.

"He's going to get himself in a whole heap of trouble with that crowd. You keeping up with the papers, Millie?" I told him I was, though probably not as much as I should. "All this business with Mr. Hiss."

"Mr. Hiss?" I asked, the name sounding only vaguely familiar to me.

"Alger Hiss. Big government man. That

Bentley woman called him a communist, and now they say he was a spy for Russia, too."

I thought about what Ruth had said last night, that Bentley would *say anything.* "Maybe Miss Bentley's lying," I said.

"Doesn't matter if she is or not. Alger Hiss is ruined now. I'm telling you, there aren't many things worse than being labeled a communist these days." He shook his head. "Look at the Hollywood Ten, rotting in jail."

I wondered what Mr. Bergman would say if he knew that I'd gone to Ethel's party last night, that the *Reds* Ed was mixed up with had been so kind to me and were our neighbors. I wondered what would happen if anyone found out about the politics they were discussing. But who would care anyway? Sure, maybe it was unfavorable to be labeled a communist these days, but there were no high-profile government men or Hollywood types in Ethel's apartment last night.

I wasn't planning on telling Mr. Bergman any of this now, though. It wasn't Ed's friends who were the problem, and I remembered why I'd come here and tears welled up in my eyes again. "It's not the politics," I said, wiping at my face with his handkerchief. "It's . . ." I glanced at David.

He stared at me intently as if he were hanging on to my every word. Was he? Did he know what I was saying even if he wouldn't acknowledge it and respond yet? I lowered my voice and leaned in closer to Mr. Bergman. "A woman came to my apartment this morning from the Jewish Children's Home. Ed called her."

"I don't understand," he said, running his plump fingers through his thinning gray hair. I tilted my head in David's direction, unwilling to say it out loud in front of him, that Ed wanted them to take David away, that he wanted to punish me and this was his way.

Mr. Bergman frowned and reached beneath the counter for his bag of gumdrops. He sifted through it until he found three more yellows and he placed them gently into David's open and eager palm.

"Ed wants them to take him," I whispered, once David was concentrating hard on the yellow candies.

"Take him?" Mr. Bergman's voice rose. "He is a happy boy. There is a shadow of your father in his eyes . . ." Mr. Bergman was right. David had my light brown eyes, my father's eyes, and very obviously Ed's square nose.

I bit my lip. "Do you really think so, that

he's happy?"

"I know so," Mr. Bergman said. "If this woman bothers you again, you call me, okay? I'll come talk to her for you. I'll tell her what a good mother you are."

I smiled at him and he patted my hand. He was very sweet, but I didn't want to tell him what I already understood, that I doubted there would be anything he could do to stop Ed if Ed set his mind on something. No matter how much he wanted to.

9

The day dragged on, and by midafternoon my stomach began to ache with worry. I worried about that Weiss woman coming back, about whether Mr. Bergman was right when he told me he thought David was happy. But most of all I worried about Ed coming home from work, about having to have a conversation with him after last night and Zelda Weiss's visit this morning. I knew the hour would turn past five and Ed would walk down Monroe Street and ride the elevator up as always. My stomach ached even more at the thought.

To make matters worse, David refused to nap, which was becoming more and more common these days, and every time I tried to lay him down on his mattress he would just kick the wall and kick the wall and cry until finally I relented and let him come back out into the living room, where I smoked a cigarette and he stacked his yellow blocks in a tower. I watched them go higher and higher. They would fall soon and he would cry again, but for the moment he was enthralled and I closed my eyes and took a drag on my cigarette.

I heard a knock at the door. "Shhh," I commanded David — unnecessarily, I thought, until, ignoring me, he toppled the blocks and began to kick the floor in frustration.

"Millie, are you in there? It's Ethel." My whole body eased with relief and I put my cigarette out in the ashtray and walked to the door to open it. Ethel stood in the hallway with John, who immediately peered behind me, noticed David kicking the floor, and then ran into the apartment past me. "John!" Ethel called, shooting me an apologetic look. "It's not polite to just barge in."

"It's all right," I said as I watched John pick up the yellow blocks, his movements calming David down. I felt an inkling of tenderness for John that I hadn't before. It was like he was learning how to understand David, to care for him, as a friend. I opened the door wider and invited Ethel in, too.

"We can't stay," Ethel said, her voice taking on that familiar nervous edge that had been absent for a little while last night while her boys slept. "Richie is napping. I don't want to leave him for long." She folded her arms. She was wearing a worn flowered housedress, a dress that might have been beautiful, once years ago before she'd given birth to her babies, maybe when she dreamed of being a Broadway star, America's leading actress. But now the pink had faded to almost beige, the left sleeve was torn, and the shoulder appeared to be stained with baby food. "I'm sorry about John barging in like that." She sighed.

I glanced at him, now rebuilding the tower with David, whose face was suddenly calm and serious. "No," I said, "not at all. David is glad for the company. And so am I." I smiled at her. "Can I get you a cup of coffee? A quick one?"

"No thanks," she said to me. "John," she said him. "Five minutes and then we have to get back to check on your brother." John ignored her and continued building with the blocks. "I just wanted to check in with you, Millie. Make sure everything was . . . all right."

I wondered how she could know about Zelda Weiss, but she didn't of course. She was asking because of the way Ed had treated me in her apartment and how I'd run out last night. "Everything is fine," I lied, and even as I said the words I realized that I didn't mean to, that I wanted to tell Ethel the truth. But I didn't know how someone whose husband loved her so obviously and completely as Julie did would be able to understand what I was feeling now for Ed.

Ethel held her shoulders up, uncertain. I sat down on our couch and patted the seat next to me until Ethel relaxed and sat down, too. Though I understood she wouldn't — and couldn't — stay long, I thought she felt the way I did, this rare moment when John and David were both content and happy, transfixed with blocks and each other, nothing more than normal little boys. And nothing less.

Our couch was our only new piece of furniture in the apartment, the only thing Ed and I had bought rather than pillaged from Bubbe Kasha's old treasures when she left her apartment and moved in with my mother just after we got married. I'd found the couch at Macy's for fifteen dollars, and Ed had said he was happy to buy it for me as a wedding gift. *This is love,* I'd thought. A fifteen-dollar couch in the most beautiful shade of royal blue I'd ever seen. How stupid I'd been to believe that.

I wanted to tell Ethel about Zelda's visit this morning. I wanted to ask for Ethel's advice. But Julie was Ed's employer. Julie had been Ed's friend first before I'd even met Ethel. And instead I heard myself telling Ethel about the silly couch and how Ed had bought it for me as a wedding present.

"It's a lovely couch," Ethel murmured, paying no attention to it. "Did you have a nice time last night?" she asked carefully.

"It was nice to get out of my apartment. To meet people . . . You know how it is."

"I do," Ethel said. "I used to see them all the time when I was younger, when Julie and I were first married. Oh, I was so involved in the cause!"

"Why were you so involved?" I asked her, wondering what had drawn Ethel, a woman now so involved in her children and her quiet life here in Knickerbocker Village, to this particular crowd of people. *Reds,* as Mr. Bergman had called them with so much disdain. I remembered Susan telling me about an article she'd read in *Look* magazine a while back that detailed "how to spot a communist" and her warning me to be careful and on the lookout, especially here in the city. But Ethel was not the kind of woman I'd imagined when Susan described what she'd read in the article — severe-looking people dressed in all black who seemed favorable to Russia. Ed, Susan had proclaimed, was excused because he'd grown up in Russia. He didn't know any better. And besides, I'd told her he was distancing himself as time went on.

"You know, I was only fifteen when I graduated from Seward Park," I realized Ethel was saying and I turned my attention back to her.

"Fifteen." I raised my eyebrows, impressed that Ethel had graduated from high school so young.

She laughed as if she were embarrassed by her own intelligence. "I got a job as a clerk at a shipping company and I saw the terrible way all the women were treated. I organized a strike of a hundred fifty women — *I* did that — and I was promptly fired of course. But boy, Millie, did I feel alive. Doing something to improve people's lives. That's when and why I joined the Party, to continue that kind of work, do some good in this country. Labor unions and fairness for workers. I thought I was going to change the world." She laughed again.

I thought about what Mr. Bergman said earlier. "But now I guess things have changed. No one wants to be a communist anymore."

"Oh, I don't know that it's the Party that's changed, Millie," she said. "It's the whole rest of the world. Julie almost lost his first job with the Signal Corps before it even began because they drummed up some petition I'd signed years ago. And then he did eventually lose his job over his ties to the Party. It doesn't matter that he's a good man and a good worker. It's all so silly. People are afraid. All this business now with the House Un-American Activities Committee. Honestly, what does it mean to be *un-American*?"

It seemed obvious to me that a woman like Elizabeth Bentley who had admitted to giving American secrets to Russia was quite un-American, but I wasn't sure what any of that had to do with men like Julie and Ed who'd lost their jobs over a silly loyalty oath. I agreed with her about that. "Is that why you're not as involved as you once were?" I asked. "You're afraid?"

She laughed. "Oh, Millie. Most days, all the energy I have goes to caring for the children. Who has time for anything else?"

I swallowed hard, Zelda's words about wanting to take David echoing in my head. Now I wasn't even sure what I'd do without him. What else was there, really, for a woman like me? A boring life spent sewing in a hot factory?

Ethel leaned in closer and lowered her

voice. "Can I tell you a secret?" I nodded, happy she trusted me enough to ask. And I immediately felt bad that I'd placed her on Ed's side, even for a second. "And you won't tell . . . anyone?"

By *anyone* I thought she meant Ed and that maybe she was picturing the way Ed had held on to my arm too tightly in her apartment last night and she knew I wouldn't tell him a thing. "Of course," I said. "I won't tell a soul. I promise."

"I'm thinking about therapy." She lowered her voice and tilted her head toward John almost imperceptibly so he wouldn't notice.

I thought of the doctor I'd met last night at her apartment and his card that had read *Doctor of Psychotherapy.* "With Dr. Gold?" I asked her.

"Who?" Ethel raised her eyebrows.

"That doctor who was at your party last night."

"Oh, no." Ethel waved her hand. "I'd never met him before last night. I'm not even sure who invited him . . . no. The Jewish Board of Guardians." The Jewish Board of Guardians sounded suspiciously similar to the organization Zelda Weiss said she worked for. "They accept payment on a sliding scale based on income" — I realized Ethel was still talking — "so we should be able to afford it."

I nodded, though I was not altogether sure what therapy entailed, exactly, nor why one went even for an affordable fee.

"But you won't tell anyone, right? I know I'm not supposed to believe in this sort of thing. But the truth is, I think I do believe in it. I think maybe if he can talk to someone . . . I don't know, he might have an easier time of things. It's been so hard for him since Richie arrived."

I wasn't sure if she meant that it was Jews or communists who weren't supposed to believe in this sort of thing. I could imagine both my mother and Bubbe Kashe pish-poshing the idea of psychotherapy, of doctors who wanted to dole out talk not medicine, and it also seemed like something Ed would be firmly against.

To look at John right now, sitting here, playing so calmly with David, one would not think he needed anything. But the restless boy who blared his phonograph late into the party last night? I understood what Ethel was saying. John was older than David and his imperfections shone more obviously for all to see. Ethel was feeling desperate. She was doing everything she could to help her son. "You're such a good mother," I said to her. And then I had to tell her about Zelda. I felt certain that she would understand. "Ed wants to take David from me. To send him away," I whispered so the boys wouldn't hear.

"What?" Ethel reached her hand across the couch for mine, grabbed ahold, and squeezed. "You won't let him," she said with an aplomb that I didn't quite feel.

"No, of course not," I murmured. Even as I said the words, I didn't quite understand how I would stop him. What was I going to do? Ethel and Mr. Bergman seemed so certain that Ed could be stopped, but what if he couldn't?

I felt tears welling up in my eyes, and then Ethel squeezed my hand again. "You'll figure something out, Millie. I know you will." She smiled at me. "We always do, don't we?"

"I don't know," I said. "I really don't."

"Listen," she said. "If you want my advice . . ." I nodded, I did. "The men are sweet enough when it comes to the children, but they're really just big children themselves sometimes. Sure, they love to play catch in the courtyard and play cowboys and Indians and all that . . ." Ed had never once done any of those things with David. "Maybe Ed just needs something to appease him."

"Appease him?" I thought of the gumdrops Mr. Bergman gave to David. If only it were that easy.

I heard a noise and I looked up. David's blocks had all crashed to the hard floor again. His curls were disheveled and his face turned in that way it did when he was upset and overtired, but before I could stand and reach for him he kicked John instead of his usual routine of kicking the floor. John's tiny nostrils flared and his cheeks turned red before he threw one of David's precious blocks in retaliation across the room at the window.

Ethel and I stood quickly and shouted at our sons in unison.

I grabbed David and held him close to me in a cross between a hug and a stranglehold and said, "David, that's not nice. You can't kick your friends."

"Good luck with Ed," Ethel said to me as she pulled a now crying John toward the door. Just before she walked out she turned back and said, "You're a good mother, too, Millie. Don't forget that."

And then as quickly as they'd come in, they were gone, my apartment was silent and still once again, a mess of yellow blocks across the living room floor, David's tangled curls against my forearm, his body limp against mine on my perfect blue couch. "Everything's going to be all right, darling." I sang the words to him like a refrain, trying to make myself believe it.

David fell asleep early, and Ed did not come home at his usual time. When darkness enveloped the apartment, I turned on the lamp and picked up David's blocks, arranging them neatly in their wooden container. I smoked a cigarette and stared down to the street below, my nightly ritual. And I felt a sadness in thinking that this small moment of the day had come to exemplify my entire life: watching the rest of the city breathe on by from too far away to truly be a part of it.

The hour grew later and the masses on the sidewalk below thinned. I wondered if Ed might not return home at all. David and I could move in with my mother and Bubbe Kasha, or maybe Susan and Sam would take pity on us and invite us into their large suburban home. But how long would Susan endure David's moodiness, his silence, before she, too, would want to suggest a different place for him?

Finally, I heard Ed's key turning in the lock and I put my cigarette out in the ashtray and smoothed back my hair. Ed walked in, removed his hat and hung it by the door, and then he stopped for a moment and looked at me as if it surprised him to see me here on our perfect blue couch looking as I always did.

"There's a plate for you in the oven," I said.

He walked toward the kitchen. I tried to judge from my place on the couch how much he'd had to drink after work and whether he was clearheaded enough to have a conversation or whether he might grab my wrist again, or worse, now that we were here alone. I stayed on the couch and watched him sit at the table and cut and chew his meat loaf. After eating a little bit Ed looked up, stared straight at me, and said, "He is gone?"

"Gone?" My heart thrummed so loudly in my chest that I was sure Ed could hear it even from across the room.

"The boy," Ed said almost casually as he took another bite of the meat loaf. *The boy?* As if David were an object, something foreign. Though Ed's tone was even, I felt my hands begin to shake. I held them together to try to steady them but I couldn't. David was our son, *Ed's son,* and Ed really didn't love him. The hatred I suddenly felt for Ed overcame me, and I had to stand up from the couch and take a deep breath so I wouldn't begin to scream.

I walked to the doorway of our bedroom, stood there, and watched David. He looked so peaceful and calm, his tiny chest rising steadily up and down. "David is asleep," I finally said, more to myself than to Ed. David was safe. Ed could not take him as long as I was here to protect him. And I would. I had to.

"Asleep?" Ed dropped his fork against the plate, and it clanged loudly enough that I saw David stir a little in his sleep.

"Shhh." I approached the table and Ed and picked up the fork to stop it from making more noise. "You'll wake him." I stared at Ed, challenged him with my eyes. I gripped the fork tightly in my hand. Should Ed move toward the bedroom — and David — I would take the fork and . . .

But Ed stood and walked back into the kitchen. I heard the sounds of ice clinking against glass, vodka pouring over the ice, the ice crackling a little bit.

I watched him from the edge of the kitchen as he swirled the liquid in the glass and then drank it down too fast. From here, in the semidarkness, he reminded me of a dangerous pouting child, one who hadn't gotten his way, and gulping vodka was his tantrum.

Ethel was right. *He is nothing more than a boy,* I thought as I watched Ed grimace at his drink. *You'll think of something,* Ethel had said. *We always do . . . appease him.*

And then I knew what I needed to do. I walked into the kitchen and dropped the fork carefully into the sink. Then I leaned against the counter and stood next to Ed, close enough so our elbows were touching. I closed my eyes. "I will give you another child," I said steadily. "But you will leave David alone."

I heard him put his glass down on the counter, the sound of the ice jumping uneasily, and when I opened my eyes, he was standing there in front of me. He put his hand on my wrist, circling it with his fingers, gentler than last night but in the same spot, so it still hurt. I resisted the urge to pull away.

"Mildred," he whispered into my ear, his fingers moving up my arms, across my back, into my hair. "Now we are understanding each other."

10

The fall moved slowly after I threw away my diaphragm. I dreaded Ed coming home from work even more. I knew now that there was bound to be another child soon, and that made the weight of Ed's body on top of mine feel even more insufferable. Each night, I closed my eyes and made myself concentrate very hard on the ceiling, counting, forcing myself to keep my breathing even.

But Ed stuck to our agreement and left David alone. In fact, he left him entirely alone. He ignored David even more than before, if possible, and did not ask about him or even acknowledge me when I spoke of David. I longed for David to talk so that Ed might begin to love him, especially as I had noticed other fathers in Knickerbocker Village playing with their boys on weekends or walking with them hand in hand to attend *shul* on Saturdays.

I ran into Julie and John playing catch in the courtyard one Sunday morning after Ed had gone to visit Lena — thankfully, without us — and David and I were off to visit my mother and Bubbe Kasha. Julie was dressed down, in casual slacks and a sweater, and he and John both wore Dodgers caps as they tossed a baseball back and forth.

Julie stopped throwing when he noticed me, and David and he motioned for us to come over, so we did. "How would David like to join us?" Julie asked, bending down to David's level to pat him on the head. Then Julie stood back up and smiled at me.

Julie's sweetness hit me as an ache, the sudden weight of jealousy and longing in my chest, and I had to force a smile. "That's so kind of you to offer. But I don't think he quite understands catch yet," I said.

"He does!" John shouted. "He does, Millie. Let him play."

John ran over and grabbed David's arm, handing him the ball, trying to explain to him how to throw it. David held the ball up in his hand, looking rather bewildered.

"Why don't you get Ed down here?" Julie asked. He lifted the Dodgers cap off his head, wiped his brow, and put the cap back down. "We'll make it a foursome."

"Ed's not home," I said. "But maybe

another time?" though even as I said the words I knew it would probably never happen.

David dropped the ball awkwardly and John shrugged, frustrated with David's lack of ability or interest in the game. "We should be going," I said, and I picked David up. I didn't want to intrude on their time, but also I couldn't bear to watch anymore. "You two enjoy your catch," I called out, trying to keep my voice even as I walked away.

"Always do, Millie," Julie said as he swiped the ball back up off the ground and threw it to his son.

The morning of the presidential election I woke up feeling awful. I barely made it to the toilet to throw up, and then when I went to stand, I felt dizzy and I had to cling to the sink for support.

"Don't forget." Ed peeked into the bathroom, not seeming to notice my terrible state. "We want Wallace to win."

"I know," I said, but what I knew was that in the privacy of my voting booth I would vote for anyone but Ed's choice.

A few hours later, I still wasn't feeling well as I walked with my mother down Monroe Street to cast our votes.

"The fog is going to kill us all," my mother said, leaning unsteadily on my arm. I balanced both her and David, one on each side, and her girth — and her constant chatter — were weighing me down, as opposed to David's lightness and silence.

"Fog?" I asked. An unbearable lightness and nausea had overtaken me. Deep down, I knew what it meant. I had felt this way only once before, when I was first expecting David.

"I saw it on the television" — my mother continued talking — "on the ABC News. There's a fog in Donora, Pennsylvania. It's killing people. There's nothing to stop it from getting us, too, you know. Pennsylvania isn't even that far away. It's even closer to New Jersey. I've warned Susan not to go outside with the twins . . ."

"Hmmm," I murmured, thinking about how my mother had become even more insufferable since Mr. Bergman had brought her and Bubbe Kasha a small television, a luxury Ed still would not consent to for us. "If the bomb doesn't get us all first, that is," I said, swallowing back the urge to vomit again, right here on the street. I focused very hard on walking, placing one foot in front of the other.

"Oh, the bomb." My mother waved her

free hand in the air as if that were an altogether ridiculous idea and this killer fog oh so much more likely. "All these politicians so worried about the communists and the Russians and here a fog can come and get you just like that. *A fog.*" I nodded, hoping that my tacit agreement would be enough to silence her, and we headed up the steps. "Dewey is going to win, you know," my mother said. "That's what they're saying all over the television."

She let go of my arm as we opened the doors to the polling place, but I still held on to David, not wanting to lose him in the rush of the crowd. It was noisy inside the library now, with everyone here to cast their votes, and David put his hands to his ears to block it out. He tried to pull away from me, but I held on tightly, pulling back. He was getting bigger, stronger, and it was harder for me to hold on to him than it was when he was a baby and a toddler. But I didn't like to think about that too much. It overwhelmed me with a terror so thick that sometimes I couldn't breathe. How was I going to manage David if he continued on like this and he grew bigger and stronger than me? *David and a baby,* I reminded myself, focusing very hard again on not throwing up. Oh, this took so much concentration. All I wanted to do was go back home and get in bed.

"Mrs. Stein, is that you?" I looked up at the sound of my name, and I squinted to make out who was calling me. Another wave of dizziness hit me and I had to hold my free hand out to steady myself against the wall. "Are you all right?" He put his hand on my arm, and I realized it was Dr. Gold. No, *Jake.* The kind man I'd met at Ethel's party.

"What are you doing here?" I asked, regaining my balance and pulling gently out of his grasp. I remembered how I thought I saw him there on the street that morning when I felt I was being followed. But Ed and I had an agreement now and I did not expect to see Zelda Weiss again anytime soon.

Jake smiled. "Well, I'm casting my vote." Of course. Everyone in the neighborhood converged on the same place today.

David yanked my arm hard and stomped his feet. "Darling, I'll be quick, I promise," I said to him. "I'm sorry," I said, turning back to Jake, "David doesn't like crowds. I've got to go and try to finish quickly."

"Would you like me to watch him while you cast your vote?" Jake asked.

It seemed like such a strange thing to say,

121

a *man* offering to watch my child? But Jake crouched down to David's level, spoke to him softly, and David's thrashing calmed. Jake was a psychotherapist, I remembered. And I thought about how Ethel was hoping therapy would help John. She'd recently made an appointment to see a woman named Mrs. Elizabeth Phillips at the Jewish Board of Guardians. But Jake was also friends with Ed.

"No thank you," I said. "I wouldn't want to trouble you."

"No trouble at all," Jake said. "We'll sit right outside on the steps and count the taxicabs going by. Wouldn't you like that, son?" Jake leaned down to David's level again, and David stopped thrashing altogether and leaned forward, maybe intrigued. How could Jake know about David's perfect fascination with taxicabs and counting? Their yellowness so attractive to him that there was barely anything David liked more these days.

"I'm sure my husband wouldn't approve of his friend going to such trouble," I said.

Jake stood back up and he stared at me. He had kind eyes. They were a brown color similar to Ed's, but Ed's eyes reminded me of stones, like the worn pebbles you might find along the shore at Coney Island. Jake's eyes were bright, more of an almond color, and they appeared to be smiling even though the rest of his face wasn't. "Make no mistake, Mrs. Stein," he said. "I'm no friend of your husband's."

"Really?" I murmured. He sounded so serious that I almost got the feeling he actively disliked Ed, which seemed strange given that I'd assumed they were part of the same circle. So he was no friend of Ed's and he wasn't a friend of Ethel's either. I wondered who had invited him to her party? Maybe he knew Julie. Ed and I had been to another party at their apartment last month, but Jake hadn't been in attendance at that one. Maybe he didn't know the group all that well.

"Come on, now. I don't mind at all," he said. "David and I will keep each other company while you go vote, won't we, David?"

No one ever offered to watch David, and here this man, this doctor, was practically begging me to do it. David stared up at Jake's face, his eyes open wide, I thought, with curiosity. I also thought if he could speak he would tell me that, yes, he would much rather count the taxicabs with this man than walk farther into the throng of noisy people with me. Another wave of nausea came over me. "You'll only be out on the steps?" I said, meeting Jake's eyes again.

Jake nodded and reached out his hand. David hesitated for only a second before taking it, and I wondered if maybe Ethel was right about this whole therapy idea and if Jake might even be able to help David. David was definitely taken with him, I could tell. And David was normally taken with no one.

I stepped into the library all alone and suddenly I felt weightless. I couldn't remember the last time I'd gone into a public place without David, without having to navigate the contours of his anxiety and silent tantrums.

"Who's that?" my mother asked, and I realized she was standing next to me again.

"Just a friend of Ed's." My voice didn't even catch on the lie. "He offered to watch David while I voted."

"He must be quite a good friend," my mother scoffed. And I pursed my lips tightly together so I wouldn't say what I was thinking, that she could've offered to watch him for a few moments given that she was his grandmother, after all. But she wasn't afraid to tell me why she didn't like to be alone with him or how his silence and his kicking for attention made her nervous. I wondered how she was going to feel about the new baby and if she might be willing to help me more if the child was *usual,* as she called it, like Susan's girls, who she was willing to ride a train to watch. I thought about Ethel's boys, about how different Richie and John were, such opposites in every way. But I pressed my lips tightly together, not wanting to think how impossible it would be if there was another baby just like David.

My mother was none the wiser, nor did she seem to notice that I had my hand on the wall to steady myself. She leaned in and kissed my cheek. "I've already voted and I can't wait for you. I've got to head home. You know Bubbe Kasha can't be left alone for long and you're taking forever. Really, Mildred . . . Choose Dewey if you want to choose the winner."

I simply leaned in to kiss her back and quickly got in line.

After I cast my vote for Truman, I walked back outside and scanned the steps. I didn't see Jake and David and I suddenly couldn't breathe. Had Jake been lying? And Ed, too? Maybe the thought of a new baby had only made Ed resolve to get rid of David even more. Was Jake somehow connected with

Zelda Weiss and here to take David from me? And I had given him away so easily, just like that. I was so stupid.

I ran down the steps, calling for David, unable to catch my breath. And then I saw them down on the sidewalk below, standing by the door of a taxicab, Jake pointing out something to David and David seeming to listen intently and calmly in response. I exhaled and ran toward them and I quickly grabbed David's hand.

"Oh, there you are," Jake said, his voice sounding so calm and easy as if he watched children like David every day. Did he? In an instant, I felt calmer, too, and I knew my thought at the top of the steps had been silly. Jake was telling the truth when he said he was no friend of Ed's. Of course he wasn't. Everything about them seemed so completely opposite. I could barely even imagine them having a conversation, much less a friendship.

Jake smiled and small wrinkles showed up around his eyes. Maybe he was older than I first thought when I met him, maybe older than my thirty years, but not by much. He still seemed young and much too attractive to be a doctor, much younger than the old, stodgy Dr. Greenberg.

"Do you mind if I ask you a question?"

Jake asked and I shook my head. "Do you know what the problem is?"

"The problem?" I repeated, though I knew perfectly well what he meant. But I was not going to tell him what Dr. Greenberg had told me, that *I* was the problem. I was too cold. I'd ruined him. And now I was going to do it again with another baby, maybe only to hang on to David. How stupid and selfish I had been to get rid of my diaphragm. Who was I helping? David? Myself? I imagined another little boy just like him floating into the world and freezing in my coldness and failures as a mother.

"Hey there." Jake put his large hand on my shoulder. "I didn't mean to upset you." I shook my head again, but I didn't speak. I couldn't. "Do you have time now? Maybe we could go somewhere quiet and talk."

"I don't think so," I said, pulling out of his grasp and holding on tightly to David's hand. "I have to get back, get dinner ready." I was holding back tears, and I didn't want this man with his kind eyes to see any more than he already had.

"Tomorrow then?" he said quickly. I didn't understand why he seemed so eager to talk with me, why he was being so nice. Maybe he saw David as a patient, though from his card I guessed he was in private practice and there was no way I could afford to pay his fees. I highly doubted he would offer a sliding scale like Ethel said the Jewish Board of Guardians would. "I'll meet you outside your building at ten a.m. tomorrow. Okay?" he said.

"How do you know where my building is?" I asked, feeling suspicious of him again. Was he really this kind? Was anybody really this kind?

"You told me that night after the Rosenbergs' party, remember?" he said gently. I remembered how I'd snapped at him when he'd offered to escort me back inside. He put his hand on David's head and patted it lightly. David didn't react, but he didn't squirm away either. "Just meet me tomorrow," Jake said, and then he turned and walked down the street before I had a chance to tell him no.

Later that night, in our apartment, Ed refused to turn off the radio. He was waiting for news of who won the election, and all I heard over David's persistent kicking of the wall was that Wallace was dreadfully behind and that Dewey was in the lead. My mother was right, and I wondered if she could be right about the killer fog, too. Maybe I would walk outside tomorrow morning and it would be hanging there on the street, or maybe I wouldn't even make it that far. Maybe it would be thick and deadly enough that it would float up and engulf us, suffocate us, even up on the eleventh floor.

"Make him be quiet," Ed said, turning up the radio, leaning in closer to listen, and blowing a thick cloud of cigar smoke in my direction. The smell of it nauseated me even more.

"He doesn't like the radio," I told Ed. "He's not going to stop kicking the wall until you turn it off." I wasn't telling him something he didn't know, but still Ed shook his head and blew another cloud of smoke in my direction. I coughed and almost gagged and had to stop myself from vomiting right there on the couch. I walked to the window and took a few deep breaths to calm myself, and then I walked back to the couch and told Ed for what felt like the hundredth time, "This is why we need a television."

"We're not getting a television," he said, and he leaned over and turned the radio up again.

11

The next morning, it was not so much a decision to take the elevator down to the street and meet Jake at ten a.m. as it was a necessity.

I felt exhausted, having barely slept from the noise of Ed's radio and David's kicking and thrashing, and then when Ed finally turned the radio off, I heard him talking on the telephone, as he sometimes did at night when he thought I was asleep, talking to his political friends about their loss, I guessed, because I heard him use words like *liberal* and *Russia.* When he finally made his way to bed, I lay as still as I could, trying to pretend I was asleep so Ed would go to sleep, too. But the combination of his vodka, his cigars, and his disappointment over the election meant he would not go to sleep that easily, and I felt his hand on my thigh as soon as I felt the weight of his body hit the mattress. "I'm not feeling well," I said. And then when he persisted, I added, "There is already going to be another baby, Ed."

"You have been to see the doctor?" Ed slurred his words, his breath thick with vodka.

"Not yet." I closed my eyes. I felt a dull ache low in my stomach, and though I was exhausted, I couldn't fall asleep. I lay in bed wide awake, staring at the ceiling, wishing I could simply dream the new baby away.

But this morning, in the pale light of the day that shone in through the living room window, I knew that was a ridiculous and terrible thought. The clock on the coffee table approached ten, the dull ache in my stomach persisted. David cried and kicked the floor, now out of sheer exhaustion. I knew we had to go downstairs to meet Jake. I knew I had to do *something.*

I let David press all the buttons in the elevator on the way down as I wondered if Jake would be out there on the sidewalk the way he said he would. But even more I wondered if he really could help us, help David. Would that change everything? If David could begin to speak and become normal, would Ed begin to love him the way Julie loved John — and Richie, too? I felt a glimmer of something small in my chest, a quickening of my heartbeat. But as we hit

131

the ground floor I wondered even if Jake could help, why would he want to?

Outside, the day was brisk and I'd forgotten our coats. The street was crowded. Men rushed by in hats that covered their eyes; women walked by in small groups, pushing strollers. I stared at them with a quiet longing. I didn't see Jake at first and I shivered in the cold, but then David tugged on my arm, pulling me to cross the street, and I spotted a man sitting on a bench, reading a newspaper. There he was. At least, I thought it was him. He had on a brown derby that shadowed most of his face and a thick long brown coat.

We crossed the street and the man put his paper down, tipped his hat, and smiled. It *was* Jake, and I felt an immediate sense of calm, though I couldn't say why. Maybe just because he'd seemed to understand David yesterday the way no one else ever did, or even wanted to, but me. Or maybe because I was so very tired, my stomach aching — my head aching now, too — that it was just a relief to understand I was not going to be alone, even if only for a few short moments.

Jake folded his paper under his arm and stood. "They were wrong last night," he said. "Dewey didn't win. Truman won."

"Oh." I felt a smug sense of satisfaction

that Ed's man hadn't won and that mine had. And also that my mother had been wrong. She seemed wrong about that silly fog, too. The day was cool, but with a cloudless sky.

"I wasn't sure if you'd come." He smiled, presumably to show his pleasure that we had.

"Me neither," I said.

He laughed. "I'm glad you did, though. It's cold out here. Should we go get a cup of coffee?"

I hesitated, now wondering how it would look if anyone were to see us having coffee, not so much that I was with a man who was not my husband, though Ed would not be at all pleased should he ever find out, but that I was with a doctor, a *psychotherapist*. Ethel had sworn me to secrecy when she told me how she was taking John to therapy as if there were something inherently wrong about paying for something like that. Not that I was paying for anything. At least, I didn't think I was.

"Is there somewhere more private?" I asked. "Your office?" Then I quickly added, "Though I'm sure I can't afford your fees."

"My fees?" He shook his head. "Oh, no, you don't have to worry about that." He paused. "I'm just setting up here in New

York and I'm afraid I don't have my office together yet. We could go to my apartment and talk there, if you'd like. It's not too far. Just down Market." He cleared his throat. "That's where I've been seeing all my patients so far."

Jake leaned down and said something to David that I couldn't quite hear but I thought was something along the lines of *How would you like to stop by my place and see the yellow cars I have there?* David stood up straighter and easily took Jake's hand, and then it seemed we had no choice but to follow Jake to his apartment.

Jake lived above Waterman's Grocery, just down the street from Mr. Bergman's shop, and I thought how we might stop and visit Mr. Bergman on the way home, though I imagined I wouldn't tell Mr. Bergman about this. This visit with Jake. Whatever this was.

I was certain Jake didn't have the steam heat and laundry facilities we had in Knickerbocker Village, though Jake's apartment was larger on the inside than I expected when I first saw it from the street. He had a back room — what I assumed was the bedroom — and a large front room and kitchen. The front room was peculiarly empty, holding only two armchairs and a tiny end table with wide spaces on either side between it and the chairs.

"Sorry," Jake said as we followed him inside. "As I said, I haven't been in the city long and I haven't had time to get things set up yet." He had been here since at least September — Ethel's party — and that seemed to me ample time to get furnishings together, but Jake appeared to be a bachelor and it always seemed simple things like decorating were so much harder for men. I was just assuming he was a bachelor anyway, as I couldn't imagine a woman tolerating a home this barren, and he hadn't mentioned a wife or any woman.

"What brought you here?" I asked him.

"Oh," Jake said, "I came for work."

"For work?" That seemed strange since he didn't even have an office yet.

"Psychotherapy is a thriving business in New York City," he said. "Or so I hear."

"And where were you before?"

Before he had a chance to answer I heard a howling and a scratching — not David, an animal sound. I turned and there was a black long-haired cat, David's hands wrapped around its thick tail.

"David! No, don't." I ran to pull the poor animal out of his clutches and David got upset and began kicking the floor.

Jake scooped the cat up and threw her in the bedroom. "I inherited her with the apartment, I'm afraid." He bent down to David's level. "Don't feel bad. She doesn't like me much either." David continued to kick and refused to look at Jake.

"I'm sorry," I said. "He doesn't mean to. He just doesn't . . ."

"Shhh." Jake put a hand on my shoulder. With his other hand he pulled a toy car from the pocket of his jacket . . . yellow. A taxicab. I wasn't sure if he'd bought it special after seeing David's fascination with taxicabs yesterday or if he always carried such things around in the pockets of his coat. Jake held it out deliberately close to David's face, and David stopped kicking to take a look. Then he took the toy eagerly and ran his fingers over it as if he could feel the yellow and it soothed him.

Jake motioned for me to have one of the two seats. I took the one closest to David, and Jake took the farther one by the window, though he pulled the chair closer toward me.

"I've studied children like David," Jake said so calmly and evenly as if to say there were more of them — many of them — that David *and* I were not alone. "Let me rephrase that," Jake said. "I've studied other children who can't or don't speak."

"And?" I hung over the edge of the chair, suddenly aware of every sound: the cat scratching against the bedroom door, the customers clamoring for groceries down below. David running the toy cab back and forth and back and forth against the same hardwood floorboard. My stomach was really aching now, but at least my nausea had subsided a bit.

"And some of them are vacant," Jake said. "Sometimes you look into their eyes and you see nothing." He paused. "But David isn't like that, is he?" I shook my head and bit my lip to try and stave off my tears. "He's inside there, but he can't get out. He can't figure out how to communicate the way the rest of us can. Something is misfiring in his brain."

"In his brain?" I murmured, thinking how different this sounded from what Dr. Greenberg had always told me, how he had placed all of the blame on me and how much I loved or didn't love David, and I'd so easily and willingly believed him. "You don't think it's my fault, then?" I asked Jake.

"Not at all." He leaned closer and put his hand on my arm. I became aware of how close he was sitting to me, how we were all alone in this empty space, and I shifted and pulled back slightly. "I see the way you are with him," he said. "It's not your fault."

"I forgot his coat this morning," I said. "It's cold outside . . . I'm too cold."

"Mrs. Stein . . ."

I hated the way that sounded in his calm tone. That I was only Mrs. Stein to him. Only Ed's wife. "*Millie,* please."

"Millie, no one is perfect," he said. "But you're not the reason why David doesn't speak." I wondered how he could be so sure. I wanted to believe everything he was saying, but he barely knew David . . . or me. "I believe I can help you. Help him," he said. "If you'll let me."

"But why would you do that?" I asked. "I already told you, I can't pay you. I don't have the money. And even if I did, Ed wouldn't —"

"I don't want you to pay me. I just want to help you, and if it works — *when* it works — I want to publish a paper about my techniques."

"I don't know," I said, thinking about how Ed would react should he find out about Jake helping us or this paper. Maybe Zelda Weiss was beyond reach now with another baby growing inside me. But what would happen when Ed got angry with me again?

What would stop him from calling her back. Or, worse, actually getting her to take David away? Her first visit had been only a warning, I was sure of that. Next time, I didn't think we would be so lucky.

"My paper would be completely anonymous," Jake said. "No one would ever know I was writing about you or David except for us." He smiled, and I noticed his two front teeth were slightly crooked. "But think of the other children and mothers like you that we might be able to help."

I still couldn't grasp it, that there were others like David, like us. I often felt we were all alone here inside this great giant bubble of a city. Sure, other children had problems. Other mothers got worn down. I saw that with Ethel and with John, in their own way. But at least John spoke and understood even if he didn't always want to listen. "What would you do, exactly?" I asked Jake.

"Therapy," he said. "I would work closely with David, one on one, trying to get him to articulate his feelings. Not through words at first, through symbols and actions, and then we would work up to words. Eventually." He cleared his throat. "And I'd like to spend time talking with you as well."

"Therapy . . . for me?" I wondered if Ethel

was also involved in the therapy she'd signed John up for at the Jewish Board of Guardians.

"Yes. Are you willing to try?"

I turned to look at David, who was methodically running his toy taxicab back and forth across the same floorboard as if he were lulled by its easy motion, its perfect color. He seemed contented here and he seemed to like Jake. If nothing else, this was a place for us to go. I turned back to Jake. "Can I ask you something?" He nodded. "Why were you at the party at the Rosenbergs' in September? You're involved with the politics that my husband and his friends are. But they don't seem to believe in the kind of work you do."

Jake laughed a little. "The Rosenbergs invited me," he said. "They knew I was new to the neighborhood. Ethel is very sweet."

I remembered what Ethel had said, that she barely knew Jake, that she wasn't even sure who'd invited him. *He's lying to me,* I thought. *Why?*

But maybe he wasn't lying. Maybe Julie had invited Jake and hadn't told her. Jake's eyes were so kind, he was so kind, I wanted to trust him, I wanted to let him help us. "Okay," I said, pushing all of my doubts aside. After all, Jake was, as Bubbe Kasha would say, offering me a *mitzvah.* And *mitzvot* were not to be questioned.

I stood and the ache in my stomach grew sharper, so sharp that I couldn't breathe for a moment, and I doubled over in pain.

"Millie," I heard Jake saying, though now his voice sounded very far away as if he were on the other side of a tunnel. "Are you all right? You're bleeding."

"Bleeding?" I said. Qr maybe I didn't say anything at all. I looked down and there was a spot of red on the top of my scuffed black shoe.

June 19, 1953

"Where's David?" Jake asks. He whispers the words in my ear, David's name, like a lullaby, still soft and sweet and beautiful. Jake steps around the barricades, away from the lights, and he pulls my arm to take me with him. But we're on the wrong side of things. I wanted Jake to take me in, not to step out here, and I propel myself forward, back toward the entrance, until he catches me and holds my arms, holding me back.

"Millie." His voice is low, even, just the way I always remember it was back when everything was still perfect. "You didn't answer my question."

But I'm not going to. I'm unwilling to tell him, to let him see what has become of me, of us, since I've seen him last. "You have to stop them," I say instead.

"I can't," he says. "It has gone so far beyond you or me . . ."

"But you know that Ethel is innocent," I

142

say, pushing harder to get away from him, to run past the barriers, but I have no plan for what I will do once I'm inside. Who will I talk to if not Jake? The names of all the men from the trial run carelessly through my head in an infinite loop. All the Irvings. Irving Kaufman. Irving Saypol. I never liked the name Irving . . . and I am certain they're nowhere near Sing Sing tonight anyway. I picture them in their large, comfortable houses, enjoying a nightcap on their back patios, watching fireflies. And it doesn't seem fair. None of this is fair.

Jake doesn't answer me, and I look up and catch his face in the orange glow of a flare, the soft yellow of the moonlight. He looks older than I remember him. He has stubble across his cheeks and chin as if he hasn't remembered to shave in weeks. I want to reach up and touch his face, to feel the coarseness of the stubble the way I once did, but now I clench my fists tightly at my sides. "You can't let her die," I say. "You just can't."

Jake looks away from me so I can't tell what he's thinking, and then the flare burns out and dusk has come on so fast that I can see him standing there next to me only as a shadow. How many times have I imagined this moment, standing this close to him again? And yet never like this. Never with Ethel's life so wrongly about to slip away from her. Above us, a helicopter begins to circle, drowning out everything else for a moment, even my thoughts.

"I'll tell them everything," I say to Jake. But now I have to shout for my voice to be heard over the sound of helicopter. "Just get me inside!"

"Millie . . ."

"Think about her children," I say. "What will John do without her? And little Richie?"

"I'm thinking about *your* children," Jake says.

My children. My throat begins to tighten at the thought. It's hard to breathe, the humidity clinging so heavy to my lungs that I think it might choke me.

1949
12

The brownstone on West Sixteenth Street was unremarkable. It might have been someone's home or any kind of doctor's office. I pulled the slip of paper from my purse and double-checked the address before walking up the steps to go inside. Ethel had written down this address for me last week on a scrap of paper she'd pulled from her purse as we'd watched the children play together at the playground. Her handwriting was perfectly legible and neat, even scribbled hastily leaning against a bench: *17 W. 16th Street.*

"How do you know about this?" I'd asked her, wondering how she always seemed to know so much more than I did . . . about everything. It was as if Ethel belonged to this secret club that I never even knew existed. A club of women who loved their husbands? But not the same club that Susan belonged to, so maybe it wasn't that at all.

Ethel was just always so smart, so aware of the world. I was sure she listened to more news programs on the radio than I did or talked to more people than I did.

But Ethel had shrugged as if this secret knowledge were something simple, something all women inherently had. *Planned Parenthood.* It sounded like something docile — welcoming, even. And I supposed maybe she knew about this place the way she knew about the sliding scale therapy at the Jewish Board of Guardians.

I hadn't told Ethel still about Jake, that David and I were seeing him two mornings a week, though I listened with interest as she told me about Elizabeth Phillips, whom she and John were going to see once a week now at the Jewish Board of Guardians. "It's helping. Mrs. Phillips gives good advice," she'd said, though I couldn't tell if there had been an air of skepticism in her voice or if she was just cold sitting outside. It was way too cold to be out on the playground — January, the dead of winter. But the sun had been shining and we were both so tired of being cooped up in our tiny apartments with restless children.

That was last week. This morning, I'd left David at Jake's apartment and I'd come here.

I hadn't been to see a doctor since that day in November, that first day David and I went to Jake's apartment. Dr. Greenberg had examined me that afternoon and had later assured an anxious Ed over the telephone that since the bleeding had begun so early, it would not affect us in the long term. Dr. Greenberg had also said no marital relations for at least three months so that my body would have time to heal. And that had been such a relief that I'd been able to swallow down my own feelings of guilt, the understanding that I might have made it happen, that I had wished it upon myself.

I pushed the thought away now as I walked up the steps of the brownstone. This morning was the first time I'd left David at his therapy alone, and I'd refused to meet Jake's eyes when he'd asked where I was going. In all these months, we had never talked about that first morning in his apartment, but I understood Jake carried around a secret about me, another secret that I hoped he wouldn't share. Only Ed knew about the baby I had lost. I hadn't even told Ethel or my mother. Certainly not Susan, who was in the family way again herself. And all I'd said to Jake this morning was, "I'm going on an errand. If you don't mind?"

I knew he wouldn't, but still I couldn't look at him, as if he might see it in my eyes where it was exactly that I was running off to on this mysterious, unnamed errand.

He'd simply said, "When you get back, maybe you and I could talk?"

I'd so far avoided any kind of therapy of my own with Jake by running out and claiming David and I had things to do, so many errands to run. My mother and Bubbe Kasha to check on. Mr. Bergman to visit. Jake hadn't pushed the issue until now. And Ethel had told me that she had also been talking on her own with Mrs. Phillips, so I was fairly sure that Jake's wanting to talk with me wasn't out of the ordinary. But I didn't want to. I didn't want to tell Jake things — deeply personal things — about myself because I had this nagging feeling in my stomach that he would look at me and I would begin to weep. Just like that. Uncontrollably.

First things first, I reasoned as I walked inside the brownstone. Nevermind that the mere act of walking inside here filled me with dread. If Ed were to find out . . . (although Ethel promised me he never would, that the women here at Planned Parenthood would be discreet, not like Dr. Greenberg). Ed had become even more

148

anxious for another child since Leo, Betty, and the girls had relocated to California last month and Lena was more focused on Ed than ever. But no one would tell Ed anything here, I reminded myself. And I put my hand tightly against my stomach, breathed deeply, and walked up to the desk.

"Mildred Kauffman," I told the receptionist, my maiden name feeling like a forgotten freedom and an awful lie. I was her once, this factory girl who never imagined a life where she couldn't want another child, where she would lie so terribly to her husband.

"The nurse will be right with you, hon." The receptionist was a blond girl, a wisp of a thing, with a kind smile. This place couldn't be more different than Dr. Greenberg's office, and all at once that put me at ease.

A few minutes later, a nurse came out to greet me and take me back into the examining room. She was young, too, and quite pretty. I wondered if that was a requirement for working here. "Come on back, Mildred," she said. "I'm Anna." Her voice was so warm, and I followed her back to the examining room.

She offered me a chair to sit in and she sat down across from me as if we were just about to have a friendly conversation. Who knew that a place like this existed? I had imagined something illicit, the kind of places you would hear whispered about among the girls who'd lived on Delancey Street when I was in high school. Harriet Edelstein was rumored to have gotten herself in trouble in high school and then to have found a butcher — not a kosher one either — who had sliced the baby out of her but had done such a terrible job that she almost bled to death, and we heard she would never be able to have children at all. It had been years since I'd seen Harriet, and now I wondered what happened to her, what had ever become of the girl we all whispered about.

"What can we help you with?" I realized the nurse Anna was asking me now and I looked up again. She was smiling at me.

"I cannot be in the family way," I said curtly the way Mildred Kauffman, a single gal from Delancey Street, might have said it once. Although I never would've said that to a stranger, never would've considered doing anything like this before I got married, and so the whole thought of it was so absurd that I nearly had to stop myself from laughing.

"Of course," Anna said. "And are you

pregnant right now?"

Pregnant. She put it so bluntly, but that was really what it was, wasn't it? Referring to the condition as *in the family way* might imply that Ed and I were truly a family, that any baby was born of love. Saying *pregnant* was clinical but felt right. "No," I finally answered.

"I can fit you for a diaphragm," she said, again so bluntly.

"Is there nothing else?" I wasn't sure if I'd be able to get this past Ed again or what he might do if he were to find out.

"There are things for men, of course," Anna said, and I shook my head. "But for women?" She sighed. "This is your best option right now. Mrs. Sanger is hoping for a kind of magic pill to be invented. Wouldn't that be wonderful?"

"A magic pill?"

"Well, not *really* magic, but she believes it can be a done. A simple pill a woman could take just to prevent pregnancy."

I nodded, but her magical pill seemed just as faraway as a killer fog or the thought of the bomb across the ocean in Russia.

When I arrived back at Jake's, I found him and David on the floor, lining up Jake's colored blocks. Jake had been trying to teach David the colors as symbols and had been encouraging me to practice with David at home. Red was for "hungry." Blue for "tired." Yellow seemed to be for everything else so far and that had been the most frustrating part. David was still — always — drawn to the yellows, and so most of the time I had no idea what it was he wanted.

David looked up at me when I walked in and then quickly looked away. He reached into the pile of blocks and he pulled out a red one, holding it up without meeting my eyes.

"You're hungry, darling?" I asked, and I felt something tugging in my chest. Was David really in there, locked up inside himself, just as Jake said he was? "Is he" — I turned to Jake — "hungry?" Or was it just an accident that David had grabbed red instead of yellow this time?

Jake pulled his pocket watch out of his jacket pocket and showed it to me. Nearly noon. I realized how long I'd been gone. Almost three hours!

"I'm sorry," I said to Jake. "I didn't realize my errand would take so long."

"That's quite all right. David and I made some progress today, didn't we, son?" David didn't answer or even look up, but I noticed he was stacking the red blocks now, forcing them into a delicate triangular tower. Red, not yellow. All at once — like that. It was no accident. It was progress. David had told me something. Or at least I thought he had.

I felt an enormous surge of gratitude for Jake, for the way he spoke to David. *Son.* He'd been saying it colloquially, from a distance — as his doctor, of course — but I had never heard Ed speak to David with so much kindness.

"I should get him home, get him some lunch." I bent down to clean up the blocks.

I felt Jake's hand on my shoulder, and I stopped for a moment. "Millie," he said. "Leave it." He stared straight at me so intensely, in a way that I was not used to a man — or anyone, for that matter — staring at me. "I have some bread and milk in the icebox. Why don't you let me get him some of that and then you and I can sit and talk?"

"I wouldn't want to —"

"Nonsense." He walked to the kitchen before I could finish my thought, and he returned a moment later with a glass of milk and a plate with some dark bread. He didn't have a dining table here, a place to eat his meals, and I suddenly wondered where he ate. Whether he walked downstairs to Waterman's Grocery to sit at their counter each night. Whether he ever had someone here to cook for him. Yet I got the impression that the only people Jake brought here were his patients, not that I ever saw any of them.

But I didn't ask. I watched David happily accept Jake's bread from his spot on the floor and he quickly took a large bite of it. He *was* hungry. He'd communicated. He'd actually communicated.

"This is amazing," I said to Jake. "Red. He actually showed us red when he was hungry."

Jake smiled and motioned for me to take one of the chairs. I did, and so did he. They were closer together than I remembered from the last time, and Jake leaned forward so he was close enough to me that I could see every crevice of his face, the tiny wrinkles around his eyes, the faint shadow of hair on his chin. He smelled vaguely of pinecones and peppermint . . . and something else, a smokiness. Not cigar smoke like Ed. Something familiar and pleasant.

"Millie," Jake said. "I've been wanting to talk with you."

I cleared my throat. "About?"

"Just about you," he said. "Why don't you tell me a bit about your life at home . . . with David and Ed?"

I shrugged, not at all sure how this was going to help David. "I don't know what to say. I'm not good at this type of thing."

He smiled and his face softened again. He pulled a pipe off the lone end table. "Do you mind?" I shook my head. He filled it with tobacco and lit it. That was the smell. *Pipe smoke.* I pulled a cigarette from my purse and Jake lit it for me. I closed my eyes and inhaled deeply before exhaling. When I opened my eyes again, Jake's face was obscured, hazy through our shared smoke.

"If it were up to Ed, David would be in some kind of an institution." I exhaled again and I felt my eyes burning. I blinked hard and hoped Jake wouldn't notice. Jake put his pipe down on the rest on the end table and he leaned in closer and waited for me to continue. "Ed would like to pretend that David doesn't exist." I swallowed hard. "He would like to replace him with another, more perfect boy." As the words came out of me I heard their awfulness, and I put my hand up to my mouth.

"It's okay," Jake said softly. "It's okay to be honest here. Nothing you say will go farther than this room, I promise." He put his hand gently on my forearm. "Have you told him about my work with David?"

"No. He wouldn't approve."

"Why do you think that?"

I thought about what Ethel said about how she felt she wasn't supposed to believe in psychotherapy but she did anyway, and I just knew Ed absolutely would not. I wasn't sure if it was because of the politics he believed in or the way he was brought up in Russia or just because he might not like the idea of me talking about him to another man about private things that we could not really even talk about with each other. "I don't know," I finally said, "I just know he wouldn't."

Jake leaned back into his chair and sucked on his pipe again. "Why don't you tell me about your circle of friends. Do you have anyone you can lean on for help with David?"

"I don't have many friends," I said, and saying it out loud somehow made the sad truth of it sink in. I'd had friends at the factory and friends in high school — girlfriends, of course. Susan and I were only a year apart, and there were a group of girls on Delancey we'd always hung around with together — Sylvia, Clara, and Elsie. But then there was the war and we all went to work. And by the time Susan got married and moved out to the suburbs, it seemed the other girls had all but floated away, out of my life for good. So maybe the truth was that they were Susan's friends all along, not mine. Then there was Addie, who I used to sometimes catch a picture with back when we worked at the factory together. But she got married and moved upstate just before I married Ed, and now we exchanged only the infrequent letter or two a year. "It's hard," I heard myself saying to Jake now. "With David . . . I don't have much time for friends."

"What about the Rosenbergs, the Green-glasses, the Sobells?" Jake asked.

"Those are Ed's friends," I said quickly, "not mine." Then I added, "Except for Ethel. She's my neighbor, as you know." She'd known Ed first, but she was mine now, wasn't she? I'd trusted her enough to ask her advice and to listen to her about Planned Parenthood. She promised she would never tell Julie and I had promised to keep her secret about psychotherapy from Ed. Which I had.

I suddenly thought of Jake that night in Ethel's apartment, in the throng of men shouting to hear one another over John's phonograph, and I wondered how he was involved with all of them. I got the sense he disliked Ed, and Ethel seemed not to know

Jake very well, so what was his role in all of it?

I looked at David out of the corner of my eye, his dark bread almost completely devoured. His red blocks stacked so neatly. And I bit my lip and didn't ask. Jake's politics and friendships were his own business, after all.

"So Ed has many friends, people to talk to, and you talk to no one?" I realized Jake was saying now.

Jake's statement startled me even though it was fairly accurate, that Ed had friends and I did not. Ed had people to call at night on the telephone and he did often. I never called anyone but my mother and Susan. But when I overheard Ed's conversations, they were always political. I'd never heard him speak of David, to anyone. Barely even to me.

"I talk to Ethel sometimes," I finally said.

"What's that like?"

"It's nice. We understand each other."

"And her husband is more supportive of therapy?"

"I . . ." I had no idea how Jake knew about Ethel's therapy, but I was certain she wouldn't have told him. Maybe Julius had? "I don't know," I finally said.

Jake picked his pipe back up and put it in

his mouth as if he were thinking. "So, mostly, you're isolated," Jake said eventually, not unkindly. "David lives in silence and so do you."

It sounded awful to hear it that way from him, but even more awful to understand how right he was. "I don't see how any of this is helping," I said, and put my cigarette out in the ashtray on Jake's table. I stood quickly and grabbed my purse.

Jake reached out and put his hand gently on my arm again. "I just want to know your world," he said. "To understand it."

I pulled myself out of his grasp. "*This* is my world," I said, gesturing toward David, his blocks, his silence.

13

Back in my apartment, I lit another cigarette while David took a nap. All the therapy with Jake, the block stacking and the communicating, had worn him out and he'd lain down without a fuss for the first time in a long while. I sat on our couch and turned the radio on low so as not to wake David, and the news came to me almost incoherently at first, a hiss of men's voices. It was snowing in Los Angeles for the very first time. Truman had a Fair Deal now, though the newsman did not say exactly what was so fair about it, and I wondered how it would make my life better. Was he advocating for the same magical pill Mrs. Sanger wished for? I highly doubted it. Alger Hiss had been indicted for perjury last month and there would be a trial in the spring. I remembered what Mr. Bergman had said about him, and I wondered what, exactly, he was guilty of lying about.

My head ached and I put my cigarette out and turned the radio off. I lay down on the couch and closed my eyes for a few moments, exhausted from the day: my trip to Planned Parenthood, my conversation with Jake. I could hear his voice in my head now saying that he wanted to know about me, about my world, and it held me like the warmth of a blanket and settled me into a sweet and easy nap.

The telephone rang and I jumped up and quickly answered it before it could wake David. "Millie." I heard a voice on the other end of the line, my name coming out in one great big hurried rush. I thought of Jake — Jake's voice, Jake's pipe smoke, Jake's warm apartment. "Thank goodness," the voice was saying, and I realized it was a woman and that I'd answered the phone still half asleep. *Ethel.* "I'm so glad I caught you at home," she said.

I sat up and tried to push the tiredness and the feeling of Jake away. Jake was back in his own apartment, probably working on therapy with someone else. I was here. Alone. "Is everything okay?" I asked Ethel.

"My father has taken a turn for the worse and I want to go see him. I can take Richie with me. He'll sleep in his carriage. I feel terrible asking, but . . ." I understood what she was asking, if I would be able to watch John while she went. She lowered her voice. "Please, Millie, just for a little while. Would you mind terribly?"

I knew Ethel's father had fallen and broken his hip last winter and that he'd been steadily worsening for the last several months. I also knew that Ethel loved her father deeply. My own father had died quickly of a massive coronary. One moment in the butcher shop he was standing up, talking to a customer, and the next dead on the floor. At least, that was how Mr. Bergman had told it to us, telling us that we should take comfort in knowing that he didn't suffer. But if I had seen it coming, I would've spent every possible moment with him that I could've.

"Of course," I heard myself saying to Ethel now, though all the while wondering what *I* was going to do with John? A boy who not only talked but argued. "David is napping, but when he wakes up, I'll set them up with some blocks . . . or take them to the playground."

"Oh, Millie, thank you. I owe you one."

"Nonsense," I said. "You'd do the same for me." Then I added, "We're friends, aren't we?"

"You're the best," Ethel said in response,

and then she hung up.

Twenty minutes later, I found myself sitting on the couch across from John while he stared at me and frowned. "Shall we listen to the radio?" I asked, knowing even as I said it that he would not be happy with the volume at which I listened to it in order to keep David happy. "Or I can take out some of David's toys for you?"

"I don't want to be here," John said curtly.

I pulled a cigarette out of my pack and lit it, my fingers twitching a little. "I know, darling, but your mother will be back soon. She just had to visit with someone for a little while." I thought it best to keep it vague in case John didn't know the details of Mr. Greenglass's recent decline.

John's frown creased even deeper. "Julie is mad at Ed, you know."

"What?" I was taken aback by his revelation, so I didn't correct his manners. He had an unusual habit of calling adults, even Ethel and Julie, by their first names, and though I'd heard him do it before it still startled me each time. But what did John mean that Julie was mad at Ed? I certainly hadn't heard a word of that from Ethel . . . or Ed.

"Julie is very angry with him," John repeated. "That's why I don't think I should be here."

Julie was so kind and even-tempered that it was hard to imagine him being very angry with anyone. I inhaled and then exhaled slowly, wishing for my cigarette to calm me the way it normally did. But it didn't seem to be working. "Well, I'm sure it's nothing," I said to John. "And besides, your mother does want you to be here. She's my friend, you know. And Mr. Stein and your daddy are at work now, so let's not worry about them." But if John was right, if Julie and Ed were mad at each other, what would that mean for me and Ethel?

John crossed his arms in front of his chest, and I heard David kicking the wall, a sound which brought me relief. John had come to adore him and certainly some blocks with David would occupy his thoughts, as long as both children could control their tempers.

I brought David out and set them up with the blocks, and David yawned and rubbed his eyes and then immediately dove in for the reds. "You're hungry, darling?" I asked. John answered that he was, so I went into the kitchen and sliced some bananas for the children. David's favorite.

I set them in a bowl in front of them and waited for David to devour them hungrily the way he had devoured his bread earlier at Jake's. But David glanced up, noticed the bananas, and then promptly ignored them. "Eat up, darling," I said, pushing the bananas toward him, but he ignored them still and instead he built the red blocks into a tower.

John took some of the banana slices and stuffed them in his mouth. "He's not hungry, Millie," he told me, pointing toward David.

"*Mrs. Stein.* And don't talk with your mouth full," I reminded him. "And he *is* hungry," I added. "That's why he's using the red blocks."

John shook his head. "He just likes red now."

Ethel showed up at my door just before five, and by then I'd already had to separate John and David, as they were throwing blocks at each other. David was in the bedroom with the yellow taxicab Jake had let him have, and John was lying on the couch, his ear pressed to the radio to listen to *The Lone Ranger.* He was angry that I wouldn't let him turn it up any higher, but he had relented finally and put his ear close. I wondered if Ethel was right, if therapy was helping him. But I felt like a fool for believing that it was actually helping David. *Progress.* Yes, now David was just fixated on a new color. John had put it so simply: *He just likes red now.*

Ethel stood in the hallway holding a squirming Richie in her arms, who struggled to be let down to run to his brother. Ethel's cheeks were flushed and her eyes were red as if she'd been crying. "How was he?" she asked.

"Fine," I lied. She half smiled at me as if to say she knew I was lying but she was grateful for it. "How was your father?"

"Not good," she said. "And my mother . . ." She sighed. "She's just never nice to me. I think she hates me, to tell you the truth, Millie."

"She's your mother," I said. "Of course she doesn't hate you."

"It's always been this way with her. I've never been good enough. Never as good as my brothers." She shrugged as if to say it didn't matter, that she was used to it by now, though I wondered if one could ever get used to an unkindness from one's own mother. My mother favored Susan of course, she always had. But I never had the feeling that she hated me.

"Do you want to come in for a little while?"

166

"I shouldn't," she said. "Julie will be home soon, and I should go get dinner ready." But even as she said it she stepped inside the apartment and I shut the door behind her. "Maybe just a few minutes," she murmured.

"Do you want something to drink?" I asked. "We have some Mogen David. And vodka."

"Vodka?" She laughed.

"Ed drinks it. It's very . . . Russian."

"I imagine it must be hard to find these days with everything Russian so out of fashion." She rolled her eyes and sat down on one of the chairs at our small table. I had no idea whether the vodka was hard to find or not as Ed was the one keeping it in constant supply in our kitchen cabinet, bringing it home in brown paper bags after work. I wondered if Ethel was right, that vodka was hard to find these days and, as such, maybe Ed kept track of how much was in the bottle. I pulled out the bottle of wine from under the sink instead. I poured two very large glasses and handed one to Ethel.

Ethel lifted her glass to toast me. "To parents," she said, and I wasn't sure whether she meant her father, our parents, or us, but I clinked glasses with her and murmured it back.

"Is Julie mad at Ed?" I asked her suddenly.

"What?" She laughed a little and took another sip of her wine.

"Nothing. It's silly. John mentioned it to me, and it's just . . . well, I wouldn't want anything going on between them at work to change things between us."

She waved her hand in the air and laughed. "Let the men be the men," she said. "Who knows half the reasons why they do the things they do."

"But Julie hasn't mentioned anything to you?"

She put her hand over mine. "Really, Millie, don't pay any attention. Sometimes John just says things." I nodded. Of course it was silly to worry about the ramblings of a child, even one as bright and perceptive as John. We sipped our wine in silence for a few moments and then Ethel leaned in close. "I think I'm going to go see a new doctor . . . for psychoanalysis."

"But you already talk to Mrs. Phillips?" I was confused how, exactly, this was different.

"Yes, and Mrs. Phillips is quite lovely, but we talk only once a week alone and only about John. I feel I need to go deeper, to do

psychoanalysis myself. To get myself together. To be a better mother. To move past
my childhood . . ." I thought about Jake's
questions about my life, about her, about
Julius, and I wondered if that's what I was
doing there with him? *Becoming a better
mother?* Ethel finished off her wine and put
the glass on the table, making sure it was
resting on a coaster even now that it was
empty. "I know I shouldn't," Ethel said,
"but I've come to believe that talk therapy
is the solution to all of our problems." She
smiled at me. "You probably think I'm
crazy, too, but you're very sweet not to say
it."

"No," I said, "I don't think you're crazy at
all." I hesitated for a moment, remembering
what Jake had said about me being isolated,
living in silence just like David. I didn't
want to be that way. I wanted to trust
someone. "I've been seeing a psychotherapist, too. Well, David has been . . . But me,
too. It's Julie's friend from the party last
spring, Dr. Gold."

"Who?" she asked.

"Dr. Gold . . . Jake."

"You mentioned him once before," Ethel
said, "but I don't really know him. I can't
picture him."

Jake seemed to know her and Julie. But

maybe he just knew Julie more, and Ethel had been so preoccupied lately, as had I, with her children and with her family, that she didn't notice a new person around.

"He's been teaching David to communicate with colored blocks. We're making progress." Then I added, "Maybe."

"That's wonderful, Millie," she said. "And Ed approves of this?"

"Oh goodness no. He has no idea that I've been doing it."

"And you've been able to pay for it without his knowledge?"

"No. Jake has offered to do it for free. In exchange for writing some kind of paper about his findings. A completely anonymous paper," I added, remembering the way Jake had phrased it that first morning I went to his apartment.

"You don't find that odd, Millie?"

"Odd?" I finished off my own glass of wine and put it down on the table. The air in the room felt thicker, Ethel's words slower, the noise of the children in the background fuzzier. "Not really . . . no."

Ethel frowned. "But nobody does something for nothing these days, Millie."

"It's not for nothing," I said. "His . . . paper." But even as I said the words aloud, I wondered if Ethel was right, if the whole thing was odd.

"Well, I'm glad to hear that you believe in all this, too," Ethel said, and she squeezed my hand. "We're lucky to have found each other, aren't we, Millie?" I squeezed her hand in return. "Someday, all this therapy will make us just perfect and we'll show them all, won't we?" She laughed, and then I heard myself laughing, too. We both knew how ridiculous it sounded, but Ethel would find a way to begin pyschoanalysis, I knew, and I was going to continue bringing David to Jake. We had to do *something.*

"It has been three months," Ed said that night in the darkness of our bedroom. My entire body tensed underneath the covers.

We'd moved around each other in a silence, a steady calm since that day in November when the bleeding had started. In the past few months I had come to understand that my marriage was nothing but a game, with points to be won and lost, and that when Dr. Greenberg called Ed and told him how sometimes these things happened early on with too much *activity,* I had won points. It hadn't hurt that I had felt a strange and infinite sadness for the sudden loss of a baby I hadn't even thought I'd wanted. *In a different life, maybe,* I kept thinking. Ed had once woken up and found me crying in the kitchen in the middle of the night and more points had been won, though that had not been my intention. I simply had not been able to stop myself from crying.

"Not yet," I said. "In one more week, it will be three months." One more week. I hoped Ed wouldn't argue with my flimsy math. I needed another week to give myself enough time to return to Planned Parenthood to pick up my new diaphragm.

Ed shifted in the bed next to me, but I didn't feel his hand reach for my thigh.

"Ed," I said after a few moments of silence, "are you and Julie fighting?" The truth was, even if they were, I wasn't entirely sure I wanted to know. Ethel was my only real friend. I couldn't lose her. And she had already brushed off this question. But I couldn't stop thinking about what John had said to me earlier, and also what Jake said about my silence. I wanted to be able to tell him at our next session that I had spoken up, that I'd tried to talk to Ed, to answer a question, to fix a problem.

"Fighting?" Ed said. "Mildred, where did you get that idea?"

"I watched John earlier for Ethel and he insisted that Julie was angry with you."

I could feel the weight of his body sigh against the mattress. "Julie is angry with me? Mildred, you are so silly to listen to a child." Ed laughed a little, and then he rolled over.

But something about the way he said it made me think that John had actually been telling the truth, and I wondered what, exactly, he'd overheard. I couldn't fall asleep for a long while, even after I heard Ed's familiar snores rattling next to me.

A week later, I picked up my small package from Planned Parenthood, and I discreetly inserted the new diaphragm every night before I got into bed. Ed moved on top of me so carefully, as if he were afraid I might break, that I felt almost bad about my deception. But not bad enough to make me take the diaphragm out.

The winter rolled on with a steady routine. Two mornings a week, I sat in Jake's empty apartment and watched him work on the floor with David. Afterward, I found myself talking to him. At first because he wanted me to, but then because I couldn't stop the words from coming. I heard myself say things I wouldn't normally say to anyone. Since Jake had seen me bleeding that morning in November, I told him about the baby, the one I'd lost and mourned — strangely, given that I did not want another baby now. I told Jake more about Ethel and how nice it was to have a friend nearby. I told Jake about John's comment, that Ed and Julie were angry with each other, and that I'd spoken up and asked Ed why. Jake let me talk and mostly just listened, but at that he stopped me. "And what did Ed say when you asked him about it?" he asked me.

"He laughed," I told him. "And he said it was nothing."

Jake leaned in closer, and I felt my heartbeat quicken in a way I wouldn't have expected. There was something so intimate about this that it almost felt wrong, more than the fact that it was *therapy.* "Do you believe him?"

"No," I said. "I think Ed was lying to me."

"And why do you think that?"

I thought about the way Ed had been talking on the phone late at night more and more. He spoke in hushed tones as if he were taking great pains to make sure I wouldn't hear what he was saying. I told this to Jake.

"Do you know who he's talking to?" Jake asked.

"No," I answered him.

His face was so close to mine, his eyes

staring at me so intensely, that I had the strange feeling that he was about to kiss me, and then suddenly he seemed to catch himself and he sat back. "Have you thought about trying to get to know Ed's friends better?" His voice was so calm and even, and he gently picked up his pipe the way he always did, that I wondered if I'd imagined his closeness a moment ago, and now I felt embarrassed. I put my hands to my cheeks to hide the sudden redness. But Jake seemed not to notice, as he was still talking, contemplating his pipe. "Other than Ethel, I mean. The men Ed works with?"

I thought of that night in Ethel's apartment, how just when I'd begun to talk with Ruth and David Greenglass, Ed had grabbed my arm and embarrassed me. Did he not want me to know his friends or was he just drunk and angry that night? "I don't know," I said to Jake. "Ed likes having a life at work and friends separate from me, I think."

"But you could just have them over for dinner," Jake said. "Get to know them a little more, see for yourself how Ed and Julius and the rest of them are getting along."

I was uncertain whether Ed would like it if I invited his friends and associates over for dinner. Yet it seemed the type of thing most women would think of naturally, an instinct that I did not seem to have as Ed's wife, or maybe as David's mother. It was something Lena or even Susan would scold me for not having done sooner. And then I felt a little silly for not having reached this conclusion on my own. "That's a good idea, thanks," I said to Jake, and I laughed a little. "Maybe I really did need this therapy for myself."

He looked away and put his pipe back down on the table and then he picked up his pocket watch. "Look at the time," he said quickly. "I have another appointment."

"Oh, right, of course. I'm sorry to have kept you too long." I expected him to say that it was okay, that he enjoyed our extra talk, but he didn't say anything else. And then I felt certain that I had imagined our closeness. Jake was a psychotherapist, and David and I were his patients. That was all.

On Sunday afternoon, Julius and Ethel and the boys arrived first, followed soon after by Ruth and David Greenglass. I'd told Ethel to invite her other brother, Bernie, who also worked at Pitt, and his wife, Gladys, but she hadn't been feeling well lately and they'd declined.

I felt a little thrill that I'd taken Jake's advice and that it had worked out so well and so quickly. It wasn't hard to get a few of the people of Ed's world all together here in our apartment. I'd only had to tell Ethel to spread the word and to offer roasted chickens — Mr. Bergman's finest ones, of course — and some Mogen David. And before I knew it, Julie and David Greenglass and Ed were perched on my perfect blue couch, drinking wine and involved in what appeared to be a very robust discussion that involved loud voices and excited, flailing hands. Ruth sat on one of the arms, smoking a cigarette, listening, but not saying much. Ethel was in the back bedroom, checking on the children.

"More wine?" I asked, bringing the Mogen David over to the couch. Julius declined, but Dave and Ed held their glasses forward for me to pour more. Ruth did, too. I envied her for the way she sat here among the men as if she belonged, but then she smiled at me kindly and I felt bad for feeling jealous. I thought about going to check on David, but Ethel was back there in the bedroom with them and I remembered the point of this little dinner was for me to get to know these people more, so I poured myself a glass of wine and sat on the edge of the coffee table.

"I think everything at the shop is coming around," Julie said to David and Ed. David shrugged, and Ed drank his wine.

"That's wonderful," I said. Ed ignored me, but Julie shot me a kind smile.

"But you shouldn't want for your own brother-in-law to be educated?" Ruth said pointedly to Julius, and I had the feeling this was the middle of an ongoing discussion that she'd jumped right back into. She blew a ring of smoke in his direction.

"Of course I want that for you," Julie said, turning to David. "But I need you there to supervise the shop. Now more than ever."

Ruth laughed bitterly. "For all the business you're having these days."

"Like I said," Julie said firmly, "it's coming around."

Ruth raised her eyebrows.

"There is business," Ed said, and it both surprised me and pleased me to hear him speak up, to defend Julius. Maybe John was wrong. Maybe it was David and Julius who were angry with each other and Ed wasn't involved at all. "We have a very big opportunity coming our way, don't we, Julie?"

Julie glanced at Ed and twirled his mustache and didn't say anything for a moment, but then he finally said, "Yes, of course. We have plenty of opportunities." He turned back to Ruth. "David will have time for night school soon."

"Right." Ruth put her cigarette to the side and looked for an ashtray. I picked one up off the coffee table and handed it to her and she thanked me. She put it down and stood. "Do you need any help in the kitchen, Millie?"

I was fine and the chickens were almost done, but I told her she could help me set the table.

"Leave the wine," Ed said as I stood up. I put the bottle on the coffee table, and Ed topped off his and David's glasses.

"What do you think they'll do to old Alger?" Ed said to the other men.

"They'll only use him," David said. "Damn government can't prove anything ever, so they blow a lot of smoke and hope to God they get lucky one of these days."

"They are so stupid, no?" Ed laughed. "But sometimes I am very worried." His voice grew more serious. "If America has too much power, the world will become very dangerous."

Julie pushed his spectacles up his nose but didn't respond to Ed's fear. "I should check on Ethel and the boys," he finally said, and he walked toward the back bedroom.

"You think too much," David said to Ed, and Ed laughed again and drank some more wine.

"Don't mind David," Ruth said to me as I handed her a stack of plates to put out on the table, but I was still thinking about what Ed said, about his concern about America having too much power. I'd never thought of it that way before. "He was stationed at Los Alamos when he was in the army," Ruth was saying.

"*Los Alamos?*" I raised my eyebrows and turned my attention to her.

"Everything was top secret, of course. He couldn't even tell me what he was doing when he was there. But he was just a machinist; he didn't know anything about anything anyway." She lowered her voice. "They didn't treat him very well — the army, I mean. Denying his leave and such. Not appreciating his skills." I tried to digest what she'd just told me, that David had been stationed at Los Alamos. I glanced back at him, sitting there on my couch, laughing at something Ed had just said to him. With his pudgy face, curly hair, and easy demeanor, he did not strike me as a man who'd worked near the bomb even in a low-level way. "Of course Julie doesn't appreciate his skills either," Ruth added.

"I'm sure he does," I said brightly. "Julie just said how much he needed David there to supervise."

"Yeah, because he can't find anyone else to work for pennies other than his family and . . ." Her voice caught and her cheeks turned a little red.

"And Ed?" I said.

"Yes." She laughed a little. "I can't figure him out, your husband. Why he stays and works at Pitt even when Julie can't always afford to pay them their salaries."

That was news to me. I just assumed Ed always got paid since he always gave me my weekly allowance for food and such. "Ed and Julie are friends," I finally said. "My husband is a loyal man." For a second, I felt something close to pride for Ed and it startled me.

"How did it go?" Jake asked me on Tuesday after he finished therapy with David and David had lined up all his red blocks. Jake offered David lunch again. And me, too.

"But don't you have another appointment?" I asked him, remembering the way he'd nearly thrown us out last week.

All he said was "Not today."

He invited me to join him in the kitchen and I followed him there. I watched him pull out bread and cheese from the icebox and I offered to help. He handed me the cheese, and we assembled the sandwiches together, quickly but clumsily, our elbows bumping into each other as we were not used to this shared job, this shared space. "Sorry." I laughed nervously as my elbow bumped him again.

But he pretended not to notice and he carried our lunches back into the other room, setting David's down in front of him first and then bringing ours to the chairs.

It was only then that I answered him about the dinner. "It went well," I said. "I mean, it mostly did. Ethel and Julie and the boys left early because Ethel's back was giving her trouble. But David and Ruth Greenglass stayed for a while, and Ruth is very kind. So is David."

"So you got to know Ed's friends a little?" Jake asked as he finished off his sandwich. "You feel better about them now?"

"Julie and Ed seemed to be getting along quite well. Julie and David seemed to be in a little bit of a row." But then I thought about it. "Maybe not Julie and David, but Ruth and Julie. She was mad about David's hours at work. She wanted time for him to go back to school."

"And that was all you talked about?

Work?" Jake asked.

"Well, yes, mostly. At dinner we talked about the kids and the weather and the Dodgers, you know?" Jake pulled his watch from his pocket, and I felt I was boring him. I tried to think of something to impress him, to let him see how hard I'd tried with Ed's friends. "Oh, I did learn that David Greenglass was at Los Alamos." Jake leaned in closer, and I thought that maybe I shouldn't have repeated this to him even though he'd promised nothing I said ever left this room. But he was leaning in so close now and I could smell the warmth of his pipe smoke, see the shadow of stubble on his chin. I wanted to tell him more, wanted to keep him here like this, so near to me.

So I kept talking. "He was stationed there when he was in the army. He was just a machinist. Ruth said he didn't know anything about anything that went on there for real. And I guess he didn't enjoy the army all that much."

Jake nodded, and then he leaned back against his chair. He glanced at his pocket watch, and I felt the sharp sense of disappointment that our appointment was coming to an end. "I'm glad you had the dinner, Millie," he said as he closed the lid to his watch and put it back in his pocket.

"Was Ed pleased?"

"Yes," I said, thinking of the easy way Ed had acted with both David and Julie, drinking wine on our couch. "I think he was pleased."

"That's good," Jake said. "And you are making more connections, Millie."

But I looked at Jake, at the distance between us now, and suddenly I felt more alone than ever.

That winter, on the days we weren't with Jake, we spent a lot of afternoons with Ethel and her boys. We alternated apartments and toys, hoping to switch things up just as the boys began to feel the brunt of being cooped up through the long cold months.

In Ethel's apartment there was the added gift of the piano, which one snowy afternoon in February I heard Ethel play for the first time.

"The first time I ever met Julie, I was singing this," she said. " 'Ciribiribin.' It's an Italian love song."

She began singing, her voice so beautiful and high and clear, the Italian words falling like confection from her lips.

"Join in," she called to me, laughing, her cheeks flushed, her eyes wide with excitement. As she sang, her entire face seemed to glow with a happiness I'd never seen from her at any other time. "Come on." She laughed. "Sing with me." I shook my head and grinned. I didn't know the song. And, even if I did, my off-key voice would've ruined it. But I loved seeing her happy.

When Ethel was singing, all three boys stopped what they were doing, stood still, and listened. The entire world seemed to stand still. It felt like a kind of magic. Her voice was the most beautiful thing I'd ever heard, and when she finished the song, I realized I was crying.

14

The morning of Barnet Greenglass's funeral, in March, I was supposed to take David to Jake's apartment for our biweekly appointment. But Ethel knocked on my door first thing. She was swathed in black from head to toe, a large, dramatic black hat shadowing her face, so it was hard to tell if she'd been crying already or not. I guessed that was the point.

"Ethel." I reached across the doorway and gave her a hug. "I'm so sorry for your loss." I'd ridden up in the elevator with Julie two days earlier as David and I were on our way home from the playground. When I'd asked him what found him home from work in the middle of the day, he'd told me about Ethel's father and about how he was gathering money to pay for the funeral. Ethel had been in bed since learning the news, and I hadn't been able to express my condolences until now.

"Thanks, Millie," she said, pulling back from the hug and straightening her hat. "Would you do me a favor? Would you mind watching the children this morning while Julie and I go to the funeral? Just for a little while." Her voice sounded hoarse, and I supposed that she had been crying.

"Of course," I said, though I felt disappointed at the thought of not walking over to Waterman's Grocery this morning, climbing up the twisty stairs to Jake's apartment. His barren living room, his kind eyes, his pipe smoke, had become familiar and quite welcome comforts in the bleakness of these winter days. I couldn't tell Ethel that now, though. Instead, I heard myself saying, "Take all the time you need. I'm happy to help." I couldn't have imagined bringing David to my father's funeral, but of course I wasn't even yet married to Ed at the time. And there would be no way I would want or be able to bring David to the funeral if it had happened now.

It had been two months since that last afternoon I'd watched John at my apartment, and as soon as Ethel left to go back to her apartment to collect the boys I began to dread the thought of another long day with him. After seeing Ed and Julie interact for myself, I felt John was wrong, that they weren't really angry with each other. But still, I hoped John wouldn't bring it up again once we were alone.

Ethel returned to my apartment after a few minutes with John clinging to her dress and a tired-looking Richie yawning in her arms.

I took Richie from her and I was surprised by the sweet and gentle way he clung to my neck. He was the opposite of John in every way: easy, calm, trusting. Ethel leaned down and whispered something to John, who stared uneasily at me. "David has a new set of cars," I said, motioning my head behind me to where David sat by the window, lining them up in rows along the floorboards. John glanced around me, then slowly walked past me into the apartment. I wouldn't mention, of course, that Jake gave David the cars last week: red, yellow, and blue. *Communication cars,* Jake called them. If John or Ethel asked, I would say they were a gift from Susan, as I had told Ed. But neither one of them did. Why would they?

"Thank you," Ethel said, peering past me to make sure John seemed to be okay.

"They'll be fine," I told her.

Julie walked down the hallway and stood behind her. "Come on, Eth," he said, putting his hands gently on her shoulders.

"We've got to leave or we'll be late." Julie kissed her shoulder, and her body seemed to relax a little, to fall into him, as if his closeness eased her pain.

"Go," I said. "We'll see you later."

Ethel blew a kiss past me at John. But John was already absorbed in the cars and didn't seem to notice.

I should've telephoned Jake to let him know we weren't coming. Our appointments had been so regular for months now. I felt they were like my days at the factory: I went when scheduled, there was never a question of *not* going. The past few weeks since my dinner party, Jake said he didn't have an appointment right after us, and David and I continued staying for lunch.

On Tuesday, I'd moved around Jake's tiny kitchen and fixed us all sandwiches, pulling ingredients out of what appeared a freshly stocked icebox, as if Jake had run down to Waterman's just before we came in the hope that we might stay and eat with him again. *Had he?* I'd wondered. But I didn't ask. Because if I'd asked, if he'd said he had, it might've seemed we were doing something wrong, that we had somehow planned a meal together, the three of us. And I didn't want to ruin it. I had come to enjoy our lunches, the way Jake and I would talk as we ate.

On Tuesday, after the sandwiches were finished, an exhausted David fell asleep on the floor, clutching his cars, and Jake and I sat in his chairs and enjoyed a smoke before David and I left.

"Are you liking life in New York?" I asked him casually, realizing I had never asked him about himself before. But, then, therapy was finished, we had just eaten lunch together, and suddenly it seemed I had the right.

"I am. But everything moves quite quickly here, doesn't it?" He laughed a little.

"I guess so. It's all I know," I said. "I've lived here my whole life."

"I grew up on a farm, in Maryland, and sometimes I do miss the country air. And the quiet."

"A farm," I'd mused, not picturing Jake at all as the farmer type.

He'd smiled. "I don't know why I'm telling you this. I haven't talked about the farm in years."

But I wanted to hear more. "Do you ever get back there?"

"Not there, no. My parents died a while back, and then my brother and I sold it."

"Oh," I'd said, processing all the new

tidbits about him. His parents were dead. He had a brother. "I'm sorry." I'd wanted to know more, but then David had stirred and I'd realized it was getting late, that I had to get home before Ed did.

I'd been so looking forward to going back today and maybe learning more about him. But once all three children were in the apartment and Richie was mobile, running through the cars, while the two older boys played, I had no time to think about anything but keeping the three of them out of trouble.

It wasn't until I got David and Richie settled for naps, and John settled with his ear to the radio, that I heard a knock at the door and I remembered Jake. *Jake.* And still when I opened the door and saw Jake standing there in the hallway, his hands resting uneasily in his jacket pockets, I was surprised to see him. Here.

"You didn't show up," he said, his voice sounding more taut than usual. He was angry.

"I'm so sorry." I quickly stepped out into the hallway and shut the door behind me. "Ethel's father died and they needed me to watch the children and . . ."

Jake nodded and put his hands on my shoulders. It reminded me of the way Julie had reached for Ethel right here in the hallway a few hours earlier. I felt my own body wanting to lean in closer to him, and I did just a bit. "I was worried that something had happened to you," he said.

Jake's hands felt so warm against my shoulders, and I knew I should step back, shake myself out of his grasp. But I didn't. Instead, I moved even closer. *He was worried about us?* I felt something I wasn't used to, a warmth spreading up my shoulders, across my neck, up to my cheeks, until I realized I was blushing. I leaned in a little closer and stood on my toes so that our faces were nearly touching. "I'm sorry," I said again, this time in a whisper into his ear. "But we're perfectly fine. Really."

The door opened behind me. Jake dropped his hands to his sides and I jumped back. "Millie," John's small but insistent voice said. "What are you doing? You're supposed to be watching us."

"Mrs. Stein," I corrected him, hoping he wouldn't notice and comment on my bright red cheeks and now trembling hands. "Go back into the apartment. I'll be inside in a moment, darling."

John ignored my instructions and stepped into the hallway. "Why are you out here with a strange man? Who are you?" He stared at

Jake with disdain the way Ed might if he were to step off the elevator at just this very moment, which he wouldn't, of course, in the middle of the day. Still, I glanced down the hallway uneasily, waiting for the elevator doors to open. When, after a few seconds, they didn't, I exhaled and turned my attention back to John. "This is not a strange man," I heard myself saying. "It's quite all right, John. I know him . . . Your parents know him, too."

John frowned as if he didn't believe me. "Go on ahead, darling. I'll be inside in a moment. I promise."

John turned and reluctantly went back in, but he didn't shut the door all the way, and I could hear his little lungs breathing in and out, seething with suspicion. Or maybe just curiosity.

Jake stared at me, his bright brown eyes catching in the dim light of the hallway. It seemed he had more to say, but he wouldn't say any of it with John listening. "Well, I'll see you next week," I finally said, and I had the thought that maybe he would tell us to come tomorrow instead, that we could make up for our missed appointment then. But he simply adjusted his hat and walked back toward the elevator, and I felt disappointed that I would have to wait five more days until we saw him again.

I turned and went back in my apartment. John stood there by the door, just staring at me, not saying anything at all.

On Tuesday, I felt nervous walking up the steps to Jake's apartment in a way I hadn't felt coming here before. Usually the walk with David was easy. I'd feel an anticipatory excitement, walking up the stairs and knocking on Jake's door. But this morning, something felt different, and I kept thinking of the way Jake had looked at me, the way he'd reached for me, in my hallway last week.

But he opened up the door and smiled and welcomed us in as if everything were exactly the way we'd left it a week earlier when we were last here. He made no mention of our missed appointment and neither did I. I sat in one of the armchairs and watched Jake work on the floor with David, speaking in the hushed and even tones that he always seemed to respond to. Until at last David presented all of his red blocks, announcing that it was time for lunch.

Jake looked up at me as if remembering now that I was still here. His eyes locked on mine.

"I could take him home and feed him?" I

left a question in my voice, hoping desperately that he would tell me not to as he had last week and the week before that and the week before that. I wasn't ready to leave now.

"I have food," Jake said, not taking his gaze away from mine. "I mean, if you have the time today to stay again."

"We do," I said quickly, and I stood and walked toward the kitchen the way I'd done last week. It felt familiar now, felt almost like something that belonged, in part, to me. I knew where Jake kept his plates and his glasses and where things belonged in his icebox.

Jake followed me into the kitchen and stood close behind me as I fixed three sandwiches. I could feel the imprint of him at my back, a shadow, and when I turned to hand him the plates, I stepped on his foot. "Sorry," I said quickly, but he smiled.

He gave a sandwich to David, and then Jake and I sat down in the chairs and ate in silence. "You do this with all your patients?" I heard myself asking after a few moments. "Lunch, I mean?"

Jake opened his mouth a little as if to speak, but then he finished off his sandwich and put the plate down on the end table. "Every case is different," he finally said.

"But you've worked with children like David before?" I pushed him.

"But no one is quite like you, Millie," he said quietly.

There was nothing untoward about his words. They could've, in fact, been something any therapist could've said to any patient, and yet the way he said it, the way his voice tilted a little on my name, it reminded me of the way wind shifts across water and ripples the waves, and I felt a different warmth building inside my stomach than I had ever felt.

"There is no one quite like you either," I echoed back.

Ethel enrolled in psychoanalysis and began seeing someone named Dr. Miller four days a week, in addition to her and John's weekly appointments with Mrs. Phillips. Ethel always seemed to have an appointment — she was always riding down the elevator to go somewhere — which left me and David going to the playground mostly without her and the boys on the days we didn't go to see Jake.

But I lived for Tuesdays and Thursdays, for the quiet, calm moments David and I spent in Jake's apartment. As the weeks went on and the weather turned warmer, we spent longer and longer there with Jake. Mornings turned into lunch, turned into afternoons, turned into me realizing the late hour and having to race home to make it back before Ed.

"Is he kind to you?" Jake asked me one afternoon while David was napping and we were talking. "Ed, I mean?"

Jake often asked about Ed, and I usually changed the subject. Now Jake leaned in close and I could hear his steady breathing, watch the rhythm of his heart moving beneath his sweater-vest. It was almost too hot for the vest and I wondered how Jake would dress come summer. "Kind?" I repeated. I wanted Jake to put his hand on my arm, as he often did now when he was trying to elicit a response from me. I wanted to feel the warmth of his fingertips against the bare skin of my wrist. And I edged slightly forward in anticipation, but, for the moment, Jake didn't move.

"I mean, does he treat you well? The way a woman like you deserves to be treated." Jake's voice was softer than usual, and then he did move his fingers to my arm, down the sleeve of my dress, to my wrist. His thumb moved gently against my skin, and all at once I had the feeling that this was not a therapy question but a question a man might ask a woman should he feel something about her.

"Ed is not really a kind man," I finally said, "but he's fine."

"Fine how?" His thumb continued to stroke my wrist gently and I didn't want to think of Ed. I wished Jake and I were talking about something different.

"You know, he provides for us, and . . . Well, I don't know what else to say." I could think of nothing else, neither good nor bad, to tell Jake about Ed that I hadn't already told him. Ed could be gruff, but even if Julie wasn't always paying him enough, as Ruth had complained, we always had money to put food on the table and pay our rent. "You know what's strange," I finally said. "I'm married to him and sometimes I feel like I barely even know him." Jake let go of my wrist quickly. "Did I say the wrong thing?" I asked him.

"There's no right or wrong answer here, Millie." Jake leaned back into his chair and lit his pipe. And then whatever had happened between us, real or imagined, disappeared just like that.

One warm afternoon in May, Ethel accompanied me to the playground and she announced, quite suddenly and with a wide smile, that she and the boys would be getting out of the city for the summer.

"Getting out?" I asked, frowning, thinking of all the long summer days without her. I would never tell her, but I felt a little jealous of all her therapy sessions now. Her need to be somewhere each day, her ability to talk to someone so many hours a week. My life had so much silence that I looked forward to every moment in Jake's apartment. And though David and I had been staying longer and longer, and Jake and I had been talking more and more, we still only went two days a week.

"The boys and I are going to spend the summer in Golden's Bridge, upstate. And Julie will come up on the weekends."

"But what about all your therapy?" I asked.

"I think that it will be the best kind of therapy for a little while. The country air!" She laughed. "You and David will come up for a visit with us, won't you, Millie?" I agreed, though I wasn't sure whether we would be able to or not. "Good." Ethel squeezed my hand, and then she started humming lightly, under her breath. I didn't recognize the song, but it seemed to me the easy sound of contentment.

■ ■ ■ ■

The next afternoon at Jake's apartment, after we'd eaten lunch, I told Jake about Ethel's upcoming trip and how I felt immensely sad at the prospect of being without her all summer. He sucked on his pipe and didn't say anything for a moment. Then he put his pipe down and said, "Millie, she may be right."

"Right?"

"About it being the best kind of therapy." Jake leaned across the small space between us and put his hand on my arm. Even after we left here, the sensation of his closeness lingered the way the smell of his pipe smoke did. "David could use a change of scenery." I realized he was still talking and I came back to what he was saying. "Out of the city, away from all the noise."

"So you think we should go visit Ethel, then?" It occurred to me as I said it that to visit Ethel would mean to miss a therapy session or two with him, and then I wasn't sure I wanted to go.

"Well, yes, you could. But we should take him somewhere I can go, too, so I can work with him there."

"We?" I tried to imagine taking Jake with

us to visit Ethel, what Ethel would even say. A trip upstate with a man who wasn't my husband? What would I tell Ed?

"I have a friend who has a cabin in the Catskills," Jake said. "And I'll be going up for a few weeks this summer anyway."

"The Catskills." I sighed. So Jake would also be leaving us this summer.

"You could take a vacation to see Ethel and stop by the cabin to see me for a few days," Jake said. "It's not too far from Golden's Bridge, relatively speaking."

A vacation? Ed and I had never been on a vacation, and I only remembered one time as a little girl taking a vacation, staying in a house at the Jersey Shore with one of my father's brother's families. My mother had hated every moment of it and had taken out her misery by yelling at me and Susan the entire time.

I allowed myself to picture this calm and quiet cabin of Jake's friend in the Catskills, maybe on a lake, where the world would be peaceful and where David would at last feel an inner stillness, an ability to find words. It seemed too easy that the Catskills or a quietness of scenery would change every-thing.

"David would enjoy the fresh air," Jake said. "I could take him fishing."

"He would love that," I murmured. Though what I was thinking was how *I* would love it. Spending a few summer days together at this cabin, away from the city. Me and Jake and David and the open beautiful country. I tingled with anticipation just thinking about it. Entire long days with Jake, not just a few stolen hours a week. And nights, too. Where would we all sleep? Then it hit me: How would I ever be able to pull this off? "I'm sure it's lovely," I said, not looking up to meet Jake's eyes. "But I don't know . . . Ed wouldn't approve at all."

"You could bring him," Jake said quickly, and I couldn't help but frown at the thought that Jake would even want Ed to come with us. Or that Jake would believe, given all I'd told him about Ed, that this could ever happen. We both knew that would be impossible, that telling Ed about David's therapy with Jake might mean the end of our sessions altogether. Ed could never know. About any of this.

"You know Ed wouldn't approve," I said, pulling casually on a string at the end of my dress sleeve. I could pull it and unravel the whole thing. My clothes were getting so worn. I tried to tuck the string in my closed palm so Jake wouldn't notice.

"Well, just consider the trip," Jake said. "Just you and David, then." He stared at me with such intensity that I felt I could hear what he was thinking, that he wanted to be alone with me as much as I wanted to be alone with him. I realized I was blushing, and then I looked away, stood, and got David ready to go home.

15

Susan gave birth to her third child, another girl, in the middle of June, two days after Ethel and the boys left for Golden's Bridge for the summer. David and I took the train to Elizabeth with my mother and Bubbe Kasha, as soon as Susan telephoned my mother to let her know her contractions were five minutes apart, and I was glad to be leaving the city for a few days, too, even if New Jersey and several days of babysitting were vastly less exciting than a vacation upstate.

Once we arrived at their sprawling two-story house, Sam left for the hospital to be with Susan, and I was suddenly in charge of everyone: the twins, David, Bubbe Kasha, and my mother.

I turned on Susan's small television, and they were all immediately transfixed, including David. Such a magical machine! If only I could convince Ed to get one for us, I imagined my daily life with David would become infinitely easier. As the adults sat on the couch, the children on the rug, and we all stared at the screen, I tried to dream up ways to negotiate with Ed, and I knew finding myself expecting another child, giving him another child, would probably get me anything I wanted. But I felt a dull ache in my stomach just thinking about it. I wondered what would feel worse: to actually have another child who I might damage like David or to lose another child in a warm pool of blood at my feet?

"Will you look at that?" my mother said, shaking her head and tsking. I looked up and the ABC News my mother was so fond of had come on the screen. "Helen Keller, a communist? Oh for goodness' sakes, the woman is a blind deaf mute."

I stared at the television, listening to what my mother was reacting to. The newsman spoke of a new FBI report that revealed that famous people were communists, too, and that they were dangerous, to be feared. I felt a little knot in my chest that the newsman was talking so harshly about communists. *Reds,* as Mr. Bergman had called them with disdain. Ed, Julie, Jake, and even Ethel once, too. But they were just normal people, my friends and family, not to be feared at all. And anyway, they'd all but left the Party behind.

Should you come across any communist propaganda, the newsman was saying now, *promptly turn it in to authorities . . .*

I glanced at David and his eyes were trained on the television screen. The images transfixed him, their ability to flicker in black and white in a multidimensional way. Helen Keller. She was worse off than David, wasn't she? She was without sight, hearing, or the ability to speak, and look at that, the government *feared* her now. It seemed almost an admirable feat.

"Who's Helen Keller?" Bubbe Kasha asked. She'd been so quiet, I'd almost forgotten she was here. As her mind had withered further and further away, she seemed to have less and less to say. "She doesn't sound very dangerous."

"She's not, Bubbe." I leaned across the couch and kissed her head. I couldn't help but think of David Greenglass's comment in my apartment that the government was just blowing smoke, hoping to get lucky. But Helen Keller? This seemed absurd. "It's just the silly government. Nothing for us to worry about."

My mother, who knew about Ed attending communist meetings when we were first married, turned to me. "Millie," she said, her voice sounding like a warning.

"What?" I shrugged. Whatever Ed's involvement was or once had been had nothing to do with me, and no one knew him or cared about what he thought the way they all knew Helen Keller.

I stood to fix everyone lunch and put Helen Keller and the FBI out of my head. That was still the way it was then. The FBI seemed like nothing that could hurt us, like something so very faraway in the remote District of Columbia. I felt no fear or disdain for them at all. I literally felt nothing. They were nothing to me.

David and I spent an entire week in Elizabeth looking after the twins, watching the television. My mother and Bubbe Kasha took the train back after three days, my mother said because Bubbe Kasha got bored in the quiet of the country air, but I guessed it was more than that: she couldn't take the three young children — the twins' shouting, David's silent tantrums. I had a headache at the end of each day, but after all the children fell asleep I enjoyed every moment of lying on Susan's couch by myself and watching her television, listening to the newsmen rattle on about the new communist report, the growing threat of the bomb should the Russians ever acquire atomic energy. I liked the way the television and the news made me feel connected to the world and reminded me that there was so much more out there beyond my tiny apartment on the eleventh floor and life with Ed. It also made me think that I was not crazy to fear the bomb so much. Russia was becoming a bigger threat. And communism as well. I'd always seen the idea of communism as something small and harmless: groups of men hanging out in an apartment complaining about Truman or smart women like Ethel organizing fights for labor fairness. But now it seemed it had become something else, something bigger and a little frightening, and I was glad the people around me had drifted away from it lately.

Despite all the bad news and fear on the television, I actually slept quite well on Susan's couch each night. The world was safer here in the suburbs, I reminded myself, and I felt so much more at ease far from Ed. In fact, I felt better than I had in years, and, after a few days, I noticed David began to seem more content, too. Maybe Jake was right. Maybe David did need to get out of the city. Maybe we both did.

"You should move out here," Susan said

to me one night as she sat with me on the couch giving the baby, Betsy, a bottle. "It has been nice to have you here, Mills. It would be nice to see each other more."

As young children, Susan and I hadn't always gotten along. But in high school and afterward we were so close in age, we were almost always together doing the same things, with the same friends. Still, I'd always felt her competing with me over something. She always wanted and needed to be the best, the smartest, the prettiest, and she always was. But now she just looked swollen and tired.

I reached my hand over to touch little Betsy's pink cheek. "Yes." I spoke quietly so as not to disturb the baby. "David seems to really like it out here."

Susan didn't say anything for a few minutes, and we both listened to the gentle sounds of Betsy sucking on her bottle. "Mills," she said. "What are you going to do about David?"

"Do?" I asked.

"What if he never talks?"

I closed my eyes and leaned back against the couch. "He will," I said. I thought about Jake. About his belief in David, in us, about the gentle feel of his hands on my shoulders. I thought about what Susan had just said

209

and I sat back up. "You think I should *do* something?" I heard my voice rising a bit. "I should put him in an institution?"

Susan shifted Betsy. "That's not what I meant. It's just . . . I worry about you, all alone in the city, and with him still not talking as he should."

"You don't need to worry about me," I said. She reached her free hand out and placed it over mine, and I understood she was no longer competing; she was genuinely concerned. "I've been getting him help," I said. "Taking him to see a doctor. But you can't tell anyone. I don't want Ed to know."

"Shouldn't Ed want him to have help?" she asked, tilting her head, confused.

"Just promise me you won't say a word to anyone."

"Okay," she said, "I promise." Betsy was asleep now, and Susan gently pulled the bottle from her lips. Then she turned back to look at me. "You know if I can ever help you in any way, I would. All you have to do is ask."

I stroked Betsy's pink and perfect arm with my thumb. "I know," I told Susan. "But we are going to be just fine."

I got by each night with only a short phone call to Ed — to ask how his day was, to ask if he'd found the food I'd stored for him in the refrigerator before I left.

"You are coming home soon?" he said to me on the seventh day, saying it more like a command than a question.

"Tomorrow," I answered, and that was only because I wanted to be back in time for our appointment with Jake. David had missed him over the past week. *I* had missed him. I wasn't sure when he was leaving for the Catskills, and now I was determined to figure out the details to make our trip happen.

16

The night before David and I were supposed to take the train to the Catskills, I was so nervous I couldn't fall sleep.

It was the end of August and the air was stifling in our apartment, the open windows failing to create much breeze. I lay in bed, sweating, dreaming up every possible thing that could go wrong, feeling something awful in my stomach, something like dread. Only, I realized it wasn't dread at all. It was an excitement I hadn't felt in so long that I'd completely forgotten the feeling. It was the way I'd felt back in high school when I'd admired a boy — Charles, his name was — a friend of Sam's. We'd made a date to get ice cream once, me and Charles and Susan and Sam, and the entire day leading up to it my stomach felt exactly this way. Until the ice cream date, when Charles barely noticed me and spent most of the time staring at Susan, which was embarrassing all around, and then the feeling in my stomach actually did turn into an awful, sinking dread.

Ed remained in the living room, which surprised me because I thought he would be in here trying one last desperate and futile time to make a child before I left. I was beginning to wonder, *How much longer?* How much longer would he wait before growing suspicious again, or angry, that it was taking so long? How much longer would David be safe? And that only made the urgency to follow Jake's advice that much stronger, to do everything possible to get David to improve, before it was too late and Ed took away my options.

David was sleeping soundly on his mattress. I could hear his rhythmic breathing, so peaceful and easy sounding. He had made progress with Jake recently, I was sure of it. He would now show me his red blocks for hungry, his blue for tired — most of the time anyway — and overall this was resulting in fewer tantrums, fewer . . . misunderstandings. But he had hit a wall, both literally and figuratively, after we returned from Susan's in June. On our first visit back, as Jake had urged David to repeat sounds, David had begun punching the wall. He was four now, and a big boy for four, with a strength that sometimes terrified me. Especially when I thought about the fact that his progress only went so far. He was *four* and he still wasn't speaking. Susan was right to be worried. I was worried.

But Jake had remained calm when David punched his wall over and over again. I'd wanted to run to David, to pull him away from everything that made him frustrated and angry, but Jake put his arms around me and held me back. "Let him be frustrated," Jake whispered, the feel of his breath against my neck warm and soothing. "We're going to take him to a place where there aren't any walls." In the cool, fresh air of the mountains, with its open spaces and colors, and no distractions, he explained, David would be able to feel in a new way without all the confines we had in the city. I wasn't sure I understood, or believed, that the Catskills would be any different, but the thought of a few days in the mountains, away from here, away from Ed, with Jake, filled me with an undeniable sense of joy that I hadn't felt in so long, if ever. And I knew I would find a way to make it happen.

The sound of Ed's voice from the living room suddenly brought me back here, to my apartment. I smelled his cigar smoke, wafting into the bedroom. The dank smell of it sickened me, blanketed me, until I could smell or think of nothing else other than the discomfort I felt with him. The way he covered me, the way he always smelled of the cigar smoke even when he wasn't smoking.

I wondered who he was talking to, and I tiptoed to the edge of the bedroom door to listen. I hoped it wasn't Julius. Ethel was involved in my deception for the upcoming few days. Ed believed that David and I were going only up to Golden's Bridge to visit with Ethel and the boys, which we were, on Wednesday. Ethel knew that I was taking David to Phoenicia for a few days first, to get him help, but she seemed to believe it was some kind of group pyschotherapy getaway, and I didn't correct her and tell her it would be only me and David and Jake. I was worried if she knew the truth she'd say, "Millie, I'm worried about you. What are you really doing, heading up into the mountains with this *Dr. Gold*?" Or maybe she wouldn't have said that at all. Ethel understood the need to want something — just right there, underneath the surface. I had the feeling that if Dr. Miller told Ethel she needed do something to be cured, she would listen and do whatever she could to find inner peace.

Ethel had telephoned me earlier this morning. "Did you hear about the riot in Peekskill last night?" I hadn't. "Anti-communist, anti-Negro, anti-Semitic . . . The whole world is becoming anti-everything. Anti- all of us." She sighed. "It seems no place is safe for us anymore. Not even up here in the mountains." She paused. "I'm worried about you. Heading up here all by yourself."

"I'm not going to Peekskill," I said, though the truth was, I wasn't exactly sure of the geography of the country towns once one got outside the city, toward the Hudson Valley and the mountains.

"If anything were to happen to you . . ." Ethel said.

"I'll be fine," I said. "And I'll see you later in the week." I wondered if I might put her mind at ease if I told her that Jake was meeting us right at the train station tomorrow. But I couldn't bring myself to tell her that, as if telling her would mean admitting something I wasn't ready to admit even to myself.

Ed's voice got louder in the living room now — he was angry. And I glanced at David to see if he was stirring, but, luckily, he wasn't. I leaned closer to the door to listen, to try to find out if he was talking about me, if he was angry with me. Was Ethel worried enough that she had told Julie my real plan and now Julie was on the phone telling Ed? I didn't think she would do that to me, but I felt very nervous as I pushed my ear to the door.

"What?" I heard him say. "You think everything we have done, it wasn't worth it?" He lowered his voice and said something else I couldn't make out, and then I heard him say, "You think our friends in Russia don't appreciate what we have done for them?"

I wondered what friends in Russia Ed was talking about. He never talked to me about friends — or the life — he'd left behind there. In fact, he had never talked to me about Russia at all. When we were first married, I would sometimes ask him, and he would say that was a life he had finished, that he wanted to forget. So it seemed odd to hear him talking about it now on the phone, and I wondered if he had a secret life, too, if he was an entirely different man when he wasn't here with me.

"So, what?" Ed said. "So they destroy us?"

I tiptoed away from the door, relieved that he didn't seem to be talking about me or about David. Then I got back into bed and attempted to go to sleep. But even long after

Ed's talking quieted down and all I heard was the gentle humming of the radio from the next room, I couldn't get his words out of my head: *So they destroy us?* He'd just tossed off the words carelessly. Destruction seemed to mean so little to Ed, as if it were nothing, that the thought of it gave me a chill even in the heat of the bedroom.

The next morning, David and I took the subway to Grand Central Terminal to board the Hudson River Line. I kept looking behind us the whole way, worried Ed might be following us, watching. Which he wasn't, of course, since he'd left for work before we even left the apartment. And, anyway, if I really was going straight to visit Ethel, as I'd told him, I'd also be taking the train.

I was surprised by the ease of my deception, the way David and I boarded the railroad car without anyone giving us so much as a second glance, the way we disembarked at Kingston and then got on the Catskill Mountain Railroad to Phoenicia just as Jake had told us to.

I scanned the platform when we pulled into the station in Phoenicia, and there were only a few casually dressed people outside. Life appeared to be vastly calmer and slower here, and I was relieved to see no signs of any kind of riot like the one Ethel had spoken of.

Jake stood there, just as he said he would, on the platform, and from the other side of the train window he already looked different here than he had in the city a few weeks ago. His shoulders appeared broader, more relaxed, and he was smoking a cigarette instead of his pipe. He had one hand on the cigarette, the other resting easily in the pocket of his brown jacket, as if this were something he did every day: waited at the train station. Though I felt certain he didn't for his other patients, that he didn't invite them up here. Just the way he didn't invite his other patients to stay for lunch at his apartment either. What did he say to me? *Every case is different. You're different, Millie.* I felt a rush of tenderness for him and I wanted to be off the train, standing next to him.

"Come on," I said to David, holding on to him with one hand, our suitcase with the other. "Dr. Jake is waiting for us outside." At the mention of Jake's name, David's eyes seemed to light up. I wasn't imagining it — at least, I didn't think I was. I hadn't told him before this moment who we were going to see when we got to the mountains. Not that he could tell Ed even if he wanted to, but, still, I'd been afraid to utter the truth out loud. David loved the train, the sway of the cars on the tracks, the blur of trees and towns on the other side of the window. Even on the short ride to Susan's house, the train was one place where he always seemed content, so he hadn't protested getting on this morning. But now I imagined the thought behind his new, wide smile — that the wonderful train could take him to Jake, too.

He yanked on my hand, and I stumbled a bit as we descended the stairs to the platform. The moment we were off the train I noticed the smell of flowers and the sudden chill in the air that hadn't been there in the city. I smiled. I had pulled this off! I had actually gotten David here, away from Ed, to a place of quiet and beauty, to a place with no walls. To Jake.

Jake seemed to notice David first and he quickly dropped his cigarette and crushed it beneath his brown leather shoe. He walked toward us and patted David on the head. "Good to see you up here in the fresh air, son." He looked past David to me, and our eyes met as if we both understood the gravity of this moment. The choice I had made by coming here, with David, with a suitcase.

"How was the ride?" Jake asked as he took

the suitcase from my hand. Our fingertips brushed for a moment in the exchange, and I pulled back and felt myself blushing.

"The ride was fine," I said. "David enjoyed it."

"No problems, then?" Instinctively, I knew he meant with Ed, not with David. I thought of Ed's anger on the phone last night and how angry he would be if he knew where we were right now. But I simply shook my head and offered Jake a smile. "Good," Jake said. "Come on, let's get in the car. It's a little bit of a ride to the cabin."

"You have a car?" I asked.

"My friend's car," Jake said.

"Your friend who owns the cabin?" I asked.

Jake hesitated and then he nodded as if I'd caught him in a lie, though I didn't care whose car it was, whose cabin it was. Only that David and I were here. That we had escaped our life in the city with Ed, if only for a few days.

The square wooden cabin sat at the end of an unmarked dirt road. It was far in the woods, at the edge of an expanse of water so clear and so blue that I felt as if I were dreaming even as I got out of the car and stood on its banks. I dipped my hand in the water just to feel if it was real, and it was colder than I'd expected. "Esopus Creek," Jake said as David clutched my hand and stared, too. His eyes followed the ducks that waltzed on the muddy shores and hopped into the water. It appeared much too big to be a creek, more like how I would imagine a lake to be, and much more blue and clear than the Hudson.

So much beauty that my son had never seen or even imagined rendered him completely still. Maybe Jake was right. Maybe by just coming here David would change and grow. "It's beautiful, isn't it, darling?" I leaned down and said to him, and for a moment I thought he might even answer but he simply continued to stare.

"Let's go inside," Jake said gently, though David resisted, wanting more of the water, the fresh air, the beautiful yellow ducklings. David yanked back on my arm hard enough so it hurt, and I let out a little cry.

"David." Jake leaned down, and he gently extricated David's hand from my arm. "We'll come back outside in a little while, I promise. I need to set your suitcase down inside. It's heavy." He paused to give David a chance to react. "Okay, son?"

Jake was so good with him, so kind, and so patient. I smiled at him, grateful, as David listened and followed us inside the cabin without any more resistance.

On the inside, the cabin was small and sparse, but not as much as Jake's bare apartment in the city. There was a couch and a table in the living area/kitchen. And there were two beds in the bedroom in back. Jake put my suitcase down next to the larger one. "You can sleep here," he said. "David can take the other bed, and I'll sleep on the couch."

"Of course." I tried to ignore a feeling of disappointment. What else had I been expecting him to say — that he would share this bed with me? It was such a wildly inappropriate thought that I felt my cheeks begin to turn red. "Where's the telephone?" I asked quickly. "I'll need to check in with Ed."

"The telephone?" Jake thought for a moment, and then said, "I'm afraid there isn't one." It seemed every place had a telephone these days, and for some reason I'd not been expecting this cabin to be so far out in the middle of nowhere. I'd promised Ed a phone call. If not every day, then at least most days, and if I didn't call him at all for the few days until I got to Ethel's, surely he would figure out something was off. "Hey." Jake put his hand on my shoulder. "Don't worry. I can take you into town tomorrow. You can call him from there, okay?"

I nodded, and I found myself biting back tears I didn't quite understand. I had an intrinsic nervousness that I'd become so accustomed to that I remembered it again, only now, when Jake rested his hand on my shoulder and it began to disappear into an unfamiliar calm.

"How about we have some lunch," Jake offered, "and then we can go out on the creek in a boat." He let go of my shoulder and leaned down and spoke softly to David. I knew that David probably didn't understand what Jake meant about going out on the creek in a boat, but, like me, suddenly David seemed to have achieved a sense of calm at last. His shoulders relaxed and he leaned into Jake — he trusted him.

We spent the afternoon in a small rowboat on the creek. I closed my eyes in the glorious sunshine, falling in and out of a half sleep, while Jake showed David how to catch fish, how to be very still so as not to rock the boat or scare them away. I opened my eyes occasionally and watched them, their bodies glowing in the overexposure of the intense sunlight. David didn't say anything. But he was smiling.

He was so tired from the day that he fell asleep back at the cabin before Jake finished cooking us the fish they'd caught. Had I stepped back and looked, thought about it, I might've thought how very strange it was to see a man, a doctor like Jake, preparing dinner for us. But he cleaned the fish in the kitchen and then roasted it over the fire with ease as if he'd done it many times before. And it felt right, like we had been doing this together for ages. I just sat there on the couch and watched, and I took the drink Jake handed me, a tumbler of gin — all the cabin had. I drank the clear liquid, even though it made me grimace, because it also made me feel warm and safe and that I had done the right thing by coming here.

"He's improving," Jake said to me, handing me a plate with some fish. He kept his voice low, presumably so as not to wake David. "I think I'll have him talking soon. I feel it. He's so close. His nonverbal cues are so much better." He finished off his gin before pouring himself another, which surprised me. I would not have expected Jake to drink anywhere close to as much as Ed did, to allow himself to become out of control. "I'm so glad you came here."

"Me too," I said. My entire body felt warm from the gin, the fire, the sound of

Jake's voice. And I let myself think what I'd been wanting to this whole time. Was that the only reason? Was David the only reason that Jake was glad we'd come up here?

I felt Jake was thinking the same thing because he looked down, put his drink on the coffee table, and then looked back up at me. His eyes appeared a softer color, almost golden, in the reflection of the fire. He moved closer to me. Slowly, almost hesitantly at first, he put his arm around me, but then without even thinking I lay back and leaned my head against his chest as if we were always this way, the two of us, as if we fit together. "You don't do this with all your patients," I heard myself saying, and as the words escaped my lips I thought maybe I should've stopped them. But the gin had made me feel warm and safe, my words suddenly easy.

"I don't," Jake said quietly, and I could hear my heart beating in my ears, as if it were loud enough to shake the room. But Jake didn't seem to notice. His fingertips stroked my arm gently, and neither one of us said anything for a moment. I just felt the rise and fall of his chest against my cheek.

"I want to know more about you," I said after a little while, both surprised and somewhat delighted in my new boldness from the gin. "You told me you had a brother once. What's his name?"

"Henry," Jake said. "We were twins. But he died a few years ago."

"Oh, I'm so sorry." I tilted my head up to look at him and his eyes looked faraway. "Did Henry die in the war?"

"Yeah." Jake put his hand on my head and stroked back my curls — almost absently, almost as if this were what we did all the time. I leaned back against him and closed my eyes, inhaling the faded smell of creek water and pipe smoke.

"And you were in the war?" I asked him. I tried to picture Jake as a soldier, in a soldier's uniform. Young and with his twin brother Henry. I wondered if they'd looked exactly alike.

"No," Jake said. "Because of my . . . Well, I was here. I was lucky enough to be able to stay here."

"But now you're all alone in the world," I said. "No family."

"I'm not alone," he said, and he shifted, sat up a little, and turned me gently so my chin was on his chest and our faces were close. "Millie," he said. "Ed is not —"

"Shhh," I interrupted him, putting my hand gently to his mouth to stop him from saying whatever it was he was going to say about Ed. "Please, let's not talk about Ed anymore."

"But I . . . Maybe we should . . ." He let his voice trail off, and he sat up, so we were no longer touching at all but just sitting close together on the couch. I thought he was going to tell me it was time for me to go back to the bedroom, to go to bed, before we both did anything we might regret. I could picture him saying it just that way, in his calm and even psychotherapist tone. He opened his mouth to speak, but then he suddenly seemed to change his mind and instead of finishing his sentence his thumb landed on my collarbone as if it were drawn there by magnetic force. His thumb traced it slowly, catching on the top button of my dress, before he pulled back a little. "I just don't want you to hate me . . . in the end," he finally said.

I put my hand in his arm. His skin was warm. "I could never hate you," I said firmly, and Jake reached up and caught my fingers as if to move them so he could continue speaking, but then his face softened and he kissed my palm instead before moving my hand to his cheek. It was rougher than I would've expected — he was in need of a shave — and I wasn't familiar with the feel of a man's face. With Jake's face. "Let's not talk anymore," I said, afraid if we continued that I would lose my nerve, or that Jake would. That David would wake up, or the world would choose to end, right at this very moment.

Jake moved in closer, and then all at once his lips were on mine, moving so slowly and filling me with a sense of warmth I had never felt before. I once had thought that Ed buying me a couch at Macy's was love, but no, this feeling, this sublime tingling that arose from my toes and traveled up my legs, my stomach, my shoulders, my neck, the length of my entire body, this was something entirely new and different and wonderful.

Jake's fingers caught on the top button of my dress again and this time he undid the button, then the next one and the next, and he lifted the dress over my head so that I was sitting there in only my underthings. "You're so beautiful," Jake said. And suddenly, without warning, I began to cry.

Jake pulled back. "Millie, I'm sorry, I didn't mean to . . ."

"No." I pulled him closer to me, close enough so I could feel his ragged breathing against my cheek. "It's just that no one has ever said that to me before."

Jake put his fingers through my curls, and then lay back, pulling me on top of him. I heard him unzip his pants, and this seemed to register from somewhere very far away, outside my body. I seemed to understand there, from across the room, what it was we were about to do, but from my spot on the couch, on top of Jake, looking down at him, I couldn't think rationally anymore, I couldn't understand anymore. All I could do was feel, follow Jake's lead, and do what my body wanted to, what our bodies wanted to do together.

I awoke to an alarm — a steady, ringing sound. *Ed's clock,* I thought. But then I opened my eyes and saw the embers still glowing in the fireplace.

Jake. The cabin, I remembered.

I sat up. I was entirely naked, my legs tangled with Jake's, who was also trying to sit up underneath me. My skin warmed again as Jake touched my shoulders to move me over, and he pulled an afghan from atop the couch and threw it over me.

"What is that noise?" I asked.

Jake stood, pulled his pants on quickly, and then he ran to the back of the kitchen, opened a cabinet, and pulled something out. The noise suddenly stopped. "Yes," I heard Jake saying. Then: "The Russians . . . Jesus . . . Tonight?"

It occurred to me what he was doing, talking on the telephone. The ringing sound had been a telephone? Yes, that's exactly what it was. But Jake said the cabin didn't have a telephone . . . He'd lied to me.

Jake finished his conversation, and he walked back to the couch and sat down next to me. He put his hand on my shoulder, but I pulled away. "Why did you lie about the telephone?" I asked. I realized how naked I was underneath the afghan. How much Jake and I had done last night. How I had felt his body and he had felt mine, and, for the first time, I had enjoyed every second of it. But if he'd lied to me about the silly telephone, what else had he been lying about?

"We have to get dressed," Jake said brusquely, ignoring my question, and me, as if last night had never happened. "I have to leave."

"Now? Tonight?" I wasn't sure if it was still night. I looked around the cabin, and darkness still seeped in through the windows. The tiny red embers in the fireplace still glowed, but only dimly.

"I'm sorry," Jake said, his voice softening a little.

"I don't understand. What's going on?"

"Millie," Jake said, "I can't tell you. But I just need you to trust me."

"Trust you?" I pulled the afghan tighter and moved farther down the couch. "You lied to me about the cabin having a telephone. What's going on here? Why should I trust you about anything?" I suddenly wanted to cry or scream, I couldn't decide which. But I could hear myself breathing very hard, ragged, uneven breaths.

"I'm sorry," Jake said, "it was just . . ."

"The Russians?" I spit back at him what I'd heard him say, and as I said it I suddenly thought of Ed. Had Ed had found us out? Had the friends Ed spoke of on the telephone the other night followed me here and told Ed everything? "Is it Ed?" I asked. "Did he find out we're here?"

"No," he said. "You don't need to worry about that. No one knows you're here." Jake reached for his shirt, which hung over the back of the couch. He threw it on and began doing up the buttons quickly, his fingers certain. He handed me my dress, and in a stupor, I took it, unsure for a moment what he wanted me to do with it. "Get dressed," he said. "I'll drive you to the train station. You and David can go visit with Ethel a few days early."

"And where are you going?" I asked.

But he didn't answer.

Outside, it was dawning slowly, and the light began to filter in through the cabin's windows, a soft and surreal pink. The world, the beauty and calm perfectness of the nature that surrounded us, none of that matched Jake's mood, what was happening here inside the cabin.

He leaned back in, closer to me, so I could hear his steady breathing. I turned back to look at him, and his shirt was on and buttoned. "Look, Millie. I'm sorry that I lied to you about the telephone. But it really had nothing to do with you . . . or us." *Us?* As if we were something now. Were we? "I didn't want to lie to you."

"But you did anyway," I said. "And you've lied to me about other things, too." I thought about the way he claimed to know Ethel when she seemed not to know him at all.

"I can't explain it to you now. I wish I could, but I can't." He put his hand on my face and traced my cheekbone with his thumb. "I have to go now. I'm sorry."

"But I don't want you to leave us," I said, my anger over the silly telephone dissipating into a sense of loss.

Jake's face softened and he put his hand

on the afghan, pulling it tighter around my shoulders. "I promise you, I'll get back to the city as soon as I can. And I'll do everything I can to keep you and David safe."

"Safe? From what?" None of this made sense. Why would he have to leave here now, at dawn, and where was he going? "Jake?" I could still feel what I felt last night, my body against Jake's, my naked skin against his, a feeling and an openness I'd never felt before, a rush of pleasure I'd never experienced, and now it all seemed unreal, like a lie.

"Please, Millie, get dressed," Jake said more sternly than he'd ever spoken to me, and I suddenly felt ashamed for everything that had happened. "We have to go."

He stood and walked into the back room, got David up, and led him into the kitchen, where I heard him talking calmly about breakfast. *Breakfast?* I clung to my dress, removed the afghan, and tugged the dress down over my shoulders. I buttoned it slowly, my fingers trembling. I understood what I'd done. It was all wrong, and now it seemed I was already being punished for it in a way I didn't even quite understand.

"Millie." I looked up and Jake was standing there again, hovering over me, while David sat in the kitchen, eating a piece of bread.

I felt tears stinging in my eyes and I bit my lip to try to keep them away. "Why won't you tell me what's happening?" I asked him.

Jake hesitated, and then he leaned down and whispered in my ear. "No matter what else happens, I need you to remember that last night wasn't a lie."

Even after he stood back up, I could feel the warmth of his breath against my skin, I could feel the warmth of his words echoing in my head. I could feel them even hours later as David and I stepped off the train in Golden's Bridge.

Outside the city, everything about Ethel seemed different, more relaxed. Her curls were looser, her skin had reddened, and her posture had eased. She told me her back was feeling good out here in the country air, that she could breathe deeper away from all the noise.

A few hours after my arrival, we lay next to each other in our bathing suits, on matching lounge chairs, on a deck that led out to the lake. I supposed it was quite beautiful here, all the green of the trees, the blue of the perfect water glistening in the sunshine, but somehow I didn't have it in me to notice.

"John has been swimming every day," Ethel said, raising her hand up to her eyes to shield them from the sun or perhaps to get a better view of me. "It exhausts him, but in a good way. He's seeming calmer here." I listened but didn't say anything. I'd been quite silent since we'd arrived. At first I said we were tired, which was true, we were. But now, in the piercing sunlight of the late afternoon, I still couldn't understand what had happened with Jake this morning at the cabin. Why he'd lied. Why he'd left. What I'd done. What we'd done. My entire body felt numb, my bare toes incapable of soaking in the warmth of the August sun.

David sat rather calmly at the edge of the lake, stacking smooth stones, and I wondered if he had begun to feel it in his chest the way I felt now, this steadily growing hole. The absence of something . . . or someone. Or maybe he didn't even understand it yet. Jake was gone. Somewhere. Something had happened in his worried early-morning phone call — I just didn't know what. It seemed so strange that Jake spoke of the Russians, and that Ed had the night before we left. It made me feel that

Jake was lying to me about a lot of things, that maybe he and Ed were friends, that they were connected in something somehow. And with the Russians? The mere thought made my head ache, and it made no sense why a man like Jake, or Ed, would have the need to be so secretive or urgent.

"Millie," Ethel said, leaning in closer and interrupting my thoughts, "are you sure everything is all right? You seem so nervous."

"Nervous?"

"Are you worried about more riots?"

"Yes, the riots," I murmured.

"We'll be safe here at the cabin. They were rioting only because Paul Robeson had a concert scheduled." I remembered what I'd heard on the radio about Paul Robeson being named a communist and being called to testify before the Un-American Activities Committee last spring. Last month, Jackie Robinson had been called in to testify against him, and now it seemed poor Robeson couldn't catch a break. Ethel laughed a little. "It's all so silly, isn't it? That a man with such a beautiful voice can't share his gift with the world. He can't give a concert in peace just because he has aligned himself with a certain political view."

I thought about Ethel's beautiful voice. She had made the choice to become a wife and a mother rather than pursue her dream to become a Broadway star, but what if she hadn't? Ed had claimed that the government was only out to get Paul Robeson because he was a Negro, and I'd felt bad that the color of his skin had made any bit of difference. "It must be hard enough to be a Negro without being a communist, too," I said.

"As if it's any easier being a Jew," Ethel said. In our own little pocket of New York City, being a Jew wasn't hard. It was what everybody was. It was who we were and what we knew, but I read the paper enough to know that it wasn't like that everywhere, that there were probably as many anti-Semites as there were anti-Negros. "Sometimes I think the whole world is going crazy." Ethel pulled her hat down over her eyes and leaned back in her chair.

I did the same. I closed my eyes, but all I could see was Jake, the way he looked buttoning up his shirt. The way he'd felt last night, his skin so close to mine.

"Something else is bothering you," Ethel said. At the sound of her voice I jumped and opened my eyes again. "Was it the therapy you attended in the Catskills? It wasn't going well. Is that why you had to cut it short?"

"Yes," I said. I couldn't tell her the truth.

"Millie." She put her hand on my arm. "You can't give up. You have to keep trying." I thought about what Jake said, that he would get back to the city when he could. How long would that be? And what were David and I supposed to do in the meantime? I bit my lip to keep from crying. "Come on now," Ethel said. "It couldn't have been all that bad. Look how contented David looks now sitting by the water."

He was stacking his rocks and unstacking them again, but his posture appeared relaxed, at ease, the way it had on the rowboat yesterday. Maybe I needed Jake more than he did. Maybe this therapy I'd had him enrolled in had become about me and the way I was feeling about Jake, not about David at all. "I'm a terrible mother," I said.

"Oh, Millie, stop it." She bit at the skin around her thumbnail. "I'm going to tell you something I'm not proud of. I have trouble controlling my temper with John sometimes." She lowered her voice. "I've spanked him before when I just couldn't take it anymore." She turned and looked off at him in the water. John waved to her, and she lifted her hand and waved back. "I didn't mean to hit him. I felt terrible about it afterward. But I can lash out, you see?

239

And I've been working on that in therapy."

"Ethel, everyone lashes out," I said.

"You don't," she countered back. "You have the patience of Job with David. You are the exact opposite of a terrible mother."

"People lash out in different ways," I said, and I wondered if that's what I'd been doing with Jake. Lashing out? *No.* I didn't think so.

She turned back to watch John gliding nearly effortlessly through the water. "Whatever you're feeling blue about today, it'll pass, Millie. It always does."

I hoped Ethel was right, but I wasn't sure how I'd ever forget what had happened between Jake and me in the cabin. I wasn't sure I wanted to. And I had no idea where I was supposed to go from here.

17

After we returned to the city, the time ticked by ever so slowly without our biweekly visits to Jake's apartment. Each Tuesday and Thursday, David and I still walked to Waterman's Grocery and then climbed the twisty stairs, hopeful that when I knocked, Jake would answer the door. But he didn't. No one did. I even began to wonder about the awful cat inside and whether she had died from lack of food and water, but I couldn't bring myself to walk into Waterman's and tell Mr. Waterman or ask him about Jake's continued absence. I knew nothing of where Jake had gone, what had become of him, or when he would return. And what if Mr. Waterman knew more? What if he told me Jake was gone, forever? I couldn't bear to hear that.

As the days went by, I began to wonder whether our night in the cabin had even been real, if it had been anything more than a dream. If Jake had been nothing but an imaginary man. David still wasn't speaking, and I'd been feeling too tired lately to keep up with the colored cars, the colored blocks. David was really no better off than he'd been last fall, I'd finally admitted to myself.

The city seemed to stand still, everything exactly as it was, except now there was no Jake in it. Ed drank his vodka and fell into bed each night, fumbling clumsily on top of me. Ethel and the boys returned to the city, and John began the school year. Ethel and I took Richie and David to the playground, trying to take advantage of the last of the warm days before winter.

And still each Tuesday and Thursday morning I set out with renewed hope that Jake would've returned, and then I found myself at Mr. Bergman's shop, just around the corner from Waterman's, when Jake's apartment turned up empty again.

"Bubbelah, boychik," Mr. Bergman cried out with joy each time we walked in through the doorway. Today we made our way carefully to the counter, and, as we approached, I nearly lost my footing, the smell of meat so strong that I thought I might be sick. "Not that I don't enjoy your frequent company," he said as he leaned across the counter to kiss my cheek and place some yellow gumdrops in David's outstretched hand, "but I am beginning to worry something is wrong."

"Nothing is wrong," I said quickly.

"Eh?" Mr. Bergman raised his eyebrows. I clutched my stomach uneasily, wishing the meat didn't smell so strong today. "Have you seen the newspaper this morning?"

I shook my head, and he pulled the paper out from underneath the counter, pushing it my way so I could see it but David couldn't. A picture of a mushroom cloud graced the front page, with the headline "Truman Says Russians Detonated Test Bomb."

"What? When?" My hands shook as I grabbed the paper and scanned it for information. The article said that the Russians had detonated their first test bomb on August twenty-ninth. A month ago. I exhaled and calmed a little at the thought that some time had passed and we were all still here.

"It is very scary," I realized Mr. Bergman was saying as he took back the paper. "Today a test. Tomorrow . . ." He snapped his fingers and folded the paper back behind the counter. "Manhattan could be dust. Just like that. Goddamn Russians."

The Russians. I could hear Jake's voice,

the urgency, as he spoke on the phone that night in the cabin. *A month ago.* The night we spent together was that very same night that the paper reported the Russians had detonated the bomb, wasn't it? Did Jake somehow learn about the test bomb then when he'd received his strange telephone call? But how? And why would someone call him to tell him? "I think I'm going to be sick," I said.

"I didn't mean to frighten you, bubbelah." Mr. Bergman reached across the counter and put a hand on my shoulder, but I ran toward the back room, where I knew from my days in the shop as a small girl that there was a sink. The meat smell was so very strong in my nose that the deeper I tried to breathe, the worse it got. Maybe some of the meat had gone bad and Mr. Bergman hadn't realized it. Was it possible he was getting too old to run the shop?

In the back room, the smell was less, and I took a slow, deep breath. The smell dissipated and the nausea calmed. "Millie," I heard Mr. Bergman's voice calling from the front. His head peeked through the doorway. "Are you all right?" I took another breath and I nodded. He smiled. "Should I congratulate you, then?"

"Congratulate me?" It was only as I said

the words that I realized what Mr. Bergman must think. "Oh no," I said, shaking my head, "I couldn't possibly be . . ." I had worn the diaphragm I'd gotten at Planned Parenthood so faithfully every single night. Every single night . . . except for one. I hadn't taken it with me to the Catskills. That night with Jake, on the couch, in the cabin. "No," I repeated meekly, "I couldn't possibly . . ."

"Let me get you some seltzer," Mr. Bergman said, motioning for me to come back out front. For a moment, I couldn't breathe. My feet refused to move, my lungs refused to move. And then I heard myself saying, "No, I don't think so. Thank you, but David and I should get back." I hustled David out onto the street.

Outside, it was windy. The leaves had begun to turn and they swirled in golden colors off the trees. The world was the color of dust, and as I walked back toward Monroe Street I could hardly see. If the bomb came and took us right now, I felt I might welcome it. That it would be an easy way to go.

18

I waited until the following week to go back to Planned Parenthood. For one thing, I tried as hard as I could to talk myself out of it, to make myself believe that this couldn't possibly be happening to me. And, for another, I needed someone to watch David. With Jake still gone, I asked Ethel and she agreed without hesitation.

"Millie, is everything all right?" she asked as I walked David into her messy apartment. She noticed me staring at all the many toys, and she bent down to pick one up as if she'd just been in the middle of cleaning and I'd caught her midway, though we both knew she hadn't been.

"Just leave it," I said, putting my hand on her arm. "The children will make a mess anyway." Though she had been the one to ask me if I was all right, I noticed that she looked especially tired this morning, her face sagging under the weight of something,

I wasn't sure what. I knew there were some things going on at Julie's company because I'd overheard Ed talking about them on the telephone. Ethel's brothers had resigned from Pitt, and seeing how ragged Ethel looked now, I wondered if this had also stirred up some bad blood in her family. I thought about the way Ruth had seemed angry at Julie when I'd had them over for dinner last winter. Had this escalated in the time since? "Are you sure it's okay if David spends the morning here?" I was hoping she would still say it was because I had no other option except to bring him with me, which I didn't want to do.

"Of course," Ethel said. "Of course it's okay." She sat down on the couch, clutching the toy she'd picked up from the floor. Richie sat quietly, playing with his cars, and John ran through them, making Richie cry and David smile. "Boys . . ." Ethel said rather weakly. "Yes," Ethel waved at me, "go on ahead to your appointment. Go. We'll be fine."

"We'll talk when I get back?" I said, and Ethel shot me a weary smile.

I blew David a kiss, but he was so busy watching John that he barely noticed. And then I left Ethel's apartment and rode the elevator down. I soon found myself in the busy morning rush of Monroe Street, caught up among all the people going somewhere, all with a purpose — all on their way, I imagined, to somewhere exciting, caught up in a life vastly more wonderful than mine.

Planned Parenthood felt less welcoming than I remembered it — darker, even — and this time neither the receptionist in front nor the nurse who took me back were smiling.

I lay there soundlessly on the cold metal table, trying to breathe, as the nurse examined me. I thought of the last time I was here, of the magical pill the nurse spoke of and how in a world where such a thing as the atomic bomb existed there should also be such a thing as a magical pill for a woman to prevent a baby.

"Well," the nurse said. Her name tag read "Nurse Ames." She was blond and pretty and, I was fairly sure, not Jewish. "There's no need to bother a poor rabbit, Miss Kauffman."

"I'm not pregnant?" I said, using their very clinical term for it, my voice riding on a small wave of hope.

"Oh no," she said, "you most certainly are. I'd guess about eight weeks along."

Eight weeks. I tried to count back, to do the math in my head, but I knew it was unnecessary. There was only one night this baby could've been conceived.

Nurse Ames cleared her throat. "You know, there are some . . . options," she said.

"Options?" I immediately thought of poor Harriet, pregnant in high school and oh so desperate. I was nothing like her, was I? I was a married woman, married to a man who wanted another child more than anything.

She scribbled something on a piece of paper and slipped it into my palm. I clasped it tightly, squeezing it, and then I gave her a small nod so she knew I understood, though the truth was, I didn't. I couldn't quite comprehend the awfulness of it, what I was somehow implicitly accepting, simply by taking her piece of paper. "Why don't you get dressed and I'll get you some vitamins to take with you," she said.

Back at Ethel's, I found the apartment dark and quiet. She ushered me inside with a whisper. "The boys wore each other out," she said. "They're all asleep."

I'd been gone awhile, and it seemed the world had changed in my absence. The day had turned gray and Knickerbocker Village had appeared menacing from the street, the elevator ride interminably long as my stomach churned, as my hand still clasped the paper Nurse Ames had handed me. Just outside Ethel's door, I'd stuffed it in my purse and then accepted her invitation to come inside and sit down.

"You look terrible," Ethel said.

"So do you," I said, and then she laughed a little and so did I.

"Have a seat. Let me make you some ginger tea," she said. "It'll help with the nausea." I hadn't breathed a word to Ethel about how I was feeling or where I went this morning, but it seemed she could sense it. And if she could, it would only be a matter of time before everyone else would, too. My mother would, certainly — I'd been avoiding her all week, ever since that morning in Mr. Bergman's shop.

I thought about refusing the tea, about denying that such a thing was necessary, but I didn't have it in me to lie to Ethel. And I knew she was right, that the tea would settle my stomach, so I thanked her and sat down on her couch, and, a few minutes later, Ethel handed me the steaming mug. "David will enjoy a sibling," she said softly.

"I don't know. Maybe." I didn't know how

David would manage when there was another child with us all the time, a baby, someone small with needs other than his. I didn't know how *I* would manage.

"They make it all worth it." Ethel had a cup of tea in her hand, too, and she blew on it carefully before taking a sip. "The children, I mean. I want them to have everything I never did growing up." She looked around the room. And I did, too, as I sipped my tea, my eye catching on the beautiful piano and all the many toys. "How's David's therapy going?" she asked.

I suddenly saw Jake, the way he looked that last morning in the cabin, the way his hand felt as it brushed against my shoulder, pulling the afghan tighter. "It's not," I said. "We've had to stop. After our trip." Then I added, trying to sound hopeful, "For now. Jake . . . Dr. Gold has had to go out of town for a while."

"But there has to be someone else you could go to in the meantime," Ethel said. I shook my head. "Is it the money? Because maybe I can talk to Julie, see if we can help out. Or I can ask Mrs. Phillips if she knows of anyone there who might help him."

"No, no, it's not that," I said, though I was grateful for her kindness, her desire to help. "It's just . . ." I concentrated very hard on my tea, willing myself not to cry, not to remember that moment in the rowboat on Esopus Creek when the sunlight had turned my son into someone altogether different — glowing, happy, at peace. "I just don't know," I finally said. "What about you?" I thought it better to get off the subject of me entirely before I confessed everything to Ethel. I didn't think she would understand what I had done with Jake. It was a terrible thing. I knew it was. What was worse was that I constantly longed to see Jake again, to be close to him again. "How is your analysis coming with Dr. Miller now that you're back in the city?" I asked her.

"It's good, I think . . . We've been talking through everything, and, you know, it all comes back to my mother. I was never good enough for her as a child. Nothing I ever did could compete with my brothers. It's all the same, even now. But I have to move past that so I can be a good mother myself. Do you know what I mean, Millie?"

"David and Bernie have resigned from Pitt?" I asked, though I already knew the answer.

"Yes." Ethel sighed.

"Is that causing problems in your family? With your mother?"

"Julie has done so much for my brothers.

For my entire family. He paid for my father's funeral, for goodness' sakes. And they don't appreciate any of it. None of them do." She moved her hand to her forehead as if trying to quell an oncoming ache. "Well, not so much Bernie . . . Gladys is sick. Did you hear?" I shook my head. "Incurable cancer."

I had never met Gladys or Bernie, though I felt a sudden wave of sadness for this poor woman, Ethel's sister-in-law. "I'm so sorry, Ethel."

"Thanks. Me too," Ethel said. "But Davey is a different story altogether. Davey always wants special treatment. He's so entitled sometimes, you know. He wants more money. Less hours. And Julie does the best he can." She sighed. "Of course my mother takes Davey's side in *everything,* always. The more things change, the more they stay the same. Isn't that right, Millie?"

"Sure," I murmured in agreement. But when I thought back on my life, it seemed to be an ever-changing thing. My life as a girl with Susan, spending Sunday afternoons in the butcher shop, even learning how to drive the meat truck, felt nothing at all like my time sewing day after day in the factory, where, looking back now, I'd been so free. Free to catch a picture with Addie whenever the mood suited me, to listen to the radio whenever I liked and as loud as I liked it . . .

"Can you count on your family, Millie?" Ethel asked.

I thought about it for a moment. Bubbe Kasha loved me, purely and deeply, and so had my father — I was certain. My mother was sometimes bothersome, and she always put Susan first, and Susan had always been so much older, wiser, better than me. But I thought of the kind way Susan had spoken to me in the summer when I was at her home and she had said she wished for me to live closer, how she would want to help me if she could. She and my mother would be excited to learn about another baby, though I wasn't sure how much I could truly count on them if the truth about what happened in the Catskills ever came out. "Yes," I finally said, "I suppose I can."

"You're very lucky, then," Ethel said. "I have never been able to count on my family for anything. And I don't think I ever will."

"But you have Julie," I reminded her. I thought of the way Julie had pulled Ethel close in the hallway just before they left for her father's funeral. Julie, who'd kissed her gently and called her *Eth* in that sweet way he had of naming her his own, someone special. "And the boys," I added.

"I know. They mean everything to me. I

love the children and Julie more than anything." She smiled and finished off her tea. She set it down on the saucer on the coffee table. "If anything ever were to happen to them, I don't think I'd survive."

"God forbid, nothing is going to happen." I quickly spit three times into my tea as Bubbe Kasha would always do whenever we spoke something out loud we shouldn't have, something that tempted fate. Ethel did the same into her empty cup. "Please do something for me," I said. "Don't tell Julie about any of this."

"Any of what?"

"That I was here. That you made me this tea. That you watched David for a little while this morning while I . . . I just don't want Ed to know about the baby." Then I added, "Yet." I wasn't sure I wanted him to know at all. Or how, or when, I would tell him if I did.

"Oh, Julie won't talk to Ed." She said it so succinctly, so matter-of-factly, that I raised my eyebrows in response.

"Well, he might."

"No, he definitely won't."

"But it could come up at work . . ." I said, my voice trailing off as I noticed Ethel was frowning.

"You don't know?" she said.

"Know what?"

"Ed hasn't worked for Julie for weeks. He left Pitt with Bernie and Dave."

I stared at her and opened my mouth to protest, but then didn't know what to say. If Ed hadn't been leaving to go to work for Julie every morning, then where was he going and why hadn't he told me? Finally I managed to say, "Why didn't you mention this before now?"

"I assumed you already knew. And, anyway, I didn't want it to come between us," Ethel said. "It has nothing to do with you and me, really, right . . . ?"

"Of course," I said quickly. "Of course it has nothing to do with us." Then I added, "Of course it won't come between us."

Ethel reached across the couch and squeezed my hand. "Of course it won't," she murmured. "Let the men be the men. And we'll be as we always are."

Later, as I waited for Ed to come home from wherever it was he was, I smoked a cigarette and looked at the words Nurse Ames had scribbled on the paper. It was a man's name and an address — in Brooklyn, I was fairly sure. The words seemed so innocent there on the paper, just scrawled out, not like something illegal, something that could kill me. I shivered at the thought.

David slept soundly on his mattress in the next room, and I went to the doorway and watched him. He was getting so big, and my heart folded with a love for him that felt larger, more all-consuming, than any other feeling I'd ever felt. What would happen to him should something happen to me? What would happen to him should I have another baby to care for?

The door opened and it startled me, and then I made my way back to the perfect blue couch. In the dark, only the glow of my cigarette illuminated the living room. "How was work?" I said to Ed as he walked into our apartment, a shadow.

He hung up his hat, turned on a light, and went straight for the kitchen, ignoring my question. I heard the vodka crackling over ice, and then he came and sat down at the opposite end of the couch from me and put his feet up on the coffee table. I took a slow drag on my cigarette and blew the smoke into the air in such a way that I could barely make out the features of his face. "How was work?" I asked again.

"Work was work." He drained the glass of vodka and put it on the coffee table. I slipped a coaster underneath it and put my cigarette out in the ashtray.

"You've been lying to me," I said quietly.

He laughed a little as if I'd startled him or amused him — I couldn't tell. "And you've been lying to me," he said with such certainty that I couldn't breathe. What did he know? About the diaphragm? David's therapy? The Catskills? Jake?

Before he could elaborate, I made a decision in an instant. It was self-preservation, not just for me but for David. "There's going to be another baby," I heard myself saying. I felt the scrap of paper in my palm and I crumpled it in my fist.

For a moment, the air was still, I could hear Ed breathing. And then he said, "You've been to the doctor?"

"Yes. Today."

"Well, then, that is very good news." He picked up his glass and walked back into the kitchen to refill it. I wanted to ask him more about what had happened at work, but if I asked him to explain his lies, then I worried he might ask me to explain mine.

I wasn't sure where Ed went the next morning, when he left in a suit and tie as he always did. For that matter, I wasn't sure where he'd been going for weeks. But I said nothing else to him about it, and I thought about how I might investigate on my own. I wondered if Ethel knew more than she'd let on yesterday. I intended to ask her.

Before he left, Ed brought me a piece of toast in bed and reminded me, his voice sounding unusually kind, to rest so what happened last time wouldn't happen again.

"Rest?" I laughed, but I felt a bit of warmth for him that I hadn't felt in so long. David was awake and had begun jumping on his mattress. His arms flailed high in the air, toward the ceiling. Someday, he would be tall enough to reach it, I thought.

"I am sending my mother over to help you today," Ed said.

"That's really not necessary." I felt suddenly overwhelmed with dread at the thought of having to navigate my day with Lena around. And today was a Thursday, a day David and I would walk to Waterman's Grocery and look for Jake, though I wondered what I would say now if we found him. What he would say if I told him about the baby. But I didn't care. It was a Thursday, and Jake might have returned and could be expecting us.

"I have already called her," Ed said. "She will be here any minute."

As soon as Ed left, I jumped out of bed, ignoring the dizziness and the nausea, and I ran for the telephone and dialed Lena's number. It rang and it rang and I knew she'd already left, a realization soon confirmed by a knock at the door.

She looked smaller than I remembered her, standing out there in the hallway. I hadn't seen her in months and, in that time, it seemed she had shrunk. Her hair was the color of dirty snow, and she had it pulled back into an imperfect bun, whisps of brown-white framing her face. "Hello," I said. "Thank you for coming all the way over here. But it's not necessary. I don't want to be a burden."

"Nonsense." She pushed her way past me and walked into the apartment. She sniffed the air. "I smell dust. You haven't been keeping this place clean, eh, Mildred?"

"I have." I suddenly felt defensive, the way I always did around Lena — though, truthfully, I couldn't remember the last time I'd dusted.

Lena ran a fingertip across the coffee table, examined closely, and frowned. "You are supposed to rest in bed," she said. "I will clean this place up, get things in order." Lena pulled a duster off my shelf and began moving it across the coffee table.

I watched David, sitting by the window, playing with his communication cars. Lena hadn't even noticed him when she'd walked in. Or at least she'd pretended not to. It was as if his silence made him invisible to her, transformed him from a little boy — her grandson — into something she wanted to ignore or even forget. He lined up the reds in rows. He was hungry. I hadn't gotten him any breakfast yet.

"I am very glad my son called," Lena said as she dusted. "I am worried about him now."

"Why?" I asked, wondering if Lena knew something about Ed's job that I didn't.

Lena looked up from her dusting. "Why, Mildred? Everyone hates Russia now. Ed still sounds so Russian. People might get the wrong idea."

Maybe Lena was right to be worried. "Has he talked to you about it?"

"Oh goodness no. He's so strong. He carries it all inside him the way men do, you know. But a mother worries." She looked pointedly at me as if I could never understand, as if David still not speaking meant that I did not worry enough, and I gave up on the conversation and walked back into my bedroom to get dressed.

I pulled a dress over my head and did up the buttons, realizing it was the same dress I'd worn that night in the Catskills, the dress Jake had unbuttoned so gently. Now I had to pull the fabric to stretch it across my swollen and tender chest. But I let my fingers linger across the buttons the way Jake's had.

I heard David banging his cars against the floor, and I walked back into the living room, quickly buttoning up the rest of the buttons. Lena stood there, in front of him now, and yelled, "Bad boy. You are such a bad, bad boy!" She ripped a red car from his hand, and he began to flail.

I ran over to her and pulled the car and the duster from her hands. "What are you doing?" I cried. David kicked the floor and started crying. I bent down and said, "Darling, I know, red. You're hungry. Just give me a minute to talk to Nana, okay?" But David was gone, past the point of reasoning.

"Look," I said to Lena, and it took all my strength not to reach over and grab her, to shake her and tell her how stupid I thought she was, how it was not all right for her to yell at David like that. I breathed in and out. "I appreciate your kindness." I spoke as firmly as I could. "But I don't need your help today. David and I will be fine on our own."

She pulled the duster away from me. "My

son asked me to come here while he was at work," she said firmly. "I will stay until he comes home."

"Fine." I crossed my arms in front of my chest. But my breasts felt so tender and swollen that I had to loosen my defiant stance a little. I walked into the kitchen to grab some bread for David, and hopefully calm him down, but the refrigerator was empty. Ed must've given me the last slice this morning. Perfect.

I walked back into the living room, grabbed David's hand, and pulled him up so quickly that I surprised him, and, for the moment, he stopped flailing. Maybe he could sense my anger, and it was something unexpected. "Darling, we don't have any bread left," I said carefully, wanting him to understand I wasn't mad at him. "We'll walk over to Waterman's Grocery and get you some food."

I wasn't sure if David understood, if he could sense what I was really saying. *Waterman's Grocery. Jake.* That today was Thursday, and Jake would have to return to the city eventually. But whether he understood or not, David stopped flailing and followed me to the door without a fight.

Lena walked over to the telephone. "I will call Ed at work," she said, waving the heavy black receiver in the air as if a threat.

"Go ahead." I was fairly positive that Lena didn't know that Ed no longer worked at Pitt. That she, like me, had no idea where he was.

The air had turned cold suddenly. It had seemed just last week to still be summer and now it was as if we'd skipped fall altogether and had headed straight for winter, though it was only October. In my rush to get away from Lena, I'd left our coats behind, and David shivered. I pulled him closer to me.

We walked inside Waterman's Grocery and went up to the counter, where I ordered David some toast, eggs, and milk. "Who're you rooting for?" Mr. Waterman asked me as he put a plate of food in front of David.

"What do you mean?"

"The Dodgers or the Yankees?" I shook my head. "The World Series, Mrs. Stein. They're one–one right now. I say the Dodgers are going to take it."

"Yes, of course," I said, willing David to eat quickly before Lena made her way over here, which I thought she might do once she realized she couldn't reach Ed at Pitt. Inwardly, I chided myself for being stupid enough to mention Waterman's Grocery, out loud and in front of her, despite the fact that it had worked to get David out of the apartment without a fight.

"Who's your husband rooting for?" Mr. Waterman was saying. "I picture him as a Yankees man. Am I right?" Before I could answer, something brushed against my legs and I looked down and realized it was the black cat. Jake's cat. She hissed at me and tried to jump up on the counter, but Mr. Waterman reached for her and threw her out back. "Damn cat," he said when he walked back in. "The tenant upstairs keeps letting her out by accident."

"The tenant?" I asked, trying to keep my voice even, steady. "Come on," I said to David. He was almost finished eating the food on his plate. I leaned in and whispered one word in his ear: "Jake." That was all he needed to hear. He quickly put his fork down and allowed me to take his hand. I paid and thanked Mr. Waterman, and David and I ran quickly out, then up the winding stairs. It was hard for me to breathe by the time I reached Jake's door. I knocked on it, lightly at first, then harder.

At last the door opened and David stood up on his toes in anticipation, squeezing my hand tightly. An unfamiliar older man stood in the doorway. "Can I help you?" he asked.

"I'm looking for Jake . . . Dr. Gold. The tenant who lives here."

"Sorry, don't know him," the man said, moving to shut the door. But I put my hand up to stop him.

"Sir, please," I said. "This is very important."

"I wish I could help you, lady, but, like I said, I don't know him. I just moved in. Rented the place from Stan Waterman last week. Maybe you should talk to him."

And that was when it hit me — when it truly hit me — Jake was gone. Jake was actually gone. He wasn't ever coming back to this place. I had no way to find him. No way to reach him.

I spent the rest of the day in bed, in and out of sleep, half dreaming of Jake and half listening to the sounds of Lena vigorously cleaning my apartment. David stayed with me, calmly sitting on the end of my bed, content to gently play with his cars among my covers. I thought he could sense it, too, that everything was wrong now. Jake was gone. He was really gone. And I didn't know or understand how he could leave us just like that. Where it was he might have gone after receiving a phone call where he spoke about the Russians. *Maybe their bomb?* I felt chilled at the thought that Jake knew too much and that then he had disappeared. Just like that. I couldn't help but think of all the warnings about communists and their propaganda, that they were somehow to blame for everything the Russians knew. That's what Jake was, a communist, wasn't he? Had he done something so terrible that he might never be able to return here? I felt tears in my eyes at the thought that he might be in danger, that he might never come back.

After darkness fell over the room, I heard the apartment door open and close. Then Ed's large voice and Lena's smaller one. I supposed she must be telling on me, recounting my horribleness, to Ed. The pitch of their voices rose. I had the door shut so the words were muffled, and I couldn't hear what they were saying. But I didn't even care.

Then the apartment door opened and shut again. Lena was gone. Ed was silent. I heard the bedroom door creak open and I squeezed my eyes shut, pretending to be asleep.

"Mildred." Ed said my name softly. I steeled myself for a lecture from him about the way I'd treated Lena, but instead I felt him sit on the edge of the bed and gently put his hand on my shoulder. "Mildred, are you awake? I have brought you a present."

"Hmmm?" I murmured, feigning waking up. I sat up and blinked my eyes to adjust to the darkness.

"Come in the other room." Ed grabbed onto my hand. I stood, and the dizziness and nausea returned all at once, so I stumbled a little, and Ed quickly reached for my arm. "Are you okay?" he asked. In his voice there was something that sounded like genuine concern — not for me, I understood, but for the baby.

"Yes, I'm fine," I said. I heard David's little feet hit the floor. He was following behind us. Ed ignored him.

Ed opened the bedroom door and an unfamiliar yellow light funneled in from just past the coffee table. I blinked, but it was still there. I turned the corner and saw where the light was coming from . . . a television! And a large one at that — I guessed it to be twice the size of Susan's — just beyond the coffee table. "I don't understand," I said, but I couldn't keep my eyes off it. A baseball player stood on the other side of the glass, a Yankee poised at bat, looking so real, as if he were almost just right here in our living room. "But we can't afford this," I finally said.

"Pitt has taken a turn for the better," Ed said. "And Julie has given me a raise."

"Ed?" I turned back to look at him, and our eyes caught as if acknowledging this thing, this giant lie he'd just told me. But then he quickly looked away. Ed no longer worked for Pitt, so where had he possibly gotten the money? But for the moment, I didn't ask. There was a giant television in my living room.

The next morning, I convinced Ed not to call Lena by promising to stay in all day and watch television with David. I almost thought Ed seemed relieved, and I wondered what Lena had said to him last night when he'd come home with a television and, as I was pretty sure she'd figured out after attempting to call him at work, no job to speak of.

I didn't lie to Ed this time. David and I did sit on the couch and watch television. David was transfixed by all of it — the baseball players, the news updates, the UN General Assembly session.

Midmorning, I called Ethel and invited her to bring the boys over to watch, and they showed up at one, just in time for *Okay, Mother,* Susan's favorite game show.

"Don't you find this all a little strange?"

Ethel asked as the host, Dennis James, addressed the audience as "Mother."

I didn't tell her that the show had pulled me in, that I knew I would tune in tomorrow to find out what letters Mr. James would read and to see what prizes might be won. I didn't tell her that I planned to telephone Susan some time today and tell her that I'd watched . . . on my new, very large television. "I don't know," I said. I turned and smiled at her. "I think we just have to get used to watching it."

Ethel laughed. "I suppose."

A commercial came on for Phillips' Milk of Magnesia Toothpaste and I turned to talk more to Ethel, wanting to get at the real reason I'd asked her over here. "Ed said that Pitt was doing well," I told her. "That Julie gave him a raise. He told me that was why he was able to buy the television."

Ethel frowned and glanced down the couch at her boys, who, along with David, appeared mesmerized by Dennis James, just back from the commercial. "I don't know, Millie. I don't want to get in the middle of anything."

"You're not," I told her.

"It's bad enough that my mother and brothers are upset with me over everything going on at Pitt. I don't want to lose you, too."

"You won't," I said. "I promise."

She hesitated for a moment, and then she said, "Pitt is not doing well. Julie's really struggling . . . We both are."

"I'm sorry," I said, "I didn't realize . . ." Though I remembered how Ruth said Julie wasn't always paying David, and I wondered if I would've seen signs of hardship in Ethel if I'd stopped to pay attention. Ethel was wearing an old, worn blue dress today with a tear in the sleeve. John's pants were much too short, and Richie was in a stained hand-me-down. I remembered her that afternoon I first met her a few years earlier when she was riding down the elevator in a dramatic red hat, so far along with Richie and practically buoyant as she was on her way to the recording studio. But things couldn't be all bad now. Ethel was in psychoanalysis four times a week. I couldn't imagine that was cheap.

"It's all right," Ethel said, and she shrugged. "Julie and I will get by. We always do."

"You're absolutely sure Ed doesn't work at Pitt anymore?" She nodded. I thought of the last job Ed had been fired from, the loyalty oath he'd refused to sign, Lena's concern about Ed, the growing distrust of Russians in New York City, which was now even that much worse since everyone knew about their test bomb. "Did Julie fire him?" I asked.

"I don't know, Millie," Ethel said. "Can't we talk about something else? The children? The weather? The Dodgers?"

"The Dodgers? You don't really want to talk about baseball."

"The children love the Dodgers," Ethel said, which I knew to be true, but I also knew she was just trying to avoid my question.

"Was it because of his accent?" I asked. "Was Ed's Russian accent bad for business?"

"Is that what you think of us, Millie?" Ethel's voice rose.

I quickly said, "Of course not." But the truth was, I wasn't sure. If Julie's business wasn't doing well anyway, then maybe Ed being so Russian wasn't helping. "The Russians blew up the bomb and everything's changing again now, isn't it?" I thought of Jake and I bit my tongue so as not to tell Ethel what I really meant.

"Maybe you're the one who's changing," Ethel said. Her cheeks were flushed and she sounded annoyed. "Come on, boys," she said, standing quickly. "Let's go. We need to walk down to Waterman's to pick up some food for dinner."

"You don't have to leave yet," I told her. "I didn't mean to upset you. I'm just . . . trying to find out the truth."

"You didn't upset me, Millie," she said, but we both knew she was lying.

JUNE 19, 1953

The inside of Sing Sing is nothing like I would expect it, at least the way Jake leads me in, past the barricades and the flares and the police officers, up a row of wide cement steps and through a large gate. The prison is a brick fortress, but there's something almost architecturally astounding about it, the way it floats here, just on the edge of the Hudson.

I look up and I see the watchtower, the floodlights, the guards hanging out. Ethel is in here, locked away inside all of these beautiful bricks, with no way out. If she tried to run, surely one of those men in the watchtower would shoot her. I wonder if that would be better or worse than being shot with electricity, and I feel ill at the thought.

Jake stops once we're inside the door and he turns and looks at me again. In the distance I can still hear the helicopter and the sounds of protesting, shouting. I'm not sure whether it's coming from outside, on the road leading up to the prison, or from inside, from the cell blocks. Or maybe both. "Are you sure you want to come in here?" Jake says softly, putting his hand on my shoulder again.

"Yes. I shouldn't have waited so long. I should've come earlier." I should've taken Ed's car months ago and done what I did tonight, but I was a coward. "I never thought it would come to this. An innocent woman. A mother . . ." My voice cracks on the word *mother,* and I can't help but think of John and Richie. *Orphans,* I think. And I bite my lip harder to keep from crying.

"Shhh," Jake says, looking around. A guard stares at me and he doesn't look friendly. "People here aren't going to take kindly to you speaking like that," he whispers.

"But it's not fair," I tell him. "It's not right. You know that."

He doesn't respond, but he takes my hand and pulls me toward the next gate. He says something to the guard, who gets out his key and opens it for us. Jake turns back to me one more time. "You have to understand, it's too late for you to change anything now."

I shake my head, refusing to believe that. Refusing to believe that everything has been for nothing. That I truly am too late. "I have proof," I tell him, and I reach inside my purse and pull out the crumpled piece of paper, dotted along the edges with drops of dried blood.

1950
19

In the winter of 1950, President Truman
announced that we were developing a hydrogen bomb. I watched his speech on the
television, the steady way he promised we
would defend ourselves against the Russians
at all costs. Across the ocean, in Britain, a
scientist by the name of Klaus Fuchs admitted to spying and giving the Russians
nuclear secrets. His arrest seemed to me the
end of something, a way to tame some of
our fear, a way for us to breathe easier
again. But then a senator, McCarthy, made
a speech that he had a list of communists
and a spy ring . . . in the State Department!
And suddenly all the world was afraid again.
As news about Senator McCarthy's speech
had come on one night as we'd eaten dinner, Ed had laughed and shaken his head.
"Idiot," he'd muttered. But when I'd asked
him what he meant, he wouldn't elaborate.

I didn't understand the idea of hydrogen

in a bomb, but it sounded terrible, worse than just the regular atomic bomb. Vastly more destructive and explosive. If such a thing were even possible.

I tried not to think about it as I headed off to Mr. Bergman's shop with David. My stomach had grown larger and my constitution stronger this past month. I felt the baby's tiny flutters now as David and I walked out of Knickerbocker Village into the frigid winter air. I rested my hand on my stomach, hoping to calm the tiny feet, and also myself. Just because they were developing a hydrogen bomb didn't mean they'd make it work, didn't mean they'd actually use it, I reasoned. It didn't mean anything at all. At least not to us.

David yanked hard on my arm, and I looked up, and for a moment, I thought my eyes were playing tricks on me. He was here again on Monroe Street, looking as he had the first morning when I met him out here, dressed in that same brown coat and brown derby hat. *Jake.* I blinked hard, wondering if he was real. I'd seen him standing here before. Or at least, I'd thought I had. But then I would run to catch up with him and he would disappear. Or I'd walk up to talk to him and he would turn and he wouldn't be Jake at all.

But this time, David saw him, too, and he let go of my hand and started running down the street. "David, wait!" I called, running after him.

David was fast, and when I caught up to him, Jake had already grabbed him. "Hold on there, son." At the sound of his voice, I knew he was real. David grabbed onto his arm, his awkward attempt at a hug. Or maybe it was his way of saying that now that he'd found Jake again, he wasn't prepared to let him go.

Jake looked up. "Millie . . ." His eyes met mine over David's head. I suddenly felt completely exposed and I tried to pull my coat tighter across my midsection, hoping Jake's eyes wouldn't fall there and notice the bulge immediately before we had a chance to talk.

"I wasn't sure we'd ever see you again." I attempted a smile, but midway my face seemed to freeze and all I could manage was half a frown.

"Can we go inside to talk?" Jake asked. "I don't have much time."

We rode the elevator back up in silence, and when the bell dinged and we stepped out on the eleventh floor, we practically ran into Ethel and her boys, waiting to step onto the elevator. Ethel glanced at Jake, as if maybe she recognized him vaguely, and she shot me a funny look.

"You know him," John turned and said to Ethel, and I remembered that morning when John had found Jake and me talking in the hallway and I'd promised him Jake wasn't a stranger.

"You remember Dr. Jake Gold," I said to Ethel. Then I leaned in and lowered my voice. "David's psychotherapist." Jake tipped his hat quickly in her direction, but I noticed he wouldn't meet her eyes.

"Of course," Ethel said, then frowned. We'd been to the playground together only once since that afternoon Ethel came over to watch *Okay, Mother.* Of course, the weather had been cold, and no one was playing outside anyway. I'd been feeling sick until the past few weeks. And David and Ruth had had a terrible accident last month. Ruth's nightgown caught the gas heater and she caught on fire, and she'd been hospitalized with severe burns. I'd read the horrible account of it in the *New York Post* and went to Ethel's right away to see if I could help. But she'd said what they really needed was O negative blood for Ruth, and neither I nor any of my family members had it. And that had been the end of our conversation.

"How's Ruth doing?" I asked Ethel now.

"Getting better," Ethel said quickly, and then pulled herself and the boys onto the elevator without any more pleasantries. Things between us had been strained lately, and no matter what we had once promised each other, I felt it was the weight of whatever went on between Julie and Ed. I still hadn't been able to figure out why Ed didn't work for Pitt any longer or what Ed did each morning when he left for work. Ed was no source of information for me, and I was pretty sure Ethel knew more than she'd told me. Ed had been friends with the Rosenbergs first, and I had begun to wonder if him unraveling that friendship somehow stunted Ethel's and my friendship. Nevermind that Ethel still seemed mad that I'd asked if Julie fired Ed because of his Russian accent. That certainly hadn't helped.

The elevator doors shut and then the hall was quiet. Jake put his hand on my shoulder, and I let out a breath I didn't realize I'd been holding and walked down the hallway and opened up the door to my apartment.

"That's quite a television," Jake said as the three of us walked in. I nodded, but didn't say anything about Ed bringing it home or about him lying about how he got it.

I unbuttoned my coat and hung it on the coat rack, forgetting for a moment about the breadth of my stomach underneath. It wasn't until I felt Jake's hand — right there, on the bulge — that I remembered again that he didn't know. "Millie." He said my name carefully, and I bit my lip to keep from crying. "You and Ed are having another baby?"

I turned and looked at him "Not Ed," I said.

His eyes widened in surprise, and then, in another instant, his face softened. I saw him the way he looked that night, on the couch, in the cabin. The way his skin still smelled of the sun, that day, and creek water and pipe smoke. "Are you sure?" he asked.

"Yes, very sure."

"A baby," he said as if it were a lark and something he had not considered as real or possible until right this very moment — that he might become a father. That he would not be alone in the world any longer. He moved his hand gently across the entire length of my stomach as if he were feeling it in order to understand that it was true. That it was his. "If I had known . . ."

"You would have come back sooner?" I asked.

"Oh, Millie." He sighed and moved his

hand back down to his side. "I came back as soon as I could." He stepped away from me and began pacing the short length of my apartment, from the kitchen to the window and back.

David watched him from the couch, his eyes wide with something, I wasn't sure what. Wonder? Happiness? He would never understand. Jake was here. And he would leave again. Just like that. I already felt sure of it. "We need a plan," Jake said as he paced. "After the baby's born, I'll come back. We'll be a family. The four of us."

"Jake." I put my hand on his shoulder to get him to stop, to stand still, to talk to me. "I need you to tell me what's going on first. Where have you been? Who called you that night at the cabin?"

"I can't tell you that," he said.

"Well, I need you to tell me something." The words came out sharper than I meant them to, but I was suddenly so tired — tired of everyone lying to me, hiding things from me, thinking I couldn't or wouldn't or didn't want to understand. It was one thing with Ed. But, with Jake, it felt . . . different. If we really were going to be a family — *a family* — then I needed it to be real, to be based in truth.

Jake sighed again and sat down on the

couch. David quickly gathered up all his cars, brought them to the couch, and began lining them up in rows next to Jake. But these rows were different than usual, the colors all mishmashed together. Yellow met red met blue. He was trying to express something he didn't understand how to, maybe feeling something he hadn't quite felt before.

I understood. I felt it, too.

"Darling." I put my hand softly on David's shoulder. "Can you go into the kitchen and go grab yourself a snack from the counter?" He ignored me, and he seemed to become more anxious, rearranging the cars, without any order and more frantically, so they were crashing into one another, tiny toy accidents. "Jake will still be here in a few moments. I promise."

David stopped moving the cars and looked to Jake, who said, "Go ahead, son. Listen to your mother."

David looked back to the cars, and perhaps their disorder was too much of a mess for him to protest any further, but I was surprised when he stood, when he listened, when he walked into the kitchen. It was as if the mere presence of Jake made him better, made him try harder.

I slid the cars over and sat down on the

couch next to Jake. He looked at me and he reached for my hand. "Can I trust you, Millie?"

"Of course you can trust me." I felt a little hurt that he had to ask.

"I mean it. If I tell you something, can you promise me you won't tell anyone else?"

"I promise. I won't tell a soul."

He leaned in closer to me, close enough so I could feel the warmth of his breath against my cheek. "I wasn't in New York to do therapy," he said.

I exhaled, his confession seeming so obvious that it was almost as if I'd already known it somewhere deep down. *Nobody does something for nothing these days,* Ethel had told me. Jake's free therapy had been too good to be true. "But you were really helping David before you left," I said.

"I know." Jake leaned down and held his head in his hands, running his fingers through his hair. "Dammit," he said.

"So why were you here?" I asked. "What did you want with us?"

"The FBI sent me."

"The FBI?" The letters sounded like nonsense coming out of my mouth, so unexpected they didn't even seem real. I'd thought maybe this had something to do with him being a communist, with all the politics everyone around me had once been so deeply involved in, but the FBI? The FBI was something far away, foreign. Part of Washington, D.C. It had nothing to do with all of us here. "The FBI?" I repeated. "I don't understand. Why would the FBI send you here?"

"I was sent to New York as part of a counterespionage task force. After Elizabeth Bentley testified in '47, well, we had reason to believe that there were people here who'd worked with her in her spy activities for Russia. And my job was to find out who."

I remembered Ruth and David speaking of Elizabeth Bentley at Ethel's party that night I first met Jake. She was that former spy who'd became an informant for the FBI, naming names of those who'd helped her. I remembered Ruth saying she thought Miss Bentley had been lying just to save herself. But was that why Jake had been there, at that party that night, because of her? Had he thought people in that room were involved? Spying for Russia? "And were there?" I asked. "People here who worked with her?" The thought seemed ridiculous. I thought about Senator McCarthy's speech, about the spy ring he said he'd uncovered, but those were people tied to the State Department. Not the ordinary men who lived here. I half expected Jake to laugh.

But instead he frowned a little, and said, "I'm afraid so, Millie."

"Who?" I asked, shocked. Jake looked away from me, down at the floor, and I tried to think of all the men who'd been at Ethel's party that night.

"Millie." Jake said my name. He shook his head a little and stared out the window, and it suddenly occurred to me what he was trying to say.

"Ed?" I asked. "You suspected Ed was involved?" Ed and his Russian accent. I'd wondered if Julie had fired him for it, and now I understood that Jake and the FBI had used this to judge him, too. My hands began to shake. "That's why you offered to help me," I said, and suddenly it all seemed so clear.

Jake hadn't cared about me or David. He'd only wanted to find out more about Ed. I'd honestly believed that Jake had made a difference, that he'd known what he was doing, that David was getting better. But maybe he was just some huckster, and Dr. Greenberg had been right about David, about me, all along. "Are you even a psychotherapist?"

"Yes." He put his hands on mine to steady

my shaking. "I do have a degree in psychotherapy. I was in practice for a few years in
D.C. before I joined the FBI. I saw some
patients like David back then, just like I told
you. And I wanted to help David. And you,"
he added. "Really, I did. All of that was
true." He paused. "But you're right. I
suspected Ed might be involved. And that
was the real reason why I approached
you . . . at first." He lowered his eyes to the
floor again, and I followed them and
watched as he shifted his feet.

I suddenly felt ill in a way I hadn't in
weeks. Jake had used me. My *psychotherapy*
with him hadn't been therapy at all. He'd
been spying on me, on my life, on my family, my friends. "So everything was a lie," I
said.

He looked at me, his eyes concentrated so
heavily on my face that it seemed they might
have the power to break me. "Not everything."

I thought about the way he'd helped David catch a fish on the rowboat, the hours
he'd spent with David on his communication cars and blocks. He'd showed David
such a genuine kindness. And me. *You're so
beautiful,* he'd told me on the couch, in the
cabin. I imagined again what our child
might look like, the way I had pictured it so

many nights lying in bed in the dark, Ed snoring next to me. I imagined how he or she might have Jake's oval face, his crooked grin, his rich brown eyes that always seemed to smile. I looked back at him, but his eyes weren't smiling now.

Jake thought that Ed was involved in something terrible. Spying for Russia. Ed, my husband, David's father, the man I shared this apartment and my bed with night after night. A traitor? But if it was true I had to know it. I wanted facts. I felt desperate to understand the world around me as it truly was, not as everyone else was pretending it to be. "What do you think Ed has done?" I finally said, my voice quiet but steady.

"We're still trying to figure it all out. Since the Russians have gotten the bomb, everything has become even more complicated. Now we're looking for someone specific. Someone who gave them the know-how."

"I thought Klaus Fuchs was already arrested for that."

"Fuchs wasn't working alone. He worked with a courier, Raymond." Jake turned to look at me. "And we think Raymond is close by."

"Not in the State Department, like Senator McCarthy said?" Jake shook his head.

Then I said, "Here?" He nodded. "But I don't know any Raymond."

"It's a code name."

"A code name?" I knew I must sound like a terrible idiot repeating what Jake was saying like this, but I couldn't help it. It was so hard to process what he was sharing with me, so far from what I'd ever imagined or thought before this moment. "And do you think Ed might be this Raymond?" I asked. "Is that why you've come back here?" The thought felt so ridiculous that I laughed a little as I said it. How would Ed have even gotten secrets about the bomb? Ed was an accountant, with a Russian accent. He wasn't a nuclear scientist. Ed was just . . . Ed. He had many faults, but I couldn't imagine *this* was one of them.

"I don't know if he's Raymond," Jake said, "but I'm fairly certain someone in his circle is involved in all this. We're just not sure who yet. Or to what extent."

I mentally tried to go through the other men in Ed's *circle,* as Jake called it, the men Ed knew from his onetime involvement in the Communist Party and the meetings he attended when we were first married, the men he'd gone to work with at Pitt. I thought of Julie, of the kind way he held on to Ethel's shoulder on the morning of her father's funeral. Of Ethel's brother, Dave, whose hands had been burned as he'd tried to rescue poor Ruth from the fire. I remembered how Ruth had told me he'd been stationed at Los Alamos, but he was just a machinist, not a scientist. He didn't know anything.

And besides, I couldn't imagine any of the men I actually knew working like this to betray our country. They were just a usual bunch of Jewish men. Men who sometimes talked too loud and drank too much. Fathers and husbands, decent and lousy. They went to work and earned a living and came home . . . or maybe they didn't? *Where* had Ed been going every day? And what would happen to me — to us — if Ed was mixed up in all this?

Jake put his hand gently on my arm. "I'm trying to figure out who was responsible, how it happened. And I will." He leaned in closer. "But remember, you can't say a word of this to anyone, Millie. Especially not Ed or Ethel."

"Why not Ethel?" I asked. "You can't possibly suspect Julie?" It was one thing to think that the FBI would consider Ed suspect because of his obvious Russian accent. But Julie? Or maybe it wasn't Julie they suspected but poor David?

"I don't know," Jake said, and I wasn't sure whether he really didn't know or if he just didn't want to tell me.

"Julie couldn't have been involved," I said. "He's such a nice man, such a good husband and father." I thought of the way he held on to Ethel, the way her face lit up just seeing him enter the room. I still saw him on the weekends sometimes, riding down in the elevator with John and Richie, all of them in their Dodgers caps.

"I don't want you to worry about this," Jake said. "That's not why I told you."

"You don't want me to worry? The Russians have the bomb, and you just told me the FBI thinks my husband or one of his friends is a traitor. How am I supposed to feel?" I cried out.

"I didn't mean to frighten you." He moved his hand down to my leg, stroking gently with his thumb across my dress. I could feel the warmth on my thigh, even through the fabric. "I just didn't want you to think I didn't care about you. I wanted you to understand a little bit about me. For real," he said. His face was close to mine, his eyes and my eyes almost near enough to touch. "After this assignment is finished, after this is all over and we've caught these guys . . . would you go away with me?"

I felt tears welling up. "We could all be dead by then. Russia could drop the bomb at any moment." It was an overwhelming sadness, the feeling that this baby inside me — Jake's baby — might never be born, or might be born into a changed world, an upside-down world.

"That's not going to happen," Jake said.

"How can you be so sure?" He pulled me against him and brushed back my hair. I allowed my body to relax into him, and for a moment I did feel safe. I did feel that everything could be okay, that Jake would make it so, that he wouldn't let me or David or this baby get lost in all that was terrible in the world — the bomb and the Russians and . . . Ed. Maybe now they were the same thing. "Where would we even go?" I asked.

"I don't know," Jake said as if my question had caught him off guard. He hadn't actually been planning any of this. Seeing me with this new baby inside me had startled him as much as it had first startled me.

"The Catskills?" I said, and my own voice sounded faraway, dreaming of that afternoon on Esopus Creek. "Maybe we could find a place just like the cabin . . ." I closed my eyes and pictured it. Jake and David out on the rowboat, catching fish. David outside in the fresh air with Jake to guide him. He would find his voice, and when he did, he would tell me how much he loved the mountains, how he couldn't even remember the city. Knickerbocker Village. Ed. *Ed.* Ed would never let me go. Or maybe me, but certainly not this baby that he believed to be his. Unless Jake was right, that Ed was involved in this terrible thing. Because surely if he was, he would be arrested. And though it may have been the most awful feeling I'd ever allowed myself to feel, the idea of Ed being arrested filled me with the smallest bit of hope. "I want to help you," I said. "If Ed did something . . . maybe I can help you."

"No. It's too dangerous," Jake said quickly. "I don't want you to get involved."

"I already am involved. That's why you approached me about therapy. You wanted information."

"You don't have any information," Jake said firmly.

"But maybe I could get some." Though even as I said the words out loud, I wasn't sure how. Ed didn't tell me anything. Being married to him, I realized now, was nothing more than sharing my bed with a stranger.

"No. Promise me that you'll stay out of

this," he said. I put my hand to his cheek, and I noticed now that he hadn't shaved, that his face was rough. "Promise me, Millie."

"I promise," I finally said to appease Jake, to keep him from worrying about me. Because staying out of this now that I had all this new information felt impossible. I would try to find out what I could about Ed — carefully, of course — but I would try nonetheless.

Jake moved in even closer, and I could feel his breath against my face. "I don't want to have to leave you here. Like this," he murmured. "But I have to go . . . I'm flying out tonight. We just had a quick stopover in New York today, and I had to come back and see you." I wanted to know where Jake had been, where he was going tonight, but I felt sure he wouldn't tell me that so I didn't ask. "Everything will be finished soon. By summer, when the baby's born, I'll find a way for us to be together," he said.

He leaned in and kissed me gently on the mouth. His lips lingered as if they wanted to stay more, do more. But then I felt his body deflate, and he pulled back a little. I held on to him tightly, the weight of his shoulders in my arms feeling exactly right. I didn't want to let go. But he stood up, and I had no choice. He took a scrap of paper from his coat pocket and pressed it in my hand. "There's a number here. In case you really need to reach me, in an emergency, call this and ask for me."

Before I could ask him anything else he shot me a wry smile and picked up his hat from the arm of the couch. He walked over to David in the kitchen, patted him on the head to say good-bye, and turned back and looked at me one last time. I gave him a small wave and bit my lip to keep from crying. I watched as he walked out the door and shut it behind him.

"No." I heard the sound, the startled cry.

It took me a moment to register where it was coming from. And then I understood and turned to run to the kitchen.

David sat there on the linoleum, banging his fists against the floor. "No!" he was shouting. "No! No! No!"

20

David screamed the word "no" for nearly half an hour after Jake left. At first I was so astounded to hear his voice — which was higher and clearer than I would've expected — that I wanted to jump up and down and scream and cry myself. "You're talking!" I shouted with joy, and I crushed his small body into mine, but he yanked away with a strength I didn't even know he had.

His *No*s became louder, more frantic, his kicks against the linoleum harder. I leaned in as close as I dared and tried to talk in soothing tones. "Darling, Jake will be back for us. I promise . . . You don't need to get this upset . . . You're talking. I'm so proud of you . . ."

At last his shouting stopped — not from anything I was saying or doing, I was sure, but because he'd tired himself out. He lay down on the floor, curled himself in a ball, his exhaustion overtaking him. He put his thumb in his mouth, and he went limp as I picked him up and carried him into the bedroom to sleep.

Just as I lay him down, I heard a knock at the door, and my first thought was that it was Jake coming back. That he'd found a few more stolen moments, maybe even an hour, and I smoothed down my hair and ran toward the door. But when I opened it, Ethel was standing in the hallway.

"Is everything all right?" she asked. "I heard such a racket when I got off the elevator. I was worried." She looked past me as if she were looking for Jake, and when she saw the emptiness of the apartment, she turned her eyes back to me.

"Everything is fine," I said. "It was David. He was talking!"

Ethel broke into a wide smile, and she reached across the doorway and grabbed me in a hug. "Oh, Millie, that's wonderful. I knew he would." She pulled back and smiled at me again, and suddenly it was as if our relationship had never been strained, as if Ed and Julie had never had a falling-out. Ethel and I were just neighbors again, two anxious and weary mothers, friends.

"Can you come in?" I asked her, opening the door wider.

She glanced down the hallway toward her

own apartment, where I guessed Richie was napping and John was listening to the radio. "Just for a moment," she said, and she stepped inside.

"Can I get you something to drink?" I asked, but she declined and sat down on the couch in the spot where Jake had been sitting not too long ago.

"So I guess the therapy really *is* helping," she said, though I couldn't help but think there was a skeptical tone to her voice.

"Yes," I murmured, "I guess so." I wanted to tell her that it wasn't just the therapy but the therapist, David's enormous love for Jake. But Ethel smiled, all traces of skepticism seemed to be gone, and I didn't volunteer any more about Jake.

"Oh, Millie." Ethel squeezed my hand. "Everything is going to get better from now on, I can feel it."

I would miss her when I left with Jake, when we went to the Catskills. I hoped she would come with the boys to visit sometime, take the train to Phoenicia as David and I had done. Though I wondered if she'd come to hate me, to judge me, when I left Ed and Knickerbocker Village — and her — behind. Or maybe she would hate me after Jake found this mysterious Raymond and it turned out to be one of the men she knew much better than I did.

"I always knew he would do it, that he would talk when he was ready," I realized she was saying. "Tell me, Millie, what did he say?"

"He said, No. He got upset when Jake . . . Dr. Gold was leaving, and he shouted, No! No! No!"

She nodded. "I thought it quite unorthodox that a therapist was coming to your apartment like that, but it sounds like he knew what he was doing."

I bit my lip to keep from telling her the truth, though suddenly I wanted to. But I couldn't, especially not her. "Ethel," I said instead. "Do you know anyone named Raymond?"

"Raymond?" She thought about it. "No. I don't think so. Why? Should I?"

"No," I said. "Never mind. Just forget I said anything."

"Okay," Ethel said, and then she laughed and leaned in closer. "Oh, Millie, I haven't told you yet. I have some good news at last."

"Good news," I murmured, thinking that maybe Jake was wrong. Ethel knew everyone and everything around us, yet she seemed to have no recognition at all of this Raymond. *A code name,* Jake had said. And Ethel wasn't really involved in politics anymore, so maybe she wouldn't know him anyway.

"Julie tells me things are going better for us," Ethel was saying. "That we may finally take our big vacation to Mexico this summer."

"Mexico?" I thought of the man who'd carried smallpox to New York a few years earlier. He'd been vacationing there, hadn't he? But all I said was, "Ethel, that's so far." If they went to Mexico this summer and then I left with Jake, it was possible I might never see her again come fall. "Why not Golden's Bridge again?"

Ethel smiled as if the prospect of going far, far away from here were absolutely divine. "I've always dreamed of Mexico. There's so much sunshine there," she said. "And the tropical ocean. Can you imagine? The children having that as their playground all summer long? I never had an opportunity like that as a child." She smiled. "And Julie will be able to be with us the whole summer this year. All of us together there as a family." She leaned back against the couch and folded her arms across her chest. I wondered how Julie would be able to manage that, leaving his business for the entire summer, but I didn't want to ask and upset Ethel, not when we finally seemed to have found this friendly rhythm again. "Of course," she said, "it's just something we're talking about now. Just in the early stages. It might not even happen . . . Ruth is doing better, thank goodness, and they think the baby will be just fine, but I'll have to make sure before I'd leave them." She tugged at the bottom of her dress's sleeves. The cuffs were lace and torn, and it seemed odd to me that they would be able to afford an expensive trip but that Ethel was still wearing such a tattered dress.

"I'm happy for you," I said. "I hope you get to go. I do."

"Thanks, Millie."

We were both quiet for a moment as if thinking about the way our worlds might change by summer. Knickerbocker Village wouldn't feel the same to me without Ethel down the hall, and maybe she would feel that same way about me after I left with Jake.

"Sometimes I think I'll look back on these last few years," Ethel said, "and I won't remember any of it."

"What do you mean?" I asked.

"The struggles we went through with money, with . . . John. Someday, I'll be old and gray, and Julie and I will be grandparents. And maybe we'll live out in the suburbs and everything that happened in Knickerbocker Village will just feel like a dream."

I wondered if that would be true. If someday I would be a grandmother, too, if I would forget all about the terrible hard years living with the silent David and with Ed. If my life would become something altogether different and wonderful and entirely unexpected. For the first time, it seemed possible. *Jake was coming back for us.*

"Oh, don't mind me," Ethel said, waving her hand in the air. "I just took the boys to visit my mother this morning and she was her usual awful self. David and Ruth are in such a state since their accident — understandably so. But my mother keeps blaming everything on Julie and the business, which of course makes it *my* fault." I raised my eyebrows, confused. "David has a new job now and he wants to sell his shares in Pitt back to Julie for the money. Julie is getting the money together, but doesn't have it all quite yet." She rubbed her temples. "Oh, if only Davey had more money, he would've been out in the suburbs by now. He wouldn't have had a gas heater in the bedroom." She elevated her voice, presumably to imitate her mother.

"I'm sorry, Ethel," I said.

"It's all right. I'm used to it by now. I remember my mother being this exact same way when I was a girl, telling me that it was my fault this thing or the other had happened with my brothers. Nevermind that Julie gave David a job when he really needed it after he left the army, or that Julie paid for my father's funeral when Bernie and David couldn't afford their shares, or that he's always loaning everyone in the family money. Oh, listen to me . . ." She laughed bitterly.

"That's okay," I said. "You might get to go to Mexico in a few months." And though I'd miss her, I kind of hoped she'd get there, that she'd find happiness in the sunshine with just Julie and the boys.

She patted my hand. "When we were walking home this morning, I just thought, Someday, I'll be older. The children will be older. Everything will be different than it is now."

"Ethel." I laughed. "I'm trying to make it through the next few months, trying to imagine myself with another baby." *Trying to imagine myself in the Catskills with Jake,* I added silently.

"I'm always getting ahead of myself, aren't I?" Ethel said, and she laughed, too.

■ ■ ■ ■

When David woke up later that afternoon, he was silent, more cranky than usual, and all my attempts to cheer him up and get him to talk again failed. He wasn't happy with food, cars, blocks, not even the television. "Jake will be back for us soon," I told him, "I promise." But he lay down on the floor and began to kick the wall. I wished he would use his anger to shout "No!" at me again, but he didn't. And after a few hours, I might have even thought I'd imagined it if it hadn't been for the fact that Ethel had heard it, too.

When darkness fell and Ed walked inside the apartment, I'd finally gotten David to sit at the table and eat some meat loaf.

I looked at Ed differently now as he walked into the kitchen to pour his vodka, staring hard at him for any sign that he could be the person Jake was looking for — *Raymond* — some crazy or evil man with secrets to the nuclear bomb. It seemed impossible this could be a person I would know, a person I might have slept next to for years. But if there was even the slightest chance, I wanted to know. I needed to know the truth.

Ed seemed unaware of my extra attention, and he carried his glass of vodka to the table and sat down. He looked just as he always did. Maybe a little older, a little more tired, a little grayer around the temples than the man I'd married. His English had gotten a little better over the years. But there he was, as he always had been. Just Ed.

"David spoke," I told him, and he raised his eyebrows.

He turned to David, and said, "So you talk now, eh, boy?"

David didn't respond or even flinch. He stared at his meat loaf, stabbing at it with his fork. Ed shook his head and laughed a little as if he didn't believe me.

"He did," I said defensively. "But now he's in a bad mood."

"And what did he say?" Ed asked, sipping on his vodka, and smiling as if he were humoring me, because this was the most interest he'd shown in David in months, maybe years.

"Never mind." I stood to get Ed a plate, piled some meat loaf on it, and set it down in front of him. "And how was your day?" I asked.

"My day?"

"At work."

He shrugged and began eating his dinner.

He had never spoken out loud the words that Ethel had, that he no longer worked for Pitt. That he had a new job now or that he did *something* each day when he *left for work* in a suit. And now, in light of everything Jake had told me, it seemed more important to know the truth. Where did Ed go every morning, and what did he do each day?

"Ethel told me that you don't work for Julie anymore," I blurted out. "That you haven't for . . . a while."

Ed put down his fork. "So?" he said. "You believe everything that Ethel tells you?"

"Are you saying that she's lying?"

"Some stupid woman who lives down the hallway tells you about my job, and you think you know everything, eh?"

"Do you know a man named Raymond?" I asked him quickly before I lost my nerve.

I expected him to react the way Ethel did earlier, so it surprised me when suddenly his eyes widened and he reached across the table for my wrist. He caught it with his hand, hard enough so it hurt. "Where did you hear that name?" he asked, tightening his fingers.

"Nowhere." My heart pounded so hard and so fast as I remembered the word Jake had used to describe what was going on — *dangerous.* "Just a man Ethel was talking about earlier." I squirmed to pull away out of his grasp. For a moment, he didn't let go. Then he seemed to catch sight of my belly and he loosened his grip on my wrist. He put his hand to my burgeoning stomach almost tenderly. "You worry about what you need to worry about," he said. "I will worry about the rest of it."

He stood and switched on the television, turning up the volume loud enough so I could barely hear myself think anymore.

All the news tonight was about the possibility of the hydrogen bomb. I watched Ed's face closely to see if he seemed to understand, to know more than I did about such things. But he paid attention only to his meat loaf and his vodka. It seemed he could care less about the possibility of the hydrogen bomb. Or David. Or me.

I could still feel the weight of his hand across my stomach long after he moved away, and I understood that Ed cared about only one thing.

The next morning, I was determined to follow Ed, to see where it was he was going each day. Though I'd promised Jake I would stay out of it, I was tired of sitting at home with the television and David, waiting for the world to happen all around me.

David and I left the apartment with Ed after I told Ed that I had a doctor's appointment. We rode down the elevator together and walked with him out to the street and then to the subway station. Ed touched my stomach lightly at the top of the steps, and then surprised me by leaning in to kiss me on the cheek before running down the steps to catch the train.

I picked up David after waiting a moment and then ran after him, surprised to feel tears burning in my eyes, as if Ed's gentle good-bye had reminded me of everything I thought I would have with him, once. Ed was not an evil man, I reminded myself. He could drink too much, and I didn't love him the way I should, but I didn't think he would spy for the Russians. He'd been glad to get away from Russia, to come to America. He would not be a traitor to a country he'd longed to be a part of for so very long.

I wiped my tears away and chalked them up to the child inside me, which more and more of late had given me the inability to control my emotions. David and I stepped on the same train as Ed, only one car back, and through the crowds of men I might have had trouble keeping track of him except that he was taller than everyone else, and I focused my eyes on his familiar black derby.

Ed exited the train near Central Park, and I followed him up the stairs and then on to Sixty-first Street, where he stopped in front of a building. The address out front read *7 East 61st Street.* I committed it to memory, and then I watched as Ed walked inside. He looked perfectly normal, dressed in his suit, his overcoat, and his hat.

The uninteresting truth of it seemed to be that Ed had gotten himself another job and he hadn't felt like sharing the details of it with me.

David and I took the long way home, walking through the park for a while before we caught the subway again. I hoped the cool air, a bit of exercise, would make me feel better, but it didn't. By the time we eventually made it back to Knickerbocker Village, I felt that Jake was wrong. That Ed was only an accountant with a new job. And that I might never be free of him.

21

The days began to grow longer again, and I began to grow infinitely larger. As the spring came, I waddled down to the playground with Ethel and the boys after Ethel picked John up from school. Most days, David was silent and sullen, and I had to drag him along. He'd gotten worse again since that morning he'd spoken, since that morning Jake had left our apartment. And we'd heard nothing from Jake. But I kept telling myself that in the summer, after the baby was born, everything would change. Everything would get better, as Ethel had said. I wanted so badly for her to be right.

Ethel began to talk more and more about Mexico as if now it were a fantasy just within her reach. I envied the way it felt so real to her in the way that escaping with Jake did not yet feel real to me. Ethel told me Julie had checked with the doctor about the shots they might need and she worried about how the boys would react, but she'd scheduled their appointments anyway. And then she made appointments to get passport photos.

"You're really going, aren't you?" I asked her.

"Yes, I think we really are, Millie." She sounded breathless, giddy, as if she were singing her response.

I, on the other hand, had no idea how close they were to finding or arresting Raymond. How close Jake and I were to being together. But I knew that the child in my belly continued to grow. And I continued to watch Ed carefully for any sign that he might be the man Jake thought he could be. But Ed's late-night phone calls had all but ceased, and most nights he lay in bed, snoring, even before I fell asleep.

As my stomach grew larger and larger, so, too, did my doubts. What if Jake had changed his mind? How would I manage here at Knickerbocker Village with two children and not even Ethel to keep me company?

Sitting next to me on the park bench, Ethel hummed a little tune under her breath. The weather had turned warm enough to leave the jackets at home, and the air suddenly smelled like springtime.

■ ■ ■ ■

One afternoon in May, just after *Okay, Mother* had come on and Ethel was visiting, I heard a knock at my apartment door.

"Are you expecting someone?" Ethel asked.

I was so large now that even a walk to the playground had begun to seem like a journey, so Ethel had been bringing Richie over here to keep David and me company before they picked John up from school. In spite of herself, she'd begun to enjoy this show, I suspected, because she managed to make it over here just before one o'clock most days just as *Okay, Mother* was coming on.

"No," I said, "I'm not expecting anyone." *Jake?* I stood and waddled as fast as I could to the door.

I opened the door and an unfamiliar man in a Western Union uniform stood on the other side. "Telegram for Mrs. Mildred Stein," he said.

I signed for the telegram and took it from him, and I noticed my hands were shaking as I ripped it open.

THE MIDDLE OF JUNE.
WE WILL BE TOGETHER AGAIN.

AWAIT FURTHER INSTRUCTIONS.
BE GOOD TO MY BABY.

I put my hand to my stomach and felt the jab of a baby elbow, or maybe it was a knee. It was sharp and it took my breath away. *Jake!* The middle of June was not that far away. I folded the piece of paper and I smiled.

"Who sent you a telegram?" Ethel was saying, and I realized for a moment I'd forgotten she was here.

"Oh, no one," I lied. "It's nothing."

"Nothing?" She raised her eyebrows. "It didn't look like nothing."

"It's just . . ." I waited to think of an appropriate and believable lie, but then I felt a sharp pain pinch my abdomen and I grimaced. Maybe it wasn't an elbow, or a knee, I'd felt at all but an early contraction.

"Are you all right?" Ethel asked.

I waddled back to the couch, folded the telegram, and shoved it into the pocket of my dress. My legs felt heavier than they had moments earlier, and suddenly the room felt warmer. Mr. James's voice, coming from the television, sounded louder. "I'm fine," I heard myself saying just as *Okay, Mother* was interrupted by a breaking-news bulletin.

"A man has been arrested as a Soviet go-between in the Klaus Fuchs case . . ." The newscaster's voice sounded as if it were coming through a tin can. "Harry Gold . . ."

Harry Gold? His name didn't sound familiar to me, and I wondered if I'd ever met him. But, for the life of me, now I couldn't remember what he looked like if I had. Did Ed know him?

"In Philadelphia . . ." the newscaster was saying.

Philadelphia, so I guessed he wasn't one of Ed's friends if he wasn't here in New York. Was Mr. Gold *Raymond?* If that was true, then Jake had been wrong. No one in Ed's circle had been involved at all. For some reason, instead of relief, I felt vastly unsettled, even nauseated.

"Richie," I heard Ethel saying. "Come on. We have to go get your brother, darling."

"Do you know him?" I said to Ethel, referring to Harry Gold, though Ethel seemed not to have been paying the television any attention, and Richie was resisting being pulled off the couch.

"Know who?"

"Harry Gold?"

Ethel glanced at the screen. "Poor man. He's probably just the latest victim in the government's witch hunt."

I tried to make sense of everything in my

head: Jake had just sent me a telegram telling me we could be together the middle of June on the very day they'd arrested the culprit in May? It didn't make any sense. Why hadn't he just come here to the apartment if his search was over? A sharp pain overtook me once more and I clutched my stomach.

Ethel didn't seem to notice. She leaned down and kissed my cheek. "I'll check in with you tomorrow, Millie," I heard her saying. "Take it easy."

I heard the door slam behind her as they left, and then it was just me and David sitting there on the couch. Dennis James was back and he was laughing now. I breathed in and out slowly and tried to relax and pay attention to the show. But then I felt the pain again, worse than before, and I looked down and noticed a drop of blood on my shoe.

It was happening again.

But it couldn't happen now, not with the baby so close to coming. Not with Jake so close to coming back for us.

Jake. I remembered the telephone number he'd given me, a way to reach him in case of an emergency. I'd stashed it away in the bathroom where I stored all of my female products that Ed wouldn't dare touch. I would get it and call him now. I tried to stand but the room twisted around me. "Darling," I said to David, "I need your help with something." David didn't seem to be listening. He was staring intently at *Okay, Mother.*

I attempted once more to stand, and this time, I made it.

"Millie." I heard Ethel's voice from the hallway and the sound of her knocking at the door. "Can you open up? Richie forgot his bear."

"Ethel!" I cried out. "Come back in."

"Millie?" Then I felt her hovering over me, and I wondered if a moment or two had lapsed. If I'd closed my eyes, between her knocking on the door and me making it to the couch, because I didn't remember seeing her come back in, hearing the door open and close, and here I was, sitting down again, which I didn't remember doing either. "We need to get you to the hospital," I heard her saying, and I let my eyes close again, relieved that she understood, that she could help me.

Then I remembered the telegram in the pocket of my dress. I couldn't let anyone else find it, a doctor at the hospital who might give it to Ed. "The telegram," I said to Ethel. Or maybe I didn't.

317

22

When I woke up, I was very cold. The room was dark, and I squinted to make sense of where I was. "Mills, are you awake?" *Susan?* How had she gotten here so fast? I'd just closed my eyes. Ethel was just saying we would go to the hospital. The hospital? Is that where I was?

I felt my sister's small hand on mine, and now that my eyes had adjusted to the light, I could see that she was sitting here in a chair next to me. "The baby?" I asked.

She leaned over and switched on a light above my head. It was too bright and it blinded me momentarily. Then I could see she was smiling. "He's fine. He's beautiful."

"He?" I asked.

"Yes, Mills. Another boy."

"Where's David?" I struggled to sit up, to stand, to look around the room for him.

"Calm down." Susan put her hand on my shoulder. "David is fine, too. He's with your neighbor, Mrs. Rosenberg."

"Ethel took him." I sighed, grateful for Ethel and her kindness. I knew David would be safe with her. "And the baby? He really is all right?"

"He's in the nursery," she said, "and he's perfect. Ten fingers and ten toes, I promise." She squeezed my hand. "It was you we were worried about. You lost a lot of blood."

"What happened?" I asked.

"There was a problem with the placenta," Susan said. "And they had to take the baby out quickly — surgically."

But I didn't care about any of that. "I want to see him," I said. "I need to see the baby. Henry," I added.

"Henry?" Susan wrinkled her tiny nose. "Who is he named after? Someone in Ed's family?"

"Ed's family? No . . . not exactly," I said slowly, remembering the way I felt that night in the cabin with Jake, everything we had shared about ourselves, of ourselves.

"You *did* lose a lot of blood . . . I'll go get the nurse." She stood and put her hand on my shoulder. She hesitated for a moment, and then she said, "Mills, there's one more thing I need to tell you."

"What is it?" I asked, not liking her serious tone.

"It's Ed," she said. "We haven't been able to find him."

"What do you mean *find him*?" I asked. "He's probably just not home from work yet." Work — that mysterious job he went to each day on East Sixty-first Street.

"Mills, you've been here a week."

"A week?" David had been without me for a whole week? I'd never even left him for longer than a few hours since he'd been born, and the thought suddenly made me feel panicky. "That can't possibly be right."

"It is," she said. "Like I said, you lost a lot of blood." *A week?* "Mother and I haven't been able to get ahold of Ed to let him know that the baby has been born. That you're here. Mrs. Stein doesn't know where he is either. We even called and checked with Leo in California. But no one seems to know . . ." She paused. "Was he going on a trip for work maybe? Or to see some friends . . . somewhere?" Her voice floundered as if she'd been going over the possibilities in her head for days and hadn't yet come up with a reasonable explanation.

I shook my head, and I remembered the events of that last afternoon in my apartment. Ethel left and then she came back. A man named Harry Gold was arrested — we saw it on the television. But he was in

Philadelphia. Jake sent a telegram. *Await further instructions,* I remembered. *Take care of my baby.*

"I don't know," I said. "I don't know where Ed is."

Susan smiled. "Well, I'm sure it's just a misunderstanding. We'll find him."

But maybe we wouldn't. Maybe Ed was gone. Truly gone. Maybe he had left me before I'd had the chance to leave him. But even as I thought it, it didn't sit right with me. Ed might leave me and David, but he wouldn't leave this baby.

Henry was a calm baby, and beautiful. I'd been right about the eyes: they were purely Jake's, and each time I looked at him, I thought about the hopeful future that surely awaited us, so soon now.

It was June by the time we left the hospital weeks later, and Ed was still nowhere to be found. Susan had to leave to go back to her children in New Jersey, but my mother took a taxi with me from the hospital to Knickerbocker Village and she promised to stay and help out as much as she could while I recovered. I appreciated the offer of help so much that I was able to tune out her constant chatter in the taxicab and to feel only grateful as she helped me and Henry get out of the car.

The weather was damp and much too cold for June, and I shivered and held tiny Henry tight to me as we walked into the building.

"The Dodgers had to cancel their games . . . This weather," my mother was saying as we walked toward the elevator.

I hadn't seen David in weeks, and as we rode up to the eleventh floor, I felt anxious to see him again, to hold on to him. When the elevator stopped, I handed Henry and the key to my apartment to my mother and I ran down the hallway to Ethel's door, which I quickly realized was too much activity for me. I put one hand to my aching stomach, as if I could hold myself together, and I knocked with the other hand — softly, at first, then harder when no one answered.

At last the door swung open and Ethel stood there in front of me, her face red and splotchy. She'd been crying. "Ethel, what is it?"

"David —" she said, and my heart began to beat quickly. I pushed past her into the apartment. Julie was talking on the telephone, frowning, but I ran past him to the back bedroom, where all three boys were sitting on the floor, racing cars.

"Darling!" I rushed to David and leaned down and grabbed him. Too hard, and it hurt to hold him so tight like that against the long incision down my stomach. David didn't say anything, but I felt his finger clutch at my dress. I kissed his head. "Oh, darling, it's so good to see you again. I've missed you so much." I stood up and held on to his hand, and I noticed Ethel, standing in the doorway, still crying.

"I'm sorry." She blew her nose. "I didn't mean to frighten you, Millie. It's David, my brother. He's just been arrested."

"Arrested? Why?"

"For espionage."

"Espionage? David? But that other man, Harry Gold, was the one who did it . . . We saw it on the television."

She blew her nose again. "Well, Harry Gold said David was involved, and now they've taken him in, too." She held her hands up in the air. "Ruth's back in the hospital with an infection, and their poor babies have no one to take care of them. Oh, it's all such a mess."

"Oh, Ethel." I walked to her and put a hand on her shoulder. "I'm so sorry. That's awful. Poor Ruth." She shrugged and bit her lip a little to keep from crying more. "This is all my fault of course, according to my mother. Julie and I got him involved with the Party to begin with. She might as well have said that we're the ones who arrested him, too."

"Do you think your brother really is a . . . spy?" I asked, lowering my voice. Did David have secrets about the bomb from his time in New Mexico, secrets that he gave to Russia? Could David Greenglass have been the man Jake had been looking for in Ed's *circle* all along?

"No, of course not," Ethel said quickly, and she blew her nose one more time. But I couldn't tell if she really believed in him or if she just had trouble comprehending that her brother, a man she had grown up with, could be capable of such a thing. "I don't know," Ethel added softly. "I don't know what to believe anymore."

"Do you know where Ed is?" I asked.

She hesitated, and then said, "I don't know where he is. But he'll be back for you soon."

"How do you know?"

She walked out of the room and then walked back in. "Here." She handed me a crumpled piece of paper and I looked at it and realized it was the telegram I'd gotten the day Henry was born. "I took this, like you asked me to, and I thought you were telling me to read it, so I did. But, don't worry, I didn't mention it to your sister . . .

I didn't know what you'd want to tell her. Anyway, according to this, Ed will be back very soon. The middle of June."

"Oh, no," I heard myself saying, "the telegram isn't from . . ." *Take care of my baby.* But I took the telegram from Ethel, looked at it, and read it again, and that wasn't what it said. *Be good to my baby.* Who wrote that? Jake? It had to be Jake, but now that I was looking at it again the words didn't sound like him. What if Ethel was right? "Ethel, do you understand what's going on with Ed? Did Ed do . . . something? Is that why he has disappeared now?" I asked. "He's friends with David. If David was involved in . . . well, maybe Ed was, too?"

"I don't know what Ed did." Ethel lowered her voice. "But I know Julie doesn't trust him."

"Doesn't trust him how?" I asked, and Ethel shrugged a little. "Is Julie involved in all this mess, too?"

"Of course not," Ethel snapped so quickly that I instantly felt bad for asking. "Julie's just trying to help. That's all he ever tries to do, and a lot of good that's gotten him." She folded her arms tightly and slumped over.

"I'm sorry. I didn't mean . . ."

"I know," Ethel said. "I know you didn't. Everything's becoming such a mess. I don't think we'll even get to Mexico this summer now. Julie's loaning David money for his legal defense, and, after that, we won't have much left."

"I'm sorry," I said again, though, inwardly and selfishly, I felt relieved that Ethel would be here in Knickerbocker Village with me until I left. "David and I should go. I left my mother with Henry."

Ethel's face softened, and she put her hand on my arm. "Henry. How lovely, Millie. I'd love to come meet him . . . soon. After we get all of this nonsense ironed out."

"Thank you so much for taking care of David while I was in the hospital. You'll let me know if I can do anything to help you. Anytime, okay?"

We hugged, and then with David holding tightly to my hand, I walked back down the hallway toward our apartment.

Later that night, with my mother having gone back to Delancey Street to care for Bubbe Kasha and with David and Henry both asleep, I walked into the bathroom to search for the hidden scrap of paper with the number Jake gave me.

In case of an emergency, he'd said. Was

this an emergency, really? His son's birth. Ed's bizarre disappearance. The arrest of Ethel's brother. Any one of those things could be considered an emergency, could it not? Or most certainly a necessity to speak to him. I wanted so badly to tell him about the soft feel of Henry's beautiful plump cheeks, the way his tiny fingers reached for mine as I gave him a bottle earlier.

I took the scrap of paper into the living room and dialed the number, my finger trembling in the rotary. And then I listened to the ringing and ringing and ringing until finally a woman's voice came on the line.

"This is Millie," I whispered, not sure why I was whispering though it felt I should be. I cleared my throat, and spoke a bit louder. "Millie Stein," I said.

"Mrs. Stein, what is the message?" she said curtly as if hundreds of other women had called and left messages for Jake. *Had they?*

"Can I speak with him?" I asked, holding my breath, longing to hear his voice, to have him tell me that everything would be okay, that we would be together soon, before Ed even came back from wherever he was. Or that Jake would tell me that he was the one who sent the telegram. That he was going to come and help with his newborn son.

"I'm afraid that's not possible," the woman said. "But I can take a message and get it to him."

A message. I wasn't sure who this woman was or what I could say to her. "Tell him I have his baby. His son," I finally said.

"His baby," she repeated, and I could hear the sounds of typewriter keys in the background.

"Yes," I said. "And I'll bring him to Mr. Bergman's butcher shop, Kauffman's Meats, on Friday morning. Ten a.m."

"Is that all?" she asked. The noise of the typewriter keys had stopped, and now I could only hear the sound of her breathing on the other end of the line.

"Yes," I said. "I think it is."

23

On Friday I woke up before dawn, my breath suspended in my chest, as if in the few hours of sleep I'd gotten between Henry's feedings I'd forgotten how to breathe. My incision ached and made it hard to get out of bed, though Henry's small cries, and the thought of Jake meeting us at Mr. Bergman's shop in just a few hours, all pushed me to stand.

I brought Henry into the living room and smoked a cigarette while he sucked on a bottle. David still slept, and the world outside turned slowly from black to pink to orange. And then David kicked the wall, and Henry dirtied his diaper and began to cry, and I didn't know which way to go first.

I'd asked my mother not to come today. Yesterday, she'd brought Bubbe Kasha with her and Bubbe Kasha had spent the day on my couch, asking me every twenty minutes or so who the children were, why David wasn't speaking. "She's gotten so much worse," I said in a hushed voice to my mother in the kitchen as she prepared Henry a bottle.

"You haven't visited us much this year," my mother said, shaking her head and tsking as if it were my fault for not noticing sooner. Maybe it was. The lines of my mother's face were ragged, her double chin heavier than it once was, and she, too, was beginning to look and sound older to me. "I don't feel right leaving you all on your own tomorrow," she said, "with your husband off to god-knows-where."

"I'm doing better," I told her. "I'll be fine on my own tomorrow. And I'll bring the children to your apartment for the Sabbath, all right? I'll bring a brisket. I'll stop by Mr. Bergman's in the morning. You need to take care of yourself, too." I put my hand on her arm, and for a moment she stopped fiddling with the bottle and stared at me.

Then she frowned. "That will be a lot for you, Mildred."

"It'll do me good. Keep me busy," I said. And finally she agreed.

She was right, though. It would be difficult on my own today, with my incision still aching as if it were on fire and two tiny people with me. But it would be worth it to see Jake again. I hoped he'd gotten my message, and I hoped to god he would come.

I changed Henry's diaper and got David cereal for breakfast, and then I tried to find something suitable to wear. Nothing fit me still. I was so much bigger than usual, and none of my nicer dresses would button. I ran my finger down the dress I'd worn that day in the Catskills so many months earlier. The buttons Jake had unbuttoned. I shivered a little, remembering that night. And then I reached for the large-flowered housedress I'd been wearing all week. I wished I could wear something nicer today, but it couldn't be helped.

After I dressed, I put Henry in the carriage. I was leaving early, but I wanted to give myself plenty of time to manage both the boys and my aching body.

Just outside the apartment door, I realized again how difficult this would be, as it was impossible to push the carriage and hold David's hand at the same time.

"Darling, hold on to the carriage handle," I implored David, but he'd already run off, toward the elevator. The possibility of getting out of the apartment was overexciting him. David had seemed not at all interested in Henry and had been quite discontented with our new life trapped inside the apartment all day long these past few days. Now that we'd left the apartment, David was full of pent-up energy, and I worried I couldn't contain him and keep track of Henry.

"Darling, wait for Mother," I called as David rushed onto the elevator without me. I ran down the hallway with the carriage, and when I reached the elevator door, I saw that Julie was inside, holding on to David with one hand, the elevator door with the other.

I exhaled. "Oh, Julie. Thank you."

He nodded, and I noticed that his face seemed strained today — new lines of worry creased around his spectacled eyes, and his thin mustache matched the shape of his frown. Another unfamiliar, suited man stood in the elevator next to Julie and he frowned, too, as he watched me struggle to pull the carriage onto the elevator and then grab David's hand. "Sorry," I said to both of them.

The stranger ignored me, and Julie said, "No need to apologize." Julie reached across us for the ground-floor button, and I shot him a grateful smile.

"Is everything all right?" I asked him. "Has all the nonsense with —"

He put his hand on my shoulder. "Let's not talk about any unpleasantness now." The unfamiliar man leaned in closer, and I suspected he was a business associate of Julie's.

We began to ride down, and the strange man put a hand on Julie's shoulder and said, "Aren't you going to introduce me to your friend, Mr. Rosenberg?"

Julie pulled out of the man's grasp, opened his mouth a little, tugged on his mustache as if considering what to do, and then he looked me straight in the eye and shook his head. "No," he said, "I don't think I will."

He must be embarrassed to introduce me, looking the way I did in this terrible large dress, and David already clearly acting up. And I looked down at my feet, unwilling to meet his eyes for the rest of what seemed like an extra-long ride.

At last the elevator door opened on the ground floor and David immediately yanked away from my hand and ran toward the front door and the street. "David," I cried, and tried to manage the carriage. "Wait."

Julie stepped off the elevator and ran after him. The other man ran close behind Julie, and as Julie caught David, he turned to the man and said, more gruffly than I'd ever heard him speak, "Give me a minute, would you?" The man hesitated, but then he walked out to the street and stood just on the other side of the door.

Julie leaned down to David's level and held on to him while I got off the elevator with the carriage as fast as I could, which wasn't very fast at all. "David," I heard Julie say. "You're a big brother now. You have to help Mother out. You have to listen, son. You have to stay close to her." *Son.* He spoke to David so kindly, the way he would speak to Richie or John. He reminded me of Jake. I smiled at him.

"Thank you," I said, and I took David back from his grip. "Sorry if I embarrassed you back there in the elevator in front of your associate."

"Oh, Millie, is that what you thought? No." Julie put his hand on my shoulder. He opened his mouth as if he wanted to say more, but then he didn't.

"Is everything all right?" I asked him. "With David — your brother-in-law, I mean."

"Of course," he said. "Nothing I can't handle." He gave me a half smile as if he wanted to reassure me, but he couldn't quite get there. "I would walk you wherever you're going. But I'm afraid I can't keep him waiting."

"That's very kind of you," I said, "but we'll be fine. David is going to stay with me now. Aren't you, darling?"

David didn't look at me. Julie waved and walked out onto the sidewalk. Once outside, he put his hat atop his head, and he seemed to make an effort to stand up straighter as he walked down Monroe Street, his business associate walking next to him.

"Listen to me," I said to David. "We're going to walk to Mr. Bergman's shop, and he's going to have gumdrops for you. And Dr. Jake might meet us there," I added, though I immediately wished I hadn't in case Jake didn't show. But all at once David stopped pulling away from me, and he reached for the handle of the carriage and held on.

We walked out onto the street. The fog had cleared, the morning was warm and muggy, and I was sweating as we made our way to the butcher shop.

"Mildred, boychik!" Mr. Bergman shouted above the din of the Friday morning rush. "And is that the baby boychik?" I couldn't help but laugh as I struggled to push the carriage through the crowded shop, and Mr. Bergman left his station at the counter to walk around all the women demanding their Friday briskets and over to where we stood by the door.

Mr. Bergman peeked in the carriage,

where Henry slept. "What a beauty," Mr. Bergman said. "How proud your father would've been, bubbelah." Suddenly I wanted to cry, imagining what my father would've really thought if he knew everything about Henry, about me, about Jake. He wouldn't have been proud at all.

I shook the thought away as Mr. Bergman took David's hand, led him to the counter, and rifled around back for gumdrops. I pushed the carriage closer to the counter, and all the old women waiting for their meat peeked inside and oohed at Henry and smiled at me. It seemed there was nothing quite like a baby to make everybody love you, even the impatient old hens who needed their Sabbath briskets right now.

I glanced at the clock behind the counter. It was quarter to ten. We'd gotten here early, but my heart thrummed in anticipation, and I looked through the crowd of women to the door. "Mildred, is everything all right?" Mr. Bergman asked. I gave him a weak smile and tried not to appear as anxious as I felt. "I worry about you with your . . . good-for-nothing husband, vanished." He snapped his fingers. "Just like that."

"It's going to be okay," I told him, and I glanced toward the door again. With no sign of Jake, I leaned in closer to whisper to Mr.

Bergman. "I'm meeting a friend here this morning. He's going to help me."

"A friend?" Mr. Bergman raised his thick gray eyebrows.

"Yes," I said, not wanting to divulge any more about Jake. I heard the bell chime on the door and I hoped it was him.

Mr. Bergman's frown creased deeper. "What is he doing here?" he muttered.

For a second, I wondered how Mr. Bergman knew Jake and why he had such dislike for him in his voice. And then I felt a hand on my shoulder, and I knew instinctively whose hand it was even before I turned around.

"You have brought my baby?" Ed's Russian accent resonated in my ear, so familiar, and now so unexpected, that I couldn't help but cry out a little.

I turned and there he was, looking as he always had, though did he appear angrier? Or was it my imagination? I wondered if he'd been drinking vodka this early in the day. But I couldn't smell it on him. His hand tightened around my shoulder. "We will talk outside," he said gruffly into my hair. "And bring the baby."

My breath caught in my chest. What were the chances of Ed showing up here when I was supposed to meet Jake? And what would Jake do when he arrived and he saw me talking to Ed? He would leave, certainly. I would miss my chance to see him. But Ed would not let go of my shoulder. He held on so tight that it hurt, and I bit my lip to keep from crying out again in front of Mr. Bergman, who most certainly would make a scene if he thought Ed was hurting me, which would be bad for business. "Can you watch David for a minute?" I asked, and Mr. Bergman agreed. I could feel his eyes on us as Ed led me through the crowd of hens and out onto the street.

I was sweating, from the heat of the June morning, from nervousness. I glanced around the street for any of sign of Jake, but all I saw were women heading to Mr. Bergman's shop.

Ed let go of my shoulder, and I reached up to rub it a little. He peered into the carriage. "He is a very beautiful baby."

"Henry." I resisted the urge to pull the carriage back away from Ed as he reached in and gently put his finger to Henry's bald head. "His name is Henry."

"Henry," Ed repeated, a note of tenderness in his voice. I tried to remember if Ed had ever looked at David this way, and I thought that he had, before it was clear that something was wrong, back when David lay beautiful and perfect and sleeping inside his carriage in much the same way Henry was now.

"How did you get the number?" Ed asked.

"The number?"

"You called for me the other night and told me to meet you here. But I never gave you the number, no?"

The number? I couldn't breathe again. I felt I was gasping for air and I couldn't get enough of it. How did this make sense? I'd called the number Jake had left for emergencies. How did Ed even know about the number? How had Ed gotten the message? Had he been listening in somehow on the party line? Jake had told me to ask for him when I called the number. Had I done that? Now I couldn't remember.

"My mother gave it to you?" Ed was asking a question, but he didn't wait for me to answer. "It must have been her." He muttered something in Russian and sighed, and then he stroked Henry's head again with a gentleness I could barely comprehend coming from him.

I thought about Ed's late-night phone calls, his strange evasiveness with where he was working now, what he was doing. That he had disappeared . . . just the way Jake had disappeared. "Are you working for the

FBI?" I said slowly. Even as I said it, it didn't make sense. Ed and Jake were on the same side, working together? Why hadn't Jake told me that? Why had Jake told me that Ed was the one they might be looking for? *Jake had lied to me.* Again. Maybe that shouldn't surprise me so, but suddenly it was as if someone had taken every ounce of hope and drained it from my body. Again, I gasped for breath.

"Mildred." Ed put a hand on my shoulder, gentler this time, the way he'd reached for Henry. "There are things you don't know about me, and I'm sorry to upset you after you have just had my beautiful baby." I shook my head unable to comprehend Ed's words, that they seemed to be salted with kindness. "You got my telegram?" he asked.

His telegram. Ethel had been right. I tried so hard to breathe, but I couldn't.

"You are hyperventilating," Ed said. "Take a breath."

I did as Ed said and tried to take a breath, slowly. I closed my eyes and focused on my lungs for a moment, and when I opened them again, Ed was staring at me with a different kind of look than I was used to. The same way he'd looked at me when he'd offered to buy me my blue couch at Macy's for a wedding present. "You've been working for the FBI?" I finally said when I regained my breath. "Why didn't you tell me?"

"There are many things I couldn't tell you, Mildred. Many things you wouldn't understand, or that might put you in danger."

"Try me," I said, but he didn't. I took another deep breath. "The FBI came to see me before Henry was born." I tried not to think about the feel of Jake's lips on mine as he sat so close to me on my couch, the way he'd made me promise I wouldn't tell anyone anything. I wasn't really, was I? Jake had lied to me again, and now I was just trying to figure out the truth. "They wondered if you are involved in all this . . . spying."

"Who came to see you?" Ed asked.

"I don't know," I stammered. "I don't remember the man's name." Ed's face remained unchanged, stoic. He didn't realize I was lying. "But are you?" I prodded, wanting answers. "Involved?"

"That is what you think, Mildred?"

"I'm not sure what to think anymore." And this was absolutely the truth. I didn't know what to think about anything . . . or anyone. Not Ed. Not Jake.

Ed nodded, but he didn't offer anything else.

"Where have you been these past few weeks?" I asked.

"I have been waiting for everything to blow over . . . Getting us a future."

"What *everything*? What kind of a future?" But even as I said the words, I knew I didn't want any kind of future with Ed. What I wanted was the Catskills with Jake. *Jake.* Who'd lied to me.

Henry began to cry, and Ed took a step back from the carriage. I leaned over and picked Henry up, bouncing him against my chest until his cries subsided and he drifted back to sleep.

Ed leaned in and kissed Henry on the head. His face was close enough to mine that I thought he might kiss me, too, and I now could smell the faint odor of vodka and cigars on his breath. "Rosenberg is going to fry for this," Ed said calmly. "And then it will all be over. We will be able to go on with our lives. I am making sure our little family will be safe —"

"What do you mean, Julie is going to fry?" I interrupted him. I suddenly thought of a raw chicken floundering in oil. And I thought of the way Julie had looked this morning in the elevator, the kind way he'd spoken to David, and then the way he'd straightened himself up on the street, heading to his appointment.

"They're interviewing him now," Ed said, and I thought about that unfamiliar man in the elevator with us, how he and Julie interacted. "But Greenglass has already turned on him. He's as good as done." Before I had a chance to ask him further what he meant, Ed looked around the street and then took a step back. "I have to go now, but I will be back for you soon, Mildred. I promise." Then he turned and quickly walked away.

After Ed disappeared down the street, I ran back into Mr. Bergman's shop, grabbed a reluctant David, and pulled him away from the counter. "But Mildred," Mr. Bergman called after me as I ran out of the store. "You didn't even get your brisket . . ."

But I didn't turn around. I ran the whole way back to Knickerbocker Village and I didn't stop. Not even when David yanked so hard on my hand that my wrist began to ache. He looked behind us, pulling and pulling. "Darling," I said to him. I was frantic, fighting back tears. "I was wrong. Jake isn't coming today. But we'll see him soon, I promise." David didn't seem to care, or believe me, or maybe he could sense I was lying. That I had no idea when we'd see Jake again. Because David struggled the whole way there, pulling against me, until finally I ignored the searing pain in my stomach, picked him up, threw him over my shoulder with one hand and pushed the carriage with the other.

My brain felt in a fog, unable to comprehend the new thought that Ed worked for the FBI, too. How was it that I was married to the man for so many years, that I slept next to him night after night, and I literally knew nothing about him at all? What was wrong with me?

By the time I reached Ethel's door, I was breathing hard and tears were streaming down my cheeks. David was kicking and Henry was crying, too.

I knocked and Ethel opened the door. She wore a tattered housedress and her hair was a mess, but I was pretty sure I looked much worse because she put her hand to her mouth and cried out, "Millie! What's wrong?"

"The FBI," I said, though I couldn't breathe at all now and I ached all over. I reached down to touch my stomach, and when I pulled my hand back, there was a little blood. I must've pulled out a stitch by carrying David — exactly as the doctor had warned me not to before I'd left the hospital.

Ethel stepped out into the hallway and quickly looked around. When she seemed satisfied that the hallway was empty, that there was no one here other than us, she invited us to come inside her apartment.

Henry was still crying and I knew he needed a bottle, but David had stopped flailing when he saw Richie on the floor, playing with a truck. I picked Henry up, and Ethel went into the kitchen, then came back with a towel. "You've ruined your dress," she said, reaching to take Henry from me. "Well, hello there, little one," she cooed to Henry, and rocked him, and for a moment I forgot why I was here. It was as if I'd just brought my new baby down the hall to meet my neighbor — my friend — as if we just might enjoy a cup of coffee together while the baby napped and the boys played.

Ethel sat down on her couch, holding a calmed Henry against her chest. I held up Ethel's towel, now dotted with blood. "I've ruined it," I said, and she shrugged to say she didn't care, it was only a silly towel.

"Yes," Ethel changed the subject back, her voice surprisingly calm, "the FBI were here this morning."

"Here?" So the man in the elevator with Julie hadn't been a business associate at all. "Did the children see them?"

She nodded. "They knocked on the door so early, before we were dressed. Julie hadn't even shaved yet."

"And what did they say?"

"They wanted to talk to Julie about this whole matter with Davey." She sighed. "So he went with them, to talk with them. But he'll tell them he doesn't know anything and this will all be cleared up, quickly."

"I don't know," I said. "Ed said that your brother *turned on him.*"

"Ed?" Ethel stood and handed a calmed Henry back to me. She paced the floor now, and bit at skin on the side of her thumb. "He's come back?"

I told Ethel some of what I knew, about how Ed and Jake were both working for the FBI and how that made very little sense. I told her about Jake's claim about someone in our circle being involved with the bomb and how I'd thought it might be Ed until today when I learned he worked for the FBI, too. As I spoke, I felt like I was betraying Jake by ignoring the promise I'd made to him to keep his secret. But now I wasn't sure who to trust. And, most of all, I didn't want anything bad to happen to Julie.

"I can't believe this," Ethel said when I was finished talking. "Ed is . . ." She let her voice trail off as if she couldn't, or didn't, want to finish the sentence.

"Ed is what?" I asked. "Tell me, Ethel, please."

"Ed is a liar," she finally said.

"About what?" I asked. "Working for the FBI? Your brother?" I leaned in eagerly, wanting more. I wanted all of it to be a lie. Ed and Jake couldn't be on the same side, working together. That just didn't make any sense. And if Ed was a liar, then maybe I could still trust Jake.

Ethel shook her head. "Look, I didn't want to get into this with you . . . Last year, Ed approached Julie and told him he had an assignment from the KGB. He wanted Julie to help him, but Julie refused. Julie didn't want anything to do with any of that. Julie's no traitor to his country."

"The K-G-B?" I spit out the letters slowly in disbelief. *The KGB?* If Ed was working for the FBI, then what would he possibly be doing with an assignment from the KGB? I remembered the night before I went to the Catskills how I'd overheard Ed on the phone, talking about destruction and his Russian friends. *A KGB assignment?* But I had called the number that Jake gave me this week — the FBI number — and Ed had gotten the message. He *must* be working for the FBI. It didn't seem fathomable that he could work for either one, much less both. "Maybe it was a trap," I told Ethel. "Maybe Ed was trying to set Julie up?"

"Why would he do that?" Ethel suddenly appeared very, very pale, as if she might faint, and she grabbed ahold of the arm of the couch. I didn't have an answer for her. I had only the information Ed had told me today and that Jake had told me weeks ago. But none of it made sense. "I don't know what Ed's done, Millie, or who he's working for. But I just don't trust him." Ethel sat down on the couch next to me and took a deep breath to compose herself. "Why'd he leave you the way he did if he hadn't done something wrong? Tell me that. What kind of husband leaves his wife when she's nine months along and then abandons her after she gives birth to his son?"

I wasn't about to tell Ethel that Henry wasn't actually Ed's son, but, of course, Ed didn't know that either. Ethel had a point. Ed had said he'd left to *get us a future,* but why couldn't he have done that from the apartment? Knowing how excited he'd been about the baby, something must've really scared him to send him away like that. Was he hiding now, worried he might *fry,* too? Or was he just on assignment with the FBI the way Jake was? I didn't know much about the FBI, but I saw the way they'd called Jake that night when Russia detonated the bomb and how Jake had disappeared for a while after that, traveling somewhere, presumably working. That day he'd come back he'd said he'd had only a short stopover in New York before he was flying out again. Was Ed doing that, too?

I wasn't sure who to trust anymore, who was lying and who wasn't. Who was good and who was bad. "Oh, Ethel," I finally said. "I don't know. I really don't."

She patted my hand.

But I couldn't get Ed's words out of my head, about Julie frying, and Ethel's words about Ed working for the KGB. "Can I ask you something?" Ethel nodded. "How is your brother involved in all this? Would he have worked with Ed after Julie refused?"

"I don't think so," Ethel said. "Davey worked at Los Alamos years ago when he was in the army."

"Ruth told me," I said. "But she said he was just a low-level machinist, that he didn't know anything."

"He didn't. But when he left, he stole a bit of uranium," Ethel said.

"Stole uranium? To try to make his own bomb?" I couldn't imagine the portly David Greenglass capable of such an enormous feat.

"Oh goodness no. Just a tiny, tiny little bit. As a souvenir." She shrugged. "Apparently, lots of the guys working there did it at the time. It was nothing. It was dumb, yes, but it didn't mean anything. He was young and stupid and that's what's got the FBI to question him in the first place." I thought about that time I'd mentioned David's stint in Los Alamos to Jake, at one of our therapy sessions, and I hoped that I wasn't responsible for all of this in some way by putting such blind trust in Jake. "That's all that Julie and I know about. And Julie had nothing to do with any of that," Ethel added.

But if that were true, I wondered why the FBI was even questioning Julie now. *Greenglass has already turned on him,* Ed had said. But how? And David was Ethel's brother. I couldn't imagine how he would *turn* on Julie, his own sister's husband, even if there was some bad blood between them over the business. "I don't know, Ethel," I said. "But I don't like all this. I'm worried."

She reached up and touched my shoulder. "You should stay away from here — from me — for a little while. I don't want you to get in any trouble over all this."

"But I don't know anything about any-thing. And you're my friend. I'm not going to stay away from you."

"Well, Julie and I don't know anything either," she said. "But the FBI still showed up here this morning. It's all becoming guilt by association. Harry Gold said he knew David. David said he knows Julie. Julie won't give them anything, of course, but suppose they see you and I talking and then they drag you in for questioning, too?"

"That's crazy," I said, but I swallowed hard. Everything else that was going on felt so crazy that I wasn't sure that Ethel's no-tion was that far-flung.

But Ethel didn't respond. She simply stood and showed us to the door. "Don't worry," she said, "Julie's going to be fine. He's going to be just fine. We all are." The way she repeated it, it was almost as if she were trying to convince herself. *Julie's going to fry,* Ed had said. But I tried to push his words, his voice, out of my head.

Ethel grabbed me fiercely for a hug. She held on so tightly, it was as if she thought she might never see me again.

Back in my apartment, I put Henry in the crib for a nap and David in front of the television. I changed my dress and ran Ethel's towel under cold water in the kitchen sink, attempting to remove the bloodstains which didn't want to budge. My bleeding had stopped, but my stomach now ached, the long, vertical wound feeling fresh again, raw, as if my body had almost ripped in two.

I lit a cigarette and paced in front of the window, watching all the people on the street below moving about as if the world hadn't changed at all. I thought again about Ed's frightening words and I worried about Julie, off somewhere being questioned by the FBI. Why hadn't Jake been able to stop that? And what did Ed really have to do with all of this?

The telephone rang and I jumped, wishing that it might be Jake, that he had somehow gotten my message after all. I had so many things to ask him now. But when I picked up, I heard my mother's impatient voice. "Mildred," she said. "Whatever happened to you?"

I remembered. *The brisket!* The Sabbath. There was still plenty of time until sundown, but I'd left Mr. Bergman's without anything this morning and now I didn't have the energy to walk both children over there again and to my mother's. "I'm sorry," I said, "I just got so very tired. You were right, this was a lot . . . too much for me to handle."

"But Mildred, you're still coming, aren't you?"

"I don't know," I said. "I don't think I can."

She lowered her voice. "There's a man here to see you. From the FBI. He knew you were coming here today. I don't know how, but he did. And now he's pacing around and pestering us. He's making Bubbe Kasha very nervous."

"A man there? From the FBI? Who?"

"He looks very . . . official." She lowered her voice even more. "Are you in some kind of trouble, Mildred?"

"Trouble?" I thought about Ethel's nervousness that I shouldn't be associated with her. Was I? If Ed was in trouble, maybe I would be lumped in with him. But if the FBI was looking for me, well, then, why wouldn't they just come here, to our apartment?

"Jack something," I realized my mother was saying. "Yes, that's what he said his name was."

"Jake," I said.

The walk to my mother's apartment felt like the longest walk of my life. Henry wasn't happy to be put back in the carriage, and he cried and cried most of the way. David wanted nothing to do with holding on to my hand or the carriage after our last outing, and I feared I might literally rip in two if I were to pick him up again. "Now we are going to see Jake," I kept saying. "I promise, I promise . . ." I gripped his hand out of fear that if I didn't he'd run into the street, away from me, and I wouldn't have the energy or the ability to catch him.

At last we reached Delancey Street, and the outside of my mother's small tenement looked run-down and gray, as it had for as long as I could remember. The upstairs window, the apartment where Ed and I had lived once, was now dark. Nothing appeared different than it had in so very long. It was hard to believe that Jake was really inside.

I found the front door unlocked, as it always was, and I opened it and stepped inside. I heard the radio, smelled pea soup coming from the small stove. Bubbe Kasha sat on the couch, her knitting needles poised in her fingers, a mess of tangled yarn in her lap, as if she were making a sweater and had forgotten how halfway through.

"Hello!" I called out. "Mother?"

"Is that you, Mildred?" To my surprise, Lena stepped out of the kitchen.

I put my hand to my mouth. Were Lena and Jake both here? "Lena? What are you doing here?"

"I stopped by to see the baby," Lena said, her voice normal and even — not the way it would sound if she'd just seen Jake, I was fairly certain. "Ed called me this morning and told me to come." I wondered what she knew about Ed, his activities, his disappearance. *My mother gave it to you,* Ed had said about the number this morning. So what else did Lena know that I didn't?

I shook my head, confused. But before I had a chance to ask, my mother stepped out of the kitchen behind Lena. "Oh, Mildred, there you are." Her voice was an octave too high. "Lena *just* stopped by for a surprise visit, and now I need you to run to Waterman's Grocery and pick me up *this* list of things for our dinner. Lena and I will watch the babies." She pressed a scrap of paper in my hand and pushed my shoulder toward the door. David, having looked around the room and realized that Jake wasn't here after all, had thrown himself down on the floor and begun repeatedly kicking and wailing. Lena shook her head in disgust, and then picked Henry up and kissed his tiny cheek. "Here is our little angel," I heard her say.

I peeked at the scrap of paper and saw it wasn't a grocery list at all, that it said: *Need to talk to you. — J.*

"I'll take David with me," I said. I ignored the ache in my abdomen and picked him up and carried him out, still kicking.

Jake was sitting at the counter at Waterman's Grocery, eating a sandwich as I imagined he had always done every night when he'd lived in the apartment upstairs. He looked just like a normal man, a handsome man, a kind man . . . the type of man I could've fallen in love with years ago before I'd even heard of Ed. I imagined I might have seen him sitting here one evening, on a stool, leaning over the counter, eating a sandwich, as I stopped to pick up groceries after my shift at the factory. That we could have met, then and there, and everything else that followed since would've been different. But of course in those years Jake was living and working in Washington, D.C., or maybe still back on the farm in Maryland. Had it not been for Ed, I would've never met Jake at all.

Suddenly David noticed Jake, and he ran away from me faster than I could run after him. He jumped on the stool next to Jake and wrapped his arms around Jake's neck.

Jake turned, saw me standing there, and offered me a small smile, which quickly turned into a worried look. He stood and rushed to me, David clinging to his arm. "You're bleeding," he said.

I looked down and saw a little more blood seeping through my dress. "It's nothing," I said, "I just pulled another stitch."

"Millie, it's not nothing." He pulled a napkin from the counter and gently held it to my dress. The feel of his hands, so close to my skin but not quite, made me want to cry, and all at once, in that smallest of gestures, I felt inherently that I could trust him. Jake was good and kind, even if he hadn't always told me the truth.

Jake looked around, then back at me. "Where's the baby?" he asked softly.

"With my mother and Lena." His face fell a little as if he'd been looking forward to seeing Henry, and I felt terrible for having left Henry behind. "You'll meet him next time," I said, though my voice caught, uncertain.

He nodded, pulled a dollar from his pocket, and left it on the counter for Mr. Waterman. "We need to go somewhere else . . . to talk. Can you walk to catch the subway?"

"Of course I can walk," I said, though as I

said it I wasn't so sure. Now that I was here, with Jake so close, I felt the exhaustion and the pain that had been coming on all day after doing so much. I felt like my entire body had deflated and that it wanted to collapse. I wanted Jake to hold me up, to help me, to take me away from all of this as he'd promised once.

Jake picked David up and held on to him with one arm. With the other, he reached for my hand. "We'll take a cab," he said.

"Where are we going?" I asked, but Jake didn't answer. And the truth was, I would've gone anywhere with him then, it didn't even matter where.

An hour later, we were in a room in the Biltmore in Grand Central Terminal City. I understood there was probably a reason we were so close to the train station. Jake would be leaving me again soon. But I didn't say anything as Jake checked us in under the names Dr. and Mrs. Zitlow. If the hotel clerk noticed the look on my face, or the blood stained across my horrible, large dress, he didn't mention it. He simply handed Jake the key and ushered us to the elevator.

David had fallen asleep in the cab in Jake's arms, and once we were in the room, Jake set him down carefully on the settee by the window. I sat on the corner of the bed and watched the gentle way that Jake maneuvered him. David shifted and put his thumb in his mouth. "He spoke, you know," I said.

"He did?" Jake smiled, and he sat down on the edge of the bed next to me.

He put his arm around me, and I leaned into him and put my head on his shoulder. The warmth of him there next to me felt exactly right, as if this strange hotel room in a part of the city I'd never been, suddenly felt like home. "When you left my apartment that day months ago . . . He shouted no. He didn't want you to leave. He was inconsolable."

"Millie." Jake leaned away from me, leaned forward, and put his head in his hands.

I wanted to pull him back toward me, to lie down here with him and pretend it was just me and him, that the whole rest of the world and all the craziness didn't matter. But it did. I had so many questions for him. So many things I needed to understand.

"Why didn't you tell me you were working with Ed?" I asked. "That Ed was part of the FBI? Why do you keep lying to me?"

Jake turned and looked at me. He ran his thumb across my cheek. "I'm not working *with* Ed," he said.

"But I called the number you gave me. And Ed knew. Ed thought I'd called the number for him."

"You must've told the operator your name, and she just assumed you were calling for Ed."

I remembered how Jake had told me to ask for him and how I must've forgotten when I called. I'd somehow messed everything up. "I'm sorry," I said. "I didn't —"

He held up his hand. "Millie, you have nothing to be sorry about. Look, I should've . . . I tried to tell you as little as possible. I didn't want you to know too much. It's better that way . . . for you." He looked me in the eye carefully. "Do you know how Ed came over to this country?"

I shrugged, confused we were starting all the way back there. "On a boat," I said. "Just the way my grandparents did."

"Yes . . . but those were different times. My grandparents came from Schedrin when my mother was a baby, when this country still welcomed the Russian Jews." In a different moment, I would have wanted to know more about Jake's family right then. I wanted to see pictures of his grandparents and his parents, and the twin brother he lost, to understand who he was and where he came from, where Henry's history began. "But that's not what I mean," Jake was saying now. "Did he ever tell you why he was able to come over in the forties, like that, during the war? When it was so much harder to emigrate."

"No, I guess not." I knew it had been a struggle, that Lena had called Ed's residence in New York a blessing — a miracle, even — but I had never thought to question how or why it had happened. It simply had. And before I met him. Ed was in Russia and then he was here. And then he was married to me.

"The FBI recruited him," Jake said. "He had some . . . ties in Russia that they were interested in getting closer to."

"KGB?" I asked, thinking back to what Ethel had told me.

"Yes, KGB," Jake said, his voice calm and even, the way it always was when he'd been helping David. "But a few years after the Bureau brought him here, they began to question which side he was really on. Who Ed was really working for."

"I don't understand," I said, frustrated. "Until this morning, I thought Ed was an accountant." I thought about the job he got fired from years ago before he went to work at Pitt — had there even been a job? The way Lena always complained that it was so hard for him here in America because he was Russian. The way Ethel had called him a liar . . .

"In 1947, the FBI began to suspect that Ed was a double agent."

"A double agent?"

"That he was working for both the FBI and the KGB." He paused a moment to gauge my reaction, but I tilted my head, still confused. "Basically, we were unsure where and to whom his loyalties lie. And that's why they first sent me to New York — to keep an eye on Ed."

"And that's why you offered David and me free therapy?" I said. "To keep an eye on Ed?"

"At first, yes."

"And then?" I asked hesitantly.

"You know," he said. But I stared at him. I wanted to hear him say it. "And then I got to know David. And you. You were so lonely, so isolated. And until we began talking, I didn't even realize how much I was, too." He kissed the side of my head gently and pulled me closer to him. "You're so beautiful. So smart and kind and devoted to David. And from everything you've told me, I know Ed doesn't love you and David the way you deserve to be loved. And it kills me." His voice cracked a little, and I curled myself into him. I stayed there for a moment, just feeling the weight of his body against mine, imagining what it might be like if we actually were Dr. and Mrs. Zitlow, sleeping here for the night, on our way to somewhere else, somewhere new.

"So is Ed a double agent?" I asked quietly, resigned to know the truth now whatever it may be.

Jake leaned up and looked me in the eye. "Millie, I don't want to upset you more than I already have, but I really do think Ed's at the root of all of this. I think he orchestrated the whole thing with Gold and Greenglass and . . ." I swallowed hard, but I thought about what Ethel said, about Ed trying to get Julie involved with the KGB, and I nodded. "But I have no hard proof. And now there's a problem."

"What kind of problem?"

"David Greenglass," Jake said. "He confessed. And he claims that Julius Rosenberg was the ringleader."

"That can't be right," I said, thinking of everything Ethel told me earlier.

"Something doesn't feel right to me here, but Greenglass is putting it all down in writing and I don't have anything else to show them to the contrary." He touched my cheek and leaned in a little closer. "I hate to ask you this, Millie, but can you tell me anything else about Ed? Anything that might suggest that Julius is innocent and that it's Ed who's behind all this?"

"Yes," I said, and then I told Jake every suspicious thing I'd noticed about Ed. Once I started talking, I couldn't stop. I told Jake about Ed's phone call the night before the Catskills just before Russia exploded the bomb, about what Ethel had said about Ed talking to Julius about the KGB, about how Ed had been gone now for weeks — I didn't know where — and even about that morning I followed Ed to what I thought was his new job on East Sixty-first Street.

"East Sixty-first Street?" Jake stopped me. "Seven East Sixty-first Street."

"Yes," I said, "I think that was it. Why? You know it?"

"The former Soviet consulate. We always suspected that was the KGB meeting place."

"So Ed *is* guilty," I murmured. "Are you going to arrest him?"

"No, what you've told me isn't enough. I need proof. Something solid we could use in court. Greenglass is going to sign a confession and testify against Julius. And that's something we can use."

David Greenglass was going to sign a

confession and testify against his own brother-in-law in court? "Why would he do that?" I put my hand to my mouth as I thought of Ethel and her boys, and I wondered what would happen to them if Julie was arrested.

"I don't know. Maybe Julius was the ringleader and Greenglass is telling the truth," he said.

"No," I said quickly, "I just don't believe that."

Jake nodded as if he didn't believe it either. "Maybe Greenglass is just cutting a deal, trying to save himself."

"But Jake." I grabbed onto his arm, "you just can't let them arrest Julie. What about Ethel and the kids?"

I suddenly felt so ill that I knew I was going to vomit. I stood and ran to the bathroom. I'd eaten nothing all day and yet I heaved into the toilet. All that came up was bile, leaving a sour taste in my mouth.

I lay on the cool marble bathroom floor and rested my head against the toilet. Then Jake came in and lifted me up. He helped me back to the bed, where I lay on my side, watching David sleep so peacefully on the settee. In his dreams, I thought he was there again, on the creek in a rowboat, all of us together, all of us happy.

Jake lay down behind me and wrapped his arms around me, his body so close to mine, so comforting, that I suddenly grew very tired. "I promise you," he said, "everything is going to be okay. I'll make sure of it." I closed my eyes and leaned against him, feeling safe. I believed him. Nothing bad would happen if he said it was so. "Tell me about the baby." Jake spoke into my hair, and I could feel the warmth of his words against my neck.

"He's wonderful," I said. "I named him Henry."

"Henry . . . Oh, Millie." Jake's voice was thick with emotion. But then he was quiet as if he needed a moment to reconcile the brother he lost with the baby — his son — who now shared his name. "What's he like?" Jake finally asked.

"He's calm and such a good sleeper. And beautiful. He has your eyes, just as I knew he would."

"He looks like me?" Jake sounded startled as if it never occurred to him until right this moment that the baby might take after him.

"He looks so much like you. I think of you every time I look at him." Jake pulled me tighter, and I could feel the weight of his body relaxing against mine.

"I can't wait to meet him." Jake rested his

face against my curls, and his closeness made me feel whole in a way I hadn't felt in so long, since that last night in the cabin. I could feel my body sliding into an easy sleep. I wanted to stay awake, but I was too tired now, too sore, I'd been through too much.

"You'll help Julie, won't you?" I murmured. "You'll make sure nothing happens to him. We'll find proof against Ed. And then we'll be together."

Jake didn't answer, but he pulled me even tighter to him so our bodies felt like one — one person, one being. *This was the way it was supposed to feel,* I found myself thinking just as I was drifting off to sleep. And then I thought that when I awoke, Jake would be gone. He would already be off, on a train, and I wanted to tell him not to leave us again. But I was too tired to say another word.

24

I was right, of course. Jake was already gone the next morning when I woke up, sunlight filtering in through the window, David's awake and silent face, staring, close to mine. There was a note on the pillow, which still held the slight impression of Jake's head. I pulled David onto the bed with me, then ran my fingers across the pillow and picked up the note.

If you need me, call the number. Ask only for Dr. Zitlow, and say you're Mrs. Zitlow.

All my love, Dr. Z.

I folded the note and sat up to put it in the pocket of my dress. As I moved, I grimaced in pain. But my head felt clearer after an uninterrupted night's sleep, the first in many nights in which Henry hadn't awoken me. Henry! How had I fallen asleep like that and forgotten all about Henry?

I left the hotel and rushed to my mother's with David in tow. He didn't fight me today as we got on the subway. His body felt limp, deflated, as if he understood now that Jake could come back, and then he could leave us, again and again. Or maybe he was just hungry. I realized he hadn't eaten dinner last night or breakfast this morning and on the way I stopped at Waterman's and bought him a bagel. The counter was empty this morning as if Jake had never even been here at all.

I ran into my mother's apartment, out of breath, and inside it was quiet and still. "Mother!" I called out, frantic. David sat down on the couch, where Bubbe Kasha had sat knitting yesterday, and he chewed his bagel carefully with a surprising calm.

"Shhh." My mother walked out of the back bedroom and shut the door behind her gently. "The baby is asleep, and so is Bubbe Kasha."

"I'm sorry, I didn't mean to leave you like that last night."

She raised her eyebrows. "The FBI man called me and told me you weren't feeling well. He said you'd gone back to your apartment to sleep, that you'd be back here in the morning." *Jake.* I wanted to close my eyes and remember the way it had felt to sleep so close to him last night. But my mother put her hand on my cheek. "Mildred, whatever trouble have you gotten yourself into?"

I thought about telling her the truth, all of it. That I wasn't in love with Ed and that I never had been, that living with him was a quiet kind of hell. That I was going to leave him very soon and begin a new life with Jake and the boys in the Catskills. That Ed was not just a bad husband but, it seemed now, a bad man, that he could be responsible for getting us all killed. If the Russians were to send a bomb across the ocean right now, it might be Ed's fault. But instead I told her, "I'm not in any trouble, Mother. I promise."

"Then what would the FBI want with you?"

"They wanted to talk to Ed," I said, reasoning that that wasn't entirely a lie.

"So he's the one in trouble?" She frowned at me. "Lena told me it has been very difficult for him, that he is hiding now because there are so many problems with him being Russian." She paused. "And Lena said they are looking into Ed's boss — your neighbor — the one whose wife watched David when you were in the hospital."

I wondered if Ed told Lena more than he'd told me. Or maybe he'd told her the same thing, that Julie was going to fry. Had Jake answered me last night when I'd asked him to help Julie? Now I couldn't remember.

"Maybe you should stay here with us," my mother said, "until all of this is straightened out. The tenant upstairs moved out a few weeks ago. You could even have your old room back. And I'll be just downstairs, to help out with the baby."

Though I appreciated her kindness, I was eager to get back to Knickerbocker Village to make sure Ethel was all right. "I'll be okay, I promise." I wondered how she would feel about me after I left the city, after I left Ed. I wondered if she would hate me then. I wanted to tell her not to, to tell her the whole story, as much of it as I knew, but I began to speak and then couldn't finish.

"What?" my mother asked.

"Nothing." I put my hand on hers and patted it gently. "Thank you for taking care of Henry last night."

When I got back to Knickerbocker Village, I paused before getting off the elevator on the eleventh floor. I glanced down the hallway at Ethel's apartment, wanting to go there

371

and talk to her, to warn her that everything was much more serious than she thought yesterday. That her brother seemed to have taken his anger over their recent business feud and had done something incomprehensible with it. But two unfamiliar men were waiting in our hallway, milling about as if they were looking for something they'd lost, and I remembered what Ethel had said about staying away, about the FBI watching them.

So, instead, I walked to my own apartment, went inside and got the children settled, and then I picked up the telephone and dialed Ethel's number.

"Hello," she answered curtly.

"Ethel, it's me, Millie." I spoke softly, though I wasn't sure why. "I've heard —"

"You shouldn't have called," she said quite brusquely, cutting me off.

"I know, but, look, I need to talk to you. I'm worried for you and Julie. Can you come over? Or can we meet somewhere later?"

She didn't say anything for a moment, and then she said, "Millie, I told you I can't. Julie and I will be just fine." The words were short, clipped, devoid of emotion. "Please don't call back again."

Then I heard the click as she hung up the phone.

25

I learned that physical wounds eventually healed, no matter how much you reopened them, no matter how many times you lifted something you shouldn't have or bled through an ugly, large housedress. I learned that no matter how much it sometimes felt that way, I would not split in two. In a few weeks time, my incision began to turn into a scar, a jagged purple line down the length of my front that made it certain in a deeply physical way that I would never forget the pain of this summer.

Henry began sleeping through the night at only five weeks of age, and I worked hard each day with David, practicing with his communication cars, forcing myself to try to have the kind of patience that Jake did with him. I noted the presence of the strange men in our hallway and out on Monroe Street in front of our building, but I neither heard from nor saw Ed or Jake for weeks. I followed the news of the U.S. entry into the Korean War at the end of June, which the newscasters blamed on this terrible espionage that had taken place and which, according to them, was being investigated with all the might of the FBI. This was a sentiment that made me laugh — *all their might* seemed to be stationed around Knickerbocker Village these days and, to me, the men appeared not mighty but bored, smoking cigarettes, reading newspapers, and I even saw them once rifling through trash cans. They were waiting for something to happen outside the normal droll life of our apartment building. And so far, nothing had. Mainly, they watched women like me, mothers struggling to pull their carriages and their older children on the elevator without losing track of anyone or anything.

As much as I wanted each day to walk down the hall and knock on Ethel's door, I followed her wishes and didn't. Partly I knew that she wouldn't talk to me even if I did. And partly it was self-preservation. I felt the men in the hallway might report anything to Jake or Ed — or, worse, another FBI man I didn't know who might begin to suspect me of something, too. So I tried to ignore the men in the hallway and concentrate on my boys.

Yet, I still paid attention to what was going on over at Ethel's. It seemed she was continuing on with her schedule of psychoanalysis several days a week, as I would hear her walk out at that time to the elevator. And Julius still went to and came home from work each day. Sometimes Ethel took the children out places, though not to the playground because I never saw her there anymore, but I guessed to go to Waterman's Grocery or Mr. Bergman's shop. They needed to eat, after all. Each time any of them left the apartment, it was immediately clear to me because I could hear the shuffle of the men's feet in the hallway as if they were racing to watch the Rosenbergs step onto the elevator. The men didn't always ride down with them, and I noticed there were usually different men on the street to follow Ethel or Julie to wherever it was they were going.

I watched the news and read the paper each evening, hoping for more than what I could gather simply from listening to the footsteps in my hallway, but the news made no mention of the goings-on at Knickerbocker Village as far as I could tell. Mostly, I read about Korea: Truman appointed MacArthur to lead the UN forces, and there were predictions of the war going on for six to nine months. All the headlines I saw now about the *Reds* referred to the ones over there. I took some comfort in the fact that the rest of the world knew nothing of the FBI watch in my hallway. It meant that nothing would come of it, I guessed, and that soon the FBI would leave for good. I wanted Ethel and Julie's life to go back to normal, but I also dreaded Ed coming back, and I hoped I would see Jake again before then so we could come up with a plan. But first I still longed to talk to Ethel, to warn her, so eventually I came up with a plan of my own.

One morning in July, after I heard the commotion in the hallway, I put Henry in the carriage and took David down the street to play in the park. I watched for Ethel and her boys to make their way back. When I saw them, I quickly scooped up David and grabbed the carriage and ran down Monroe Street after her. I bounded onto the elevator behind her just as the door began to shut. I put David next to the buttons, and I didn't try to stop him as he pushed every single floor.

Ethel's face turned in surprise, and then she seemed to realize what I had done and her features softened. We were completely alone in the elevator. Just me and Ethel and our boys. All at once, she leaned across the carriage and gave me a hug. "Millie," she said, her voice breaking a little on my name, "I've missed you."

"I've missed you, too," I said, my voice catching. Life had been so lonely without Ethel. I'd been keeping the television on nearly all day and all night just to feel I wasn't completely alone.

"Every floor?" I heard John say to David. "Really?" I laughed a little and pulled out of Ethel's hug. I wiped away tears from the corners of my eyes. John shook his head, and from the peculiar look on his face it seemed clear to me that he understood something wasn't right, that the adults in his world were acting strangely.

I patted him on the head. "We've missed seeing you, Johnny," I said. "Haven't we, David?"

David didn't answer, of course, but he stared at John, his eyes open wide. John shrugged my hand away and folded his arms across his chest.

The elevator door opened to an empty first floor. The sound of the ding startled Ethel and she immediately jumped back as if she had never even spoken to me at all.

"I'm sorry, Millie," she said when the door

closed again and we rode slowly up to two. "I haven't wanted to ignore you, but it's for the best. For your own good. We shouldn't want those FBI men to see us talking, to know we're friends. They might start to follow you, too."

I remembered how Jake told me to not get involved and I worried that Ethel might be right. With Ed gone, the FBI should want nothing of me right now, and it occurred to me for the first time that maybe Ed had left to protect me. The thought didn't sit easily with me and I tried to push it away and get back to Ethel. I had only a short time before the elevator made it up to the eleventh floor. "Jake told me that your brother blamed Julie for getting him involved in espionage," I blurted out. "David told the FBI this was all Julie's fault."

"No, Millie," she said. "Absolutely no. That's not true."

"Ethel." I reached for her hand. I thought about how there was so much about Ed that I never knew, that I still didn't know. How well could you really *know* a person, even your husband or your own brother? "David's your brother. Why would he lie?"

"No, Millie. Your information . . . it's just plain wrong. We've just been to see Ruth, who's finally home from the hospital, thank goodness, and she said David has it all worked out with them now. He's struck some kind of a deal with the FBI. Everything's going to be fine. For all of us."

"But Jake said . . ."

"Millie, you can't trust Jake."

"No, I can," I said, but even as I said it I felt a flicker of doubt. I wanted to trust Jake. I really, really did. But could I?

"He's been lying to you all along," Ethel said. "And he's FBI."

I knew what Ethel said was true, but I also felt in my heart that Jake loved me and David. And Henry, even though he hadn't met him yet. But he was going to adore Henry. "But now he knows me," I told Ethel, feeling desperate to make her understand. "He might have lied before. But he wants to help me. He wants to help all of us."

Ethel frowned. "Millie, the FBI is out to get us. They don't want to help any of us. Julie thinks Jake is the worst of them. And the way he lied to you about helping David —"

"But he *did* help David." My voice faltered a little as I glanced over at my still-silent son, now staring hard at John.

Ethel put her hand on my shoulder. "Trust no one but yourself. Please, Millie."

"Ethel," I said, thinking about what she'd

just said, that David had worked out a deal, that everything was going be fine — for all of us. I wanted to believe that. "If your brother has fixed everything, then why are the men still in the hallway upstairs?"

"I don't know," she admitted. "But Julie thinks they have it in for us just because we're Jews who used to be involved in the Party." She lowered her voice as the door opened up to an empty third floor. "We've gotten our passport photos now. Julie thinks we can go to Mexico. Maybe for a longer . . . vacation than we'd anticipated."

"You mean run away?" I asked.

"Mortie and his family did."

"The Sobells went to Mexico?" I thought of Mortie Sobell, and he did not seem like the kind of man who would take kindly to so much sunshine.

"It doesn't matter that we didn't do anything wrong," Ethel was saying, "everybody in this country is so afraid of Russia and the bomb. And they need someone to blame. They need to feel like they're doing something. How silly is it that they've focused in on our little Jewish family here in Knickerbocker Village?"

"But are you sure that Julie wasn't involved?" I said quietly.

"Yes, Millie. I'm absolutely sure. He told

me he wasn't and I believe him." She looked at me and then quickly away. "We're not like other couples. We tell each other everything. And Julie's a good man."

I thought of the way he helped me that morning in the elevator, the kindness he showed to David. "Jake thinks Ed was involved, but he doesn't have any proof. Ed and I aren't like you and Julie. It seems I don't know much about my husband at all."

Ethel frowned again, maybe at the mention of Jake's name, maybe because I was telling her that I knew nothing real about Ed. But all she said was "They don't have any proof about anything these days. It doesn't stop them."

The elevator rode up a few more floors and we rode in silence. Henry let out a little cry and I pulled him out of his carriage to comfort him.

"Millie," Ethel said as we headed toward the ninth floor, "I want you to know that you've been a good friend to me. I'll miss you. The boys will miss David. And little Henry." She squeezed his chubby little leg. "I'll want to write you from Mexico. But I might not be able to . . . It might not be in your best interest to receive letters from me." She squeezed my hand, and I squeezed back.

When the elevator doors opened on the eleventh floor, Ethel quickly moved away from me, grabbed John's and Richie's hands, and walked off brusquely, her head held high as if we hadn't ever spoken to each other at all.

The next evening, after I'd put the boys to bed, I found myself smoking a cigarette in front of the television. I closed my eyes, listening to the voices of the men reporting the news without watching. As if I were just listening to the radio, not enjoying my television, which I wasn't enjoying now anyway remembering how Ed had brought it here. For me.

Suddenly, I heard noises in the hallway. Louder than just the two men. Many, many sets of footsteps, a banging on a door, a woman screaming from somewhere down the hallway. *Ethel?*

I cracked open my door and peered down the hall. There were so many men by Ethel's door. I counted one, two, three . . . twelve? Was Jake there? I arched my neck, looking for him, but I couldn't see clearly enough, and I was afraid to actually open the door and walk out into the hallway.

The men entered the Rosenbergs' apartment and then they came back out carrying things — papers, a typewriter. "You can't take my record!" I heard Ethel yelling. "I made that for my son." And I remembered that morning when I saw her about to ride down the elevator — so carefree, it seemed — off to the studio. How could they dare take that away? What possible use would they have for it?

I heard more shouting, more commotion, the sounds of *The Lone Ranger* on the radio still playing in their apartment. I heard Julie complaining that they didn't have a warrant. "You have no right!" he kept shouting. And yet the men continued, in twos, carrying out things and riding down the elevator. If Ethel was right about her brother striking a deal, then why were all these men here taking things from their apartment?

At last, when it seemed they couldn't take any more things, two men came out with Julie. I gasped as I watched them walk him out of the apartment, holding on to his arms, his hands in handcuffs. I couldn't make out their faces, but, from the back, one of the men vaguely looked like Jake. *It couldn't be him.* Suddenly Julie noticed I was watching and shook his head a little. I quickly shut my door before the FBI men saw me staring.

I remembered what Ethel had said: *Trust*

no one but yourself. Was she right? Was that really Jake out in the hallway? Arresting Julie? It couldn't have been him. No matter what the rest of the FBI were doing, Jake would not arrest an innocent man. I wanted to believe that so badly.

The hallway was silent now, and I opened my door and walked out. No one was there, and if any of the other neighbors were home and had noticed the noise, they were now pretending not to.

Ethel's door opened and she stepped out, holding on to one boy with each hand. "Ethel," I called down the hallway. She looked up and tears streamed down her face. "What's happened?"

"Julie's been arrested," she said. The words sounded unreal coming from her. She said them almost without emotion as if she couldn't even comprehend what she was saying. Tears kept falling down her face, but she made no attempt to wipe them away.

"Oh, Ethel . . ." I walked down the hallway toward her, but she let go of John's hand to hold up her hand to stop me. "Where are you going?" I asked.

She shrugged and bit her lip. "The FBI men are driving us to my mother's," she said, and then she turned toward the elevator and stepped on.

"Wait!" I called after her. But she didn't answer, and I heard the elevator door closing.

Back inside my apartment, I held the piece of paper with the FBI number on it in my hands. Julie had been arrested. Ruth must have lied to Ethel about the *deal* Davey had struck. Or maybe the FBI did have some other proof, although I had no idea what that proof could be. And I thought about what Ethel said in the elevator — that they didn't even need proof. But that made no sense at all. This was America. I needed to call Jake and talk to him. Ethel had said I couldn't trust him, but what other choice did I have?

Still, a little bit of doubt crept up inside me, a small, annoying itch that I couldn't quite scratch. Even if he wasn't here tonight among the men pulling Julie and Ethel's possessions out of their apartment, he'd let Julie be arrested. But maybe he'd had no choice. Or maybe he was less involved than I thought and things had gotten beyond his control.

I dialed with shaking fingers. I could still feel the panic in Ethel's voice as she'd yelled about her record that the FBI men stole.

"This is Mrs. Zitlow," I said when the

386

woman answered. "Tell Dr. Zitlow to call me as soon as possible."

I hung up before I could say, or she could ask me, anything else, and I sat there and stared at the telephone, waiting and waiting and waiting for it to ring.

I fell asleep on the couch with my hand still on the black receiver, the television still on, its muted yellow light flashing on and on.

The next morning, I awoke late to the sounds of Henry's cries and David's kicks. I was stiff from sleeping on the couch so awkwardly, and as I sat up and stretched, I remembered the way Julie had looked as the men had pulled him to the elevator in handcuffs last night: smaller than usual and very grim. I thought about Ethel now and how she must feel this morning, waking up without him, at her mother's. It seemed an unfathomable sort of sadness and fear. When Ed left, it was of his own accord. And, anyway, I didn't love and need him the way Ethel did Julie. These past few weeks without him had been a relief.

The telephone finally rang as I was fixing a bottle for Henry. I put the bottle down and I ran to answer it.

"Mills." Susan's voice, not Jake's, rang

through the line rather clearly. I stretched the telephone as far as it would go to grab Henry's bottle off the table and put it in his mouth. "I saw on the news about your neighbor being an atom spy. I can't believe it. You were friends with such a person . . . Has the FBI been there to question you?"

"Slow down," I said, and I tried to take a moment to process what she was saying, that now the entire world believed Julie to be an *atom spy.* It sounded like such a silly phrase, almost harmless like a science project, but I knew exactly how terrible it was. The FBI believed Julie to have given Russia secrets about the bomb. And now that it was reported in the news, the entire world would believe it, too.

"Well?" Susan said, sounding a bit out of breath as if she'd run to the telephone immediately upon seeing the news. I heard one of the twins calling for her in the background, the words so clear and obvious in her childish voice. I glanced at David, who was concentrating very hard on eating his cereal — silently, of course.

"No," I said, thinking about Jake, who hadn't returned my call. "No one has been here."

"They say they've set his bail at one hundred thousand dollars."

"One hundred thousand dollars? That's absolutely crazy." There was no way Ethel and Julie would be able to pay anything close to that. I was pretty sure that meant Julie was going to have to wait in jail until this was all resolved. I couldn't imagine what Ethel was thinking right now. Or feeling.

"Well, apparently they believe him to be a very dangerous man. Who knows what else he might do should they let him out while he awaits trial?"

Dangerous? Julie? "That's ridiculous," I said. "He's so kind, and such a good father." I thought again of that morning on the elevator, him talking to David so sweetly, reminding David to help me. "And very good with David, too."

"Look, why don't you and the boys come out here and stay with us for a little while. Until this all settles down."

"I don't think so," I said. "I should go check on Ethel."

Susan inhaled sharply on the other end of the line. "I read she's inviting the press into her home today."

That didn't sound like Ethel at all. Inviting the press, here? "Let me call you back," I said, and I hung up despite her protests.

I put David in front of the television and

turned it back on. Henry was finishing his bottle, and I picked him up and took him with me down the hall to Ethel's apartment. I knocked on the door and I was surprised when she answered with a flourish and a huge smile. As soon as she saw it was me who'd knocked, her smile faded rather quickly.

Ethel wore a brightly flowered dress today — one of her nicest, though, I noticed her bra strap was slipping free, down her shoulder, and I wanted to tell her to fix it, but she interrupted my thoughts by leaning out toward me and chiding me, in a hushed voice, "Millie, what are you doing here? The press are coming. I'm really in quite a rush, trying to get this place cleaned up. And I need to go out and buy a chicken."

"A chicken?"

"For dinner."

"You're making chicken for dinner? Ethel . . . ?" I slung Henry under one arm and reached up to fix Ethel's bra strap with my free hand.

Ethel pulled back quickly and finished fixing the strap herself. "I have to show them this doesn't mean anything. That I'm not worried . . . because Julie's innocent. I have to present a strong front." Her eyes welled up with tears and she stopped talking to desperately wipe them away. "It's what Julie wants me to do."

"But Ethel . . . you *are* worried." She bit her lip and wiped a stray tear off her cheek. "I've called Jake," I said. "He'll get this straightened out. I know he will."

"Please, Millie, stay out of this."

"I want to help you," I said. "You took care of David the whole time I was in the hospital, and now you need a friend." I put my free hand on her bare arm. "Let me help you." Ethel's features eased. I noticed her strap had slipped again, but I didn't move to fix it. "At least let me go get you a chicken from Mr. Bergman." She bit her lip again and didn't say anything. "Come on," I said. "No one will fault a neighbor for getting you a chicken on a day like today. And I was just about to go see Mr. Bergman anyway," I lied. But I felt desperate to help her. To do *something.* And however small, this seemed to be it.

She nodded, but then she quickly shut the door.

Outside, the sun was shining brilliantly, the cars driving across the Manhattan Bridge, small and glittering like colored stars over the sparkling East River. It was almost incomprehensible the way the world beyond

Knickerbocker Village appeared so exceedingly normal this July morning.

The children were surprisingly calm on the walk to Mr. Bergman's. They understood nothing but the warmth of the sunshine upon their faces, neither one of them seeming to comprehend the shift in the air or to sense that something enormous and almost entirely unbelievable had happened on the eleventh floor last night.

I wondered how much *press* would be there this afternoon. And I wondered if she could pull it off, acting, as she'd said, as if nothing were wrong, preparing a chicken for dinner for herself and the children. I remembered how she told me once that her high school class had named her most likely to be America's leading actress by 1950 and it made me sad to think that *this* was it.

Mr. Bergman's shop was fairly empty this morning, though when he saw us walk in, he didn't call out his normal buoyant greeting, and I guessed that he had heard the news, too.

I pushed the carriage up to the counter, and David jumped up, had a seat, and held his hand out expectantly, waiting for the gumdrops. Mr. Bergman leaned across the counter, patted him on the head, and pulled a few gumdrops out of the bag and put them into David's hand. In his other hand he had an envelope, which he placed in my hand. "Mildred." His voice was low, more serious than usual. "I was going to come find you after work. Your friend . . . a Mr. Zitlow . . . dropped this off for you this morning."

I exhaled. *Jake had gotten my message.* Thank goodness. I ripped the envelope open and pulled out the letter inside:

I'm doing everything I can but cannot find any evidence yet for what we discussed. Things are getting bigger than me now, and I can't contain them. Search your apartment and see what you can find to implicate the suspect we mentioned at our last meeting.

I have a plan for us. Will explain in person . . . making arrangements. Meet me in the lobby of the place we were last together. Will send word when. Until then . . .

With love,
Dr. Z

I turned the paper over in my hands, wanting it to say something else, something more. Excitement rose in my chest but then quickly subsided. Jake had a plan for us. But he hadn't mentioned Ethel and Julie. Was he not able to help them? He was not able to prove that Ed had done anything wrong, that he might be at fault for this whole horrible mistake. It was up to me to find something on Ed.

"Mildred." Mr. Bergman's voice sounded like a warning, and I wondered if he'd read the contents of the letter. I tried to imagine Jake here in his shop, just hours, or maybe moments, before I was. I sniffed the air to see if I could catch the faint waft of pipe smoke, pine trees, but all I could smell was raw meat.

I remembered why I'd come here, and I folded the letter up and put it in the pocket of my dress. "I need a chicken," I told him. "For my neighbor Ethel. And one for myself, too. Two chickens."

Mr. Bergman looked at me sternly. "Have you got yourself tangled up in this mess, Mildred? Atom spies?" He lowered his voice on the last two words as if he were almost afraid to say them out loud. "Is this Ed's doing?"

"This is all a terrible mistake," I said in a low voice. "That's why Ethel needs a chicken. She's going to prepare one while the press watches, show them that none of

394

this is worrisome to her. That Julie's completely innocent."

"A chicken?" He raised his eyebrows. "What they need is a good lawyer. Do they have one?"

"I don't know," I said, "I suppose they must." I wondered how expensive a good lawyer was and whether they were able to afford one. Ethel had already said Julie was paying for David's lawyer, and now he would need one for himself, too. They were supposed to be using that money to go to Mexico this summer.

"All right, I will get you your chickens," Mr. Bergman said. "But first, let me tell you a story." He cleared his throat. "When your father was still alive, back in '28, and the slaughterhouses were trying to gouge us, do you know what he did?"

I vaguely remembered that time, when I was a little girl, before the market crashed, before the war, when people still had it in them to get all up in arms about things like the price of meat, but I didn't remember anything specific my father did. "No," I said. "What?"

"He organized all the kosher butchers in the city to call a strike. He was the one who said he wasn't going to stand for it. He was going to make a difference. And do you know what happened?" I shook my head. "Even after the strike was over and things were resolved, the slaughterhouses were very angry with us. They wanted to get even. They sent us terrible meat for months. If it hadn't been for the chickens — we always have had the best chicken" — I nodded, listening — "it would've put us out of business for good."

I thought about my father, standing up and organizing all those butchers to fight for something that wasn't right, and I felt a proud of him in a way I hadn't ever felt before. Then I remembered why Ethel said she'd been so involved in the Party to begin with — to help organize labor unions, fairness for workers. My father would've understood that being a communist once didn't mean you were a spy. "I miss him," I said, my voice breaking.

"So do I, bubbelah." Mr. Bergman reached across the counter and squeezed my hand. "But you know what he would tell you if he was here now?" I shrugged. "He'd tell you to go give Ethel her chicken and then get the hell out of Knickerbocker Village. Go out to New Jersey, stay with Susy for a little while. Keep away from all this."

I was fairly sure that wasn't what my

father would tell me at all. "I can't do that," I said. "I'm not going to abandon my friend." I lowered my voice and leaned in closer. "I don't understand everything that's gone on. I know Ethel's brother David got into some trouble and he's somehow dragged Julie into it now." I paused, wondering whether I should say this next thing to Mr. Bergman, whether I should bring him into this at all. His brown eyes were fixed so heavily on my face as if he were imploring me to continue, so I did. "But I don't think Julie would've given atomic secrets to the Russians no matter what the FBI or the papers say. He's so kind, and he's such a good husband and father. He's always playing baseball in the courtyard with his boys." I said it firmly as if this were all the evidence anyone might need. But wasn't it? A man like Julie, who loved his children and his wife so, he would never want them murdered, just like that, by the Russians suddenly dropping the bomb.

"You gotta look out for yourself in this world. You can't worry about everybody else. I have a bad feeling about this, Mildred. They're not going to stop with arresting just Julius Rosenberg."

"What do you mean?"

He shrugged. "Everyone is so afraid. The

Russians have the bomb now. We're at war with Korea. The House Un-American Activities Committee is looking into so many supposed communists, and that Senator McCarthy keeps talking about all the spies in the State Department, changing his mind about how many of them there are. The government needs to look like they're doing something or else how will everyone sleep at night?" He sighed. "What do I know? I don't know," he said. "Listen to me. I'm just an old man talking."

"You're not that old," I said, though I worried about the tense lines around his eyes, the way his hands shook a little bit as he wrapped my chickens in brown paper.

He handed the chickens across the counter. "I'm just saying, Mildred. You're such a nice girl. You've always wanted to help everybody else. You do such a good job with your boys." He said all these things about me as if they were fact, as if everyone knew and believed them, not just him. He patted David on the head. "But if you have to choose between helping your friend and saving yourself, you save yourself, you understand me? You save yourself."

"Don't worry," I told him, and I knew he wouldn't hate me if I left with Jake. And that if my mother did, maybe he would help her understand that it was what I had to do. "Really." I squeezed his hand. "I'll be fine, okay? And if Dr. Zitlow comes back, you'll tell him I got his message?"

He frowned a little, but then he agreed. I put the wrapped chickens into the carriage, and then I grabbed David's hand and we walked back to Knickerbocker Village.

Back on the eleventh floor, I knocked on Ethel's door and this time John answered. He stared at me and then held out his small hands as if Ethel had told him to take the chicken without saying a word to me. I bent down and put the brown package in his hands. "Does your mother need anything else?" I asked.

"Johnny, shut the door!" I heard Ethel yelling from the kitchen, where I guessed she was cleaning.

'It's okay," I said to him just before he did what Ethel asked and shut the door. "Everything is going to be okay."

In my apartment, I read Jake's letter again, and I wondered where I could find the evidence he needed. After I laid the boys down for their naps, I searched the kitchen cabinets, not quite sure what I was looking for. I pulled out Ed's half-empty bottle of vodka, but, behind it, there was another full one. I quietly rifled through his bureau drawers but found only clothes, then looked under couch cushions, between the pages of an old copy of the *New York Times* on the coffee table. But I found nothing of any consequence. If Ed had anything that might incriminate him, I didn't think it was in our apartment.

I stopped searching as I began to hear noises in the hallway, people walking down the hall. *The press.* They were coming to watch Ethel prepare her chicken. I felt nervous for her and I sat on my couch and lit a cigarette. I closed my eyes as I inhaled and exhaled the smoke, wishing for the moments to pass quickly until Jake sent word again.

In the days that followed, most of what I learned about Julie and Ethel's situation was from other sources. I heard news in worried telephone calls from my mother and Susan, and I read bits on my own in the paper and watched it on the television. Ethel went to visit Julie in jail the Sunday after he was arrested, which I learned when I got onto the elevator as she was getting off, in tears, her face so red it seemed she had been crying for years.

"Ethel," I said, reaching for her arm to embrace her, but she ignored me and walked off the elevator past me.

Mrs. Greenwald, an older woman who lived down the hall, stepped onto the elevator with me only after Ethel had slammed her apartment door shut. "It's better we shouldn't be seen on the elevator with her, eh?" Mrs. Greenwald cocked her eyebrows at me. "I waited to make sure she was gone before I came on."

I pressed my lips tightly together, remembering what Mr. Bergman had told me, not wanting to make my own enemy.

As August came, I learned that there was going to be a grand jury hearing in Julie's case. In the nights after I put the children to bed and the apartment was quiet, I watched the television turned down low, and I began drinking what was left of Ed's vodka. I couldn't even stand the taste of vodka or the way it burned my throat as it went down, but I enjoyed the warmth I felt immediately after — the feeling, at last, that everything could be okay. Maybe that was why Ed had always drunk so much of it.

Ed had been gone so long now that I convinced myself it was possible he'd left us for good. If he was never coming back, he

would never miss all his vodka I was drinking. But deep down, I knew he wouldn't
have left Henry behind for good no matter
what. I hoped and prayed for Julie's ordeal
to be over, for life to go back to normal and
for the FBI to forget all about Knickerbocker Village, but I was pretty sure when
that happened Ed would mysteriously re-
appear, and I could not imagine life here as
it once was, me and Ed, living in this apartment as husband and wife.

The Saturday night before Ethel was called
to testify in front of the grand jury, I stayed
up late, drinking more vodka than usual,
watching a report on television about a
bomber plane that had crashed into a
neighborhood in California, killing and
injuring innocent people. I imagined it
would be like the bomb, coming out of the
sky out of nowhere. And I shuddered at the
idea, and stood up to turn the television
off.

I was dizzy; I'd drunk too much vodka,
and I reached out for the top of the television to steady myself. My hand caught on
something odd, and, once I'd regained my
balance, I ran my hand across the top of the
television again. It felt like a small door built
into the wooden casing surrounding the

television. I turned on the lamp and came back to examine it closer. I tried to pull it open with my fingernail and realized I'd need something stronger, so I grabbed a steak knife from the kitchen and then pried the small door open.

Inside was an envelope. I opened it and unfolded the paper inside it. It was a sketch: large circular objects that were unfamiliar to me. It appeared to be a giant bull's-eye, with numbers — calculations — on the left side.

I held it up to the lamp as if seeing it more clearly would help me understand it better, and I noticed something was written on the back. I turned it over and there, in Ed's very familiar large block handwriting, were the words *For Raymond.* For Raymond? My fingers trembled as I traced the letters. I was still unsteady and I had to sit back down on the couch. Was this what Jake was looking for? Was this the evidence that could show Ed was actually the man the FBI wanted?

I picked up the telephone and quickly dialed the number, that by now, I had memorized. "Tell Dr. Zitlow I found something," I said when the woman picked up.

After I hung up, I wondered if I really had. I wondered if this one piece of paper that

Ed must've hidden in the television could have the ability to change everything.

Two days later, on Monday morning, August seventh, a Western Union man knocked on my door just after the children awoke. As I stood in the hallway, Henry on my hip, and signed for the telegram, I saw Ethel leave her apartment, her boys in tow. She was in a nice dress I hadn't seen before — I wondered if it was new just for this occasion — and she wore one of her spectacular hats, like the one I'd seen her in that first morning I'd met her when she was dashing off to the studio to make her recording for John. I knew from the news reports that she was on her way to testify in front of the grand jury in Julie's case today.

I thought about waving to Ethel or calling out to wish her good luck, but then I thought I better not, especially with the Western Union man standing at my door. And besides, I was still dressed in my nightclothes and had thrown on only a robe to answer the door. She went into the elevator, and I felt a sense of sadness that we couldn't even smile at each other in the hall anymore. That I couldn't even tell her that I was trying to help her.

I looked down at what I was signing for

and remembered the last telegram I'd gotten on the day of Henry's birth. Ed's message, which I'd mistaken for Jake's, and my heart fell at the idea that this was Ed contacting me now as if he intuitively knew about the paper I'd found hidden inside the television on Saturday. But I hadn't seen or heard from Ed since that morning in Mr. Bergman's butcher shop, and my new theory was that he'd run off to Mexico, too, just like Mortie Sobell. And besides, I'd carefully left a message specifically for Jake Saturday night. I was fairly certain that, this time, the telegram was from him. It had to be.

Back inside my apartment, I put Henry down on the floor and opened it up.

MEET ME FRIDAY 4 PM.
DR. ZITLOW

Friday was only a few days away, and there was so much to do. I would need to pack our things and make sure to say a quiet good-bye to my mother and Bubbe Kasha and Mr. Bergman. And . . . Ethel . . . if she would let me. I hoped her grand jury testimony would go well today and that the jury would have no choice but to let Julie go. How couldn't they? Even according to the press, there seemed no real evidence to hold him other than David Greenglass's word.

And on Friday I would bring Jake what I found Saturday night. I hoped it would be what he needed to put this on Ed, wherever he was, and then they'd have to let Julie go no matter what. Ed would be arrested. Julie and Ethel would be free. And then Jake and I would be together. I held the telegram against my chest and exhaled.

26

I woke up on Friday morning feeling lighter than I had in some time. I sat up and smiled, remembering that today was the day my life was going to change. At last. While the children still slept, I walked around the apartment, readying our last-minute things in a suitcase. I thought we wouldn't need much in our simple, beautiful new life in the mountains, and last night I'd packed only the basics: clothes for the children, a few dresses for myself, bottles and formula for Henry, David's communication cars, and, of course, the paper I'd found in the television. I felt paranoid just having it in my possession, and all week I'd felt the overwhelming dread that Ed would choose just now to return for it. Last night I'd even taken the time to draw a duplicate sketch and I'd placed it back in the envelope, back inside the secret compartment in the television, just in case Ed were to come back looking.

Now I stood by the living room window, looking down and watching the tiny men rushing to work on the street below, and I realized this might be the last morning I'd ever have this view. Instead of sadness, I felt relief. I was more than ready to leave Knickerbocker Village, this world in the shadow of the Manhattan Bridge, behind.

I heard a knock at the door. Another telegram from Jake maybe? I ran to the door. Then I thought, *Or from Ed?* And I hesitated for a second before turning the knob and opening the door. I was surprised to find Ethel there on the other side, her face as pale as fresh snow.

"Millie," she said, "I need a favor." She was dressed in a crisp, light blue polka-dot dress and she held on to a pair of white gloves in her hands, wringing them together uneasily as she spoke. "I have to go back to testify before the grand jury again today. And I really need you to watch the boys for me." She looked down at her feet. "I can't take them back to my mother's again. There was so much . . . unpleasantness on Monday."

"I'm sorry." I put my hand on her arm. "Of course I'll watch the boys. It's just . . . I have an . . . appointment later in the afternoon. At four p.m." I didn't say more. I couldn't tell Ethel here, like this, that I might be leaving her forever, or even that I found something that could possibly implicate Ed, because I didn't know what was going to happen yet.

"It shouldn't take that long," she said. "I'm pleading the Fifth Amendment to everything they ask, just like the lawyer said."

"What does that mean?" I asked.

"It means, I'm answering nothing," she said. "It means, this is all a waste of everyone's time." She held her hands up in the air and then let them drop back down. "I wouldn't have anything to tell them even if I did answer."

"I know." I put my hand on her shoulder, and she didn't push me away. The hallway was empty and we were talking softly, so none of the other neighbors could hear us. "I've been following everything in the newspapers. And after this silliness today, they'll have to let Julie go, right?"

"I don't know. It seems they don't have to do anything, Millie." She shrugged. "I've made an appointment for later today with the Jewish Homemakers. For . . . help with the children . . . should Julie not be coming home anytime soon."

"The Jewish Homemakers?" I thought of that odd and frightening woman, Zelda Weiss, whom Ed had called years ago to take David, and I tried to remember if that was the same organization. But Ethel wouldn't give her children away. It had to be something different.

"I need help," Ethel said, sounding apologetic.

I opened my mouth to offer more help, whatever she needed, but I remembered I might not be here past this afternoon. And even if I were going to be here, Ethel probably wouldn't let me help more, that today, it seemed, she was here asking only because she had no other option.

"I can't take the children with me today," she said, "and I can't take them back to my mother's again, I just can't." Tears sprang up in her eyes, and I leaned across the doorway to hug her. I wanted to tell her that everything was going to be fine, to apologize for running away today before her entire ordeal was finished. *But I have to go,* I wanted to say to her. *I have to save myself.* And this piece of paper I had to give to Jake could save her and Julie, too. I was going to help her, I reminded myself. But all I said was "Of course. Bring the children over. I'm happy to watch them this morning."

"You're such a good friend, Millie," she said.

"I'm so sorry this is happening to you. It is isn't right . . ."

She pulled back and wiped away her tears. She stood up a little straighter. " 'A coward dies many times before their death. The valiant never taste of death but once.' " She gave me a half smile. "It's from *Julius Caesar*. It was a line in a play that I was in once when I was still just a girl. Oh, isn't it silly that that's what's running through my head now?"

"No one is going to die," I told her, and she laughed a little, wiped away the rest of her tears, and then she walked down the hallway to collect her boys.

A few minutes later, she was back with John and Richie. I ushered them in, and John raced to turn on the television. Ethel looked past me into the apartment, watching them for a moment. "They'll be fine," I said. "We'll have a nice day."

She pulled her white gloves on her hands and blew a white-gloved kiss as she backed up toward the elevator. I waved in response. I didn't say good-bye to her. I thought I would do that when she came back to pick the children up.

■ ■ ■ ■

After Ethel left, Henry began to cry. I went into the bedroom to pick him up and get him his bottle and I found David just sitting up on his mattress, looking out of sorts. "What is it, darling?" I asked him as I jostled Henry a bit to try to calm him down. Then I remembered I'd packed David's communication cars, and David always reached for them first thing now when he woke up. I walked into the living room to retrieve them from the suitcase.

"Where are you going?" John had turned around and was peering at me over the back of the couch, his eyes wide with suspicion. Richie still faced the television and watched eagerly, sucking his thumb.

"Oh," I said, startled. "Just a little trip with the boys, that's all."

"To Mexico?" John asked. He must've overheard Ethel and Julie talking about the possibility of their trip. I didn't answer him. "I don't think you should go to Mexico. It might not be very safe there," he said. "David could get hurt."

"You don't need to worry," I told him. "We'll be fine."

"Mortie and his family were kidnapped

by bandits just like on *The Lone Ranger.*"

"Oh, were they?" I murmured. I pulled the cars from the suitcase and brought them back to David in the bedroom. His entire body seemed to ease with relief as he took them out of the box and began lining up the reds to show me he was hungry.

"They really were," John said, and I realized he'd followed me back to the bedroom. He sat down on the edge of my bed and stared at me expectantly. He was calmer now that he was seven . . . or maybe now that he'd been in therapy for a little while. He was bigger, too. The babyish look seemed all gone from his face, and I could see the beginning of what he might look like as a man. Something like Julie, only with Ethel's spark thrown in.

"You don't need to worry. We're not going to Mexico," I told him. "We're just taking a short trip," I lied, "that's all." As soon as I said it, I felt bad. I imagined John repeating this conversation some time later to Ethel, her frowning and wondering, *Why didn't she tell me?* But, for now, I pushed the thought away. "Come on," I said, "let's get some breakfast and then we'll go to the playground."

If I thought two children were hard to manage on a walk outside, four were nearly impossible. I had John hold on to David while I held on to Richie and pushed the carriage. Just out on the street, I thought about turning around and going back inside, but I wanted to stop in to see Mr. Bergman. Yesterday, I'd taken the boys to see my mother and Bubbe Kasha, but I hadn't had a chance to visit the butcher shop all week and I couldn't leave the city without saying good-bye.

The shop was crowded this Friday morning, as it always was just before the Sabbath. It occurred to me that I would meet Jake at the Biltmore before the Sabbath came tonight and that I wouldn't need my usual brisket today, that it might be the first time in years, except for when I was in the hospital, that I hadn't observed Shabbat, except for that last night I'd been at the Biltmore with Jake. I'd kept up the weekly ritual on my own even after Ed had left because it seemed important that something should be the same. Tonight would be the end of that something, I thought. I felt vaguely sad until I remembered it would be the beginning of something, too.

As we walked inside the butcher shop and the little bell rang above the glass door, I marveled at how the rest of our neighborhood appeared entirely unchanged today. Julie had been sitting in jail for weeks, Ethel was *testifying* at a grand jury hearing, I'd found what I was pretty sure was evidence that Ed was the real man the FBI wanted and I was about to bring it to Jake, yet all the other women on the Lower East Side bustled about, buying up meat for their Sabbath dinners as they always did.

Mr. Bergman noticed me walking in with all the children and he caught my eye and shook his head a little as if he were saying he didn't want me to come closer, to bring all the children up to the counter, to draw so much attention to myself. He moved his hand in a shooing motion to motion me back toward the street, and I did what he was asking and walked back out.

"What are we doing here?" John complained. "I'm hot." The air was stifling, even for August, but I ignored John's complaint. David noticed a taxicab drive by and tried to run into the street to catch it. I let go of Richie and quickly grabbed David before he could run. I hugged David tightly to my chest, against the sweaty fabric of my dress, and then Mr. Bergman walked outside.

"Bubbelah," he said, and he leaned over and kissed my cheek. I noticed he seemed smaller out here than usual, shorter and frailer now that he was not behind the counter. "He was here this morning," he said.

"Jake was here?" I asked. "I mean, Dr. Zitlow?"

"Who's that?" John asked.

"No one," I said to him.

"No," Mr. Bergman said. "Ed. Ed was here."

"Ed?" Deep down I'd known that Ed was still here, in the city, somewhere. I understood that he wouldn't have possibly gone to Mexico without Henry. But hearing that he was here in the neighborhood still, at Mr. Bergman's shop this morning, made me feel suddenly ill.

"Mildred." Mr. Bergman put his hand my shoulder. "He came to ask me what you've been up to and where you are going."

"Going?" I laughed nervously.

He cocked his head to the side. "Lena told him your mother said that you were going somewhere today with the boys."

"Oh, my mother and her big mouth." When we'd visited her yesterday, I was vague, told her I was considering taking the boys to see an old friend this weekend. She'd assumed I meant going upstate to visit Addie from the factory, and I'd let her rest with that assumption. I hadn't specifically told her not to tell Lena, but it hadn't occurred to me that Lena would be speaking regularly to Ed, when I hadn't seen or heard from him in weeks. Now I felt like such an idiot.

"You *are* going somewhere? For good?" Mr. Bergman said.

"Yes," I said softly. "But you didn't tell Ed that, did you?"

He didn't say anything for a moment, and then he put his hand gently on David's head. "Of course not, I know nothing about that. I told Ed you are up to what you are always up to — being a mother, taking care of your family, no thanks to him."

I leaned in and gave him a quick hug. "I'll miss you," I whispered in his ear. "I'll try to telephone or write."

He stepped back. "Boychik." He kissed David on the head. "You take good care of your mother."

After we left Mr. Bergman, we walked to the playground. I watched the children play, and then I looked around, suddenly having the creeping feeling that I was being watched, that Ed was here — or everywhere. But I saw only some of the other mothers from the neighborhood, who refused to meet my eyes when I looked at them. They all turned and moved to the other end of the playground, pretending not to notice me at all, their eyes and scowls trained steadily on John and Richie.

I wondered how long this would follow them, the notion that their father was an atom spy, that their family was tainted by communism. Even after he was cleared and let go from jail, I wondered how long it would take for these silly women in the neighborhood to forget all the lies they had read and heard and told one another. Ethel and Julie might have to move, too.

After a few hours we made our way back to the eleventh floor. Even John was quiet and seeming rather tired as we walked inside and rode the elevator up. It was nearly two, and I knocked on Ethel's door, figuring that she was most likely already home. I knocked a few times, but she didn't answer.

As we walked back to my apartment, I was beginning to feel anxious. I needed to get out of here and meet Jake at the Biltmore. Four o'clock was coming soon and I wanted to get there early.

I put my boys and Richie down for a nap and turned on the television for John. He stared at it, but I didn't think he was watching because he said to me, without turning to look at me, "Ethel should've been back by now."

"I'm sure she'll be back soon," I murmured. She had to be, after all. How long could this testimony about nothing possibly take? And didn't she say she had an appointment this afternoon with the Jewish Homemakers? Maybe she had left the courthouse and gone straight there. But she knew I had an *appointment* of my own at four. She'd promised she wouldn't be long at all, and I knew she would've come back here for her boys the moment her testimony was over.

At half past three I began to pace my apartment, and then I decided to place a call to the Biltmore and leave a message for Dr. Zitlow that I might be running late and that he should wait for me. Then I tried to telephone Ethel's apartment just in case she'd come back when we were gone after all and had maybe fallen asleep, but there was no answer.

At four I went down the hallway and tried knocking on her door again, but there was no answer then either.

Richie woke up from his nap at four thirty and joined John on the couch. He leaned against his brother and sucked his thumb, and I didn't know what to do. How much longer would Jake wait? And what if he didn't get my message? Ethel had promised that she wouldn't be gone this long. Something felt wrong.

At five o'clock I was certain that court had to be over for the day and I knew I couldn't wait here any longer. "John," I said, "do you know your Grandmother Greenglass's address?"

"Sixty-four Sheriff Street," he said carefully. He frowned, and I wondered exactly what had happened on Monday when Ethel had taken the boys there.

"Your mother is running late. I'm going to have to drop you off there for a little while. The boys and I need to take our trip now. We'll leave a note for your mother on her door and she'll come pick you up at your grandmother's in a bit, all right?"

His small face fell and I expected him to argue, but it seemed he had grown used to disappointment this summer and he quickly grabbed onto his brother, stood, and went to the door. He stretched his shoulders up as if trying to make himself appear taller, older. Then he turned back to look at me. "We're not going to see you anymore, are we, Millie?" he asked quietly.

I didn't correct his manners, but I leaned down and gave him a hug as if that were an answer. Then I woke up David and Henry and quickly gathered our suitcase.

Sheriff Street was just on the other side of Delancey, and as we approached number 64, I noticed the outside of Ethel's mother's tenement building appeared grayer and grimmer than my own mother's. I considered for a moment that maybe I shouldn't leave the boys here to wait for Ethel. But I couldn't take them with me to see Jake today at the Biltmore . . . or wherever we might go after. And besides, Ethel couldn't possibly be much longer. Maybe Julie was being released and that's what the holdup was. In which case, both their mother and father would come for the boys shortly. I'd already waited long enough, and I hoped that Jake had gotten my message, that he was there in the lobby of the Biltmore, waiting for me.

I knocked on the door, and after a few moments Mrs. Greenglass answered. I could see little resemblance to Ethel in her peaked face. None of Ethel's ebullience, her charm, her warmth, appeared to have come from her mother. Mrs. Greenglass caught sight of John and she narrowed her eyes.

"I'm Ethel and Julie's neighbor," I said. "Ethel asked me to watch the boys while she went to court today, but she hasn't come back yet, and I'm afraid I can't keep them any longer. Can you watch them? I'm sure she'll be back soon."

"Eh?" Mrs. Greenglass cocked her head to the side. "I wouldn't be so sure. She refuses to talk. She's going to burn with her good-for-nothing husband."

I quickly rushed to cover Richie's ears, but I wasn't fast enough to avoid him hearing what she said. John looked down at his sneakers, and I noticed he was shuffling his feet together.

I couldn't leave the children here with this woman. I couldn't believe what she had just said in front of them. But she was their grandmother, and what other choice did I have? Ethel would be back soon. This was only for a very short time.

I heard a car pull up on the street behind us and I let go of Richie to instinctively grab for David, whose eyes wandered toward it. I didn't turn to see if it was a taxicab but guessed it was as David's eyes widened. I held on to him tightly so he wouldn't run toward it.

John grabbed ahold of Richie's hand, turned, and looked at me. His gaze was stoic now, the face of a man, and I missed that boy he once was. That boy who played his phonograph too loud and too late. It was as if the FBI had stolen the recklessness of his childhood along with the record his mother had made for him. As if his grandmother's words had instantly transformed him, pushed him, into a maturity he hadn't needed before. John looked away and he turned back to enter his grandmother's house with his brother.

A horrible coldness seeped into my chest, making it hard to breathe. I sensed that Ethel wouldn't want me to leave them here for however short a time. She'd watched David that entire time I was in the hospital after Henry was born and I owed her something. I owed her this much. Her children! As much as I wanted to leave right now, run to the subway and ride it to Grand Central Terminal City to find Jake, maybe I could telephone the Biltmore and tell them to tell him I would meet him later tonight. Or even tomorrow? I ignored Mr. Bergman's voice in my head, reminding me to save myself. Ethel was my friend, and John and Richie were just children. Just sweet, innocent little boys. Ethel would not have abandoned Henry and David, I was certain.

"Wait," I heard myself saying, but Mrs. Greenglass moved to shut the door as if she hadn't heard me. "Wait," I said again, and I began to run toward the door before it closed. But then I felt a hand on my shoulder, pulling me hard, and I stopped to turn around.

"Hello, Mildred," Ed said.

I gasped and tried to pull away from him, but he held on so tightly to my shoulder that it hurt. "What are you doing here?" I tried to keep my voice even, though I could feel myself trembling.

"I went to the apartment and I saw the note you left on Ethel's door." He pointed to the suitcase that I'd left on the ground next to the carriage. "You are taking a trip?" His other hand still held tightly to my shoulder.

"Let go of me," I said, trying to sound strong and certain. But I was sure Ed could hear the trembling in my voice, sense the fear that I felt jumbling my brain. What was going on? Why had Ed gone back to the apartment? Now? Today?

He pulled me closer to him as if we were in a dance. The only time we ever danced together was the night we were married. After the rabbi performed the small ceremony, Lena invited everyone to her cramped apartment, where she played Russian music on the phonograph and insisted Ed and I dance together while she took a photograph.

You will want this to show your grandchildren, she'd insisted, and at the time I'd laughed, thinking the picture would be so schmaltzy I would never want to show it to anyone.

Now I could feel Ed's breath against my neck. He smelled of soap and toothpaste, but I couldn't detect even the slightest smell of vodka. "I've come here to save you," he said.

"Save me?" I tried to suppress a laugh but couldn't quite, and it came out as a strangled cry in my throat.

"Ethel has been arrested."

"Arrested? I don't believe you."

"It's the truth," Ed said evenly.

"Arrested for what reason?" I still didn't believe him. He was lying. He was a liar. Ethel had said so herself, hadn't she?

"I don't know," Ed said. "For being married to Julius."

"That makes no sense," I said.

"As soon as I heard I came back to the apartment to save you, but you had already left."

"Came back from where?" I demanded. "Where have you even been all this time?"

"I told you," he said, his voice remaining calm and even, "getting us a future. Staying safe." He hesitated. "Until today, I thought you would be safer here without me. But they arrested Ethel to get Julius to talk. And they will do the same for you."

"What?" I could not make sense of what Ed was saying. "But he has nothing to say. Neither does she. And I certainly don't." I felt blood rushing to my brain as I thought about the paper from the television that I'd copied the other night. Did that make me guilty of something I didn't even quite understand?

"Do you think they care?" Ed's breath was warm on my neck, and he was suddenly breathing hard, but it made me feel chilled, feeling it against my skin, so close like that. "What do you think Jake is planning to do to you if you go to meet him now?"

"I don't know what you mean," I said as if I had no idea who Jake was, but I could hear my own ragged breathing now. How could Ed know? My mother had no idea, so there was no way she'd shared that with Lena.

"I know you've been talking to him recently. Maybe you even think you've become *friends* with him. Jake is good at playing games, no?" He laughed a little, but I kept my lips pressed tightly together and glanced at Henry. From the way he spoke, so casually and calmly, I was fairly certain Ed knew much less than he thought he did. "But he has been on me — on both of us — from the beginning. He can't have me, so he now he is trying to get you." I was unwilling to process or believe what Ed was saying.

"You're wrong," I said. "I don't even know what you're talking about."

"Okay," Ed said. "I hear the FBI chatter that a woman has been calling for Jake from a party line in Knickerbocker Village. It's you or Ethel, and Ethel is in jail and you are standing here with a suitcase." He was breathing hard, almost as if he'd been running, even though he was just standing here next to me. "You are just a pawn in his little game. Just like Ethel." He finally let me go, so suddenly that I stumbled back and grabbed onto the carriage to steady myself. Henry began to cry, as my grabbing hold shook the carriage, and David stared at Ed, his eyes so wide it looked as though he might burst. "He has been after us the whole time," Ed repeated.

"And why should he be after us?" I asked. "What have you done?"

Ed hesitated for another moment, and I thought he was going to tell me the truth, tell me everything. Then he said, "The less you know, the better. But you have to trust me on this, Mildred. Jake will arrest you."

"No." I shook my head, back and forth

and back and forth, as if I could shake away the words Ed said. Ed couldn't know what he was talking about. Jake *was* after Ed, he'd admitted that to me. But Jake loved me and David. And he would love Henry, too. He wanted us to be together. I thought about the paper tucked so carefully in my suitcase. I would give it to Jake, and he would make sure that Julie and Ethel — if Ed was even telling the truth — were let go. He'd make sure Ed was arrested for all of this.

I remembered Ethel's warning: *You can't trust Jake,* she'd said. *Trust no one but yourself.* The words echoed uneasily in my head now. Could I trust Jake? I wanted to so very badly. Jake had promised me that night in the Catskills that what we had done wasn't a lie. But had he really meant it?

"I've got us a car," Ed said, pointing toward the street, "a Fleetmaster. Very reliable. We'll get in it and drive over the bridge tonight into New Jersey. I have found us a very nice house, with very nice new names to live under, until this all blows over."

"I'm not getting in the car," I said. "And I don't need a new name."

"I am only trying to help you, Mildred. All I have ever wanted to do is to help you."

That was a lie, too. I felt sure it was. But

428

before I could say anything else, I heard a terrible sound from inside Ethel's mother's house, a scream like the cries of the feral cats that lived in the alley off Delancey Street, only louder, more horrible, and it seemed to be in John's voice.

I grabbed David and ran back up to the door, and I knocked, then banged, on the door until finally Mrs. Greenglass opened it again. "You are still here?" She scowled at me.

"I think I should take the children with me," I said breathlessly. "I'll keep them until Ethel gets back." I didn't turn to look at Ed, though I swore I could feel his eyes on my back, an added heat to the humid night air.

"Ethel won't be coming back," Mrs. Greenglass said matter-of-factly. "She's just called. She was arrested on her way back from testimony today." She leaned in closer and she smelled like cabbage, and I had the sense she'd been in the middle of cooking dinner before I'd come here. Life was normal and then suddenly it wasn't. "If I were you, I would run away from here and never look back. You don't want nothing to do with my daughter and her lousy husband. You should pretend that you never even met them."

Before I could protest, she slammed the door in my face. I felt Ed's hand on my shoulder, gentler this time.

I turned. He had taken Henry out of his carriage and he was holding on to him, rocking him almost sweetly. So Ed was right when he'd said Ethel was arrested. Was Ed telling the truth about Jake, too? Was Jake really waiting at the Biltmore to arrest me, not take me away from all this? And if he was, what should happen to David and Henry?

I walked back down the steps and looked up at Ed, still holding Henry. "Are you an atomic spy?" I asked, my voice quiet but steady now, resigned to know the truth.

"Things are much more complicated than that." He rocked Henry a little more. He stroked Henry's cheek gently. "I am Russian. I was born in Russia. You always knew that about me."

"But you wanted to come to America so badly," I said. "You're American now."

"I am," he said. "But that doesn't mean America having so much power in the world doesn't scare me. That doesn't mean I don't have certain loyalties to where I came from."

"The KGB?" I asked.

"Mildred," he said. "Please. Just get in the car."

David yanked on my arm, and I turned and looked at him. Though he was almost five, he suddenly seemed so small. What would happen to him if there was a chance Ed was right? What would happen to him should I have to go to jail?

My heart pounded so furiously and tears welled up in my eyes, making it hard to see, but I felt myself following Ed to the street.

The dusk came as we drove. The Sabbath began as Ed maneuvered the Fleetmaster across the bridge, leaving the lights and the bustle of the city behind us, maybe forever. And I wouldn't let myself turn around and watch it all disappear. I wouldn't let myself think about Jake waiting for me in the lobby of the Biltmore or about the possibility that Ed was right. That Jake wasn't waiting there to run away with me but to question me or use me or even arrest me. Instead, I thought about what Ethel had said to me this morning, that line she remembered from her play — about a coward dying many times — and it felt like I was dying as I left the city behind.

Henry fell asleep in my arms, and I turned around to the backseat, where David was sleeping, too. Again I thought about what would happen to them if I were not with

431

them. Would they go live with my mother and Bubbe Kasha the way I'd just taken John and Richie to Mrs. Greenglass's? Would Susan offer to take them? Henry? Maybe . . . But David? No. Ed, or probably any one of them, would lock David away in some sort of facility. They would never awaken in him what I knew was in there. What Jake knew was in there.

Jake. I didn't believe he could possibly be waiting there at the Biltmore to arrest me.

Just on the other side of the bridge, I asked Ed to stop the car, to turn it around, to go back. "I think I've made a mistake," I cried out.

"We can never go back now, Mildred," Ed said, and then he kept on driving, into New Jersey, into the darkness.

June 19, 1953

"I waited for you all night when Ethel was arrested," Jake says. He has taken the crumpled piece of paper from my hand and now he examines it closely, trying to hold it up to the minimal light in the very bare room he has led me to. He grimaces when he seems to notice the dried blood, but he doesn't comment on that.

The room is empty but for the two of us, and we sit across a metal table, not meeting each other's eyes. "I sat in the lobby of the Biltmore until six a.m. the next morning," he says. "I was worried something terrible had happened to you."

"I didn't know what to do," I say. "Ed came for me. And I didn't know if I could trust you."

"And what? You trust me now?" He folds the piece of paper back up and hands it back to me.

"Should I?" I ask. "Trust you?"

433

Jake leans in closer and under his breath murmurs, "You have a crude sketch of the atomic bomb. You have no way to prove who drew it. It could've been you, for all I know."

I remember how easy it was for me to copy the drawing and I bite my lip. But this one is real. "It wasn't," I say. "And turn it over. Look on the back." He does, and he holds it close to his face, reading the words in Ed's handwriting — *For Raymond.* "Ed wrote that. That's Ed's handwriting," I say. "This proves he —"

He puts a finger to his lips and moves closer to my ear so I can feel his breath on my neck as he whispers, "Proving one person's guilt does not prove another's innocence. The only thing you will do with this is get yourself arrested. Hell, I should arrest you right now." He pulls back, stares at me hard, his features stoic, unmoving, and I think he might really do it here after all this time. Ed was right back when we left the city — Jake would have arrested me.

I hold my arms up in the air as if to surrender "Go ahead, then," I say defiantly, daring him to.

He moves his hands a little as if he's going to reach for me. But then he seems to think better of it and he stops himself. "I'm going to walk you back out to your car now.

I want you to get in, turn around, and drive back to New Jersey. Go home to your husband and your children."

"You knew I was in New Jersey?"

"Of course I knew." He laughs drily.

"And you didn't come to find me?"

"I didn't think you wanted me to," he says.

"But you could've come and arrested Ed . . . and me. It's been three years," I say.

He folds his hands together on the table and looks down at them. "The Rosenbergs were found guilty. They refused to talk or implicate anyone . . ." I think of that terrible day in the spring of 1951 when I learned the outcome of the trial. Until then, I kept telling myself they would be found innocent and that I'd go back to the city, to Knickerbocker Village, and I'd tell Ethel how sorry I was for leaving the boys at her mother's, for leaving her. I would invite them all to come stay in New Jersey with us, where no one knew who we really were, where no one bothered anyone else. But of course that never happened, and now I feel like a fool. "We had no more evidence on anyone else," Jake is saying. "No reason to keep looking for anyone else."

"So what are you even doing here now?" I ask.

"We've got men waiting with an open line

directly to Mr. Hoover should there be any last-minute confessions." He looks down at my paper, then back up, at me. "That's probably the only thing that could stop this now. And even that . . . I don't know."

"But Ethel has nothing to confess." I throw up my hands, urgently wanting him to realize what we need to do. "And I'm here. Confessing, aren't I? Call Mr. Hoover and let him know that."

Jake puts his finger to his lips again. "Millie." His eyes look just the way I remember them still, the way they looked that night in Phoenicia in the cabin. "You need to go home to your children. You need to burn this piece of paper. You need to forget all about the Rosenbergs."

"I can't," I say. I try to bite back tears that have been so long coming. I close my eyes, picturing the muted curves of David's face, the soft feel of Henry's curls against my arm. I remember the last thing I ever said to Ethel as she stood in my doorway in Knickerbocker Village. That no one was going to die. "I want to see Ethel," I tell him. "I'm not leaving here until I see Ethel."

1951–1952
27

In New Jersey, our only neighbors were cornfields as far as the eye could see. It was the country, the noiseless air I'd wanted for David, and yet for a little while David refused to go outside his small, windowless bedroom. Even after Ed left us again for a few weeks to go back to the city, to *tie up loose ends,* he said, I had a hard time getting David to come out of his room even to eat.

Then the corn was harvested, and there was so much of it I was cooking corn for weeks. Bright yellow kernels that brought a reluctant David back to the dinner table again.

I often considered telephoning Jake at the number I'd memorized, especially when Ed was back in the city. We didn't have a telephone in the house, but there was one at the general store in the small nearby town. I could walk there with the children on a nice day and I could use the telephone for a dime. I used it once to call Mr. Bergman and tell him that we were safe, and I asked him to let my mother and Susan know we were all right despite Ed's warnings before he left to not contact anyone.

Months had passed, but I still asked Mr. Bergman, "Has Dr. Zitlow been back to look for me?" I tried to keep my voice light so he wouldn't understand the weight of what I was asking and become worried about me.

"No," Mr. Bergman said, "Mr. Zitlow hasn't been here." He lowered his voice. "But there have been some FBI men here, asking questions."

"What kind of questions?" I asked.

"About you, and about Ed. Where you are. How well you know the Rosenbergs." He coughed a little and cleared his throat. "I didn't have anything to tell them. I know nothing." I tried to imagine it, and the thought of these FBI men there, pestering Mr. Bergman, made me think, in some deep place in my heart, that maybe Ed was right, that all Jake had been interested in that night was arresting me, too.

"If I send you a letter," I said quietly, my mouth close to the receiver, "can you keep

it safe for me until I might need it someday?"

"I would do anything for you, bubbelah,"
he said. "You know I would."

Ed returned after a month away, in March
1951, with a ragged-looking Lena and the
television set from our apartment in Knickerbocker Village. I wondered if he'd checked
the secret compartment and noticed the
slight differences in the paper I'd put in his
envelope, but he didn't say anything to me
about it so I guessed he hadn't, that he
believed everything was just as he'd left it.
I'd already sent the real paper in a letter to
Mr. Bergman, and, anyway, I was just happy
to have the television again and be recon-
nected to the world just as Ethel and Julie's
trial was wrapping up.

Until then, I'd followed the trial by walking to the general store and buying the local
paper. Removed from the city, I couldn't
help but feel the news was watered down.
But from what I could tell, both Ethel and
Julie, and Mortie Sobell, were accused of
conspiracy to commit espionage, which
sounded to me like a fancy way of saying a
whole lot of nothing. The prosecutor, a man
by the name of Irving Saypol, claimed that
Ethel and Julie conspired to get weapons to

the Soviets, weapons which could destroy us all. There seemed to be very little evidence, other than David and Ruth Greenglass's testimony that Julie passed information and that Ethel helped by typing up notes. Ethel had been so sure that Julie hadn't been involved, when we'd spoken in the elevator, that I knew even if there was the smallest chance he had been, she most certainly had not had anything to do with espionage. She had never typed up notes like that, and I felt it was so obvious her brother was lying. I wondered what was more painful for her, to be accused of such terrible things — to be *on trial,* to be away from her children, to have her husband accused and in peril — or the fact that her brother had betrayed her so. The thought of being away from my children for days felt unbearable, much less for months, and I imagined that was the worst of it for Ethel. That was worse than anything.

After the arrival of the television, I turned it on and watched the news unfold, so close and so real, right there. It was unusually cold for the end of March, and the tiny house did not have the steam heat we'd grown accustomed to in Knickerbocker Village. I sat wrapped in a blanket, shivering, the television on all day. Henry was crawling, and he made circles around the tiny house, while David stacked dried corn ears and pennies in lieu of the blocks I'd left behind in our apartment.

On March 28, 1951, the trial ended at last. On the television, in grainy black and white, I saw Julie and Ethel being led out of the courthouse, holding on to each other tightly as they were plunged into the bitter cold. Someone ripped them apart, and Ethel appeared to cry out to stop them. I put my hand up to the television, wishing I could push them closer, back together, just like that. But I felt only heat and static and I pulled my hand away. I thought about the paper I'd found hidden in this television and how I might go now to the city and get it back from Mr. Bergman. I wanted to help Ethel so badly, but I glanced at David, stacking his pennies in silence, and I knew I couldn't risk it.

The next day, everything happened so quickly. The jury came back, and then it was announced that they were all found guilty. My hands shook and I started to cry.

Ed and Lena were sitting on the couch and had been watching with me. Lena was unusually quiet, and even when the verdict was announced by the newscaster, she only looked up from her knitting for a moment, looked at Ed, and then looked back down. Ed drained his glass of vodka and put it down on the table. "At least it is over now," he said. "Ethel will be shown leniency. They won't do anything to a woman. A mother. She'll be free in a week," he said.

"And Julie?" I said bitterly.

Ed didn't answer me, and he stood and turned off the television.

A week later, the newscasters read Judge Irving Kaufman's sentence with stoic faces. I began watching with the hope that Ed was wrong and that *both* Julie and Ethel would be let go, that this would all be over. And then I began to listen to what it was Irving Kaufman said, what Ethel had heard him say to her, somewhere across the bridge, inside the bleak courtroom. *A crime worse than murder . . . Ethel knew what she was doing . . . Julius and Ethel Rosenberg . . . sentenced to death.*

The valiant never taste of death but once, Ethel had said.

No one is going to die, I told her.

"You have to stop this," I turned to Ed and said in agony.

"Me?" Ed sucked on his cigar and looked down at his feet. "And what do you think I should do that would stop this?"

"You know the truth about what really happened, don't you? You work for the FBI . . . or the KGB. You can come forward and tell them the truth."

"You should want *me* to come forward?" Ed said. "And what do you think they would do to you?"

Lena grimaced at her knitting needles. "You would not last one day in jail, Mildred. You are much too soft."

I opened my mouth to protest, but then Henry crawled up to the couch and pulled himself up to stand, wanting me eagerly to pick him up. I pulled him into my lap and put my face into his sweet baby curls.

Lena was wrong. Jail didn't scare me. Not being here to take care of Henry and David did.

In the little house in the cornfield, Henry turned one and began to walk and chatter and utter nonsense words. David turned six and stayed shrouded in silence. In the summer he spent hours in the backyard, watching the crows fly over the cornfields, and I remembered the way he looked in the rowboat in Phoenicia. I couldn't help but think it wasn't the country air that had helped him at all but rather the presence of Jake.

I often thought about John and Richie, living with their unforgiving grandmother on Sheriff Street. Later, I would learn that they were there only a short time until she gave them away, first to an orphanage, then to their other grandmother. I'd like to think if I'd known what was to come, I would've gone back to the city to rescue them, to bring them out here to live with us. I'd like to think I never would've taken them to Sheriff Street at all, that I would've taken them with us from the start and taken care of them. I liked to think I would've done the right thing just once. But I had no idea what would happen to Ethel. It was unimaginable to me back then.

For months, though, I had nightmares about Ethel's children. Especially John.

In my dreams, I kept seeing him walking around Monroe Street, all bundled up in his old brown winter coat but without any shoes. Without his mother there, he'd forgotten to put them on. Or someone had forgotten to buy them for him.

When winter came again and snow fell upon the corn, there were appeals to the higher courts. All denied.

I thought so often about the paper I'd sent to Mr. Bergman that very well could implicate Ed, but I felt he was right that it would somehow implicate me, too. I couldn't let them take me away from David and Henry the way they'd taken Ethel away from John and Richie. I couldn't bear the thought and so I kept quiet, living in the cornfield, protecting my children, listening to Lena complain about David, listening for Ed coming to bed at night. There was no Planned Parenthood out here in the middle of nowhere and, luckily, I'd packed my diaphragm that night when I left. I couldn't imagine finding myself with more children, all the way out here, all alone.

At the end of December 1952, the papers reported that Ethel's and Julie's death sentences had been handed down. They were set to die in three weeks.

And then there was another stay and they weren't. Their deaths came and went, something unreal, something that began to seem like little more than a threat.

I never thought it would actually happen.

June 19, 1953

"It's too late to see Ethel now," Jake says. He stands and puts his arms on my shoulders to move me toward the door. "Ethel can't have any more visitors." He lowers his voice, and he stops pushing me forward to hold on to me. It feels something like a hug, and it still gives me warmth the way it always did when Jake touched me.

"She can't die," I say. "I should've come sooner. I should've brought you this that night years ago."

Jake moves his arms back to his sides. "Ed was right," he says, "I would've arrested you if you had shown me this back then. I would have had no choice."

"I don't believe you," I say, because now that he has stood so close again, now that I have given him a chance to turn me in again and he hasn't taken it, I think he's lying just to get me to leave. "You never would've taken me away from my children,

446

would you?"

Jake looks down, refusing to meet my eyes. "How are they? How's Henry? And David?" The way he says their names, the way his voice is soft and still filled with kindness, I know my instinct is right, and I hate myself for knowing this so solidly only now. When it is too late.

"They're gone," I say softly. "I thought I was saving the children by leaving with Ed. But I wasn't."

"What do you mean *gone*?" he asks. "Where are the children now?"

"I don't want to talk about it," I say. I can't tell him what has happened. I can't. "Where are John and Richie?" I ask. "Are they here?"

His face turns as if I've hurt him by not answering his question about my boys, but he still gives me an answer to my question. "No, they were here earlier. Now they're in New Jersey. With friends."

"Will Julie be with her?" I ask. "Will they get to die together? As they lived," I add.

"No," Jakes says slowly. "Julie will be executed first. Then Ethel."

The word *executed* sounds so cold and calculated, as if he's already accepted it and moved on. But I don't understand how the Jake I once knew possibly could. "Ethel should have a friend with her," I say. "She shouldn't die alone. There should be a witness here who loves her." As I say the words, it's as if I've understood them for the first time. *Ethel is going to die.* For no good reason. For nothing. There is nothing I can do or say now to stop it. Maybe Jake is right and there is nothing I could've done or said all along. I've held on to this stupid paper and Ed's guilt. I've let go of my children. All for nothing.

Jake doesn't say anything for a few moments, and then he says, "I'll get you a press credential. If anyone asks, you're with the *Times.*"

"A woman here, covering this for the *Times?*"

"Don't worry," Jake says, "no one will ask. No one will notice you. Everyone's eyes will be focused on her."

In the end, Ethel is led into the room where she will die in a thin green prison dress and prison slippers. I want to call out for her, to tell her that I'm here. Much too late. But still, I want to tell her that I know that she's innocent. That I understand that she has tried so very hard to do the best for her children. That none of this is her fault. But we have been instructed not to speak, and a forbidding sign over the door reads *Silence.* It feels as if it were directed just at me — harshly.

Two women lead Ethel in, and she leans up to kiss one on the cheek before they cover her eyes. She doesn't look at the people watching, sitting here on the hard wooden benches. She doesn't see me. She doesn't know I'm here. As I watch them strap Ethel in, I find myself paralyzed, unable to move.

The jolt of electricity seems to come fast, to be over quickly. Just like that. They move her dress a little, put a stethoscope to her chest, and then the doctor shakes his head and they began to reattach all the electrodes to her all over again. "What's happening?" I whisper to Jake, forgoing the instruction of silence for an answer.

"She didn't die," he whispers back. "The normal amount of electricity didn't seem to kill her."

I begin to shake as if I were out in the snow without a coat on, though I'm also sweating. It's so hot in here. But I keep my eyes straight ahead, trained on Ethel's face. I think I know what's in her mind, in her thoughts, in her final moments. She's with them again, John and Richie. Maybe John is playing the phonograph much too loud and

Ethel is holding on to Richie, dancing across her living room, singing along. I imagine her singing her Italian love song to Julie.

They jolt her again, and I close my eyes and picture her singing there, at her piano in her apartment. I hear her voice pitched with joy and happiness.

When I open my eyes again, smoke is funneling from her head, whispering toward the ceiling, the skylight up above.

The world outside Sing Sing is just as loud and as steamy as it was when I entered, though now I watch one of the men who'd witnessed Ethel's death standing out front, recounting to reporters what we'd just seen. *Ethel has met her maker,* I hear him say, *and now she has a lot of explaining to do.*

I want to run through the crowd and scream at him how wrong he is, to tell him that it is only people like him who have the explaining to do. The people who let this happen. Everyone who knew better and didn't come forward. *Like me.* Everyone who might have stopped this before it got away from them. *Like Jake.* Everyone who was guilty of something real. *Like Ed.*

Jake hears the man talking, too, and it's as if he can sense my thoughts because he holds on tighter to my arm, unwilling to let me run or do anything too crazy. He leads me through the crowds, back out to the road, where I'd left the Fleetmaster stalled in a long line, and when we reach the car I stop walking.

My entire body feels numb, my skin impenetrable. I no longer feel the heat or smell the dank water of the Hudson. All I can see is the smoke, all I can smell is burning flesh, all I can hear is the sound of a body crunching against gravel.

"Millie?" Jake says. His voice sounds strange, far away and alarmed all at once. He is bent down in front of the Fleetmaster as if sizing up the damage to the front fender. I lean down, too, and see what he sees: blood. "Did you hit a deer on the way up here?"

"A deer? No," I say very quietly. "Not a deer."

1953
28

Ed returned from one of his many trips to the city for what he called meetings. I imagined him there on East Sixty-first Street meeting with the KGB, so obviously in front of the FBI's noses. One day they would arrest him, I thought, and he wouldn't come back here. And maybe then we would be free. Or maybe the FBI would come for me, too. I had a plan to grab the children, to run into the cornfields and hide. Maybe it was a silly plan, but I felt better practicing it in my head, imagining how fast I could grab them both and where, exactly, I would run into the maze of corn to lose them. But Ed always came back and the FBI never did.

Tonight, he made his way back into the small house, and he walked into David and Henry's room, where I was already sleeping on the floor. I slept here often now to avoid him in the bed we were supposed to share.

He startled me awake by pushing on my shoulder, and I jumped up in the darkness, awakening from a dream about Ethel trapped in the women's death house at Sing Sing with no way out. Every time she was supposed to die, there was another appeal, another chance. Now Supreme Court Justice Douglas had granted a stay of execution, and I'd gone to sleep with the feeling that, finally, there was going to be good news. Ethel was going to be set free.

"Mildred," Ed said. "Wake up. Come with me."

I sat up, rubbed my eyes, and tried to focus. My back was sore from lying on the floor, but I stretched and stood and followed him into the living room. "What's going on?" I asked.

"Get dressed," he said. "We are going to the city."

"The city?" I felt confused and wondered for a moment if I was dreaming. "But the children are sleeping."

"My mother will watch them," he said. I wasn't going to leave David and Henry with Lena. He leaned in closer to me. "Your grandmother has died, Mildred. Your mother is asking for you. The funeral is in the morning. You cannot miss that."

"Bubbe Kasha?" I hadn't seen her for

nearly three years, and even the last time I saw her, she hadn't seemed well. But still, I'd imagined her living forever, sitting there in my mother's small apartment, on the couch with her senseless knitting needles. Now I understood I would never see her again. I began to cry.

"Come with me," Ed said. He put his hand on my shoulder. "I'll take you to say good-bye."

"I'll wake the children up," I said, though even as I said the words I dreaded the thought of dragging them out of slumber now and taking them into such sadness.

"Let them sleep. They'll be fine," Ed said. "They will sleep for a while longer, and you'll be back just after the funeral by lunchtime tomorrow. They are in the middle of nowhere out here. They couldn't be safer."

Ed was right. There was nothing here, no dangers of taxicabs for David to chase after as in the city. And as much as I disliked Lena, I knew that she was capable of watching them for at least a few short hours.

"But is it even safe for us to go back into the city now?" I said, though I couldn't imagine not being there for Bubbe Kasha's funeral even if it wasn't safe.

"You will be fine," Ed said with what

seemed to be a new confidence. I wondered if he knew something I didn't. Or maybe it was just the sound of a terrible relief in his voice, the feeling that whatever he'd done he truly believed now that he'd gotten away with it.

Ed dropped me off on Delancey Street and he promised to return before noon. "You're not staying?" I asked, and he said he couldn't, that he had more business to attend to in the city. As I watched him drive away, I felt strange and out of sorts here all alone without Henry and David.

I found my mother's door unlocked, as it always was, and as I stepped back into her apartment it was as if nothing had changed, as if no time had passed at all. Even the smells of chicken fat and grease lingered in the air as if they had hung here through every Sabbath since I'd left.

I walked to the small lamp on the table and pulled the chain to turn it on.

"Mishe?" a familiar voice said. "Honey, is that you?"

I turned, and Bubbe Kasha was lying on the couch, her face in a smile at the sight of me. "Mishe," she said again, mistaking me for my mother.

I rushed to her. "I thought you were . . ."

I didn't let myself say the word. She looked smaller than I remembered. Her frame was frailer, but I could hear her breath catching in her chest, the breath of an old, but very alive, woman.

My mother ran out from the bedroom, wrapping her robe around her chest. I noticed that she had grown so much older-looking in the past three years: her hair had gone completely gray, her double chin had folded over once more into another layer. "Oh, Mildred," she said, "you've come back to us."

And that's when I realized what I'd done. Ed had lied to me as he lies to everyone. Ed was a liar. I'd left the children. I'd left them all alone with Ed and Lena.

Mr. Bergman's butcher shop hadn't changed much in the past three years, though it was virtually empty when I walked inside. I wondered if business had slowed or if just today, this early in the morning, it was slow.

"Bubbelah," Mr. Bergman exclaimed when he saw me walk through the door, and I noticed his hands and jowls shook constantly now when he talked. He, too, was older. "Where are the boychiks?"

"I've ruined everything!" I cried out, and

then I couldn't stop myself from breaking into tears.

"Bubbelah?" Mr. Bergman put his shaky hand on my shoulder and pulled me into a hug. "I'm very sorry about your friend, Mrs. Rosenberg," he whispered into my ear.

I pulled back and wiped at my tears, realizing that that's why Mr. Bergman thought I was crying. "There's been a stay by a Supreme Court justice," I said. "I think Ethel might be set free this time."

"No, Mildred. Not anymore. It was thrown out today. I just heard it on the radio."

"No, not again."

"I'm afraid so," Mr. Bergman said.

I took a deep breath, and I thought about why I was here, in the city now. The way Ed had lied to me. The way Ed had always lied to me, been cruel to me, ruined the lives of people I loved. And I knew what I needed to do. "Do you have that letter I sent you?" Mr. Bergman nodded, and he walked into the back. He came back a moment later with the envelope, still unopened, and I took it from him and stuffed it in my purse.

"You are not going to do anything stupid, are you, bubbelah?"

"I'm just going to do what I should've done years ago."

■ ■ ■ ■

Ed returned to my mother's house just before noon. Just as he said he would. I felt I was going insane waiting for him, pacing by the door, until my mother put her hand on my shoulder and asked me not to wear her floor out. "Everything will work out the way it's supposed to," she said to me. "You'll see." I didn't tell her that nothing worked out the way it was supposed to, that her old expression was lost on me now.

I didn't want to wait for Ed. I wanted to hire a taxi to drive me back to the house, the children, as soon as possible. But the truth was, I didn't think I'd know how to get back there on my own. And anyway, I didn't have the money to hire a taxi for such a long ride.

I was relieved when I saw the Fleetmaster pull back up at last, just as he'd promised. And I wondered if maybe I'd been wrong about Ed's intentions, if all of this was just a silly stupid mistake and my fears for the boys were overblown.

"You were wrong about Bubbe Kasha," I said as I got into the car, hoping that Ed would be as surprised as I was.

"Was I?" Ed asked, seeming unconcerned.

"Well then," he said, "you should be grateful you got to spend some time with her. She is getting old, no?" His voice sounded like a threat.

"Are the children okay?" I asked him.

"Of course they are okay," Ed answered.

We didn't talk anymore as he drove over the bridge, and then the city roads turned into empty, winding country ones. I paid attention this time just in case I might ever need to get back here on my own from the city.

At last we found the middle of nowhere, the certain end of the earth. Ed pulled over and stopped the car right in front of the tiny, ugly house we now thought of as home.

I got out of the car and ran inside the house before Ed even turned off the engine. "David!" I called out as I entered. "Henry!"

The house was dark and felt unusually still, and I closed my eyes and I sunk to the floor. I noticed the television was on as if someone had rushed out of here in a hurry and had forgotten to turn it off. Ed? Or Lena and the children? I imagined David kicking as Lena pulled him away. And I remembered that day when she yelled at him so harshly. She didn't understand him at all. She wouldn't be able to keep him safe. She might not even want to.

"There is something we need to discuss, Mildred." Ed had walked into the house behind me. He put his hands under my arms and pulled me back up to standing. He pulled me close against him, and his breath felt hot on my neck. I struggled to get away from him, but he twisted my arm back behind me. "Mildred, are you listening to me?"

"Where are the children?" I asked, my voice sounding much calmer than I felt. "You told me they were okay. You lied."

Ed pulled my arm tighter, and I let out a little cry. "It seems we each have something the other wants," he said.

"Where are the children?" I repeated.

"Where is the real paper?" Ed countered.

"I don't know what you mean," I said, the thought that it was now inside my purse and not safe at Mr. Bergman's terrifying me a little. I wondered how long Ed had known.

He twisted my arm harder. "I would not give you so much credit. Not only did you steal from me but you tried to cover it up."

"You're not making any sense," I said, though I felt a nervous heat rising up my neck, my face.

"You are the only one who could have that paper, Mildred. You are the one who copied it and tried to fool me. My mother searched through all of your things here and she could not find it."

"Lena searched through my things?" I imagined her thin fingers poking into my stuff and imagined the look on her face as she'd come across the diaphragm. "Well, then, you know I don't have it," I said defiantly.

"What I know is, you are lying to me." Then he dropped my arm suddenly, and I shook it a little to ease the shooting pain running straight down my wrist and through to my fingers. "If you should not hide something here, I asked myself, where would you hide it? At your mother's house? With that crazy butcher you like so much?"

It frightened me a little the way Ed seemed to know me better than I thought, better than I ever knew him. I opened my mouth to protest, but suddenly Ethel's and Julie's pictures flashed on the television screen and I reached across Ed to turn up the volume. "The Supreme Court Special Session has denied Justice Douglas's stay of execution," the newscaster read from his paper and then looked at the camera. "The Rosenbergs will die tonight at eight p.m. at the death house at Sing Sing Prison, shortly before the Jewish Sabbath begins."

"Tonight?" I cried out. "No, they

can't . . ." Ed turned the television off and grabbed my arms again and pushed me up against the wall. "Why do you want this paper of yours so badly?" I asked Ed. "Why now? Julie and Ethel are already going to die."

"So what?" Ed spat at me, his breath warm against my face. "You think they wouldn't kill us, too?" I shivered on the word *us*. "You think your friend Ethel knows any more than you do about what has happened? They don't care."

Ethel. I wasn't sure what Julie had done, if he'd done anything, but I knew Ethel believed he hadn't. I was sure that Ed was right about this one thing, that Ethel knew and understood as much about this whole thing as I did. And she was going to die tonight. For real, this time. For nothing. "No," I moaned. "This can't be happening. You conspired to commit espionage and you're letting Ethel and Julie take the fall for you?" My voice trembled but grew louder as I kept speaking. "You want Russia to bomb us? You want us all to die? You won't be happy until you destroy us all, will you?"

"I will make it very simple for you," Ed said, speaking in a calm, even tone. "You give me the paper you took from me and maybe I will let you see the children again."

I thought about Ethel. She'd been separated from her children for almost three years. *Three years.* I wanted to save her. I wanted to give this paper to the FBI today and I wanted her to live. I wanted her to go back to her children and love them and care for them. But more than anything, I wanted to hold on to Henry's soft curls and give David a silent hug.

"Mildred," Ed said. "The paper."

"I will give you this paper, and then you will give me the children?" I said, trying to match his calm tone. If I could just get him to take me to the children, I could figure this out. Ed nodded and loosened his hold on my arm.

I pulled the paper from my purse and I held it up above my head, and then, before Ed could react, I pulled away from him and ran outside. "Take me to the children," I shouted at Ed as he ran toward me, "and then I'll give this to you."

"Stupid woman." Ed laughed, shoved me hard so I fell to the ground, and he grabbed the paper from my hands. Ed's words stung more than the fall. I *was* stupid. I really was. I never should've trusted Ed. I should've gone to Jake with this paper all those years ago. But I was not going to let

Ed take away my children now. I was not going to let this all be for nothing.

I pulled myself up from the ground and dusted the dirt off my dress. "Where are the children?" I said, trying to keep my voice even.

Ed looked at the paper, seeming satisfied that this was what he needed, that he had won. "You should think I would let you have the children now that I have them?" He grimaced. "You are a terrible mother. I will not let you ruin them both the way you have ruined one."

"You promised," I said, annoyed with the way my voice trembled. Ed laughed again. The afternoon air was stifling and I couldn't breathe.

I looked toward the car and I noticed that he'd left the keys in the ignition. He must've forgotten to take them when he ran in the house after me. If I took the car, he would be stuck here, in all the corn, in the middle of nowhere. He would have to tell me where the children were if he wanted to get the car back, if he ever wanted to leave.

My heart pounded as I ran to the car, got in, turned the key, and heard the ignition sing. I hadn't driven anything since the meat truck back when Kauffman's Meats still had one, when I was only a teenager, and that was so long ago now. But my feet shifted below me, finding the pedals, remembering.

"You stupid woman!" Ed was shouting. He was behind the car, waving his arms in the air. That's all I was to him? That's all I ever was to him.

I put my foot on the gas and gunned the engine. The tires squealed a little in the gravel since I hadn't remembered to take the car out of park. Ed ran to the side and he knocked on the window. "Get out of the car!" he shouted.

I put the car in reverse, backed up, and then stopped and turned the wheel so I was facing Ed straight on.

"You will never see the children again if you don't get out of the car!" he shouted at me. *A coward dies many times before their death, but the valiant never taste of death but once,* Ethel had said to me.

No one is going to die, I told her.

"Mildred, I'm warning you!" Ed shouted.

I couldn't lose the children. But Ed was a liar, and Ethel was going to die. Tonight. I had to help her.

I put my foot on the gas and pressed down on the pedal. Ed didn't have time to react, or maybe he thought a woman as *stupid* as me would never think to hit him with a car. But I did, as if by instinct. I wasn't going

465

very fast, but it was fast enough. With the power of the car, Ed did not seem large or menacing. I knocked him to the ground, just like that, as if he were a domino I toppled over with the flick of my forefinger.

Then I heard the thud of his body against the gravel, and suddenly it hit me. What I'd done. And I let out a scream.

I backed up and got out of car. Ed lay on the ground flat on his back, but his chest still rose and fell, up and down and up and down, and his eyes were open. His pants were torn, his leg was bleeding, but just a little. "Mildred?" he said, looking up at me, his voice ripe with surprise. "My leg."

"Can you get up?" I asked him. I watched him struggle to stand, but he couldn't put any weight on his leg.

"I think it's broken." He lifted up his hand for my help, but instead I reached down, plucked the paper from him, and ran back quickly to the car.

"Mildred!" he yelled. "Come back here . . . If you leave me here, I will never let you see the children again."

But I was not a stupid woman. Ed was a liar. He'd always been a liar. If I helped him up right now, he wouldn't tell me where the children were anyway.

"Give me your keys," Jake says.

"Why?" I ask, though I know why.

"Just give them to me." He holds out his hands, and I hesitate for only a moment before throwing the keys to him.

I don't care about the keys or the stupid car. Ethel is dead. My children are gone. I imagine myself now going to find John and Richie, telling them that I will take them, that I will care for them and love them the way their mother always intended for them to be loved. But they will hate me now for leaving them the way I did back at their grandmother's. I'm sure of it. They will hate me for being unable to stop their mother's death, for staying hidden away for so long. They should hate me. I hate myself. I am a terrible mother and a terrible friend. And besides, I will be no good to them once Jake arrests me for what I did to Ed. *A coward dies many times.* Here I am, dying again.

"Come with me," Jake says, and he puts his arm around me and leads me back the way we came. He leads me to an unfamiliar black car, opens the passenger door, and tells me to get in. I do. I'm shivering, though somehow I understand it's still hot outside.

Jake pulls a blanket from the trunk and throws it over me.

Suddenly I am so very tired. It feels impossible that I would be able to or want to sleep after what I have done and what I have seen in the past twenty-four hours. After what I have lost and who I have become. And yet it is as if my entire body were surrendering under the weight of all of it and the warm blanket Jake has covered me with. As soon as Jake begins driving back down, moving steadily on Route 9, I lean my head against the window and I fall asleep.

Jake awakens me by gently shaking my leg once the car has stopped. It feels like only minutes have passed. But maybe it has been hours.

I open my eyes and look around, squinting at the familiar shapes in front of me. Susan and Sam's house . . . in Elizabeth?

"I don't understand?" I say. I'd thought Jake was taking me somewhere to arrest me. He already threatened once and that was for something I hadn't even done.

Jake moves closer to me. "You need to get out of the car and go inside," he says. "Pretend nothing else happened today before I drove you here."

"I can't pretend that." I know I will never forget the image of that whisper of smoke coming out of Ethel's head. Or Ed waiting helplessly in the gravel. Him screaming at me that I would never see my children again.

"You have to," Jake says.

"What if I don't want to?"

"You just have to." He pauses. "Go inside. I'm going to take care of the rest."

"The children!" I cry out, and Jake reaches up and puts his hand on my cheek. His hand still feels exactly the way I remember it, and for a moment I close my eyes and try to fight back tears. I think about Richie and John somewhere here in New Jersey. *Orphans.* Their parents gone forever. I think about Henry and David hidden away somewhere by Ed, and it feels almost wrong for me to wish that I will find them, that they are safe. I don't even deserve that much. I have done this life of mine all wrong. Every choice I've made has been the wrong one. A tear escapes onto my cheek, and Jake brushes it away with his thumb.

"I want you to know that I wanted to stop this," he said. "I did everything I could, but it got so much bigger than me so fast. The best I could do was to save you. And the boys." I wonder if this is what he's doing even now — saving us. He looks at me for

469

another moment, and then he leans across me and opens up the passenger door. "Go," he says. I shake my head. I don't want to leave him. "Go," he says again.

Somehow I get out of the car. I walk up the front lawn and I stand on my sister's porch, but only for a few seconds before the light turns on and she opens the door. "Mills?" I hear her voice through the screen. "Is that you? Oh my, look at you. You're a mess. Mother called me . . ."

I turn around and look back at the street, but Jake is already gone.

29

Ed is found by a corn farmer two weeks to the day after Ethel died.

The animals have found him first, and by the time the farmer makes the discovery, Ed, the police tell me, is unrecognizable. Lucky for all of us, they say, his car was parked nearby and it had his wallet, emptied of everything but his New York driver's license, sitting right there on the passenger seat. For that reason, the authorities believe that Ed was robbed, but because of the license they are able to find me quickly, his next of kin. I am sleeping on Susan's couch in Elizabeth when the officers come in the middle of the night to notify me of my husband's tragic death. I do not cry or scream or put up a fuss the way Susan does. I think of the way the smoke escaped from Ethel's head, so quietly and yet so precisely. And then I ask them about the car and how damaged it is.

One of the officers says, "The car? It's in mint condition, Mrs. Stein." And he hands me back the keys that I handed to Jake two weeks earlier.

"Then how did he die?" I ask them. The officers glance at each other, and Susan looks at me as if I were crazy.

"There's evidence he struggled during the robbery and . . ." But he doesn't finish his sentence because I gasp and suddenly begin to cry.

Susan puts her arm around me and tries to comfort me. "It'll be okay," she tells me over and over again.

I let her believe my tears of sadness are for Ed. But really they are tears of understanding the weight of what Jake did . . . for me. Tears of knowing that I'd been right about him all along. Jake only ever wanted to protect me. Jake loves me. But I am also sure now I will never see him again.

A few days later, they find Lena in a hotel room in Philadelphia with Henry and David. Actually, it is the FBI who find Lena, and an unfamiliar agent comes to Susan's house to tell us of her whereabouts. He also tells me how strange it is that they have become involved in such a thing. "Children in a hotel room with their grandmother?"

He shrugs. "Isn't normally FBI territory. My boss called this one in as a special favor."

Susan and I drive to Philadelphia in the now perfect Fleetmaster and we knock on Lena's hotel room door. When David is the one to open it, I grab him and promise him I will never let him go again. Lena cries, but then she lets me take Henry from her arms.

"Where is my Ed?" she asks me coldly. "You don't have his permission to take his children, Mildred."

I stop a moment from kissing my boys to look her straight in the eyes and say, "These are my children. You're the one who took them." Then I say without even blinking, "Ed has died."

"I don't believe you," she says, but her voice falters.

"It's true. The police say he was killed in a robbery." I keep my voice steady on the lie. And as time goes on, I will even begin to believe this as truth myself.

Lena's face falls, and she suddenly appears small and frail and old. "A robbery," she says meekly. "But Ed had nothing."

I remember that Ed was her child and that she has lost something, too. We've all lost something. I picture her rifling through my things, trying to help Ed cover up his espionage and then helping him steal my children away. I want to hate her. I have so many reasons to hate her. But suddenly I feel bad for her.

"You'll come for the Sabbath one night soon," I tell her. "The boys will be glad to see you."

But I never see Lena again. A few weeks later, Mr. Bergman tells me he heard that Lena died in her sleep of heart trouble. Without her children, it seems that Lena died of a broken heart.

The boys and I never move back to the city.

For a little while, we live with Susan and Sam, and then once Henry is old enough for school I get a job selling shoes at Little's Department Store and eventually we move into a tiny house of our own only a few miles away from Susan and her family. My boys grow up near their girl cousins, playing in the long yards of the suburbs, never knowing a world where you don't have half an acre to stage a baseball field. They also never know a world where there is a kosher butcher shop just around the corner filled with the familiar smells of meat and family and the Sabbath.

What surprises me most is the way the days sometimes feel so long and yet the years so short. It's all the hours between that count. All the endless weary and wonderful hours in which I raise two boys on my own, neither one of them ever knowing their fathers. But every birthday, every milestone, I find myself thinking not of Ed or even Jake who are missing all of it but of Ethel, of all the hours she missed with her sons. Of all the hours that were stolen from her.

I try to keep track of Ethel's boys, but the last news I hear comes in the mid-fifties when I read they are taken in by a childless couple, then adopted. The boys changed their last names, became new, and, I hope, happy children. That is what Ethel would've wanted for them, after all, if she couldn't be with them.

After this, the newspapers stop reporting about the children. As if the Rosenbergs never even existed at all, not even through their sons.

By the mid-fifties, Senator McCarthy is censured and, a few years later, he dies. It falls out of fashion to hate the communists so, and people start to forget about the espionage they once so greatly feared. People seem to forget about Ethel and Julius, too. But not me. I know I will never forget everything Ethel and I shared in our apartments — our children, our families, our fears — and especially not that night in June 1953. I know the memory of Ethel's last breath will stay with me forever.

In the late fifties, Henry brings home a comic book from school and a description of the air raid drills where he hides under his desk should the bomb ever come. And suddenly it all seems ridiculous. Fear is the worst thing of all. Fear is what killed Ethel. You cannot live your life being afraid. "The bomb isn't coming to New Jersey," I tell Henry, but nonetheless he learns how to use his desk as a shield.

Still, the world moves on and on, the bomb never coming.

In 1960, everything changes for us. Not only do women have the Pill now but also a special government-owned school opens nearby for children with problems and they come to me, inviting David to attend. At the ripe old age of fourteen, David at last gets the kind of intensive therapy Jake started with him years earlier and he suddenly begins to talk the way Henry did at age two and a half, one delicious word after another, as if he were gulping them down and spitting them back out. If you were to

476

see him now from the outside, you might understand that there is something not quite right with him, but then he might tell you to stop staring. *It's not polite.* Dave is, to this day, meticulous about politeness.

In the seventies, Henry gets accepted to medical school at Penn and he finds himself with a government scholarship. Dave gets a job working for the IRS. He is painstakingly thorough with the filing and the order of life, and before long he enrolls in a night school program to become an accountant himself.

And I find myself living in my small house in Elizabeth, New Jersey, all alone. In the mirror I begin to see an old woman with a double chin identical to the one my mother and Bubbe Kasha once had. I have the Sabbath dinner with Susan and Sam each week, but otherwise the world passes all around me in quiet. I eagerly await my Fridays with my sister, my weekly phone calls from Henry, and Dave's Sunday visits.

But I stay away from the neighbors. I don't let myself make friends. Even now, after all this time, I prefer to keep to myself.

In June 1978, I find a small mention in the *Times* that there is going to be a march in

Union Square on the nineteenth, the twenty-fifth anniversary of the execution.

Twenty-five years since the murder, I think.

Henry has a wife now and lives in Philadelphia, and Dave doesn't like to travel beyond his normal range, but, still, I guilt them both into driving me up to the city. I know I could take the train, but then I might not have a reason to make the boys come with me. And they have to come with me. "You might not remember," I tell them each over the telephone several nights in a row, "but you were friends with the Rosenberg boys. You lived down the hall from them. Their parents were innocent and they were murdered," I add.

Henry sighs heavily, in that way he has, and I can picture him running his hands through his brown curls in that way that reminds me so much of his father. I know that he will drive me there. And he does.

Henry drives, I sit in the front, and Dave is in the back. I think of how this is so very different and yet so very similar from the car ride I took with Ed that summer evening so very long ago. And then I close my eyes and remember that drive I took alone on this day twenty-five years earlier.

After Henry finds a place to park, we mill around the crowds of people. I haven't been

478

to the city in years, and now it is familiar and unfamiliar to me all at once. Mr. Bergman and Bubbe Kasha died in the early sixties, and my mother sold the butcher shop and used the proceeds to buy herself a little condo in Miami Beach, where Susan and I try to go every winter to visit her. I've had no reason to come back here since, and even the smells and the sounds of the taxicabs are so foreign that they make me feel as if I don't belong here anymore.

Then, as we pull up to the gathering of people, I see the reason I came. The boys. *Ethel's boys!* I would've recognized John and Richie anywhere. All these years later, I would've known it was them. They are so tall now, such . . . men, but they look just like Ethel and Julie, a wonderful combination of both of them. *You would be proud,* I say to Ethel in my head. *So handsome!*

I start to walk toward them. I want to tell them so much. That I am here. That I am sorry for everything. That after all this time, I still remember their mother, how much she loved them. I still believe in her innocence. I want to tell them that I was there the night she died. That she did not die alone. That someone paid for everything that happened even if I am the only one to remember that part now. I want to tell them that when I close my eyes at night I can still hear their mother's voice, imagine the way she looked, so full of life, riding down the elevator in her wide red hat.

I take a step toward them and then I feel a hand on my arm.

"I wouldn't talk to them," a voice says and I turn around. *Jake.* Older, grayer, slightly heavier, but undoubtedly him. His almond eyes are smiling. "Let it be," Jake says gently. "They're different people now." Then he adds, "So are you."

I wonder if he means my double chin and I put my hand to my face, self-consciously. Jake smiles as if he finds this amusing, and I realize that wasn't what he meant at all. Of course I am different than I was that night, that last time he saw me. It has been so very long and yet it feels like yesterday.

Henry lets go of my arm and stares at Jake, then looks to me and raises his eyebrows. Henry is a piece of Jake, the one good thing that came out of all those terrible years.

"You probably don't remember," I say to him, "but this is Dr. Gold. We knew him once a long time ago back when —"

"Actually," Jake interrupts me, "it's Dr. Zitlow. But please, call me Jake." He holds out a hand for Henry to shake and they do.

480

Jake holds on to him for a second longer than he should, and then Dave holds out his hand to shake, and Jake lets go and turns to him.

"Pleased to meet you," Dave says, ever so politely.

"David," Jake says. "My goodness, son, is that you?" He smiles and clasps Dave on the shoulder. Dave appears wary and pulls back, and he asks Henry if he wants to go look for something cold to drink. Maybe they can sense I need some time alone because Henry agrees and the two of them walk away. And then there we are, Jake and I, by ourselves.

"So," Jake asks me, "what are you doing here?"

"What are *you* doing here?" I shoot back.

"I figured you would be here."

"Even after all this time?"

"Even after all this time," he says. Neither one of us speak for a moment. Jake's eyes trail off in the direction of Henry and David, but they are lost among the crowd, and he turns back to me. "The boys are good?" he asks.

"The boys are very good," I say. He nods and smiles.

I've thought of Jake so often in the last twenty-five years, between thinking of other things like air raid drills and putting food on the table, getting the boys to school on time, making sure David kept up with his therapy, making sure Henry's baseball uniform was clean. At Henry's wedding last year, I couldn't help but think that Jake should've been invited, but of course by then I was long past knowing how to reach him.

"You know, I've retired from the FBI," he says now. "Last fall, actually. I bought a little cabin up in the Catskills a few months ago."

I close my eyes and remember the pieces of that one perfect day, those most perfect hours in the cabin, just before Russia exploded the bomb and the entire world went crazy. "I haven't been there in so many years," I say. And I haven't, even in my memories.

"It's the same," Jake says. "All the rest of the world has changed so much. But there, everything is exactly the same. Beautiful. Quiet." He smiles again. "I take a little rowboat out on the creek now and then and try to catch some fish."

Suddenly I hear someone else talking. I look up and see Richie has taken ahold of the microphone. He talks about justice for his mother and his father even now. There are many people here and they nod and holler along with him. It reminds me of the crowd that night in front of Sing Sing, the commotion, the restlessness. The inhumanity. It's a different world now. Stalin and Khrushchev are dead. Jimmy Carter is president, and, with his soft Southern accent, I can't imagine him allowing a mother to be executed for something she didn't even do. But still, I hear the shouting all around me, and I realize I'm not the only one. Other people haven't forgotten. Even after all this time.

"It gets lonely up there sometimes," Jake is saying now. "It can get too quiet."

"I feel the same way, now that the boys are grown, and I live alone."

Jake looks at me for a moment, and I can see the way he looked that last night I saw him, the night Ethel died. The way he put his hand on my face in the car and promised me he would take care of everything else. I know what I have always known — that from a distance, working for the government, he brought my children back to me. I smile at him and he reaches for my hand.

We stand there together and listen to Ethel's children. They speak so well, they are so impassioned. They have become men in spite of what happened. Maybe because of it.

"On the day she died," John is saying, "my mother wrote us a letter and asked us to never forget their innocence . . ."

In my head, I can still hear Ethel's voice, the way she sounded singing at the piano in her apartment, clear and sweet and high as a bird. Now I imagine she is singing again for me and for Jake. For Henry and for David. But, most of all, for her children.

AUTHOR'S NOTE

I remember learning briefly about Ethel and Julius Rosenberg in a high school American History class. Years later, I had only the vague recollection that they were a married couple executed in the fifties for spying. As it turns out, they were the only civilians ever executed in the U.S. for conspiring to commit espionage. As it also turns out, the more I read about the case and the trial and the Rosenbergs themselves, the more convinced I became that Ethel was innocent, and that Julius might have been, too. I began to believe that neither one of them had deserved to die, that their executions were more a result of the political climate of the time than of anything they might have done. Of course, I wasn't there, and I don't know the inner workings of what happened, but the Ethel Rosenberg I read about struck me as a wife and mother just trying to do the best she could for her two young sons. When she was executed in 1953, her sons were only six and ten — quite similar to the ages of my own sons as I began writing this book. When I read the letter she wrote to her children shortly before her execution, it moved me to tears, and it made me want to create a novel around her, the woman I saw in that letter: Ethel the mother.

This book is entirely a work of fiction, and Millie and Ed Stein and their families, as well as Dr. Jake Gold/Zitlow, are all completely fictional characters. Ethel and Julius Rosenberg did live in an eleventh-floor apartment in Knickerbocker Village in the 1940s with their two young sons until their arrests in 1950. Though I've researched factual details of their lives and have drawn on them, this book represents only my fictional reimagining of the Rosenbergs and their time living there.

On August 11, 1950, the second day Ethel testified for the grand jury — and the day she was arrested — Ethel really did leave her children with a neighbor, who, when she didn't return, took the children to Tessie Greenglass, Ethel's mother. But that neighbor wasn't Millie Stein, nor is there any indication that she and this neighbor were close friends as Ethel and Millie are here, and everything I've created about

Millie's life here is completely fictional. I also changed the timeline a bit for the purposes of my story. From what I've read, it seemed the neighbor spent the night with Ethel's children and took them to Tessie Greenglass's home the following morning. Ethel *did* call and speak to her older son after she was arrested and he reportedly let out such a loud scream that it would haunt Ethel for the rest of her life.

I've centered the fictional events of Millie's life around real events that happened between the years 1947 and 1953: the smallpox outbreak and telephone operators' strike in 1947, the election and the killer fog in 1948, the World Series between the Yankees and the Dodgers in 1949. The Soviets exploded their first nuclear bomb on August 29, 1949, and it was announced in the papers a month later.

I've also structured Millie's fictional events around real ones in the Rosenbergs' lives: Ethel made a recording of her voice for her older son just before giving birth to her younger one in 1947. She took her older son to therapy with Mrs. Elizabeth Phillips at the Jewish Board of Guardians, and she later went into psychoanalysis herself with Dr. Saul Miller. Julius's business, Pitt Machine Products, was struggling, and there was tension in the family after Ethel's brothers left the company in 1949. Ethel and her boys spent the summer in Golden's Bridge in 1949 and Julius came up on weekends.

David Greenglass, Ethel's younger brother, was arrested first, in June 1950, and he quickly confessed, implicating Julius, and then Ethel, saying she typed up Julius's notes. Years later, in the nineties, Greenglass admitted he perjured himself when implicating his sister, Ethel, but said he was doing it to spare his own wife, Ruth, from being arrested. Just before David was arrested, his wife did suffer burns in an accident, and she had been rehospitalized for an infection when David was arrested. David had stolen a bit of uranium from Los Alamos as a souvenir and reportedly that was what first put him on the FBI's radar. Greenglass served nearly ten years in prison. After being released, he and his family continued to live in New York under assumed names. He died in July 2014 at the age of ninety-two. The *New York Times* learned of and announced his death in October 2014 when they called the nursing home where he'd been living under an assumed name.

Julius Rosenberg was taken in for questioning by the FBI on the morning of June

16, 1950, the day after David Greenglass was arrested. The FBI came to the Rosenbergs' apartment early that morning while Julius was shaving. Twelve men came back a month later, on July seventeenth, to arrest Julius and take things out of the apartment, including the record Ethel had made for her older son. The night her husband was arrested, Ethel and the children went to her mother's house to spend the night, but the next day she invited the press into her apartment in Knickerbocker Village, and she prepared a chicken while the press took pictures.

In early August 1950, Ethel was called to testify before the grand jury. She consulted with Julius's lawyer, Emanuel Bloch, and on Monday the seventh she went in and took the Fifth Amendment. She was called back on Friday, August eleventh, and again took the Fifth. She'd left the boys with her mother that Monday, but when she went to pick them up there was unpleasantness between her and her mother, who Ethel felt was taking David's side and did not believe in Julius's innocence. For that reason, Ethel found a neighbor to watch her boys on Friday, August eleventh. She was arrested by the FBI after her grand jury testimony as she was leaving the courthouse.

I changed the names of Ethel and Julius's sons for this book, though I kept their ages accurate. The boys in the pages of this book are fictional characters based loosely on what I read about the real Rosenberg boys. On the twenty-fifth anniversary of the execution, there was a rally in Union Square. I came across a picture of one of the Rosenberg boys there, all grown up, and I knew Millie had to see him again there, too.

Though Dr. Jake Gold/Zitlow was not a real person, the idea for him came from stories I read about FBI informants infiltrating communist groups. To the best of my knowledge, however, there was no one like Jake, or Ed, in Ethel and Julius's circle of friends. Though, there were other people at the time who passed information to the Soviets who were never prosecuted, much less executed. One of the most interesting accounts I read was a *NOVA* interview with Joan Hall, the wife of Ted Hall, who was a scientist at Los Alamos and who did give secrets to the Soviet Union. Joan knew about Ted's involvement, but he was never arrested, and the truth did not come out publicly until shortly before his death in 1999. Though, unlike my fictional Ed and Millie, Ted and Joan Hall didn't know the

Rosenbergs.

Of course, the fictional Jake was not actually at Sing Sing the night of the Rosenbergs' execution. However, the FBI had reportedly set up a secret command post at Sing Sing with an open line to J. Edgar Hoover in case Ethel or Julius should want to *confess* at the very last moment. I was very much extending fictional liberties to allow Millie to be an observer to the execution. I read that Julius's brother came up for one last visit with him that evening and was turned away, so Millie being able to get inside the prison, much less witness the execution, would've most likely been impossible. However, there were witnesses to the execution. A quick search on YouTube turns up a very graphic and horrific videotaped description from an actual observer, and the awful details of Ethel's execution, including the fact that she refused to die after the normal amount of electricity, are true. Also, the execution was moved back from the usual time of eleven p.m. to eight p.m. to take place before sundown and the start of the Jewish Sabbath. But Ethel was pronounced dead at eight sixteen p.m., three minutes after the Sabbath officially began.

In the course of writing this book, I read

and/or consulted the following books and I recommend them for further reading: *Ethel Rosenberg: Beyond the Myths* by Ilene Philipson, *We Are Your Sons: The Legacy of Ethel and Julius Rosenberg* by Michael and Robert Meeropol, *An Execution in the Family: One Son's Journey* by Robert Meeropol, *The Brother: The Untold Story of Atomic Spy David Greenglass and How He Sent His Sister, Ethel Rosenberg, to the Electric Chair* by Sam Roberts, *The FBI–KGB War* by Robert J. Lamphere, and *Final Verdict: What Really Happened in the Rosenberg Case* by Walter Schneir, as well as many of the death house letters of Julius and Ethel Rosenberg, a collection of which can be found in *The Rosenberg Letters,* edited by Michael Meeropol. Any historical inaccuracies in these pages, intentional or otherwise, are strictly my own.

Over the years, many people have written about the case, trying to shed new light on it, and there are many sources detailing the trial. That was not my intention here. Through fiction, I wanted to reimagine Ethel as a person, a woman, the mother whom I pictured her to be. I can't definitively say what Ethel knew or what she didn't, what she did or didn't do, but the more I learned about her and the case and the trial, the more I personally came to believe she didn't deserve to die the way she did.

There were a few ideas I kept close to me as I wrote this book and I'll leave you with them: Ethel was only accused and convicted of typing up notes, which later her brother admitted was a lie. She was a wife who seemed to love and respect her husband deeply. And she was a mother to two young sons whom she loved greatly and was forced to leave orphaned when she was executed on June 19, 1953.

ACKNOWLEDGMENTS

An enormous thank-you to my wonderful and talented editor at Riverhead Books, Laura Perciasepe. I am so grateful for her support, guidance, and infinite wisdom, starting from the moment this novel was just a spark a few years ago. It has been such a joy to work with her, and I feel so fortunate to have had her by my side for this entire process. Thank you also to everyone at Penguin Random House and Riverhead Books for supporting me and my novels and always making me feel like a part of their amazing publishing family, with special thanks to Geoff Kloske, Jynne Dilling Martin, Margaret Delaney, Meagan Brown, Craig Burke, Kate Stark, and copy editor Tony Davis. You are the best!

Thank you to Jessica Regel, my brilliant agent extraordinaire, whose insights helped get this book going. Her belief in me continues to amaze me, and I'm so grateful that I have her on my side! Thank you also to the team at Foundry, who have welcomed me, and this book, into their fold.

Thank you to my family and extended family for their love and overwhelming support: my parents, my sister, and especially my husband and children, who always go along for this ride with me — often literally; they have been to more book events than I can count and still pretend to find it interesting. Thank you to my writer friends who keep me sane on a daily basis, especially Maureen Lipinski, T. Greenwood, and Laura Fitzgerald, to whom I owe an extra thanks because she has been telling me for years that there was a story here.

Last but certainly not least, thank you to all the readers, librarians, bloggers, and friends, both old and new, who supported me and *Margot* and who allow me to keep writing stories and doing what I love. Thank you for inviting me to your cities, your homes, your book clubs, and your schools and libraries, and, most of all, thank you for inviting my characters into your hearts.

ABOUT THE AUTHOR

Jillian Cantor has a BA in English from Penn State University and an MFA from the University of Arizona. She is the author of award-winning novels for teens and adults, including, most recently, the critically acclaimed *Margot,* which was a Library Reads pick. Born and raised in a suburb of Philadelphia, Cantor currently lives in Arizona with her husband and two sons.